CHRYSALIS

B. GALLAT

Published by B. GALLAT

ISBN 978-0-578-85402-1

Table of Contents

Prologue

The clock read 4:00 p.m. and Simon Blake was in the Amsterdam Schiphol International Airport making his way up the ramp that led to the Airport Sheraton. Back home in Cincinnati, Ohio the time was 10:00 a.m. and he was tired. His day had begun 30 hours earlier, waking up at 4:00 a.m. in Paysandu, Uruguay to start his trip home, a journey that took an unexpected turn. Noises from the airport and its train station disappeared behind him as he entered the tunnel which would take him to the hotel 100 yards away. He scrutinized the shops along its length, noting a procession of travelers going both ways. It was a wide tunnel, at least 35 yards, and there was plenty of room for what little traffic there was this time of the afternoon. International flights were done for the day with only local hops remaining, and his suitcase wheels clacked over granite tiles as he trudged toward his destination.

By now he should have been safely at home in his kitchen having coffee. If all had gone according to plan, he would have finished his journey from Uruguay to Cincinnati approximately 28 hours after he started. He shook his head at how the day had turned to garbage. The six-hour bus ride from Paysandu to Montevideo went smoothly and his plane took off on time, an event you couldn't always take for granted in South America, but a volcano eruption in Guatemala combined with a hurricane stalling out over the East Coast of the United States rerouted his plane to Europe two hours into his journey. Going back to South America wasn't an option since the winds were directing ash fallout across the continent. It was the second eruption in a year for this volcano, Fuego, and the airlines learned from their mistakes the first time. Get the planes with their expensive engines as far away as possible.

Too tired to rehash the events of the day, he concentrated on what lay ahead. *Check in, whiskey and dinner.*

Registration went fast after Blake flashed his membership at the desk clerk, and he rode the elevator up to his room to deposit his luggage before going back downstairs to the bar. Tomorrow's flight left at 7:00 a.m., plenty of time to have dinner followed by sleeping off the marathon that he had just been through.

Safely ensconced in the bar and more relaxed than he had been at any point in his trip, Blake was sunk back into a leather chair, watching the waiter approach with his drink. Johnnie Walker was heading his way, and the show was about to start.

The waiter was carrying a silver tray that held a rocks glass, silver ice bucket with a pair of silver tongs, a silver shot glass with a set of wings on the sides and a bottle of Johnnie Walker Black Label Scotch whiskey that was half full. There was also a curvy bottle of Coke in the old-style green glass with ridges down the sides. Stopping before him, the waiter balanced his tray in the air, using the tongs to place an ice cube into the rocks glass followed by lifting his eyebrows at Blake. Blake flashed two fingers to signify his desire, watching a second cube drop on top of the first.

The wings on either side of the shot glass were meant to allow its positioning over the rocks glass, a placement which the waiter performed next. He then unscrewed the cap on the whiskey bottle. Having observed this same ritual in various countries during his travels, Blake often wondered if the whiskey bottle was designed to fit the procedure or if the procedure was designed to fit the whiskey bottle. Taking hold of the whiskey with a flourish that involved raising the bottle nine inches above the shot glass, the waiter poured a generous measure, letting the shot glass overflow into the receptacle below so that Blake received more than a full allotment. Blake watched in appreciation, signifying his approval with a thumbs up. Using the OK sign of thumb and forefinger forming a circle was unwise when traveling internationally because it could sometimes be construed as an insult, but a thumbs up was universally accepted.

Placing the glass of whiskey on the table, the waiter proceeded to uncap the Coke bottle and place it alongside the whiskey. An empty glass intended for the Coke was also on the tray, but Blake waved away the waiter's attempt to set it down. Blake preferred to mix Coke into his whiskey himself, but that concept was difficult to communicate when traveling, so he waited for the empty glass to be offered and then declined its use. The waiter left after bowing in acknowledgement and Blake set about adding Coke. He didn't use much, and one bottle of Coke easily served to doctor four rounds of whiskey.

Blake took his first sip, the mixture burning a trail down his throat to launch a delicious unwinding from the stress of traveling. *Yes.* He took another, feeling the knots loosen at the same time a voice penetrated his awareness.

"Excuse me, sir. Might I inquire about your cochlear implants? My mother is considering this operation and I was wondering if you could possibly tell me how you like them."

Lowering his drink Blake saw a character that he recognized from baggage claim, a 6'-7" Irishman with flaming red hair and the build of a Viking. *Hard to forget that dude.* Blake's shaved head made his cochlear implants stand out and he was accustomed to people asking about them. He was more than willing to share his experiences and the whiskey was triggering a relaxation that let the words flow. "I've had them for a year now and they've changed my life."

"How so?"

Blake swirled his glass, enjoying the clinking of ice and the generation of foam. "I can give you the short answer or the long answer. Are you eating here?" He inclined his head toward the restaurant attached to the bar, an inviting room with lighted chandeliers, large pots of greenery and dark wooden tables covered with white linens. The Sheraton chain was always classy, wherever they were located. It wasn't his practice to seek company on the road, but something about the Irishman struck him as a like-minded soul.

His fellow traveler bowed his head in thanks, "Yes, indeed, I was planning to. My name is Andrew McNaught." He extended a massive hand in friendship.

Blake stood up to clasp the offered hand, "Simon Blake. Let's have dinner and I'll tell you what I know."

Chapter 1 – Reality

A continuous procession of lightning, thunder and wind filled the nighttime hours, and morning arrived with inclement weather firmly established. Even so, Simon Blake wasn't bothered by the storm because he slept soundly without his hearing aids. Once they came off, he didn't hear anything.

Rain and humidity were dominating the forecast in Cincinnati, causing mid-September to be unseasonably wet. Coming after a string of recent rainfalls, last night's storm helped to create a portentous atmosphere for Blake's appointment this Friday morning.

Having fortified himself with a breakfast that included four cups of coffee, Blake was now driving on I-275 East toward the Montgomery Road exit in a hard rain. Road spray generated by highway traffic obscured the signs, but Blake was familiar with this drive. Slipping into autopilot, his mind drifted back to the beginning.

Born in Chicago, his family moved to the Mt Healthy suburb of Cincinnati when he was four years old. It was his second day of kindergarten when a teacher suspected he might have a hearing problem. Her intuition was correct and led to Blake receiving a hearing aid in 1962.

Soon after Blake made the mistake of telling a classmate that his new earmold was making his ear itch. His fellow student deemed this fact hilarious and promptly began blurting out, "Simon has itchy witchy ears!" to whomever would listen. That was the day when Blake realized sharing his feelings could backfire, and the incident made it clear that kindergarten offered lessons besides the standard curriculum.

Like any four-year-old, Blake thought his hearing aid was more of a hassle than a benefit. He developed a habit of taking it off at the bus stop and putting it in his pocket for the trip to school. Once at school he would slip it back on with nobody the wiser. One day though, he reached in his pocket and it was nowhere to be found.

The loss didn't upset Blake too much. He was bright enough to know that he couldn't hide the fact that it was gone and even volunteered the information to his teacher. In the meantime, he was hoping that he would have a temporary break until a replacement materialized.

His mother showed up at school within the hour, having received a call from Blake's teacher. Blake was happily sitting in class sans the undesirable implement when his mother appeared at the classroom door with a face that conveyed she was on a mission. He was pretty sure he knew the focus of her mission when she politely requested his removal from class. The teacher, having already ratted him out, was more than happy to surrender Blake to his mother. Once out of the classroom they sat down, and his mother began to grill him over his movements between the time he left home and when he arrived at school.

Upon learning that he had been playing tag while waiting for the school bus with his hearing aid in his pocket, she hauled him off to the bus stop where they began an intense search, at least on his mother's part. Blake's contribution consisted of shuffling his feet through the grass in an aimless manner which he hoped would convince his mother that he was trying to help. Inside he remained hopeful that his goal of freedom would still be realized.

When she stood up with a sigh of thankfulness, Blake was dismayed to realize his dream was gone. He was in shock at how his mother's determination to track down the hearing aid proved so successful. Her investigation located the missing unit in no less than 35 minutes, raising his respect for her capabilities to another level. What he didn't realize was that in 1962 a $500 hearing aid was big money, and she was highly motivated to find it.

After the bus stop episode Blake's mother began using an adhesive disk to fasten his hearing aid onto his scalp. He didn't dare complain of discomfort, feeling grateful that he managed to avoid any episodes of yelling or swatting, especially when his father came home. Blake only had to endure a measured gaze along with the delivery of a few pointed comments. The message was received, and from then on Blake made sure that he was always aware of his hearing aid's location.

Blake's parents did him a service by emphasizing that his disability was no reason to accept failure. Not knowing any different, he proceeded as if he had no limitations, an approach which was responsible for much of his success as he grew up. Presented with a problem, he kept searching for a workaround until he solved it, applying his mother's advice that she repeated ad nauseam, "If at first you don't succeed, try, try, again." Wired to keep on plugging away, he developed a unique combination of optimism and orneriness that served him well.

His natural tenaciousness honed by the constant necessity to cope with the world around him proved to be an asset. Forced to battle for comprehension with each interaction, he developed a perseverance which few people could match, learning early in his youth that outlasting people was sometimes enough. The daily challenges also led to a high degree of self-discipline. Along the way he deduced that most people were uneasy in the face of those two qualities, helping Blake learn the value of subtlety.

Navigating his way through the rain, Blake felt the rear end of his truck shimmy on the wet pavement. Unhappy about having to slow down, he grudgingly lowered his speed by 10 mph and kept on with his recollections.

Wearing a hearing aid meant being positioned in the front row of class for his entire education. Blake came to consider the situation quite unfair. He often fantasized about the adventure and high jinks of the back row; an adventure him denied forever. The seating arrangement was especially painful in high school when he felt that it significantly diminished his cool factor.

Blake's hearing impairment prevented him from developing a large circle of friends, but there were a few close buddies that he could count on, starting with three or four in Mt Healthy. This was a pattern that repeated as he grew up. He would latch onto several persons that he saw regularly and make the most of them. The awkwardness that stemmed from needing a couple of extra seconds to process the spoken word was a relationship killer for most people, and they would choose to direct their interactions towards a person without communication issues.

Blake also encountered those who would make fun of him because he presented such an easy target. Those people provided him with an involuntary education in human nature. Starting with kindergarten, he learned that not everyone could be trusted to put his interests first. His reaction to the possibility of mistreatment was to start off his interactions as agreeably as possible. The effect was to position himself as unthreatening and easy to defend if any bystanders were so inclined. In doing so he stumbled upon a system which greatly reduced the number of situations where he might be singled out for abuse by his peers.

Forty-nine years old now, Blake recalled a backpacking trip out West during his high school years. His group of 12 travelers had arrived in Seattle too late to have a choice of campgrounds and had to settle for a location close to the Seattle - Tacoma International Airport. Nobody gave the location a second thought while they unpacked, pitched their tents and made dinner. After dinner Blake saw that it was late, said goodnight and crawled into his sleeping bag. In the morning he found out that the campground was located almost directly under the airport's East - West runway where a succession of planes kept the rest of his group awake until exhaustion took over somewhere around 2:00 a.m. Once the noise situation became obvious, they gathered around the campfire in various states of disbelief, discussing whether to wake up Blake. As he learned in the morning, the majority voted to cut him a break and let him sleep, in no small part because he was considered a good guy.

This Friday morning Blake was traveling to a 9:00 a.m. appointment with his audiologist, Pamela Henry. His hearing aids were losing their effectiveness, and he was not happy about having to invest time in yet another adjustment. Heavy rain beat down on the truck's roof drowning out the radio. He could barely understand the radio under the best of conditions, much less now with the rain producing an overwhelming roar of white noise. The situation began to aggravate him as he drove through what was becoming a fierce downpour. As the intensity of the rain increased and the vehicles around him began to slow down en masse, he couldn't even go the speed limit, a situation that added to his annoyance.

He grimaced with impatience. Driving was an activity he enjoyed, as long as he could use the accelerator the way it was meant to be used. Being forced to travel at someone else's pace irritated Blake, making him search for any chance to whip around the offending turtle. An entire pack of cars was being forced to a crawl by the rainstorm, with him trapped in the middle.

Ugh!!! he growled. *I might as well be caught in traffic leaving a Reds game!*

If Pamela couldn't improve his situation by reprogramming his hearing aids, he would be facing two new units and a $5,000 charge. He didn't want to lay out that much money if there was another option.

Stuck in traffic that was going to be slow for the near future, he continued reflecting.

In 1981 he graduated from the University of Cincinnati with a bachelor's degree in Civil Engineering to start working as a maintenance supervisor at the Seagram whiskey plant located in Lawrenceburg, Indiana, 22 miles from Cincinnati. Blake vividly remembered taking his pre-employment physical at Seagram, scoring perfect except for his audiogram. After the plant nurse evaluated his scoring, she sadly told him that he didn't do well. He jokingly told her that it was probably one of his better days! Fortunately, the test didn't become an issue and Blake's first job started off normally.

It wasn't long before his career took a turn for the worse. Faced with the realities of the working world, it was clear that his disability was responsible for problems. Blake found it hard to assimilate with some of the other managers, finding himself being accused of arrogance because it was difficult for him to join in the normal camaraderie. Smart enough to figure out most problems by himself, his inability to effectively participate in discussions would cause him to appear stupid. He would answer the wrong questions, switch topics at the wrong time or wind up on the wrong side of the group consensus. Needing to blend in and achieve some measure of success, he soon determined that it was critical for him to form personal alliances.

There were occasions in the beginning when Blake would have visions of being forced into janitorial work because he couldn't do his job without relying on the kindness of others, but these days those visions were happening weekly. Hearing loss affected each decision that he made. He was shying away from controversial options since he knew that he couldn't hold his own versus animated opposition. Blake needed people working with him instead of against him or he was doomed.

Over a 24-year period noise exposure from the industrial environment gradually worsened his impairment from severe to profound. Profound is a loss of 80 db (decibels) or more. The clinical definition of a profound loss is listed as difficulty hearing and understanding, even with amplification. Blake viewed his loss as an affliction that affected every second of his day and any plans that he made for the future. A daily collection of missed comments was responsible for engendering a constant anxiety, taking a tremendous toll on his wellbeing.

Traffic sped up and for an instant Blake thought he might break free from the pack's uninspired crawl, but it proved to be a false alarm.

The rain was starting to get on his nerves. Driving was now a stop and go affair as the road accumulated water faster than the drains could remove it. Blake was alternating between the gas and the brake, feathering the pedals to the point where his right foot was developing a cramp. Attempts to rotate his ankle in between helped only slightly. Heavy rain was pushing humidity through the cracks in his vehicle's weather proofing and creating condensation on the windshield. He switched on the defroster and the air conditioner as he continued down the road, thankful that he was getting closer to his exit.

One coping mechanism that Blake relied upon heavily in his current situation was the ability to present a specific demeanor. Trapped in a group where it was too difficult to understand the conversation, he would direct his energy toward efforts designed to control his outward appearance. He would note the body language and mood within his group of companions in addition to other factors such as relationships and context. Combining his observations, he would determine which appearance to project. Sometimes he would choose to blend in and sometimes he would choose to stand out, switching presentations to check reactions from the group.

Projecting a particular pose was especially beneficial in dealing with any ridicule that came his way. Since he failed to act upset and his tormentors were deficient at mind reading, they would perceive him as unruffled, causing them to lose interest. He could easily reinforce their interpretation by standing up straight, speaking clearly and moving with deliberate slowness.

Blake also employed his posing as a protective strategy when he was unable to follow the conversation, but people expected him to contribute. If he kept his mouth shut it was natural for others to assign him points of view based upon body language and facial expressions. An appropriate bearing when combined with a lack of commentary would lead them to classify him as competent, agreeable or some combination of the two, when the truth was that he couldn't understand enough to be confident voicing an opinion of any kind.

The random occasions when he was lucky enough to say the right thing at the right time reinforced the value of timing. Wary of sharing too much since that day in kindergarten, he taught himself to understand how nonverbal cues could telegraph intentions and emotions. For Blake, survival depended upon employing a comprehensive suite of coping mechanisms rather than trying to scale the wall of the spoken word. He employed his strategies in the background, invisible for the most part since the immediacy of speech consumed the attention of his companions.

An exit sign appeared for Montgomery Road. Traffic was stop and go with the rain showing no signs of letting up. *One more mile,* Blake thought in relief. *Then I can get out of this crush.*

For as long as he could remember, Blake's biggest problem at work or at play would defeat him time and time again. Dependent as he was upon the goodwill of others, he invariably found himself in a predicament where he was limited by someone's inability to imagine an alternate method of communication. He employed notepads, emails, quiet zones and a host of other methods to facilitate communication only to run up against the same brick wall. Faced with the complications presented by Blake, people would often avoid the interaction, choosing to implement easier solutions that excluded him.

When people did choose to engage him, it wasn't long before a chain of events began where Blake would miss some comment, ask for a repeat, receive a reply, ask for another repeat, receive a shorter reply and so on. After enough false starts the conversation would die a miserable death as both parties transitioned to seeking a way out. It was a depressingly predictable sequence that would occur without fail whenever he attempted to communicate. The futility was endless, and he could sense it slowly suffocating his spirit.

Blake understood enough of human behavior to anticipate people taking the path of least resistance, but it was forcing him to inhabit an undesirable place. The path of most resistance was his route by default, and these days it was becoming a lonely slog. Creative workarounds could help him accomplish tasks, often better than most, but they could not offer the fellowship that developed from close relationships.

Unwilling to let hearing loss claim victory, Blake could see his isolation increasing as less and less sound entered his world. Desperation and depression easily found entry on his unprotected flanks, piercing his heart with a sword that he chose to bear in silence. He could not bring himself to share his pain with anyone, being reluctant to even acknowledge its existence. Blake feared that merely entertaining the possibility of being defeated by his handicap would bring that defeat closer to reality. So he fought with all the tools he could muster, determined to resist with every ounce of energy that he had.

Reaching the exit for Montgomery Road, Blake observed a long line of cars in front of him. *So much for that.*

Turning off the highway, Blake gave thanks that Pamela was available to fix his problems. For the last 14 years she had provided him with the latest technology by introducing him to portable FM systems, loop systems, cell phone telecoils and a succession of increasingly powerful hearing aids with better programming features. Her services allowed him to keep functioning at work and in the world despite his profound loss. He was already feeling grateful that another round of relief was on the horizon, even if it meant spending major bucks. Worst case, he would be ordering two new units this morning and be back to normal in a couple of weeks.

Thank God I'm almost there, Blake brooded while he watched for Pamela's office sign. *Things will be better after today.* Traffic was no better on the secondary roads, the rain causing his fellow drivers to become tentative and move at a snail's pace. *Safety first, let's take all day about it.* Flexing his fingers away from their grip on the steering wheel, he rolled his shoulders to ease his tension.

Arriving at his destination, Blake navigated to the entrance, parked and shut off the engine. Then he sat in his truck watching water flood the windshield so heavily that he could barely make out any lettering on the office door in front of him. Rain came down with a savage drumming as he remained inside, bogged down in his ruminations.

Blake was finding it necessary to avoid interactions that were not one on one in a controlled environment. His aids functioned on the edge of ineffectiveness, making conversation without lip reading infeasible. It was easier to never begin, and that was depressing. The momentary acknowledgement encouraged the sword he carried inside to twist in deeper, generating an icicle of fear.

Unable to participate in a group setting, Blake was letting himself drift off into daydreams. His default approach was to observe the people around him and try to understand how they were relating to each other. As he knew it would, his silence was causing his own invisibility.

There were group occasions when he needed to listen and respond, leading to a situation where he could perceive the sounds of speech but was powerless to solve the puzzle by himself. His frustration would grow, a living organism thriving in its optimum environment.

He could feel himself getting overstressed fighting the nonstop battle to understand. Years of frustration were responsible for creating a reservoir of unresolved rage which would overflow for seemingly no reason to spawn violent reactions in the face of minor annoyances. Driving, a plumbing job gone awry, waiting on a slow cashier, the wrong pizza, any of them could serve as the trigger, generating a response way out of proportion to actual events. Powerless to choose a different path, the constant need for adjustment took its toll on his mental state, sustaining a perpetual boil in response to the injustice of his situation. Blake was aware of this, could feel it reaching critical mass, but the rage could not be held at bay forever, eventually erupting to consume some undeserving victim. In the aftermath he would apologize. Those who knew him could see it coming and would get out of the way, reasoning that it was part of his cycle.

Explode and explain.

Temporary relief was available through racquetball, fishing or drinking whiskey, all of which served to help him decompress and come out the other side feeling renewed. Of the three options, racquetball was the most effective because it provided him an opportunity to haul off and smash something as hard as he possibly could, leaving him drained in the end. He needed the catharsis of focusing so intensely that his problems dissolved into the ether. Fishing brought the same kind of escape. Afterwards Blake would be ok for a while, could even laugh off some of the situations in which he found himself, but an extended period without one of the three was risky for himself and those around him.

He spent a minimum of energy considering the true reason behind his outbursts because he was unwilling to analyze that part of his life at anything more than a superficial level. Like the pain of isolation, he felt that to achieve a better understanding would only serve to highlight the state of his deterioration. Blake knew the struggle for comprehension was reason for his explosions, but he also wanted to blame a short temper to convince himself that he was halfway normal. All he would concede was that, yes, hearing loss was partly responsible for the blowups and, yes, he needed a regular safety valve. That made the difficulties more bearable in the long run. It was a personal compromise to achieve peace of mind and allow him to keep going.

Technology was his savior, allowing him to bypass the spoken word and still communicate. The advent of email was a tremendous improvement, giving him the ability to dash off a missive to replace the phone conversation that was impossible or eliminate the walk to a co-worker's office. He fantasized about the day that voice recognition would be a feature on his cell phone so that he could read a conversation without the possibility of misinterpretation. His hearing would always be substandard, but Blake saw technology as the light at the end of his tunnel. Somewhere in the world someone was working on a solution that would make ears obsolete. A brain treatment to kickstart ESP would fit the bill nicely.

Interrupting his train of thought, the cumulative effects of a useless radio, creeping through the rain and a looming probability of laying out $5,000 chose that moment to intrude. *This is not turning out to be a good day.* The thought slammed him back to the present. *Just like every other day.*

Blake felt ashamed thinking how close to the darkness he flirted, wondering if he was a danger to himself and others. Was he doomed to go overboard at some innocent event, lose control and violate the standards of propriety? The scary part was the number of ruthless scenarios alive in his mind, great white sharks lurking in the mix. His daydreams had teased him with so many inappropriate fantasies of getting even with the world that he could probably turn one loose without a second thought. An unpleasant suspicion that he would enjoy it unfurled itself with a hiss of evil glee. *Great.*

Sitting back, Blake inhaled the dampness brought by heavy rain as water vapor permeated the truck. *That's enough.* After traveling clear across town with no change in conditions, it appeared that the storm was going to last for a while. Placing his hand on the door handle, he readied himself for a dash through the rain. *Think positive,* he admonished himself. *It's going to get better. Pamela is my lifeline.* Without her help he would have lost hope a long time ago.

Blake unlatched the door of his truck and pivoted out of his vehicle in a graceful flow. Swinging the door shut, he sprinted towards the portico less than six feet away while shielding both hearing aids against the downpour. Despite his haste in covering the short distance, by the time he ducked under the awning he received enough of a dousing that his clothes were pasted to his skin.

Stopping in front of the doorway, Blake shook off the water and fluttered his shirt to release its grip. Standing 5'-8" at 150 pounds, with a muscular and symmetrical build, his defined shoulders and tight waist were the result of a weightlifting regime that started in middle school. Regular exercise ensured that his muscles were still compact and hard, although not quite the same as in his twenties. A receding hairline was rendered inconspicuous by the choice to shave his head.

He was wearing slim-cut grey jeans with a silky long-sleeved t-shirt that hung down without being tucked in. His shirt was black, a frequent choice. The effect was clean and understated, not form fitting, but tight enough to avoid appearing sloppy. A pair of Hugo Boss sneakers in black leather purchased during a trip to England completed his efforts.

An electronic bell chimed twice as he walked through the doorway, the air-conditioned office offering a sharp contrast to the dampness outside. Pamela's place of business consisted of dedicated offices for two audiologists, a centrally located reception desk and a waiting area offset from the entrance. A hallway behind the receptionist led to a small room with a testing booth, a kitchenette and a unisex bathroom. The decorating scheme of warm earth tones and low pile industrial carpet directed visitors to the waiting area where the chairs and couches were comfortable sinkholes of walnut brown leather.

He walked up to the receptionist. "Morning Val, it's nasty out there." His years at Seagram taught Blake to learn and use people's names as a means of gaining their cooperation. It amazed him that some of the managers would ignore such an easy strategy.

"Glad you made it," she replied. "I have you down for 9:00 a.m., with Pamela."

"Perfect," he responded. Blake eased himself down into the sanctuary of the nearest chair, fluttering his shirt to help dry it out. Picking up a magazine, he settled back to wait.

"Good morning, Simon!" Before he could finish paging through the magazine, a cheerful Pamela Henry strode out of her office to approach Blake. She was holding her coffee in one hand while offering the other in a welcoming handshake. He stood up and met her hand in a firm and familiar clasp. Captured by the self-assurance radiating from his attractive audiologist, Blake was boosted by a surge of optimism.

Nine years younger than Blake, Pamela held herself to her full 5'-7" height. She smiled and notched up her eyebrows at him. Warm brown eyes gazed comfortably into his as she said, "Shoot any teenagers lately?"

"Not today," laughed Blake. "But there's time!"

"Is there ever," she said, then turned to lead him back to her office. Like Blake, she had three kids, but, while his were mixed between college and high school, hers were all in high school. They were on the same wavelength with regards to raising children and often faced common problems with their respective offspring. As they walked back to her office Blake appreciated how Pamela's figure was still worth a perusal after three pregnancies. Shiny auburn locks bounced across her shoulders as she approached her office doorway.

Of the many audiologists whom Blake had encountered, he respected her the most. She was not pushy, knew her stuff and made sure to ask about his family, making visits more like two friends getting together than an office appointment. Blake respected how Pamela focused on what her patients needed instead of what she could sell them. Pamela understood the problems faced by those who were hard of hearing and made a practice of speaking slowly, clearly and pleasantly. If the rest of the universe spoke the same way, Blake would be fine reading lips for the rest of his life.

For her part, Pamela enjoyed a professional relationship with Blake that also included friendship. Blake provided a welcome change of pace to those of her patients presenting various combinations of whininess, and she appreciated how his efforts to get the most from his hearing aids made her job easier.

Pamela entered her office and waited for him to pass through the doorway. "Sit down and bring me up to date, Simon." After he walked in, she shut the door and proceeded to her workstation to take her own seat while Blake settled into his customary spot to the side of her desk, leaning back on the padded chair.

"I'm having problems again."

"Go on," she said, facing him with a comforting smile. Golden hoops dangled from her ears as she waited for his next words, letting him set the pace.

Blake started off, "I was wondering if you can boost my speech frequencies because I think that I'm missing more than normal." An engineer to the core, Blake would interrogate Pamela about how his hearing aids were supposed to work and how they were programmed. He knew that his aids had a total of twelve frequency bands, but he mostly cared about the frequencies dealing with speech. Speech frequencies typically ranged from 85 to 180 Hz (Hertz) for men and 165 to 255 Hz for women. His goal was to maximize his ability to understand speech, not being too concerned about environmental sounds such as cars or singing birds.

Pamela studied him with an appraising eye. She strove to treat all her patients the same, however with Blake she was willing to push the boundaries because he gave her useful feedback about results and didn't complain if an adjustment needed reversing. Many patients were incapable of properly analyzing their condition for her purposes because they had trouble describing their symptoms. Their descriptions centered on discomfort and dissatisfaction without defining the specific situation or equipment settings that were involved.

Taking some cables out of her desk drawer, Pamela said, "Let's check your settings and find out if the diagnostics tell us anything useful." Outside her office rain beat against the windows, with unbroken clouds offering a gloomy backdrop. There was a dullness to the atmosphere inside as the grayness from outside blended with artificial light from the ceiling.

She held out her hand, "Give me the left, please." Blake surrendered his device and Pamela began connecting it to her computer, embodying a calmness as she worked. "How is Emily?" she asked, referring to his wife.

"She has an open house this weekend." Blake's wife had been a realtor for the last ten years, a job that suited her.

"Always busy! Now the other."

Blake handed it off and said, "Good thing too. College is killing us this year with two kids at University of Cincinnati."

"You have my full sympathy," she commiserated. "Not looking forward to that." Pamela stood up and replaced the hearing aids on Blake's ears, carefully looping the cables around his shoulders and positioning the extra lengths on her desktop. Her closeness and easy manner instilled a familiar sense that an improvement was in the works. Blake could feel the tension exiting his frame as he relaxed in anticipation, his aids directly connected to Pamela's computer with a couple of thin wires.

"Here we go," she cautioned him. "The computer will run its diagnostic scan and then we'll have a conversation while I observe the frequency bands oscillating within their ranges." She took pains to narrate each step knowing that Blake wanted all the details.

"Let 'er rip!" responded Blake, eager to benefit from whatever magic she might pull from her bag of tricks this morning. He had yet to leave without a spring in his step after she miraculously bailed him out. She was a superstar. On those days when he agonized over going deaf, he sought reassurance in the wonders that Pamela performed.

While the computer ran its diagnostics Pamela reviewed her files on Blake's history, occasionally monitoring the computer screen. Blake took the opportunity to close his eyes and focus on relaxing the muscles around his neck and shoulders. The computer was blocking all reception from his devices, making it easy for him to drift off into a peaceful place.

The brief respite recharged him, leaving Blake burning to get on with it, opening his eyes to turn towards Pamela. After a few minutes the diagnostics finished, sounds flooding back over his world. He was aware of the rain pounding the office window and a slight hum, the origin of which he had no clue. Pamela was bent forward, closely focused on her computer screen. She nodded to herself slightly and then turned toward him with a smile, "OK. Let's talk!"

With a burst of ebullience, Blake snapped off his opening line, "How 'bout them Bengals?"

"You know that I come from Pittsburgh, don't you?" she replied. Pamela sat up in her chair and flipped back her long tresses while fixing him with a disapproving glare.

"That was your parent's choice. I can't hold that against you," Blake was grinning.

"You can't win against us either," she retorted. "You can try but it's free entertainment!" Her eyes were flashing at him now.

Blake laughed out loud. He was feeling better, the gloom and doom from this morning starting to fade. Pamela peeked to the side and adjusted some parameter on the screen with her mouse. With her other hand she absently tapped on the desk as she continued, "My husband is going to the game this weekend. I told him if he's going to wear a Pittsburgh jersey in downtown Cincinnati that he better tone down the loud stuff." Her eyes were smiling this time.

"Smart move," said Blake. "I might pick up some tickets off the street if the rain clears out."

"Could work," said Pamela. She returned her attention to the computer screen and began to click in various places, her face going blank with concentration as her fingers moved rapidly. Blake quietly watched her work the magic. His hearing seemed better already but that was par for the course since Pamela took pains to ensure that her office minimized environmental noises.

Won't be long now, he thought. Blake didn't think that Pamela would be able to modify the programming for his hearing aids and he was already resigned to spending money. His current units were purchased three years ago, a lifetime for advanced electronics. He interlaced his fingers together and spread both arms outward in preparation for the news, a ballet in slow motion. The rain drummed onto the glass in foreboding.

Pamela rotated towards him, glancing at the rain outside the window. Then she studied him closely before saying, "You already know that you have a profound hearing loss, 97 dB, and your hearing aids are set to optimum power."

"I thought so," Blake sighed. *Big surprise,* he told himself.

Pamela continued "Any power increases for the speech frequencies will increase distortion. The result will be less speech comprehension, not more." She inclined her head in the direction of the file laying open on her desk. "My records show these units are three years old."

"That's what I remember too," responded Blake. He moved his hands to grip both armrests. "So what's the latest and greatest available today?" Pamela was responsible for providing a continuous flow of solutions, and he was already anticipating her recommendation.

Pamela didn't respond. She smoothed her skirt with both hands before leaning forward with her hands clasped in her lap. Her eyes conveyed resignation as she spoke firmly and clearly, "The latest and greatest available today is exactly what you are wearing now."

Blake swallowed, "What do you mean? There haven't been any improvements for the last three years?" The news was unexpected, and his posture shifted as he began to sit up straighter. "That's a first," he added. A medicinal scent assaulted his nose, taking Blake by surprise.

"There have been improvements," she answered. "Unfortunately, the changes have been focused on speech algorithms, background noise and directional microphones instead of more power. None of those will help you if the sound can't register in your brain to begin with." Pamela shifted further back in her chair. She crossed her legs while putting a hand behind her neck to gather the length of her hair, getting ready for the backlash.

"So why doesn't Phonak put those features on a more powerful model?" asked Blake. He turned his palms up and continued, thinking out loud and progressing to what seemed like a logical conclusion. "That way the sound is loud enough for me and the processor enhancements give me better speech comprehension."

"Sure," Pamela began explaining, "The problem is that hearing aids have a limited amount of processing power. Phonak does not put those improvements on a stronger unit because processor design is a compromise between modifying sound and boosting sound. To incorporate processing improvements and more power the hearing aid would wind up being too large to fit behind your ear." She was watching Blake carefully now, this being a topic that gave him difficulties in the past. "We talked about this before; there is a limit to what I can do for you." *And this is it,* she thought, with a twinge of sadness. Pamela fell quiet as Blake looked toward the window.

Rain slammed against the glass in powerful surges, generating a fatalistic backdrop for the elephant materializing in front of them.

Blake broke the impasse. Turning away from the window back to Pamela he began to speak. "Doesn't Siemens have a unit with the same amount of power?" He was in problem-solving mode now with his back straight up in the chair, feet flat on the floor, elbows on the armrests. Aware that his heart was starting to pound, he kept going,

"I'd be willing to give Siemens a shot if theirs might be a little better." *Tell me that works,* he said inwardly.

"Siemens has 1 dB more power than your Phonaks," countered Pamela. "As we discussed three years ago, the two are virtually identical. You have the most powerful Behind-The-Ear (BTE) hearing aid on the market." Her voice was soft and resolute as she waited for the words to filter through.

Blake stared down at his feet and then back up to Pamela. Her warm eyes met his with the same competence as ever, except that this time they stoked a fear that he was afraid to acknowledge. Was she saying that there was nothing for him anymore? *What's happening?* There was a tightness in his neck and his ears were filling with a roar that blocked out any noise from the rain. "Why don't we try it anyway?" Blake suggested, unwilling to surrender after so many years of resistance.

Pamela tightened her lips and responded, "I'm sorry Simon. I became an audiologist to help people. Letting you spend your money on a diversion that has, in my professional opinion, no reasonable chance of improvement is not an avenue that I am willing to pursue." Her voice modulated in the soothing rhythm that Blake had come to associate with relief, but her meaning rocked his core. He sat there in disbelief, the sting of betrayal starting to emerge.

No more magic? The roaring was louder now. He could not think of anything to say, his eyes traveling around the room to land on a painting, a mountain somewhere. His mind was lost in the foothills, stumbling through the scrub in a futile search to regain the trail. Dimly, he became aware that Pamela was talking.

"What was that?"

Pamela sat forward to repeat herself, "Simon, there is another option available to you." Her face was calm and her voice gentle.

"Oh?" Thinking far too slowly, his response slipped out before he realized where she was going.

Pamela pounced on the opening, "It's time you were tested for a cochlear implant." In the quiet office her request resonated with the force of a gong, and she watched him disconnect.

No! Slicing through his psyche, Pamela's words caught Blake unprepared, cratering his spirit upon impact. In a flash his world was annihilated, eyes falling to the floor as his face went flat.

Earlier this morning he was living a crappy life, but it was a familiar crappiness with familiar problems. Pamela's words generated an unknown world where every activity was called into question. He felt sick as a dullness took hold, a dullness so pronounced that a fortuneteller would have recoiled at the hopelessness in his aura.

Throughout the years he had known people with implants. They talked funny. They looked weird. Maybe it was his imagination, but they held themselves differently. Each of them said that sound from the implants was better than nothing, but Blake secretly felt pity for them. He desperately wanted to avoid an implant, fearing it to be the end of his physical integrity. The idea that he no longer had a choice left him frozen to the chair, with the roaring in his ears replaced by silence. His awareness retreated to form a tiny ball, from which issued a keening wail.

Wrapped in a fog of disbelief, Blake's thoughts looped over the same refrain, *How can this be?!* Accustomed to steamrolling past obstacles, Blake was caught off balance at how suddenly his fortunes were being struck down by a mortal blow.

Blake panned his gaze around the room, unwilling to meet Pamela's eyes, trying to breathe. The rain and gloominess outside the window resonated with his mood. *Appropriate,* he thought. His face adopted a passive mask without a hint of emotion as his eyes transitioned to an impenetrable blackness. He replayed the devastating words, not yet trusting himself to speak.

The idea of an implant was detestable. He loathed it with a passion, unable to decide if it scared him to death or if he despised it. Fear, hate and rage braided themselves together into an unholy vortex, his heartbeat pumping the foul mixture with each beat.

His emotions ran amok, swelling his chest with the power to destroy. If he could have thrown a switch to destroy the planet, he would have done it.

I hate my life. He slowly shook his head. It was no idle thought. Malevolence was running wild inside, threatening to breach his clamped lips. His eyes became hard and flinty, hostility oozing to the surface. Unwilling to target Pamela, Blake purposely directed his gaze downward, knowing that he was at the end of the road through no fault of hers. With an angry exhalation he shoved his hatred into a box and slammed the lid, a string of epithets coursing through his mind.

Pamela reached out, "Simon, I know this is difficult, but implants have improved significantly in the last couple of years. One of my former patients is hearing better than she ever did with hearing aids." Her words filled the office with a familiar encouragement, making him wish for better days. As much as Blake wanted to lash out, his emotions were curbed by their mutual respect and friendship.

Even so, he couldn't hold back his rejection. *Big deal. I don't want anything to do with them.*

Blake had the ability to present an inscrutable exterior and the stronger his emotions the easier it was to do, channeling negativity so that it worked for him. He was busy constructing an outer shell that was strong enough to repel a line of tanks, ensuring that the world would see nothing except what he saw fit to release. His breathing slowed and his body entered a silent stillness. Pamela had saved him many times in the past and the least he could do was keep himself under control. It was a given that she would have spared him if possible. The day had come, that was all there was to it. Determined to remain in control, Blake could feel his turmoil growing, but there was plenty of power in his rage to flip that switch to the off position and keep it there long enough for him to leave the office. Some unfortunate soul would receive a killing blast later.

Sitting in the chair, Blake broke away from the turbulence inside to cross an ankle over his knee while his arms squeezed the ends of the armrests. Aware that a response was long overdue, he raised his eyes to Pamela. She met his gaze, waiting.

"I don't know." All he could get out was the same nonsense that drove him crazy coming from his kids. It was true though. The emotions in his mind were gyrating through fear, bitterness, indecision, action, rage and hopelessness, with every third heartbeat bringing a new perspective. His thoughts were a jumble, bouncing between schemes like a barefoot person trapped on hot blacktop.

To Pamela's credit, she did not push any further. Having said her piece, she knew Blake needed the gift of time. Implant candidates cycle between fear and hope. Their minds have to process surgery, rehabilitation, doctor visits, financial issues, work performance and the specter of the unknown. On top of all that was the possibility that the procedure might not work. In that event there are no further options, and life can easily degenerate into a depressing fusion of silence and isolation.

As if on cue, the rain switched to a light pattering as both Pamela and Blake remained quietly sitting in place. Minutes passed, the steady tap of the rain serving to solidify a fresh reality. The drama was exhausted, grey light from outside mirroring a subdued atmosphere inside the office. Waiting, they both understood that their 14-year relationship was coming to an end.

It was Pamela who broke the silence, offering Blake a path forward, "Think about it, Simon. I can connect you with a cochlear audiologist up at University Hospital when you're ready." Her eyes expressed compassion. Still on his side, her task was to present the most appropriate solution and she was determined to do exactly that. She would miss having him as a patient, but her job was done; it was somebody else's turn to work the magic.

Her words affected Blake like a favorite blanket that suddenly ripped. Their relationship was ending, that much was clear, sorrow mixing with shock to knock him off his feet. Facing an unknown future, he was losing his treasured audiologist. *What a morning.* He addressed Pamela, "Give me a few days. I'll let you know." *Or not.* Blake stood up, having no desire to stick around for any wallowing, starting to feel painfully awkward in her presence. *How could I have been so stupid?*

Pamela rose with him and said, "No problem. We can proceed when you're ready. Contact me anytime." She moved to her office door and opened it, "Let me walk you out." Moving ahead of him to the main entrance, she turned with warm brown eyes that said he would be remembered as one of her dearest patients. Her smile was genuine and full of caring as she presented her hand in goodbye. A professional and friendly smile that Blake knew he was going to miss.

Chaos cluttered his thoughts, preventing him from offering much of a farewell, so he clasped her hand and weakly croaked, "Thanks Pamela. For all of it." It was too early for the finality of today's events to sink in. With effort Blake forced out a regretful smile, thinking that he must seem pitiful indeed, and walked out the door, passing under a gentle rain. A few steps more and he gracefully pivoted into his truck the same way that he pivoted out. But he landed in a different world.

There were times in the past when Blake was faced with problems that dominated his life in a way that could not be ignored. The worst were searching for a job, selling a house and wrestling with infertility, each of which he hoped to never experience again. This was all that and more, bulldozing him so completely that he was too numb to consider the next step.

Right when he was getting ready to fly Pamela grounded the plane permanently. Earlier today he was hoping to get a good start to the weekend, but that expectation was gone, left behind with the remains of his old existence.

The nightmare was real, and it gripped him with a sickening paralysis.

Chapter 2 – Resignation

Blake sat in his truck with both hands on the steering wheel, molding his fingertips into the leather. A dwindling patter indicated that the rain was ending. As he watched another patient enter Pamela's office, Blake wished for a do-over. *Not a chance,* he told himself. *It's done. I was lucky to last this long.* His eyes darkened and a sneer fell across his face.

With a scowl he started the engine in preparation for the drive to work. Luckily it was Friday, because he needed to lick his wounds, starting with a generous pour of whiskey.

After work he would have a chance to examine the whole mess with his wife, Emily. She was the love of his life, his place of refuge. They met during senior year at the University of Cincinnati where the two of them blended together into a steaming cup of coffee and creamer.

As it came about, one Tuesday evening Blake and his fraternity brothers were shooting pool and knocking back shots in the Fat Cats pub off campus. By that time Blake was wearing two hearing aids, having received the second one during his junior year of college. They had been there for a few hours when the vibrant and beautiful Emily Heather Harris wandered in with her sorority sisters. With a mane of raven hair falling in lustrous waves over a voluptuous body, her entrance was noted by most of the pub occupants, but Blake was focused on the game, unmindful of her arrival. Emily noticed him bending across the pool table and maintained a subtle observation until she made up her mind that she liked what she saw, polling her sorority sisters to arrange an introduction.

The next day after class Blake stopped by the sorority house for a surprise visit. Emily was delighted. Their chatting escalated into a spontaneous dinner date as they both started getting interested and before long they were part of each other's daily schedule.

Taken with her beauty, Blake was enthralled by Emily's natural empathy and musical laugh. They found themselves to be kindred spirits, and friends were soon commenting on their peaceful intimacy. The budding relationship lifted them both up to a plane of existence that neither thought possible and once there, it was a natural decision to join their lives together. Their union simply worked, and Blake proposed after two months. Three kids and 25 years later the relationship was still working.

Emily was a partner who placed a high premium on loyalty, jumping in to be his ears whether they were at church, traveling or anywhere else. Whenever she got wind of anyone being inconsiderate they would receive a blast of rebuke and those who failed to conform to her expectations soon found that she was willing to escalate. Their three children, in particular, had all experienced her commitment to supporting her husband.

Blake checked the back-up camera and began to exit his parking spot, maneuvering through the lot to get back on the road. The pavement was wet and slippery but at least the rain had stopped, leaving behind a sky of solid grey that matched his dull mood. He was caught in the grip of his nightmare and the emotional upheaval had paralyzed his thoughts. Pulling onto the highway, he began heading in the direction of his office.

For a change Blake was one of the slower drivers on the road, having so much to think about that he was not thinking much at all. His truck tires hummed over the pavement as Blake navigated in a haze, functioning purely on autopilot and arriving at work without being conscious of the journey. He found himself sitting in his vehicle in a different parking lot, without the rain this time. A single-story office building stood before him; grey brick interspersed with vertical windows that extended from grade level to the roofline.

Blake had stayed at Seagram until 2005, when the company went up for sale. His ability to get along with different people worked in his favor, allowing him to establish a reputation for accomplishing results by enlisting the cooperation of others, and he advanced to a level one step below the position of Master Distiller. Deciding to investigate his options, Blake was fortunate enough to land a position at Worldwide Ethanol Fuel Technology (WEFT), a company that focused on designing industrial plants to produce ethanol used in automobile fuel. WEFT's reach was international, with clients in North America, South America, Asia, Europe, Africa and Australia. It was a good match since the fuel ethanol process is similar to the whiskey process, making an ethanol product of higher alcoholic content without the requirements of aging.

Proficient in the operations of cooking, fermentation and distillation, Blake was able to create a favorable impression in the quiet offices of WEFT. The president was enthralled, considering Blake's hiring a home run. Blake walked out the door at Seagram for the last time marveling at his luck in securing a better job with a hearing loss of such magnitude.

Worldwide Ethanol Fuel Technology was a small company with 15 employees. Peering around, Blake saw that the car of his boss, George Petropoulos, was absent. It was lunchtime, but his appetite was nonexistent. He was thinking to put in several hours and then leave without getting involved in any task requiring serious effort, unsure whether he would even last that long. If George stayed away, chances were good that he could make an early escape.

As he sat in his truck Blake watched a group leave for lunch, laughing as they exited the building. Others left on individual errands and he saw the opportunity to duck inside with minimal interaction. Above him the brooding sky matched his mood. His hands remained fixed to the wheel, their network of veins drawing his attention as the warmth of the seat welded his legs into place. He could easily stay captive to his paralysis.

Forcing himself to action, Blake exited his truck and approached the entry. As he glided across the blacktop, the tinted glass of the door prevented him from inspecting inside. He hoped there would be a minimum of people left by now. *Get ready,* he warned himself. Blake put one hand on the cold steel of the handle and slipped through the doorway, scanning the area as he entered. The door swung open soundlessly and he walked into the foyer.

One side of the foyer held a seating area while the other contained a reception desk that currently displayed an out to lunch sign. Two hallways branched off from the foyer. The office layout was a rectangle consisting of perimeter offices surrounding a common area in the middle that was taken up by a conference room, kitchen and break room. *So far, so good.* Nobody was in sight and Blake made his way down the right hallway. Grey walls and grey carpet continued the same color scheme as outside. Although muffled voices floated through the air, he made it to his own office without encountering anyone. *Never hurts to be lucky,* he breathed, as he ducked inside.

"Is that you, Simon?" A high-pitched sing song followed him through the doorway, accompanied by a smiling face as Angela Townsend, the office administrator, showed up to stand in the hallway. "You missed the lunch expedition," she informed him. "I think they're going to Skyline if you want to catch up." Angela was in her late sixties with gray hair and was prone to supplementing her official duties with a little mothering. Her hands were occupied with a cup of Coke in one hand and a salad plate in the other. She often referred to her drink as 'evil Coke' because of its double whammy from caffeine and sugar.

"I think I'll pass on lunch today," Blake answered. "Trying to finish up and start the weekend early." *Because I can't think straight anyway and need to leave as fast as possible.* As he spoke Blake settled into his chair and repositioned his computer keyboard, hopeful that Angela would take the hint and disappear. He liked Angela, sharing with her a common philosophy of building people up instead of tearing them down, but he wanted no part of a conversation.

Not so easily put off, Angela came back with "So what's the weekend schedule then?" Standing there holding her lunch she was too relaxed to interpret his weak suggestion. Her loose skirt flowed around her ankles as she swayed back and forth in front of his door.

"Emily has an open house scheduled for Saturday and Sunday. I promised to help her with staging this evening."

"Oh, a working weekend! We're going down to Oktoberfest. Gonna do the Chicken Dance!!" Angela gave a small shimmy as she said the last part. Coke sloshed around her cup and she lifted her eyebrows while displaying a perfect 'O' with her lips.

Faced with Angela's impromptu jig, an involuntary laugh escaped from Blake, "Ha! Don't think I can dance like a chicken!" *I might be able to stomp on one though.*

"I'll give you the update on Monday," Angela turned to go. Her skirt swished as she peeked back over her shoulder. "Don't pull any muscles. You're no spring chicken anymore!" She walked down the hall, laughing. From his chair Blake contemplated an empty doorway as her giggles tailed off. He wondered how he would feel after the weekend. *This might take more than a weekend.*

Blake considered shutting the door only to decide against it. Closing the door would guarantee isolation, but as soon as he opened it people might show up with a bunch of last-minute questions. *Don't need that.* He booted up the computer and started to go through his email. Finding a Snickers bar in his drawer Blake absently tore open the wrapper. The scent of chocolate and peanuts gave rise to a suppressed hunger and he devoured the candy with an indecent ferocity.

By 3:30 p.m. Blake was seriously considering going home. George was still gone, his attempts at productivity were proving fruitless and several people had already passed by with coats in hand. Outside his window sunshine was attempting to break through the cloud cover as rays of sunlight would come and go, occasionally beaming inside his office to cast a pleasant warmth. On the other side of the window tree branches were bent over, revealing the presence of a brisk wind trying to blow this morning's storm into history. Blake considered that the sun would be setting in a few hours, causing him to make up his mind and shut down the computer. *That's enough.*

Blake walked out of his office, down the hall and out the door, throwing off goodbyes as he bailed. Immediately upon his exit the trailing wind from the storm started to knife through his clothes, chilling him with an unrelenting intensity until he gained the sanctuary of his truck. *Finally! The day is over!* He needed to share his angst with Emily and feel the comfort of her embrace. They couldn't talk on the phone anymore and texting was a poor way to discuss serious topics, leaving her in the dark about this morning.

Pulling out of the parking lot Blake felt better knowing that he would soon be home. Once he hit the highway, he smashed down the pedal in his urgency. Courtesy of the strong winds, no water was left on the road and afternoon sunshine was circumnavigating the clouds that remained, producing an emerald glow wherever the rays touched grass.

Blake habitually drove above the speed limit. Currently there were zero points on his driving record so he figured that allowed him a little leeway. Flying down the road at 85 mph it wasn't long before someone interrupted his momentum, making his temper rise up in response. *Come on you brain dead steer monkey! Move out of the way!* It lacked his normal punch, but he wanted to fly. He wondered what it would be like not to be the fastest driver. *Way more relaxing, probably.*

Taking a deep breath, he tried to disengage, flashing back to when the family had taken their camper through the middle of Utah with scarcely any traffic and no speed limit. *Such a blast!* Not many gas stations either, but it all worked out in the end.

Memories of Utah took him through downtown Cincinnati and the suburbs of Delhi to park in his own driveway where for the last time that day Blake took a moment of refuge in the familiarity of his truck. His youngest daughter, Mackenzie Hannah, was 17 and lived at home. The other two, Madison Hailey, 21, and Matthew Hunter, 20, both attended the University of Cincinnati. Madison lived with a girlfriend in Cincinnati's Over the Rhine district, OTR, a revitalized area of downtown, while Matthew roomed on campus. Blake's thoughts shifted to breaking the news to his family. *Somehow.*

Getting out of his truck to walk up the front sidewalk, Blake hunched his shoulders against the wind attempting to cut through his clothes. As he approached the door, a golden warmth flowed from the sidelights, beckoning him inside. Blake turned the knob to catch a glimpse of his oldest daughter, Madison, disappearing into the kitchen. The house was filled with an enticing aroma, and shutting the door, he made his way across hardwood floors towards the kitchen where Madison had vanished.

Blake and Emily owned a three-bedroom ranch built in 1958. The walls were thick and the plumbing was copper, but the electrical system was woefully unsuited to the demands of the modern world. Blake spent four years remodeling the rooms one by one, updating them with additional lighting, adding extra circuits for an expanding universe of electronics and painting the walls and ceilings. He finished up by polishing the hardwood floors and including special projects for each room.

The crown jewel of their home was the kitchen, everyone's best-loved place, measuring 38 feet by 20 feet with a cooking area at one end and a brick fireplace at the other. Off to one side was a Dutch door that opened onto a screened-in porch looking out over a private backyard of two acres. In the middle of the kitchen stood a massive table constructed from black walnut, merging with pine cabinets and red brick walls to create a homey atmosphere. As Blake entered the kitchen he saw both Mackenzie and Matthew sitting at the walnut slab engrossed in their cell phones. Mackenzie's head came up long enough to give him a smile and a nod while Matthew stayed glued to his phone. Madison and Emily were standing together at the stove monitoring a simmering pot of stew from which wafted up a delicious promise.

"Hi peeps!" Blake announced, drifting toward the stove to move up behind his wife.

"Hey babe!" Emily turned from the stove and slid into his arms, tucking herself in under his chin. Giving him a brief hug, she leaned back to expose a silky curve of neckline. In the next second her hands pulled Blake down to a set of full lips that embraced him with demanding intensity. Her greeting was short but powerful, claiming him as her own.

"Lighten up Mom. We have children in the room." Madison watched her mother's greeting with an amused smile.

"Watch and learn then!" Giving her husband's face a gentle caress, Emily twinkled at her oldest daughter and swiveled back around to inspecting the stew. Curls of lustrous hair swirled in her wake, settling to her shoulders as she completed her turn.

"How is it that we have the whole crowd in one place on a Friday night?" Blake inquired. Standing close enough to his wife that a stray hair floated across his face, his gaze tracked the lines of her neck. *Yeah.* Reluctant to separate, he rested a hand on the curve of her waist.

Emily turned in his direction so he could read her lips, "Last night's storm knocked out power and cancelled classes at the University. This morning I asked Madison and Matthew to help set up my showing for the weekend." She bent down to peek in the oven at her biscuits and continued, facing Blake again, "The good news is that we have tonight free for ourselves!" No one else saw the suggestive wink she slipped in.

"Works for me," Blake responded. "I'm ready for a drink. Who's in?" A chorus of agreement came his way, and he headed to the liquor cabinet in the other room.

Blake's philosophy on drinking differed from accepted practices. He was OK with his kids experiencing alcohol while underage because he wanted to observe how they reacted. If by chance one of them was prone to losing control Blake wanted to know so that he could take preventative measures for the future. Another goal was to teach his children how to enjoy alcohol in moderation rather than dangling the forbidden fruit for years and risking an orgy of overindulgence when they came of age. In the case of his girls, Blake wanted them to be at ease with alcohol so they could focus their energies on how they were being treated. From what he could observe, the approach was working. Madison, in particular, was immune to the mystique, having taken a six pack to Florida for Spring Break and returned with half of them unopened.

Taking his approach a step further, when they reached the age of 18 he had already taken Madison and Matthew out to the porch to sample the heady combination of whiskey paired with a cigar. He would do the same for Mackenzie next year. It wasn't so important for Matthew, but if the girls encountered someone who tried to impress them by lighting up a stogie, he hoped that their reaction would be somewhere along the lines of, 'been there, done that'.

Oldest of the three, Madison arrived after four years of trying to conceive, each more stressful than the last. Combating infertility proved to be a miserable time for Blake and Emily. The surge of optimism gained from seeking professional help dissipated into hopelessness when month after month passed without results. Infertility is with you daily, a cloud that follows you around in the background, growing to a thunderstorm that drenches you with the arrival of the dreaded period, shrinking down to a smaller puff of white as hope creeps in afterwards, only to return with a vengeance the next month. Eventually hope fades to a pinprick of light and a black cloud looms overhead constantly, the sole difference being whether or not it pours. There is a striking similarity to hearing loss.

After fourteen months of disappointment Blake knew to the day where Emily was in her cycle, a concept outside the limits of his imagination when he decided to propose. It was hellacious for Emily. Each day would find her agonizing over an empty womb, unable to escape the presence of women with cooing babies in their arms.

Then one memorable day Emily was pregnant and they both prayed for her pregnancy to hang on past the critical three-month mark. Afraid to share such news too early, they held their hopes between the two of them, dreading the consequences of a miscarriage.

Three months became four, then five, and they were on their way. Today their oldest daughter was a 5'-9" willowy blonde with short hair, sparkling blue eyes and a finely chiseled face. Madison was attractive, both physically and because of an unshakable confidence. Graceful and sophisticated, she could rock a pair of high heels in a way that was unforgettable.

Matthew followed, bypassing the infertility angst. Unlike his father, he was not inclined towards physical activity or spending time outdoors. On the thin side, he chose to dress in dark jeans and t-shirts, seeking to fit in at grunge clubs where the dark venues gave a translucent cast to his white skin. With hair the color of midnight inherited from his mother he was a perfect contrast of white and black. His son had a habit of talking in choppy sentences with long pauses in between, a speech pattern that robbed Blake of the ability to interpret context and often made communication difficult.

The baby was Mackenzie, who inherited curves and olive skin from her mother plus physical aptitude from her father. Her extracurricular activities at Oak Hills High School were dancing and cheerleading, and at 5'-3" she was the perfect size for the requisite lifts and throws. Like her sister, Mackenzie chose to wear her brown hair cut short, pairing it with a million-dollar smile that brightened up the room. Eleven years of dancing and cheerleading had perfected her primping skills so that Mackenzie could achieve the most dramatic transformation with the least effort.

Blake loved all his kids, but there was no denying he shared a unique bond with Mackenzie. When she was a toddler, the two of them had instinctively developed their own unspoken language. Somehow she figured out that words could be more of a hindrance than a help and they developed a system to communicate by glance or gesture. Mackenzie also had the advantage of watching her mother berate her two siblings for not facing Blake when speaking to him. Of his three children she was most in tune with her father's impairment and put the greatest effort toward adjusting her speech patterns for him.

Opening the liquor cabinet, Blake evaluated the choices and decided to go with Woodford Reserve. Uncorking the bottle, he took a sniff. *Perfect.* Twenty-four years at Seagram gave Blake an appreciation for all kinds of whiskey and his inventory contained Scotch, Irish, Canadian and American expressions with multiple variations among each category. Sometimes he drank whiskey neat for the purposes of tasting it, but otherwise Blake mixed it with Coke. He viewed drinking whiskey neat the same as sex that dragged out too long – the burn overrode any sensation of enjoyment.

Bringing his bottle into the kitchen, Blake began to make the drinks. Mackenzie was arranging place settings for dinner while her older sister and mother were attending to the salad and biscuits. Matthew continued to busily punch at his cell. Although it was quiet in the kitchen, Blake was having trouble picking up the conversation between Madison and Emily. He lifted his eyebrows at Mackenzie and she supplied, "Madison is going to an FC Cincinnati soccer match tonight and is telling Mom that you guys would enjoy it."

Blake nodded in acknowledgement and started to revisit the events of the morning. He had the whole family here and was trying to figure out how to bring them up to speed. "Did she say what time the match starts?" he inquired.

"8:00 p.m." Mackenzie finished setting the table and sat down in her spot. "I have to be at the basketball game by 6:00 p.m. We're doing a sleepover afterwards." She gave a giggle and continued, "Not here though! I don't think that fits in with Mom's plans!" Blake shook his head as he carried the drinks to the table. *Full time romance radar.*

Blake sat down with Mackenzie and Matthew, then took a swig from his glass. *I need that!* The smooth sweetness of Woodford and Coke trickled down his throat with an effervescent tingle that helped to loosen the tensions of the day. He held the short glass up to his nose, allowing the scent of vanilla to caress his senses, grateful that he was sitting in his kitchen surrounded by people he loved. Another taste added to his resolve and he decided that his best opportunity was either during dinner or immediately after. *Sometime after bourbon number two,* he told himself.

Still chatting, Emily and Madison loaded up the center of the table with a steaming pot of beef stew, hot biscuits, butter, honey and a fresh salad made with spinach, carrots and red bell peppers. Taking her place, a smile bloomed across Emily's face. The spread of home-cooked food together with the whole family present made the atmosphere resemble a holiday. Observing the joy in her expression Blake lifted his glass and gave an impromptu toast, "Here's to family time!"

As a unit the family lifted their drinks and a resounding "Cheers!" drowned out the staggered clinking of their glasses.

Blake's toast triggered a festive atmosphere and suddenly there were dueling conversations taking place. Madison and Mackenzie began a discussion about their respective plans for the weekend while Emily took the opportunity to ask Matthew how his classes were going. Just like that their words collapsed into a game of pick up sticks, leaving Blake lost in the jumble.

He was used to dealing with isolation around co-workers or strangers, but it was a biting pain to encounter the same futility at home, causing a sadness to creep over him. *They're only acting naturally,* he reminded himself. The fact that his deafness limited interactions with his family was a bitter pill. Hearing loss was such a powerful curse that it could even transcend loving relationships.

The bitch slap that never stops stinging.

Left to his own devices in the midst of the family gathering, Blake took a nip of Woodford and switched to his habitual pattern of observation. It was obvious to him that Emily was trying to pump Matthew for information and equally obvious that Matthew was being uncooperative. Focused on her son's intransigence, Emily was temporarily distracted from the rest of the group while Matthew's energy was occupied with resisting his mother's probing questions. Mackenzie and Madison were engaged in an animated discussion punctuated by hands flying through the air. Knowing his daughters' proclivities, Blake would bet money that boys were involved.

Summing up his observations, Blake determined that his isolation had no obvious break point. He loaded his plate, took another pull of whiskey and settled back to wait.

With a sigh of exasperation Emily gave up on Matthew and turned her attention toward the rest of her family. A pang of sorrow touched her heart as she took notice of her husband quietly eating. No explanation was required. She had seen it before and would no doubt see it again. Then she remembered his visit to the audiologist today. The hectic pace of rounding up helpers, staging tomorrow's open house and preparing dinner had totally consumed her time. Mentally chastising herself she inquired, "Simon, what happened with Pamela this morning?"

Blake looked up from his plate to meet Emily's eyes, gazing into a face with long black eyelashes framing a pair of hazel irises flecked with green that were surrounded by brilliant circles of pure white. It was easy for him to get lost in those eyes, especially when they were gripping him with such an unwavering focus.

With a small sigh he straightened up to put both hands on the armrests of the chair. Shifting to one side and then the other, Blake gave another sigh and shook his head as he lightly clamped his lips together. Not one to glorify negativity, he had no idea what to say. It wasn't the type of information that he wanted to blurt out, but he couldn't decide how to begin.

Before he could start, Mackenzie became aware of the mood shift and switched her attention to him. Holding up a single finger she stopped Madison in mid-sentence and sat there watching her parents. Blake was now front and center whether he liked it or not.

Sitting in the chair Blake's face was naturally controlled and flat. His daughters frequently said that they had a hard time reading him. Emily would usually have to clue them in since she had the advantage of knowing him and his moods much longer. Blake's emotions were telegraphed by a flickering of his eyes, a twitch of the eyebrows or a light pursing of the lips in conjunction with a minute movement of his head. The tells could be hard to spot, appearing and disappearing in the space of one or two breaths.

Blake was scared, upset and confused, paralyzed by a muddle of distress. He was having trouble expressing himself because his emotions were swirling together, each one competing to break free of the pack.

Emily knew how to pull him out of it so she softly coaxed, "Tell me a little."

"OK," responded Blake, grateful for the opening. "Pamela told me that my hearing aids are as powerful as they can get. There's nothing better available." He picked up his half-finished drink. Encircling the cold glass with his palm, he swirled the mixture around, causing the ice to produce a musical tinkling and creating a foamy layer on the surface of his drink. That was his favorite part, and he took a second to slurp the foam off the top. "My hearing is getting worse, but the aids are maxed out."

Putting down her fork, Emily's eyebrows knitted together in concern. All three children were now paying close attention, Matthew accepting the diversion as a welcome release from his mother's interrogation. Emily addressed her husband, "What does that mean?"

"Well," Blake sat back in his chair swirling his glass, the regular motion helping him to stay on an even keel. *Here it comes.* His swirling got a little faster and he watched foam collect on the surface of the whiskey. Four pairs of eyes waited in suspense. He met the concerned visage of his wife, wishing he could let those eyes take him somewhere other than the place now rushing up.

"She said that I should get tested for a cochlear implant."

As he said the words Blake was rattled by a gong in the halls of his consciousness, made worse because of Emily's widening eyes. For the second time that day he was shocked with a mixture of fear, confusion and anger. In the cozy kitchen surrounded by his family, fear won out, squeezing his heart and cause it to skip a beat. Anger linked arms with fear as he was overpowered by his new reality. *This is me now.*

Knowing how Blake felt about cochlear implants, Emily slowly sagged back into her chair. Pamela had called her earlier, but it went to voicemail and she didn't get around to checking it. The food was forgotten. *Of course, it would happen today!*

Madison, Matthew and Mackenzie took in their father's announcement along with their mother's reaction and were left in confusion. Mackenzie was first to speak, saying, "Dad, what is that? Another type of hearing aid?"

Turning towards his daughter, Blake was grateful for the query, finding it easier to answer questions than to come up with something to say. He and Emily had discussed cochlear implants before, but the children didn't know that implants even existed. Gathering himself together he began to explain, "A cochlear implant is a medical device that bypasses the ear and stimulates the auditory nerve directly." Blake pronounced each word slowly as he spoke, waiting for the concept to register. Gradually comprehension began to dawn on the three of them.

It was Madison who figured it out first. "Do you need an operation?" She had adopted her Dad's habit of swirling her drink and was now slowly slurping off the foam like he would do. The animation displayed during her discussion with Mackenzie was gone, replaced by a questioning frown.

"Yes," Blake answered. "I know that much. There's plenty to learn though." With his burden out in the open he was starting to relax. He drank from his rapidly disappearing whiskey and gave Madison a reassuring nod, "Some of my friends have them so it's an established procedure." *Which I have no desire to be part of.*

Emily broke in, "Your dad hasn't needed to consider an implant before, so we haven't brought it up." She was mad at herself that she had not gotten ahead of the day's lightning strike. "Simon, let me get you another drink." Rising from the table she took his glass and went to the refrigerator, jamming his glass under the ice dispenser in silent frustration.

"What does that cost anyway?" Matthew entered the conversation.

As soon as the words left his mouth Mackenzie turned on her brother with undisguised contempt. "It doesn't matter what it costs dope! Shut up!" Green eyes drilled her brother with deadly force, her expression capable of dropping a rhinoceros in its tracks. Next to her mother, she was her father's best advocate.

From the counter Emily pinned Matthew with her own stony expression. "We have insurance for that," she said firmly. She finished making her husband another drink and walked across the kitchen with it. Bending down, Emily curled her hair back behind her neck as she offered him the glass. Blake was struck at how inviting she appeared to him in that moment.

Recovering from her shock, Emily attempted to redirect the conversation. Standing by her husband she announced, "Regardless of cost or any other details, we will support your father the way he supports us." Three heads nodded in agreement. Keenly aware of their mother's reaction when someone mistreated their father, all three knew that the wrong response would take them to a place they had no desire to visit.

Emily took her seat and turned in the direction of her husband. Unknown to him, a couple of years ago Pamela had shared with her that getting an implant was a matter of time, but she had also told Emily that it was a significant decision and Blake needed to get there at his own pace. Trying to figure out where he was at in his mind she said, "Simon, tell me what you're thinking."

Blake regarded his wife across the table. His meal had been abandoned, replaced by his second drink, and the alcohol was having a calming effect. Thanks to 24 years at a distillery, he could drink a fair amount before it started to show. The kids were returning to their dinner, but he was on the whiskey train. "I guess I need to investigate. Maybe contact Pamela on Monday and go from there." *There's not much of a choice any longer.*

He tried to smile and lighten up the mood. "On the bright side, there's still plenty of whiskey to drink between now and then!" Blake held up his glass in a silent toast. He had no idea what to expect but it appeared that he was going to get educated. *I'll even know the answer to Matthew's butthead comment.*

***

"**B**ye Matthew!" Emily shut the door behind her son. The two girls had left after dinner, but she kept Matthew back for a discussion.

Appalled at his insensitive comment, she wanted to emphasize how heartless it made him appear. Emily, like her husband, tended to quickly go ballistic. On a smaller scale her blowups matched Blake's pattern of rage, release, repent. The similarity allowed her to view his upsets as temporary blips and it was one reason she understood him so well. Fortunately, by the time she got Matthew alone Emily had calmed down, not liking to lose control with her children.

Matthew was immature, the family member most likely to do or say something dumb. She hoped that he had gotten the message and would be more supportive in the future. Emily could see Blake trying to find commonality with his son, but Matthew was focused on loud music in dark clubs, not exactly an optimum situation for his dad. Empathy was a skill Matthew needed to work on. As far as her daughters went, Madison connected easily with her father and loved to

55

discuss whiskey while Mackenzie bent over backwards to accommodate him.

Emily was determined to be Blake's champion for the duration of this journey. She loved and respected her husband, and the fact that he made a good living impressed her. Many of the hearing impaired experience stalled careers because of their disability. There was an alpha force about him that came from not giving up and this made her feel secure. Early in their relationship Emily recognized that Blake would be a reliable partner come what may, appreciating his natural optimism and the way he made things happen for her.

Going back through the house Emily went in search of her husband, heading towards his office where a light shone out into the hallway. She peeked inside. "Hello," she purred. "I have you all to myself tonight!" Hazel eyes with heavy lids locked onto Blake with swirling flecks of green going every which way. Blake looked up from his desk, to be captivated by her gaze. He swore up and down the unique flecks changed depending upon her mood, and tonight they were glowing and dancing in a ballet produced just for him.

Taking in the sight of her, Blake was transfixed by the symmetrical mounds of her breasts pushing out the front of a grey cashmere sweater that disappeared inside tight black jeans. Her belly made a gentle rise and fall before descending into a flat splay of hips. In the plunging neckline of her sweater an inviting swell of cleavage displayed a tantalizing valley of silky skin. His breathing took a sudden hitch as her beauty and availability hit him full force.

Emily stood in the doorway, one hip jutting sideways, a real-life fantasy standing six feet away. "How long are you going to be?" Low and husky, her unspoken invitation hung in the air between them as her eyes pooled with desire. With her head tilted back, golden earrings flashing against the arch of her exposed neck and an arm stretching up against the doorjamb, Emily was a showstopper. She knew what she wanted and how to get it.

Blake's mouth turned dry as he was captured by the intentional distraction. "I'm waiting for you," he responded. The seductive allure of his dazzling wife flooded his thoughts. He watched the hazel in her eyes whirl with eddies of sparkling green, even gold. *My God is she gorgeous!*

"In that case I guarantee you'll forget all about this morning." She turned sideways in the doorway to offer him her outstretched hand. "Follow me." Shiny falls of raven hair lay across her breasts, accentuating her voluptuous curves. Willed forward by the power in her eyes, Blake rose to her summons and Emily smiled as he approached. Towing him behind, she led her husband to the bedroom.

Chapter 3 – Evaluation

The following Monday morning at 6:30 a.m. Blake was at his desk drinking Starbucks, relishing the jolt from three shots of espresso. When not traveling overseas, Blake's breakfast was a triple, venti, nonfat, no-whip mocha. If the right barista was on duty, his drink would be waiting when he arrived at the register, and on those days Blake would sometimes receive a jealous dagger from the customer preceding him. He would throw the barista a thumbs-up and slide on out the door. *Gotta learn those names, dude!*

Over the weekend his ability to sleep uninterrupted helped him recharge from Friday's emotional wallop. The capacity to shut down noise and encase himself in silence was a great benefit of deafness. *Maybe not so great for a hotel fire though.* Blake sampled his coffee and scrolled through the week's schedule. Early morning was a treasured time when his energy belonged to him alone. Later on he would have to handle the demands of interpreting what was issuing forth from everybody's pie hole.

Blake considered the schedule on his computer as he fingered the knot of his tie. The years of avoidance were ending today and it was time to raise his sword to confront the dragon, because an unpredictable future with an implant was better than a predictable future without one. This morning he was wearing tailored grey pants, a white dress shirt patterned with red pinstripes, black wingtip shoes and a Jerry Garcia tie that pulled it all together using intermingled waves of red, grey, black and white. He made a point of starting each workday with the sense of positivity that came from dressing sharp.

When his children were infants and prone to spitting up, Blake would quickly hand them off to Emily if he thought they were approaching an eruption. The prospect of sullied clothes mortified him, making his wife roll her eyes and watch his panics with amusement. Today he felt invincible after giving himself a haircut last weekend, leaving his dome as smooth as an egg and glowing with a caramel hue. Bolstered by his meticulousness, Blake felt energized to direct full resources toward addressing his dilemma. He texted Pamela asking for a contact number and settled back with his Starbucks. *And away we go!*

Traffic moved down the hallway as his co-workers began to arrive, Blake reflecting on how being hard of hearing made it necessary to temper his behavior at work to avoid conflict. He couldn't afford to have dysfunctional relationships at WEFT, because he needed assistance from his co-workers on a regular basis. His primary focus was to cultivate loyalty for those instances when he failed to understand. Sometimes he walked a troubled line, supporting positions that he would consider unacceptable under different circumstances.

Angela was a bright spot. She had a natural empathy for the underdog and was considerate of Blake's loss, providing him with a relationship that offered honesty instead of artificiality. He relied on her to let him know what was going on behind the scenes and to keep him up to speed during meetings.

Blake was doubly careful in his relationship with his boss, George, making sure that their interactions didn't reach a point where the two of them were irrevocably at odds. George had no clue about the compromises Blake made to stay on his good side, but neither did anyone else in the office, not even Angela. That was by design because Blake saw no value in revealing vulnerabilities to his coworkers.

With so many relationships to juggle and his hearing decreasing over time, Blake was increasingly aware that he was living on the edge. Pamela's rejection meant that his options were now reduced to a single solution, because he knew of no alternate fix waiting in the wings.

A stab of panic pierced his heart at the realization that an implant might very well be his last chance. He surveyed his office with engineering manuals filling the bookshelf and drawings spread out over his worktable. One wall displayed a prominent picture of yeast cells, a memento from Seagram. Blake had years of experience making whiskey and fuel ethanol, but his expertise and people skills were useless if he couldn't communicate.

If an implant doesn't work, I'm screwed. My life can only get worse and it already sucks. Putting down his coffee Blake stood up to head for the kitchen. *I can't think!* Angela brought in donuts on Monday and he needed the diversion of a chocolate bomb.

Walking heavily down the hallway Blake considered the ways his life would change if things kept getting worse, none of them good. As he got closer the smell of fresh pastries and coffee filled the air until, turning the last corner, he saw the kitchen was already occupied by two of his co-workers. Dan Henderson, with whom he maintained the barest of relationships, was standing by the sink located at the far end talking to Robert Nolan, whom Blake considered a buddy. The long and narrow kitchen had a grey tile floor and white cabinets. A table and chairs were set against one wall and a full-length grey countertop ran along the other. Blake called it a one-man kitchen because its long length and short width permitted only a single person to comfortably perform meal prep at a time.

Dan was in a position that served to block access to both the refrigerator and the sink. *A normal situation for him,* Blake observed, *getting in somebody's way while being oblivious to it.* He was a thin and gangly engineer with white skin and straggly hair who had a propensity to be clumsy. Unmarried, Dan spent his days living in his own world and indulging his own idiosyncrasies.

"Hey Simon," Robert nodded in his direction, "What was your choice of whiskey this weekend?" A former Navy mechanic, Robert was 5'-6" and 135 pounds, fit and trim due to an exercise regime carried over from his military days in Scotland. Robert and Blake both shared an appreciation for whiskey, often discussing the merits of Scotch versus bourbon.

Blake considered the question for a minute, knowing that it didn't matter what he said, because no one at WEFT believed that he could make it through a weekend without drinking whiskey anyway. A denial would be met with disbelieving guffaws. "The sweet touch of Woodford," he answered, flashing a brief smile, "and this morning I need the sweet touch of chocolate!"

"Amen to that!" said Angela, as she entered the kitchen carrying paper plates. "I have more supplies from the bathroom for you guys!" Blake rolled his eyes at the comment. WEFT was the only place he knew of where kitchen supplies were stored in the ladies bathroom. Having been thoroughly trained in the consequences of sexual harassment at Seagram, he would never need something bad enough to get it from the women's bathroom.

"About time," Dan broke in, wandering over to the counter where the donuts were laid out and standing directly in front of it. A sloppy dresser, his shirt was already starting to pull out in the back. Blake regarded Dan with an internal boil. On different occasions Dan had offhandedly remarked that Blake probably heard more than he let on and the clueless comment invariably propelled Blake into a seething turmoil. Sometimes he got lucky and figured out a few tidbits. *Then this ignorant turd accuses me of hearing more than I do.* He fantasized about watching Dan screw up on some remote jobsite and ripping him a new asshole. *One that he won't forget.* No revenge could ever compensate for having to put up with Dan spewing forth his ignorance though, and Blake had assigned Dan a place on his shit list a long time ago.

"Sorry Dan. The chocolate one has my name on it." Blake reached around Dan to take possession of the sole chocolate donut with chocolate frosting, slipping it onto a plate while turning to leave the kitchen. Raising his eyebrows at Dan he continued, "The rest of them are up for grabs." *You stupid self-absorbed bastard.* A slight wink to Angela belied his bland expression and she returned a knowing grin.

Returning to his office, Blake laid the plate on his desk, swinging into his chair before taking a bite. He savored the erotic sensation of rich chocolate cake mingling with sweet chocolate frosting, the diversion clearing his mind. Hot coffee chased down the sweetness with a bitter aftertaste. Then he wanted to do it again, and, flipping his tie out of the way, he moved up closer to his desk to finish. It was a challenge trying to eat while wearing a tie and getting food on his tie was guaranteed to throw him off kilter for the rest of the day. *So don't.* Coffee and chocolate celebrated with a party in his mouth, Blake's thoughts drifting to his boss, George, with whom he checked in on Monday morning.

In a much better frame of mind after the donut, Blake rose from his chair to grab his coffee and navigate down the hallway to George's office. The panic attack of earlier was gone, replaced by resolve. George was already here; Blake had noted his car through the window. Massively built, George was 6'-9" with a barrel chest and wide shoulders. At the age of 62 he was proud of his thick grey hair that he wore long, covering his ears and part of his neck, giving him the illusion of grasping after youth. Long hair on older men was tough to pull off and George wasn't one of those who could do it. Possessing large hands studded with thick fingers, he evoked an image of a bear trying to hold a candy bar whenever he used a cell phone. Blake often marveled how he ever got the buttons to work.

In keeping with his physical presence, George was a blustery character who preferred solving problems aggressively, not caring to soft pedal his approach. Most of the time Blake's sole choice was to go along whether he agreed or not because there was no way to mount a rebuttal when George's rapid-fire delivery overwhelmed his ability to keep up. Unable to form an opposing opinion within the turbulent flow of oration, Blake found it easier to roll with

George's plan. The part that aggravated him was the implied perception that he agreed when in reality he sometimes thought differently. Those were the days that triggered a need for racquetball therapy. Blake silently celebrated the rare occasions when he could orchestrate events ahead of time so that his ideas were presented as a done deal.

As soon as Blake appeared in his doorway George waved him in and started speaking before Blake could enter. "Simon, perfect! Come on in!! I got a problem for you!!" His voice boomed out to fill the hallway and his eyes were wide in a display of agitation, but it failed to make an impression on Blake. George didn't need much to get excited.

Blake stopped short of entering to support himself against the doorway with his coffee, knowing that if he sat down the tirade would only be prolonged. He preferred to appear as if he was on the verge of having to visit the bathroom. "What's up?" Both he and George shared an exhaustive experience with the mechanical and biological considerations involved in making ethanol, enabling them to bypass the red herrings and identify root causes better than anyone else in the company. It was a significant connection and they worked together well. *Even if he always gets the last word,* thought Blake. *Then again, he does own the company. I'm pretty lucky to be here.*

"Our Austrian plant has developed a fermentation problem," George explained. "I need you to analyze the data and figure it out. They've been crying about it since Saturday." He raised a thick arm in the air and waved it around as he spoke.

"Since Saturday," Blake replied, "Did they send all the supervisors to a seminar and ignore the lab results for a week?" Thanks to his time at Seagram, Blake was the fermentation expert at WEFT. A detail he regularly emphasized was the need to analyze fermentation data as soon as it came out of the lab, having learned that conscientious attention to the data went a long way towards heading off fermentation issues.

"Something like that," George grimaced. "I'm not trying to say they're blameless. We need to steer them in the proper direction though." He nodded at Blake, bobbing his head in confirmation, "Tell me the problem and I'll call them back." Loosening his tie, George looked like Monday was already getting the best of him.

"Could be more than one, you know."

"Tell me the most important, that's all I need." George shot down further discussion, large hands flying to either side for emphasis.

Blake sighed in defeat, *OK, Mr. Black and White.* "Give me an hour, I'll let you know." He gracefully rotated off the doorjamb and cast a glance backwards. "I was reviewing their lab results last week and I already have my suspicions." At Seagram he had learned to think ahead in an attempt to discover hidden problems, a habit that paid off repeatedly. Sometimes he made it seem too easy because nothing bad appeared to happen, but that meant problems got solved while they were still small. *Time to earn my keep!* Heading back to his office, he was grateful that George was willing to forgive Blake's inability to make the phone call himself.

*****

Later that afternoon, Blake was done for the day and ready to get out of Dodge, amazed at how much more taxing Mondays could be from the rest of the week. Taking Pamela's recommendation, he had scheduled a 10:00 a.m. appointment for next Monday with Dr. Susan Archer, a cochlear implant audiologist working out of University Hospital at the University of Cincinnati. His thoughts lingered on Pamela with regret, remembering the easy give and take they shared and wondering how Dr. Archer would compare.

Lost in thought, he drifted down the hallway towards freedom. Because he missed so much verbal information, Blake had been forced to develop his skills and strategies with minimal input from other people. He did a lot of reading to help fill in the gaps and the rest of it came from on the job training. *The crucible of life,* he contemplated, *you pass or you fail.*

Blake had a track record of solving problems by himself, a situation that made him his own hero, with an unwavering confidence in his decisions. A few people had attempted to point out that his confidence sometimes bordered on arrogance. *Tough shit,* Blake said to himself. *I'll do whatever it takes. Nobody else is going to step up for me and I'm the one who gets screwed when I back off.* His ability to overcome obstacles without help was a defining strength. *However, whenever and wherever,* Blake firmly told himself. This cochlear thing was simply the latest challenge, and he was determined to kick it in the ass so hard that it would collapse at his feet.

***

Seven days later Blake and Emily were waiting for Dr. Susan Archer in the audiology department of University Hospital. As they marked time, the receptionist directed additional arrivals to their area, which consisted of nine chairs arranged in a horseshoe pattern. They had arrived separately, both coming from work. Emily was elegantly dressed in black heels, beige pantyhose and a navy-blue suit that was paired with an ivory blouse. Fingernails done in a French manicure complemented her professional appearance and raven tresses curling around her shoulders teased at other dimensions beneath the businesslike image. Blake was in dress pants, button down shirt and wingtips with his customary Jerry Garcia tie. Evaluating their poised attitude and business dress, a casual observer would easily assume that they were there to make a pitch to the hospital staff.

Except one of us has a major problem. The assessment dominated Blake's mind as he rotated his head toward Emily, who was paging through a magazine. Sitting with scissored legs and a copy of Vogue magazine laid across her lap, his wife appeared engrossed in an article, but the magazine was just for show. Emily's awareness was tuned into her husband's mood and movements while her thoughts were reviewing possible outcomes for today.

Intimately familiar with her husband's years of angst, Emily was excited to be moving forward. They were finally trying a different solution, taking a chance that she had been waiting to pursue, and anticipation was strumming her pulse in a regular rhythm. Noticing his slight movement, she counted a few beats before casually glancing up from the magazine. Connecting with her favorite pair of chocolate brown eyes, Emily gave her husband a reassuring smile.

At that moment a petite blonde in her early thirties came out of the hallway to approach the horseshoe and call out, "Simon Blake?" The announcement was loud but modulated enough to avoid crossing the line into rudeness. Blake and Emily broke eye contact to see a slim woman standing in a relaxed posture with both hands in the pockets of a white coat. Her warm smile and friendly blue eyes projected across the room.

"That's me," Blake responded, getting up from the chair in a smooth motion. He extended a hand in greeting as Emily stood up also, "This is my wife, Emily."

"My pleasure," the blonde returned. "I'm Dr. Susan Archer and I will be taking care of you today." As she introduced herself Susan shook both of their hands with a firm clasp followed by a quick release. Short hair trimmed to closely hug the contours of her head and neck displayed a pleasing symmetry. Her close-cropped hair and petite size complemented each other perfectly, red lips combining with a smooth complexion to create an arresting image. Underneath the white coat she was dressed in black slacks and a black sweater. "Let's go on back and get you situated." Dr. Susan Archer did an about-face to enter the clinical area as Blake and Emily followed close behind. Walking alongside Blake, Emily took his hand with a supportive squeeze.

And so it begins, Blake thought, as the three of them journeyed down the linoleum track.

Dr. Archer arrived at the exam room and swung around to face them, inviting Blake and Emily to enter with the sweep of an arm. "Here we are. Call me Susan," she offered. "I reserve the doctor title for presentations." Susan smiled pleasantly as she stood by the door with a confident air, gold earrings in the shape of tiny seahorses sparkling from her earlobes.

Blake entered first with Emily a close second, scanning the room to observe that the floor was a continuation of the creamy linoleum in the hallway with the rest of the décor comprised of grey walls with an eggshell finish and a white drop ceiling. Directly across from the doorway was a corner occupied by a computer workstation with two file cabinets lining the wall perpendicular to the doorway. Sunlight came from a window on the far side of the computer desk and on the near side of the desk, directly in line with the door, sat three black leather chairs with silver legs. All the furnishings and the window occupied an L shaped area that traced two edges of a 15-foot square room. The remainder of the square was taken up by an audiometric booth with two double pane windows, one in the entrance door and one in the wall.

Sitting down in the chair closest to the computer workstation, Blake inhaled the scent of rubbing alcohol. *Some things never change.* He detected an outflow of air coming from the ceiling duct as Emily settled in next to him. Closing the door, Susan took her seat at the desk and turned towards the two of them. Through the window behind her Blake examined a patch of blue sky as sunshine came pouring in to backlight her honey blonde hair, flowing over her shoulder to illuminate specks of dust floating in the air. "Why don't you give me some background before we start?" Folding her hands on her lap, Susan adopted a composed expression, waiting for the saga to unfold.

Blake paused, the enormity of his future in sharp contrast to the futility of his past.

Where to start.

Blake began to tell his story, starting with kindergarten and ending with the 14 years he spent with Pamela. Susan seemed competent enough up to this point. As he recounted the various steps along his pathway Blake was glad for Emily's presence, because he wasn't sure that he would portray events the same way later. He would either leave some comment out or shy away from the same depth of feeling. In the habit of holding back emotions, he tended to minimize his own reactions, especially after the fact, so it was better that she was hearing his narration firsthand.

Both women concentrated intently as he spoke, Susan listening with a professional interest and Emily occasionally coming across a new anecdote.

Sitting in the institutional chair, Blake's gaze drifted to the audiometric booth, causing his voice to peter out. Focusing on his feet where the sunlight illuminated cracks in the linoleum floor, he thought, *How did I ever get here?* The finality of his predicament rendered his vocal cords useless, and Emily touched a hand to his back as the silence stretched on.

How is this going to end?

Susan gave him time, knowing each patient needed to process reality in their own way. Emotions came out frequently. Some were joyful, some were sad, all of them were deeply interwoven throughout her subject's lives. There were no casual feelings in her line of work, but she was unable to get a read on Blake. There was a remoteness to him that she found puzzling, his pauses being the sole indications of emotion that she could detect. It was easy to tell that he and his wife were on the same page, but that was her only insight.

Blake stared at the floor, gearing himself up before acknowledging the truth, "Pamela told me she was out of options and that my next step was a cochlear implant." *Or nothing.* As he finished Blake came back to Susan, appreciating her silence. Calm and professional, her blue eyes projected acceptance, giving him encouragement that he was in the right place. *Maybe.*

"Thank you," Susan began. "From your history it appears that a cochlear implant may be a possibility and the first step in making that determination would be an evaluation by a cochlear implant audiologist such as myself."

Emily spoke, "Could you please tell us what that means? This is all brand new to us."

"Of course," Susan answered, relaxing into her chair as she began to explain the basics. "A cochlear implant has two components, the internal unit which is surgically implanted under the skin and the external unit which is located outside the skin. The internal unit consists of an electrode which is threaded into the cochlea, a computer chip which is placed under the skin and a magnet which is also placed under the skin. On the outside of your head is the external unit which consists of a battery, processor, a short cable and an external magnet." She stopped to let the information sink in.

"The surgery implants three elements then?" Blake posed his own question.

"Correct," Susan replied. "The internal components come from the manufacturer already connected together and encased in a protective covering. Four weeks postop, after incisions have had time to heal, we give you the external unit. At that time power is supplied to the internal components from an induction loop created between the external magnet and the internal magnet. This induction loop is created by positioning the external magnet on the outside of the skin over the location of the internal magnet." She pulled a diagram out of her desk drawer and offered it to them. "Here you can see the internal and external parts and how they connect together." Blake and Emily grasped the diagram as one, bending their heads together as they inspected it.

"Fascinating," Blake commented.

Continuing with her explanation, Susan added more details. "The external processor is powered by a battery. Two microphones on the external casing capture sound which is converted to electrical pulses by the external processor. The pulses are transmitted along the cable to the external magnet where an induction loop passes them through the skin to the internal magnet, the computer chip and down the electrode to the cochlea. Electrical pulses passing between the magnets power the internal chip while at the same time providing the signal to be sent to the auditory nerve."

"What happens then?" asked Emily, her eyes wide with interest.

"Then the magic kicks in!" Susan replied. "When the internal electrode sends electrical pulses into the auditory nerve the brain interprets them as sounds. The internal electrode functions the same as a pickup from an electric guitar."

"Wow!" Blake exclaimed. "How cool is that!!"

"Yes!" Susan agreed. "Once I discovered how implants worked, I knew that I wanted to focus on this area of medicine." She nodded her head for emphasis, "It's so gratifying to help someone's hearing be restored and I feel privileged to be involved." Her face glowed and Blake felt a loosening inside, remembering Pamela.

"I had no idea how these things worked," Emily said. "It's mind blowing!"

Susan smiled in agreement, "Yes, and they are getting better all the time! Each version is an improvement over the last!" She paused, waiting for any questions. "Now then, let's talk about the evaluation process. At University Hospital potential recipients are evaluated by a cochlear audiologist first, then by a surgeon and are also required to undergo an MRI to diagnose potential issues affecting surgery. If all three examinations turn out to be satisfactory, then the person is considered qualified to receive an implant." Continuing, she said, "Of course there are additional issues to consider such as risks from the operation, insurance coverage, family support and personal motivation." The professional demeanor was replaced by a grin as her blue eyes began to sparkle, "You two seem to have the family support part figured out!"

"Oh yes," Emily returned, "That's a done deal." Her hand gave Blake's leg a squeeze and she smiled at her husband. Excitement at being here with him was difficult to contain, especially after learning how implants worked. She was trying hard to stay low key and let him set the pace.

Blake met Emily's eyes, then returned his focus to Susan. "Will we have the results of your audiologist evaluation after today?" The question was designed to focus on logistics. He could sense Emily's optimism, but wasn't ready to surrender his misgivings.

"Yes, you will," Susan replied. "We can begin anytime." Her tone was encouraging, and a reassuring smile spread across her face.

Blake was struck at the comment and how similar she sounded to Pamela. *Forget it.*

"Is that what the little room is for?" Emily jumped in.

Susan chuckled in amusement. "Yes. I take it you're not familiar with a hearing test?"

"Not me. My daddy used to say I could hear a bug pissing on a flat rock at 50 yards!" Both Susan and Blake erupted with laughter, the raunchy comment sounding hilarious coming from someone so elegant. Emily appeared pleased with herself as she observed them both laughing. "We should start whenever you two get yourselves under control."

"OK, then!" Susan rose from her chair to open the door of the audiometric booth, still laughing at Emily's comment. Blake was becoming more comfortable around her, thinking she might turn out to be an acceptable replacement for Pamela. Entering the booth, Susan grabbed some wipes out of a box to busy herself cleaning headphones and a handheld pushbutton before sticking her head back out of the doorway to address Blake, "Simon, I am sure you have been inside a booth before, but I need to ask whether or not you are claustrophobic before we begin."

"Not a problem," Blake answered. The levity dissipated as he stood up and moved toward the door, his face taking on a flat expression and his eyes turning dark. Audiometric tests invariably turned into depressing episodes. Missing the shift, Susan slipped out of his way and shut the door behind him, moving to her desk while Emily watched curiously.

Blake surveyed the interior of the cramped box, spanning six feet square and seven feet high. All four walls, the ceiling and floor were constructed from soundproof panels that were 1" thick and covered with metal cladding perforated with thousands of pinholes. Heavy rubber linings surrounded the doorframe and the two windows, while the door itself was fabricated from another soundproof panel. In the middle of the booth, where Blake would be sitting, was a metal stool with rubber feet and a thick cushion serving as the seat. On the wall next to the stool hung a pair of headphones and a handheld control, both connected to cables that disappeared into the ceiling. With a little padding the place could serve as an isolation room for mental patients.

The wrong place for claustrophobics, thought Blake. He could see Emily through the window in the door and Susan through the second window in the wall. Both windows were patterned with circular scratches, so although they could observe each other, the finer details were obscured. Taking his seat on the stool, he faced a speaker mounted three feet high aimed directly at him. An antenna was mounted above the top of the speaker's wide mouth, and he could easily imagine that the speaker was giving him the finger along with a taunting sneer.

The wrong place for me.

Blake had been in many audiometric booths and hated the devices. Once the door closed he lost the use of context, body language, lip-reading and any nonverbal cues that helped him communicate. Hearing impaired people are experts at interpreting the world without sound, employing facial expressions, gestures, dress and posture to evaluate situations and determine how to react. In a testing booth with its electronic voice those signals were unavailable. Sometimes Blake would escape stressful situations by slipping into daydreams, except that wasn't an option here. This was a harsh environment requiring intense focus, and he performed terribly under its restrictions. Stripping away nonverbal clues, the booth presented a formidable challenge.

Survival demanded that Blake be able to read situations without understanding speech, and this proficiency was why he functioned so effectively overseas. It was a useful skill when dealing with the logistics of a foreign language, a predicament which simulated hearing loss perfectly.

He remembered being in Frankfurt and working in the control room when ten Germans began an animated discussion in the corner. Clueless about the actual words, he could nevertheless determine the general idea by observing where they pointed and who was included in the discussion. Another tipoff was the fact that the group formed immediately after an operator discovered a malfunctioning valve. After observing a few glances in his direction, the smart move had been to put his task on hold until the discussion was resolved.

Lowering himself onto the stool, Blake wished there were ten Germans to observe.

Susan's robotic voice came out of the speaker, "Simon, we are going to test you with both hearing aids first and then do each ear separately without assistance. For your initial test with both hearing aids, please leave the headphones on the wall." The mechanical sound was barely understandable, an ugly portent.

"Got it." Blake was on the stool with his hands resting on his knees. He knew the drill by heart without needing to hear Susan or read her lips. "Ready when you are."

Susan busied herself configuring the computer to test for speech comprehension. The program was designed to issue 25 words from the speaker, spaced ten seconds apart. It was Blake's job to listen and repeat back as accurately as possible while Susan recorded his responses. After completing the words, 25 sentences would be issued in the same manner.

With a click of Susan's mouse, the speaker began its relentless barrage, "Dog"

"Bog," Blake repeated.

"Duck," was the second word.

"Dock," replied Blake. He was pretty sure he missed that one, but it wasn't hard to throw out a guess.

"Wrestle"

"Trestle," Blake shot back. *Bastard.*

"Lane"

"Rain?" *I hate you.*

"Better"

"Better!" *Got it, you weasel!*

"There"

"Chair??" The words continued, one every ten seconds until all 25 were finished. Blake tried to offer up an option each time, aware that he was mostly guessing. With no way to read lips, he was lost. Ten years ago he might have performed poorly, but today was a train wreck. He sat on the stool with his heart pounding, feeling inadequate, knowing that he was failing miserably.

I'm dying here.

Out of the corner of his eye Blake snuck a glance at Emily, who was sitting still with her hands clenched together. *Just wait. You ain't seen nothing yet.*

"Sentences are next," Susan spoke up.

"Yeah, let's go," Blake responded wearily. *Straight to hell. Let's do it.*

The speaker began another emotionless attack, designed to expose his vulnerabilities, "She bought seashells at the seashore."

"She, uhh…" Blake was already behind.

"Dad bought me a baseball," followed almost immediately.

Trying to put words together Blake spit out, "We want to play in the hall??" This was way harder than before, and it was all he could do to get a response out before the next sentence began. Words were hard enough, sentences had him drowning from the start.

"It's a blustery day in Minnesota."

Blake sat there. *No way.* "Pass." Maybe he could grab a few seconds to get ready for the next sentence. Now he was the one with clenched hands, knowing full well how feeble his hearing was and how much help he needed to function. It was no surprise to him. His performance in the booth was an unwelcome acknowledgement of what was hammered into him daily. He considered the hateful details better kept secret, but today his weakness was in full view.

"They were in such a happy mood that they decided to throw a party."

"We need food for ... whatever?" *That's a major fail,* Blake acknowledged. *This whole procedure is a disaster.* He sat back to wait it out. Rage took control and he imagined himself knocking the speaker with its fuck-you antenna off the wall.

Sitting on the stool with eyes of stone, Blake adopted a protective stillness. He had started hiding his feelings in kindergarten, and unsure where to fix the boundaries, his strategy evolved to hiding all his emotions. The price was steep, especially now. A tempestuous rage scoured turbulent paths through his veins as his heart pounded with a violent rhythm. His thoughts went off on their own to lay down a track burning with malevolence. Fantasies of crushing the speaker into millions of tiny pieces with his bare hands followed by kicking the booth into smithereens came front and center. Blake channeled some of the negative energy for the purpose of maintaining his outward shell, but there was plenty left over to rocket his insides into a storm of chaos.

Breathing deeply, he struggled against the physical toll of negativity running amuck inside of him. Daily suppression of his emotions produced a constant turmoil of his own creation that was never far below the surface. The stress was boiling his insides, putting his physical self under vicious attack and turning his mental core distressingly hateful. *Nothing good is happening here.*

Blake realized long ago that hiding his feelings created problems, but he didn't know how else to react. Embarrassed at the depth of his internal ugliness, he was constantly on guard to avoid unveiling the true extent of his personal darkness. He fought a daily war on two fronts - a battle to control his external reactions and a battle to combat the internal stress that was generated.

Striving for control, Blake's thoughts shifted to racquetball. *I need to hit something.*

The excruciating prompts finally ended and Susan's voice flooded the booth, "Thank you, Simon. Now we are going to test for sound thresholds in each ear without your hearing aids. We will not be bothering with word or sentence comprehension. Please put on the headphones and use the pushbutton to indicate when you detect a beep." She spoke as slowly and clearly as she could, facing him through the window so that he could read her lips. *A lot like Pamela,* he decided. *Yeah, I don't think we need to worry about comprehension either.*

Taking off both hearing aids, Blake laid them on a small shelf and slipping on the headphones, he turned to look at his wife who was partially obscured by the blur of scratches on the window. Emily was sitting straight up with both hands covering her mouth, eyes wide with dismay. Their eyes met and Blake gave a shrug. His wife shook her head in disbelief and he could tell that the real scope of his loss had just been shoved down her throat. Blake was an expert at compensating for his disability, but the booth was exposing his deficiencies with a savage authenticity.

Watching her husband inside the booth, Emily took in the shrug, his performance a heartbreaking disclosure. Her eyes were brimming with tears remembering the many times when he had been defeated by a difficult situation. It was painful for her to think that she had sometimes settled along with him instead of helping him to fight back. *I was his best hope and all I did was quit on him!* She continued to stare through the hazy glass, shocked at the brutal revelation. Tears leaked out, blurring the view of her husband, and she was gripped by a wrenching heartache.

Blake concentrated on Emily through the window and gave her a tight smile. *What a day.* The shock displayed on her face spoke volumes. *It's hard to explain the emotions,* thought Blake. *It's easier to describe the logistics. Despair and futility don't easily translate into words.*

Turning away from his wife, Blake settled back on the stool. The remainder of the testing only required him to activate the pushbutton whenever he heard a beep. Susan checked each ear individually, running various volume and frequency combinations. As he expected, Blake's responses were less than minimal. Most of the beeps were undetectable.

Strike out. Blake got up as he saw Susan approach the booth. Feeling defeated, he hung the headphones back on the wall and recovered his aids from the shelf, the accumulated tension making his movements stiff and uncoordinated. Susan unlatched the door and Blake exited the booth with eyes of cold steel. Pretense was useless now that the testing had shown how little he could hear, and in the face of such vulnerability he felt unclean.

Returning to his chair, Blake slipped down into the leather cushion. *I hate that booth.* Emily firmly took Blake's hand in hers, and he squeezed back once, not wanting to talk. *There's no way to describe it. Thank God she's here today.* Drinking in the solace from her touch, Blake felt an upwelling of tears as her contact eased his pain. Whatever happened Emily would be there with him. Exhaling a long sigh, he managed an initial comment, "That was poor, I guess."

"Oh my God!" Emily blurted out. "It was awful!" One hand clutched his with fierce energy while the other wiped her face. "I had no clue your hearing was so terrible!"

Susan ran a finger down the score sheets in her hand before turning in their direction. "All right," she addressed Simon, "At this point I would venture to say that you must rely heavily on lip reading because your auditory capability is almost nonexistent. Word comprehension with your hearing aids is 7% and sentences are even lower at 2%. In order to detect sounds, you require a minimum power level of 105 dB, and some frequencies you can't hear at all." She evaluated Blake's demeanor while delicately waving the sheets back and forth, seeking the best approach but receiving no help from him. Taking the direct route, she said, "You have almost no hearing." The words seemed harsh, but he could tell from her tone that she was just trying to be truthful.

"You're right," Blake responded. "If I couldn't read lips, we wouldn't be having this conversation. I've been getting by for a long time now without hearing much." The admission triggered a physical wave that started at his neck and went down to his toes, any objection to implants melting away along with it. He dropped his gaze to the floor where the rays of sunlight highlighted the linoleum to callously expose each crack and scuff mark in the flooring. Time slowed down and he could feel his heartbeat pulsing in slow motion as he focused on the refuge offered by Emily's touch. *I'm scared. Scared to do it. Scared not to.*

Lost in a haze, he returned to Susan, "What else do you need to do?"

"My evaluation is complete," Susan assured him. "The magnitude of your impairment definitely qualifies you for a cochlear implant. Your next step is to be evaluated by the surgeon." She paged through her appointment book. "I meet with Dr. Samuel Rickerson on Monday. Let me brief him on your results and then I'll contact you." Regarding Blake with a thoughtful expression, she said, "Given the fact that you have a functioning auditory nerve and are able to compensate for such a tremendous loss, you may benefit greatly from an implant." Sunlight reflected off her lab coat making it blindingly white, the implied imagery so obvious that Blake wondered if he was the only one aware of it.

"I hope so!" Emily breathed. She had a firm hold on Blake's hand and he felt she was going to hang on for a while. "Thanks for your help."

"Thank you for being here with your husband," answered Susan, getting up from her chair. "It's sad to watch some patients try to navigate this procedure without support. I'll email you with several options to meet with Dr. Rickerson."

Standing in front of them she added, "We're fortunate to have a cochlear support group here in Cincinnati. I'll forward you their contact information so that you have the chance to talk with some implant recipients. They're willing to share their personal experiences to help you decide on a course of action."

"Thank you," said Blake quietly. Grateful to move forward, he was overwhelmed by what lay ahead with his thoughts bouncing back and forth between surgery, insurance and recovery. He was applying for membership in the implant club, an option he could no longer avoid. There would be questions to answer, but at the same time he was also thinking that Susan would be a good partner. Blake was impressed by her straightforwardness and sensitivity. *No worries there.*

After shaking hands with Susan, Blake and Emily exited the examination room and walked through the reception area on the way to the elevators. Thoughts of the future filled Blake's mind as they arrived at the elevator bank and waited for their ride. They were both silent in the vestibule, but as they entered their car and the doors closed he turned to his wife.

Emily was already facing him. In one step she closed the distance between them, slipping both hands around his waist to pull herself to him so that he found himself looking down at a sorrowful face. A tear escaped to trail down her cheek and the elevator started its descent, unnoticed by them both.

Her eyes sought permission and he opened the door, their souls linking together in the most intimate of connections. A protective shield rose up to surround them and Blake felt the power of a promise that went back to their beginnings. The entreaty visible on her face searched out his heart and enveloped it in a regretful caress, "Simon, I'm so sorry that I never understood." Her voice faltered at the end as the elevator hummed its way down.

"Not your fault. I couldn't find a way to explain it," Blake said, tears filling his own eyes. "Today fixed that problem." He pulled her in under his chin and Emily shuddered against his chest, choking down a suppressed sob.

Blake's voice cracked with accumulated sadness, "You're wonderful to me."

He paused, "It's just how it is."

Emily tightened her arms around his waist, then slipped an arm free to snake it upward. Reaching behind his neck she splayed apart her fingers to tenderly grip the back of his head. As she pulled him down toward her Emily tilted her own head back and raised herself up on her toes. The kiss she offered was gentle and intimate yet the pressure of her hand behind his head lent a demanding quality to it. They stayed that way until Emily broke free to fix him with a pair of shiny eyes that held resolute strength.

"No," she replied softly. "I will move heaven and earth to get you an implant. THAT'S how it is."

Chapter 4 – Decision

Two weeks after meeting with Dr. Archer, Blake was in his kitchen on a Saturday morning slamming down a third cup of coffee before heading out to a cochlear support group meeting at the Sisters of Charity Convent. Emily was busy shepherding a client around, but that was OK since Blake welcomed the opportunity to be alone. Implants were dividing his attention among multiple avenues, and even though Blake was leaning toward getting two, his mind was filled with questions. One minute he was worried that he might not wake up from the operation and the next he was obsessing about getting insurance approval. Then there was the question of whether the procedure would work. Hopefully he could address some of his concerns at the meeting. *What a mess.* Deep down he still held onto a wild hope that the newspaper would bring news of a breakthrough releasing him from his quest, but the day of reckoning was getting closer.

Blake was familiar with the meeting location, which was located close to his home in Delhi Township. Dating to the 1800's, the Sisters of Charity Convent was a massive conglomeration of red brick surrounded by a large expanse of manicured grounds. After negotiating a winding driveway to arrive at the parking lot, he got out of his truck and peered around. It was one of those radiant mornings that autumn would pull out to make people wish that summer was still an option, with the grass exuding an emerald glow, the sky a sheet of Arizona blue and the gardens displaying their last profusion of blooms. The only indication of what lay over the horizon was a crispiness in the air. He stood on the blacktop by his vehicle, soaking up warm sunshine on the back of his neck.

Across the parking lot Blake could see a rectangle of yellow plastic suspended above the ground by a couple of metal rods. Walking closer for an inspection, he saw that it was a sign with directions to the cochlear meeting. Following the instructions led him to another sign in front of a weathered portico connected to the rear wing of the building. The entrance was guarded by a pair of tall doors capable of withstanding assault by a Sherman tank. A third sign taped to the doors instructed him to walk on inside, so he took hold of the handle and pushed.

His thoughts flashed over the people he expected to find here, cochlear recipients, potential recipients and family members who were there to provide support. Today's gathering would probably be an accommodating group and he wouldn't have to worry about using his defense mechanisms. In unfamiliar situations he conducted himself with a reserved manner until he got the lay of the land, behavior that caused people to perceive him as cold and unfriendly. Blake was long past caring whether he made a good impression, although he could be charming when it suited him. *I should probably try to be nice today.*

As the door reluctantly yielded to his push, Blake considered how providing communication tips to hearing people for connecting with the hearing impaired was a waste of time. He had learned that those people who were going to be considerate would do so without prompting. The others didn't change just because you asked. After a few awkward attempts at accommodation, the latter group went back to their chosen state of oblivion, an observation that made

Blake exert minimal effort to explain his situation. *The world is divided into angels and assholes. It's only a matter of waiting for them to declare their identity.*

When he judged it necessary to identify himself as hard of hearing, there would occasionally be some cynic who saw his announcement as an attempt to gain special consideration. Such an idea offended him so deeply that he would reject attempts at reconciliation if they changed their tune later. An accusation of that sort minimized the futility of his daily routine and displayed a lack of charity and compassion. To him it was an unforgivable offense, agitating his internal boil. *The worst kind of arrogance.* In a perfect world Blake would have a front row seat to see those individuals get their just desserts somewhere down the line. *We're all temporarily able-bodied whether we realize it or not.*

Blake was OK with explaining his situation once. He viewed the adjustments as common sense, similar to moving away from the path of a blind person. What transpired after his explanation served as a window to someone's character and provided him a way to evaluate the motivations and capabilities of people. While some fell short due to lack of empathy, others were incapable of adjusting because they were overwhelmed with their own affairs. Then there were those who were unaware of the needs that other people had because they weren't even aware of their own. Those people who could see past themselves and compensate for someone else's weakness were the gemstones of humanity, and Blake treasured each one that he met.

Blake was constantly evaluating people, not for the purpose of criticizing, which was a guaranteed trip to nowhere, but to make his way through the forest of interpersonal relationships as effectively as possible. In many cases the understanding gained allowed him to direct the initial stages of communication. Of course what usually occurred once interaction sped up, especially in a group, is that he was left behind and left out while attempting to interpret tone of voice, body movements and a whole host of nonverbal cues to follow the discussion. At that point conversation became a lost cause and he would shift to accumulating observations about the people around him.

Bending his legs to lever the door open, Blake peeked inside to see a rectangular table piled with pastries beyond which groups of people were scattered throughout a large foyer. Some of the attendees were standing in huddles while some were sitting down at round tables. In contrast to the sunny warmth of outside, there was a coolness to the interior. The meeting area was expansive with high ceilings and tall windows, and he noted painstaking craftsmanship from another century on the moldings and trim. He realized with dismay that the room was full of reverberations from sounds bouncing off the high ceilings and hardwood floors.

This is where people with hearing loss meet?

The unexpected complication triggered an automatic rundown of his prerequisites for communicating. Number one was his desire for people to politely get his attention before trying to talk to him. Yelling to get his attention was flat out rude and would either make him mad or in some cases wind up scaring him, an occurrence which made him even madder. For the same reason physical jabs or violent waving were a no-no. Facing him, speaking slowly and leaving the lips uncovered were important items on his list.

He desired speech to be at normal levels without shouting and words to be pronounced without exaggerating their enunciation. Changes in topic should be telegraphed on the spot and a quiet environment was a definite plus.

Blake got upset when people would talk exclusively to his hearing companion and treat him like a piece of furniture. Likewise, he did not appreciate being ignored on the infrequent occasions when he finally comprehended enough to make a contribution. If someone tried answering for him that never failed to set him off. He was fully capable of answering for himself and did not appreciate the insensitivity of someone who was able to chime in three seconds faster.

He understood himself enough to realize that he would inevitably overflow his reservoir of grievances. *So now and then I go nuts. Of course, if I make a polite request and people ignore it, they're really saying that they need to be told in a more forceful manner.* Ready to enter the meeting, he entertained a fleeting thought, *Poke me at your own risk.*

Easing past the heavy door, Blake felt its momentum reverse as he released his grip. Inside he counted about 35-40 people, the majority on the downhill side of 50. Blake figured that he was close to being the youngest in the room. *I'm the baby here.* An elderly woman noticed his arrival, detaching herself from one of the groups.

Blake observed that the welcoming committee approaching him with a steady smile was a petite woman of 65ish with steel gray hair. He detected a slight hitch in her walk as she came toward him. She was dressed in brown jeans, tennis shoes and a white sweatshirt patterned with bluebells. *OK,* he thought, *we have contact.*

As she moved closer Blake maintained a neutral stance while observing her movements and the expression on her face. Upon meeting people Blake would analyze their body language, facial expressions and speech cadence. Often forced to observe in place of participating, Blake used those opportunities to become proficient at understanding himself and those around him. Constant practice fostered an ability to quickly evaluate situations and people. He was in evaluation mode now, trying to determine how much he wanted to interact with this woman. The last thing he wanted was to get sucked into a discussion that would waste precious time without answering his questions.

His greeter stopped in front of him and introduced herself in a manner that implied she was confident in her role. "Good morning! I'm Mary Beth Lunsford." Her clear voice was easy to understand and she took pains to face him and speak slowly.

"Simon Blake. I got this address from Dr. Susan Archer?"

"Ah, yes. You must be a potential recipient then?" Mary Beth studied him quizzically. A grandmotherly voice evoked memories of cookies and fresh bread. Pausing to wait for his response, she seemed content to let him take the lead, and Blake dove in.

"I guess so. This is all new to me. I'm not even sure what questions to ask." He made a snap decision to surrender himself and see how the discussion went. *Let's do it.* Blake decided to take a chance that Mary Beth would be helpful and not interested in pushing an agenda.

It wasn't a decision that he made lightly. Blake had observed that people with excessive egos fought to control the narrative, desiring to choose the topic of discussion and the direction of the conversation. Trapped in such an interaction, people with hearing loss were forced to stay silent, since they found it difficult to intervene. How people without his limitations could keep their mouths shut, he had a tough time understanding.

Of course, if he didn't give a rat's ass what people thought, then there was no problem. *If it doesn't work out, I'll cut her off at the knees and find someone else.*

"Let's sit down and start with the basics," Mary Beth replied. "I have two implants and can answer most of your questions." She motioned to an empty table with folding chairs and they both went over to sit down. Blake was unsure how much the background noise would interfere, but fortunately she intended to talk one on one.

Blake sat down wondering where to begin when Mary Beth fixed that problem by starting off with a personal comment, "Before I got my implants, the only way I could converse was to read lips." Displaying a blank face, Blake immediately recalled his appointment with Dr. Archer. *That's me.*

For the next 30 minutes Blake listened to Mary Beth describe her results and what to expect from cochlear implants. He learned what they could do and what they could not do, at least in Mary Beth's experience. A few times he asked her to go into greater detail.

He was surprised that he could not easily see her implants, but then realized the gray color of the components matched her hair, blending in perfectly. The processor hung over her ear the same as a hearing aid and in Mary Beth's case her hair was the same color. Her hair also did an effective job of concealing the magnet and the cable connecting to the processor. Blake's hair was cut close to his head and any implant would be completely visible. Not that he cared. *It just needs to work. People can already see my hearing aids.*

Blake asked her if there was any discomfort from the coil rubbing on the skin and learned that the coil magnets came in six strengths to adjust for that issue. If the magnet sizing required further adjustment, the magnet could be rotated within the coil to increase or decrease the attachment strength.

He learned that when the implant was first turned on voices sounded tinny and mechanical. That effect went away soon, although each person's experience was different. Mary Beth informed him that after several weeks the sound quality changed to become the same as normal hearing. "Your brain will take care of that for you," she commented. "But you do have to practice listening to vowels, consonants and sentences with the computer program. The more you practice, the better you will get at understanding speech."

"I can do that," Blake responded. "Why go to the trouble of having surgery and not try to make the implant work as well as possible?"

"Absolutely!" Mary Beth nodded. "Think of it as learning a foreign language. Your brain will require training to recognize words and environmental sounds. I still find myself tracking down specific noises to figure out what I am hearing."

Their conversation was an easy give and take with Mary Beth stopping her narration to address Blake's questions as they came up. He was gratified at how Mary Beth focused on his queries without going off on some tangent that he considered useless. She was also making it easy for him to read her lips. Eventually it dawned on Blake that she was focused on responding to his specific needs. Once he made that determination, he started to realize that he was enjoying her company. Blake found himself in a conversation where he could fully participate, and he was loving it.

"Tell me," he asked, "Do you have any regrets about the implants?"

"Heavens no!" she replied. "I can hear without any effort at all. You know how hearing aids wear you out by the end of the day?"

"Do they ever!"

"That doesn't occur with implants. They just work and I listen without thinking about it. I can talk to strangers anytime; it is so easy." Mary Beth was sitting in her chair with a contented smile.

She sure looks happy, Blake thought. He raised both hands in defeat, "Most of the time there's no way I can talk to someone unfamiliar without saying something stupid."

Mary Beth leaned in closer, "Implants produce a clearer sound than hearing aids. They allow you to get past the background noise and focus on the actual words."

"Yeah, background noise is a killer. I have to stop talking in restaurants when they fill up because I can't understand." Blake shook his head in despair, "I watch everyone else have fun." He had already noticed that Mary Beth wasn't bothered by the noise level in the room.

"That won't happen anymore. You'll also stop sounding stupid because you missed something."

"Yeah," Blake acknowledged, "That's me." They exchanged knowing glances and Blake nodded his head.

"Cochlear implants will make a difference at work too," Mary Beth volunteered. "You can do a better job when you know what's going on."

"So true." Blake was getting a ton of information from Mary Beth and he was discovering that implants were much better than he had imagined. *There must have been significant improvements in how these implants work.*

Another woman approached them and Mary Beth stopped to make the necessary introductions. "Simon, this is Peggy Dennison. She also has two implants and can give you a different perspective." Peggy was similarly dressed in jeans, tennis shoes and a sweatshirt with a Charley Harper print portraying cardinals in winter. *Must be the uniform around here.*

With brown hair falling to her shoulders, Peggy was approximately ten years younger than Mary Beth. A pair of wire rim glasses perched halfway down her nose. The glasses were connected to a gold safety chain that looped behind her neck. In one hand she held a large cup of Starbucks coffee and in the other was a pastry. Seeing that there were no more chairs, Peggy chose to perch on the edge of the table.

Shielding her mouth with the pastry, Peggy let out a yawn, "Excuse me!" She shook her head to dispel her lethargy and continued, "I would be happy to answer your questions. Implants have completely changed my life!"

"Any way in particular?" inquired Blake. Watching Peggy, he was wishing that he had thought to bring his own

Starbucks. He also envied her faith in the stability of the table.

"Oh yes!" Peggy replied. "I used to say 'What?' all the time and it would drive my husband nuts. Now I can hear perfectly!" She threw her head back and laughed, "I love it, love it, love it!"

I say 'What?' all the time, Blake brooded to himself. *These women are hearing way better than me!* Blake listened to Peggy laugh in delight. Tilting back in his chair to rest on the rear legs he prompted her again, "Anything else?"

Peggy took a pull of coffee and got serious. "Probably the biggest improvement is that I can control my interactions instead of settling for what is given to me. If I get tired of a conversation, I end it and go somewhere else." Mary Beth nodded her head in agreement. Even though Mary Beth was sitting alongside Peggy and was unable to see her face, Blake realized that she was understanding whatever Peggy said. The noise created by multiple conversations didn't seem to be a problem, both of them appearing at ease. Blake rotated the chair back down to all four legs. As the chair legs touched the floor, he got hit with the revelation that while his hearing was pretty much useless, it might not have to be that way.

Mary Beth and Peggy appeared to have normal hearing or at least something close to it. Blake was amazed. He had thought that implants might possibly improve his situation, but implants were starting to look like the Holy Grail.

Maybe the last few years I've been digging myself a hole for no reason. He remembered the times when Pamela tried to steer him toward implants and he blew her off.

Stubborn and stupid at the same time, a deadly combination. Blake was cynical enough to viciously criticize the actions of others when he thought they deserved it. Applying the same standard to himself, he acknowledged that he might be responsible for making his problems worse.

Idiot.

Blake's practice of observing his environment was automatic, almost subconscious. Even while talking with Mary Beth and Peggy he was sneaking glances around the room to observe the actions of individual people and the compositions of various groups. He paid attention to whether people were happy or sad, polite or abrupt, noticing when they tried to participate and when they shrank back, evaluating the group dynamics on a continuous basis.

He was coming to an inescapable conclusion. The people with implants stood out because they were moving around and participating in multiple groups and side conversations. These people were laughing and smiling. Those who were present to get information stood out in a different way, staying in one spot and waiting for people to come to them. There was little cheer in the second group, but a great deal of angst.

I don't have to put up with this! All these people with implants don't have problems!!

Blake's heart started to beat faster and he was overtaken by an unexpected surge of hope. Watching the implant recipients work the room he yearned to be the same. His breath caught as he realized the possibilities. *What if that was me?!*

Remembering his restless night before proposing to Emily, Blake recalled how sick he had felt at the prospect that a random accident would end their relationship before it began. He wanted to marry her more than anything in the world and had been terrified that his life would become a train wreck of regret if he missed his chance. His insides contracted as he came to a wrenching realization.

Not again.

***

Next Friday afternoon, six days later, Blake and Emily were ensconced in the University Hospital horseshoe, this time for an appointment with Dr. Samuel Rickerson. Blake was tied in knots. Attending the support group meeting had spawned a yearning that would not go away, and dreams of being able to hear as well as Mary Beth danced through his head constantly. The things he could do! *It would be a new life.*

The cochlear meeting had set Blake on fire. Stealing time from work, he began to shut his door at lunchtime to research implants with a passion, investigating surgery, recovery, insurance and whatever else he thought relevant. His head was spinning with information and he was having a hard time thinking of anything else. It was fortunate that Blake had only recently discovered what he was missing, because with more lead time he would have driven himself crazy.

Returning home from his meeting Blake had described to Emily how easily Mary Beth and Peggy could hear and finished up by telling her that he was sold on getting implants. She was thrilled. After observing both women in action, Blake was upset that he had wasted so much time being stubborn.

What have I missed?

Even though he didn't have every detail, Blake was all in, having been around long enough to know that people mostly regretted the actions they failed to take. True to form, he was sorry enough already. Blake had seen what he needed to see and wanted at least one implant, preferably two. He tried to keep from dwelling on the possibility that he might not qualify. Last year he had placed implants in the same class as amputation, but now he desperately wanted to be in the club.

Late afternoon sunshine was barreling through the windows, toasting people wherever the rays made contact. Emily had moved several times already, finally giving up to stand against the wall. Blake was too distracted to think about the temperature, consumed with the desire to have today's appointment go smoothly so that he could move on. A baby could have thrown up on the floor without bothering him. For one of the few times in his life he was blind to Emily, able to acknowledge her presence, but that was pretty much it.

He was facing Emily with a gaze that went straight through her to loop back to his own meditations. She smiled encouragingly, but it was lost on him. A nurse appeared in the doorway to call out, "Simon Blake?" Emily reacted, pushing herself away from the wall and motioning to Blake that it was their turn. Blake got up and blindly followed his wife to where the nurse stood holding the door ajar. Observing his detachment the nurse said, "OK then, come on back with me." Depositing them in an exam room, she closed the door after telling them the doctor would be in shortly.

Their room was small, 15' by 15' with the entire wall opposite the doorway a tinted window looking out across the hospital's medical campus where an assortment of brick buildings were crammed together over hilly terrain. The curtains were pulled back to display the full view against a backdrop of sunshine and no clouds, with any greenhouse effect mitigated by the tinted glass. In the center of the room stood an examination chair upholstered in grey leather with stainless steel trim and an extended footrest. Blake sank down into it noting two other chairs in the room, a folding chair set against a side wall with a wheeled stool next to it. Emily took her seat in the folding chair and they both settled in to wait. A small sink with a cabinet lined the same wall as the doorway while the two side walls were adorned with pictures of the human ear.

Time downshifted into another gear as they took in the beige walls and creamy floor tiles, waiting for Dr. Rickerson to make his entrance. The massive window went a long way toward making the room feel bigger than it was. Emily lifted her eyebrows at him, "Nervous?"

"Of course. I don't want some problem to keep me from getting an implant." Blake hated verbalizing the fear, afraid of encouraging disaster, but it was the only thought on his mind. Rays of sunshine angled through the window to bathe his left side in a soothing touch, a positive omen, he hoped.

"Same here." Emily was sitting in the shady part of the room, dressed in professional garb. One leg was crossed over the other, balancing its high heel off her toes. Blake allowed himself to become mesmerized by the pendulum, thinking how supportive she had been during the last 25 years, hoping that the end result of today would be a positive outcome and not a blow from which they had to recover.

I don't know if I can handle disqualification after learning how great these implants can be.

These last few weeks had forced Blake to face up to the fact that he was unable to communicate without reading lips, and it had become frighteningly obvious that his only path forward was a cochlear implant. Although he never mentioned it to Emily, one of Blake's greatest fears was to become both deaf and blind. It was such a terrifying prospect that he was unwilling to broach the subject, burying the horror deep inside. Ten years ago it seemed a remote threat, but now he was halfway there, the possibility no longer something he could ignore. One unfortunate accident of biology or circumstance could take his sight tomorrow, the fearful scenario skewering him with its direness. If blindness ever entered the equation, he visualized his life turning into a nightmare as his skills and relationships fell apart and his existence became a lament of the past.

Blake shuddered inside. The trepidation shadowed his soul with despair, darkening his daily routine. Unable to share his fear, he was fraught with a need to find a way past his torment. *This has to work.*

A sharp rap interrupted his agonizing and the door swung in, "Good afternoon, I'm Dr. Samuel Rickerson." Blake turned toward the door to observe a doctor in his late forties wearing the requisite white coat. Hair the color of coal was matched with olive skin and dark eyes, Mediterranean heritage evident. As Dr. Rickerson entered the room he brought with him an aura of movement and action, one hand gripping a clipboard in slender brown fingers.

Without wasting any time, he offered a quick handshake to Emily, plopped himself down on the stool and wheeled over to Blake. Sliding up directly in Blake's face, Dr. Rickerson abruptly began, "So, you are considering an implant?" The no nonsense delivery was combined with an intense expression and piercing eyes, his manner designed to get events moving.

"I am," responded Blake. "Dr. Archer said your examination was the next step." Automatically retreating in response to Dr. Rickerson's abruptness, Blake offered the bare minimum in response.

"Please take off both hearing aids and let me have a look."

Dr. Rickerson started by inspecting the inside of Blake's ears. Then he proceeded to perform a series of motor skill and balance tests more appropriate for a physical. The doctor also performed several examinations related to implants, probing the bone structure of Blake's skull and holding a tuning fork up to each ear. Alternately prodded, poked or manipulated, Blake submitted passively to the procedures. *I have no clue what's going on here. Is this a hearing exam or did he argue with his wife this morning?* Blake's eyes sought Emily for guidance. He was completely deaf without his aids and the doctor was moving around so much that reading lips was out of the question. Emily shrugged. She was as perplexed as him. Finishing up, Dr. Rickerson motioned to Blake that he could put his hearing aids back on.

How about that, we get to talk, Blake thought as he slipped his earmolds back in.

"At this point, your physiology is OK," Dr Rickerson announced. "We need to do an MRI to detect potential issues with surgery."

Emily jumped in, "What would those be?"

"The MRI will tell us if there are bone masses that may cause difficulty with drilling or if the ear is misshapen. We check a number of variables."

Blake spoke up, "What are the surgical risks?"

The doctor responded, "With any procedure using general anesthesia there is the danger of not waking up. The risk is small, but it does exist."

Blake continued, "My research revealed that sometimes a patient has nerve damage from the operation?"

"Yes, that's another reason for the MRI," Dr. Rickerson explained. "There is a low probability of damaging two major nerves. One controls your ability to smile and the other controls your ability to taste."

"That's scary!" This comment was from Emily, who was now gripping the arms of her chair.

"One patient failed to fully recover her sense of taste," Dr. Rickerson volunteered. "That was my most discouraging case. For the last five years I have been performing two operations a week without significant problems." As he talked, he swiveled between them. "I keep my patients in the hospital overnight for observation and discharge them the following morning. We check for balance problems before you leave since a small percentage of patients have temporary dizziness afterwards."

Resting both hands on his knees, he offered more information, "The surgery itself takes about three hours. During the operation we make an incision behind your ear and pull back the skin. Then we drill a hole at the top of your cochlea – the part of your ear that is coiled up like a snail." They were both listening intensely, and he kept on talking, "An electrode assembly is threaded into your cochlea. Connected to the electrode are a sealed magnet and a computer chip. Those are imbedded in a shallow depression that we hollow out from your skull and then your scalp is stitched back up." As he explained the surgical details Dr. Rickerson got up and walked over to a picture on the wall where he traced the procedures on a cutaway view of the human ear.

"Does it hurt?" Blake asked. *Wuss!*

"Not much," Dr. Rickerson answered. "The surgical area has a minimum of pain receptors. We send you home to heal for four weeks and then you return to get the implant 'activated' or turned on."

He walked back to his stool and sat down. "Dr. Archer will be performing the activation for you. My job is done once you leave the hospital." Dr. Rickerson surveyed each of them to see if they were following him. During the short lull, Blake considered making a 'turned on' joke, but the opportunity came and went. *Just as well.*

Perceiving no questions, the doctor returned his eyes to Blake. "My office offers help navigating the insurance maze to get approval for the procedure. Keep in mind we still need to approve your MRI results before surgery."

Blake exploded with an internal cheer, "Does that mean I passed step two?" His heart was doing back flips. On the outside he showed a blank face, but inside there was a brass band striking up music.

"Yes, you did," Dr. Rickerson told him. "Do you intend to get one or two implants?"

"Two of course!" Blake exclaimed. He looked to Emily in his elation to find her smiling broadly. "My insurance will cover two and that's what I want." *Yee Haa!* He allowed himself to start smiling. *Thank You God!* His thoughts shot to Pamela. *If you could see me now!* Blake exchanged smiles with his wife and a river of tension broke free. *Never hurts to be lucky!*

Emily sat in her chair, watching her husband. Her practiced eyes took heed of his frame losing its rigidity and she could detect a vibrancy dancing in his pupils. *One step further,* she rejoiced.

"Most of my patients can expect to achieve speech comprehension of at least 80%." Dr. Rickerson was talking but Blake was floating in the clouds. He turned and Dr. Rickerson repeated his comment.

"80%? That's light years ahead of what I have now."

"It's not unusual," Dr. Rickerson commented. "We have patients that perform worse than that. I don't know why it happens to some people and not others."

"Are you saying the operation could be a failure?" inquired Blake.

"Unfortunately, yes," the doctor answered. "In the rare case of infection we have to go back in and remove the implant."

"Huh," Blake responded. "What about recovery?"

"You will be given a prescription for antibiotics and need to keep the surgical area dry for five days. Most people go back to work in one week." Dr. Rickerson continued, "Driving is a personal decision. We recommend waiting at least seven days before attempting to drive."

Emily sat up straighter in her chair, "No problem. We have enough drivers in our family. I'm sure we can figure that out."

Dr. Rickerson shifted back to Blake, "There is a 75% chance that you will be able to use the phone. A lot depends upon how much effort you put into rehabilitation."

Blake eyed the doctor, "That would certainly be nice." *Right! I'll believe it when I see it.* Happy to be moving on, he was wary of riding a roller coaster of expectations and disappointment. It was enough to keep going forward. "When should I get the MRI?"

"We'll schedule it today," Dr. Rickerson informed him. "I'll send the nurse in to set it up for you, maybe Wednesday or Thursday. Do either of you have any more questions?" With that comment Dr. Rickerson's attitude shifted and he seemed ready to make an exit.

Blake mentally reviewed his list. "Nope," he answered. "I think we're good." He reached out to shake hands and said, "Thank You! I'm thrilled to be moving forward."

"I hope you do well." The doctor shook hands with them both and disappeared as fast as he entered. Blake and Emily were left alone as the door closed behind the doctor's flying white coat.

Blake turned to Emily, breathing a sigh of relief. "Two down. One to go." He didn't want to get too excited, but a positive vibe was starting to build. The doctor had been abrupt, almost rude, but Blake didn't care, focusing on his upcoming MRI. Meeting her eyes in solidarity he said,

"Things are starting to look up." Emily met his comment with an enthusiastic nodding, returning an unspoken acknowledgement.

For better or for worse, Blake and Emily were joined together as victims of hearing loss. Opportunities to chat had been growing fewer and fewer as Blake's hearing worsened, and intimacy was a direct casualty. Emily, especially, mourned the easy way they used to share their lives. In their world today, conversation required a purposeful effort and could frequently be exhausting. The sad part was that one, the other or both sometimes chose to pass on putting in the necessary effort.

"I love you," he told his wife. As he said the words he got out of the chair and crossed the room to open his arms. She rose to meet him and silently slipped her arms around his chest to nestle in tightly. They stood together, each seeking refuge in the other, seeds of hope begging for permission to sprout and grow.

Holding his wife in a secure embrace, Blake promised himself that if he passed the MRI it would be full steam ahead. Nothing would stop him after that. *Forget the risks. This is my last chance.*

***

Leaving the hospital to enter the parking garage, Blake and Emily were chattering in excitement. It seemed incomprehensible that Blake's hearing could improve to the level mentioned by Dr. Rickerson. Blake hadn't known 80% comprehension in his life. Emily slipped behind the wheel, not trusting Blake to talk and drive simultaneously.

Whenever Blake attempted to drive and carry on a conversation, his companions were petrified to see him take his eyes off the road and try to read lips. She had laid down the law years ago. If he wanted to talk he was riding shotgun and if he was driving she was not interested in anything he had to say.

After getting on the road, Blake turned to face Emily and started rehashing his research findings. Blake had learned that the operation rendered the affected ear completely deaf, but as he mentioned to Emily, he wasn't concerned about that issue. He couldn't have a conversation without reading lips, so he didn't think deafness was much to worry about. If the procedure failed his life would be no worse.

The possibility of nerve damage affecting his sense of taste and ability to smile was more daunting, but he was ready to take the plunge. Emily listened with growing excitement, praying for a miracle that might be within reach.

The electrifying possibilities consumed their conversation on the way home, with Blake talking so animatedly that Emily found it hard to get a word in edgewise. A mile from home, they drove past Skyline Chili, a Cincinnati chain serving up a weird concoction of chili, spaghetti and cheese. Emily passed the sign and made an offhand observation about not having been there recently, but her remark went over Blake's head. Searching his phone for details about implants, Blake kept on talking. Shortly thereafter he commented, "You know, we should go to Skyline soon."

Emily regarded her husband out of the corner of her eye and suppressed a grin, "You don't say?"

A quirky aspect of hearing loss is that a hearing impaired person's brain will subconsciously register a comment – for example, let's stop playing cards and check if it's still raining outside – and then prompt them to verbalize it shortly afterwards. What they fail to realize is that they are repeating something voiced a few seconds earlier. Bewilderment ensues as the hard of hearing person suddenly sees people laughing at a secret joke.

"Yeah," responded Blake. "I could go for it."

"Sounds good to me!" Emily bit her lip, trying to keep a straight face. "Maybe this weekend."

Five minutes later they arrived home and pulled into their driveway. As they got out to walk up the front sidewalk Madison rolled her Honda Civic in behind them, tooting the horn. Blake turned around to see Madison and Matthew, with Matthew holding up a box from Adriatico's Pizza in Clifton, Blake and Emily's eatery of choice during college. His mouth started to water at the sight of the familiar brown box, visualizing a thick crust Sicilian pizza topped with pepperoni, sausage and hot banana peppers.

Emily waved at her children and turned to Blake, "I gave Madison a call to bring over Matthew and a pizza once we left the hospital. It's not Skyline Chili but will have to do!" Her eyes sparkled with delight and a pair of dimples framed her smile.

"Perfect!" Blake answered. "I'll find a whiskey to match!"

The four of them filed through the front door with Matthew in the lead, steering the pizza down the hallway to the kitchen and leaving a tantalizing odor in his wake. Mackenzie was perched at one end of the walnut slab working on homework. She stopped writing as they entered and announced, "It's about time! I'm starving!!" Her face made a cute circle of pretty on top of a petite frame.

Madison shook her head, "The smallest body and the biggest stomach. I hate you."

"I'll get drinks," Blake said. "Anybody?" His family enthusiastically expressed their approval and Blake headed to the liquor cabinet. *This crowd is expensive at a restaurant. My fault.*

Blake poked around the cabinet to select a bottle of Blanton's Single Barrel whiskey. Blanton's was 93 proof with a sweet profile that offered up hints of caramel, vanilla, raisins and blackberries, all four flavors equally balanced. The nose held mostly vanilla with a touch of oak and the finish incorporated a small burn that lasted less than a second before fading away. He was eagerly anticipating how the medium proof would mingle with the fats in the pizza, creating a delectable interplay of flavors. *Love it!* It was one of his jewels, with the bottle formed in the shape of a miniature whiskey barrel.

Blake carried the whiskey back to the kitchen and pulled a bottle of Coke from the refrigerator before setting both items down on the table. Next he dumped some ice in a bucket and put that on the table also. Grabbing a glass, he plopped in four ice cubes from the ice bucket. After that he lifted up the bottle with its rounded shape and took a moment to enjoy how it nestled perfectly in his hand before pulling out the cork and taking a sniff that resulted in a murmur of approval.

Mackenzie had put her homework to the side and was watching him with her chin cupped in both hands. Whiskey was part of her Dad's identity and she loved watching his rituals. With a playful tilt to her head she addressed her father, "That one's for me, right?"

Standing before his daughter, Blake gave her a mischievous smile, "Sure! I might mess up the first drink so you may as well get that one!" The rest of the family laughed while Mackenzie shook her head ruefully. Blake gave her a wink and tilted the Blanton's down to pour. Twenty-four years at Seagram working among farmers and mechanics included a daily gauntlet of verbal jousting that made him prone to wisecracks.

Coming to her daughter's rescue, Emily said, "Hurry up, Simon! Pizza's getting colder by the second!" Feigning impatience, she pulled out a chair and sat down, hazel eyes challenging him to respond. Mackenzie, Matthew and Madison watched with interest to see who would come out on top.

Affecting a deadpan gaze, Blake responded, "It's very polite of you to hold off. I don't remember asking anyone to wait for me, though. You're welcome to start while I make drinks." He threw his wife a deliberate wink and poured the Blanton's over ice, measuring with his eye. Putting the whiskey back down, he gestured with one hand as an invitation to dig in while he picked up the Coke with the other. They all took the hint and began reaching for a slice, Emily smiling as she made her selection. Pouring the Coke over ice and whiskey, Blake watched it start to fizz, timing his actions to stop pouring and deliver the drink to Mackenzie in one continuous motion. The foam reached overflow level right when he placed it in front of her and she bowed her head down to slurp it off just in time. "Perfect!" Blake exclaimed. "That's the best part!"

"Uummm!" Mackenzie agreed. Not willing to waste any more time, she lifted a slice of pizza to her mouth and chomped down with a moan, rolling her eyes in a mixture of relief and pleasure.

Blake prepared the remaining drinks before sitting down to eat, passing them out individually to a series of appreciative thanks. His family could easily make their own, but watching his ritualistic flair was part of the fun.

Mingled sounds of clinking ice and light conversation filled the kitchen as Blake took a bite of pizza to groan at the spicy explosion of flavor. The deliciousness chased around his mouth finding every spot capable of acknowledging its presence, a chaser of bourbon the perfect complement. Finishing his first piece, he moved on to the second, alternating bites of pizza with pulls of whiskey, a swell of contentment starting to build. Halfway through his third piece of pizza, Blake reached a point where he felt satisfied.

He stopped eating and took a few seconds to swirl his bourbon and sample the diluted contents. His family was finishing up and the mood was relaxed. Seeing that he could easily gain the floor, Blake began, "I guess you guys already know that I passed the surgeon's exam. Insurance should cover two implants also." Surveying his family he continued, "There's not much left to do except get an MRI and schedule the procedure."

Madison broke out in a broad smile, "Terrific news, Dad! Calls for the good stuff!"

"You better believe it!" Blake laughed. "It's a relief to have come this far. I'm not in the clear yet, but it's pretty close."

Mackenzie expressed a happy, "Yay!" beaming at her father.

"Nice!" Matthew chimed in around a mouth full of pizza.

Emily regarded her family with contentment, happy that events appeared to be moving in the right direction. She met her husband's eyes, catching a subtle lift to his chin, the silent message indecipherable to their children but full of meaning for her. It was a signal that covered a lot of ground, years of shared struggles condensed into the minuscule gesture.

The group was almost done demolishing the pizza, a single slice remaining in the box. It was then that Matthew, overtaken by the lassitude of a full stomach, blurted out, "It would be a shame if you failed the MRI and couldn't get an implant."

Conversation in the kitchen came to a stop, the upbeat mood fading off to become an ominous silence. Four pairs of eyes shifted. Three of those pairs regarded Matthew with incredulous expressions loaded with disapproval, while the fourth pair, which belonged to Blake, was searching the group to verify that he had heard correctly. Taking in three stormy visages and Matthew's widening eyes, Blake concluded, *Close enough.*

A few beats passed then Madison stepped in to deliver a volley of criticism. "OK buzz kill, it's not necessary to prove your stupidity constantly. You might want to consider taking a day off now and then." Blatant censure dripped from each word.

Emily was consumed by a slow burn, upset that her earlier session with Matthew had proven to be so fruitless, thankful that Madison had beaten her to the punch. If she responded to Matthew's comment, there was no doubt that it would become an event worthy of memorializing. Buttressing the stance taken by her older sister, Mackenzie's eyes were flashing in pure hostility.

Blake remained silent. He instantly recognized the potential for piling on and thought it wiser to stay quiet. Observing his wife and daughters, he knew Matthew was in for the worst sort of humiliation, the kind which came from family.

Trying to back his way out of trouble, Matthew offered up a weak defense. "But it's true," he protested, his normal pallor turning crimson. The words left his mouth of their own volition, even as he recognized they would only make his situation worse.

Taking charge, Madison unloaded onto her younger brother without a vestige of sympathy. "It's probably true you had a bowel movement today too, but it doesn't add much to the discussion." The brutal comment was designed to preclude further remarks, challenging Matthew to admit defeat before he dug a deeper hole.

At a loss to counter Madison's vicious rebuttal, Matthew surveyed the remainder of the group in rapid succession. Eye to eye with his son, Blake lifted his eyebrows in disappointment. Cowed by the universal condemnation, Matthew bent his head down to his plate. *It is true!* He repeated the thought to himself with a stubborn single mindedness but didn't dare go any further. What did come out as he slouched down in disgrace was, "Sorry. That was a dumb thing to say."

With that the kitchen fell silent as they all tried to regroup. Blake picked up his glass with its comforting heft and swirled his whiskey, ice clinking in a familiar cadence. The soothing rhythm helped ease the tension. Emily lifted her glass, closing her eyes to take a drink. Matthew took another bite of his pizza and as he did Blake mentally coached his son from where he sat. *Put some food in your mouth, smartest thing you can do.*

Blake figured people were correct when they said that boys matured slower, Matthew being a perfect example. His son was so emotionally immature that he couldn't offer much in the way of empathy. Blake did what he could to maintain a positive attitude in the face of his disability, but it was frustrating when forced to counter negativity from a member of his own family. *I only have so much energy.* Blake wasn't surprised by Matthew's faux pas, because he lacked an understanding of people. Growing up with hearing loss had forced Blake to mature quickly and it was painful for him to watch his son create unnecessary difficulties for himself and others. *Unfortunately he didn't have the advantage of growing up with a disability. As stupid as that sounds.*

A pause hung over the kitchen, broken by Madison's phone skittering across the table in an onslaught of buzzing. Grabbing it up, she announced to no one in particular, "Downtown is calling my name. Soft opening at the Octopus bar tonight!"

Rising from her seat she moved her willowy frame alongside Matthew and addressed him good naturedly, "Come on doofus, I have to go and you've done enough damage for one day. I'll take you back to campus." Having vented her outrage, she was the least upset among the three women. Abandoning his last bite of pizza, Matthew drained his drink and quickly got up, grateful for a chance to escape.

He hung his head as he stood next to Blake, "Sorry, Dad!" Black hair fell off to one side, hiding half of his face.

He did look sorry, Blake reflected. *Sometimes sorry was all you had to offer.*

"Sure," Blake responded. "Don't worry about it. Water under the bridge."

He and Emily walked their two kids to the door, Blake kissing Madison goodbye and clapping his son on the back. Emily, still visibly upset, gave Matthew a light smack on his cheek as she fixed him with her eyes and softly sighed, her meaning clear. Gently kissing his cheek on the same spot, she sent him on his way with Madison.

Closing the door, she backed up against it to face Blake, shaking her head in defeat. "Don't worry, he's dumb, not mean."

Blake burst out laughing as Emily threw Matthew under the bus. *She would only say that to me!* If it was someone outside the family Emily would apologize and leave it at that. "Luckily Madison was there to straighten him out. You would have torn him up!"

Emily raised her eyebrows in relief, "Yes. Thank heavens she jumped in."

The shared intimacy took them over the hump and Blake hooked an arm around Emily's waist as they returned to the kitchen. "I have a hunch about the MRI. Don't ask me why but I think it will turn out fine. This whole process is moving so fast it's almost preordained." He pulled her closer as they squeezed through the kitchen doorway. "I'm starting to get excited about being able to hear. It was hard to imagine the slightest chance before, but now..." Blake stopped talking to examine her upturned face. A stray curl hung in front of her eyes and he brushed it back behind her ears. "Now it's starting to look like a miracle might pan out." His voice choked off as he dared to give life to the dream.

Emily grasped his face in both hands to bring it close to her own. "It just might. I pray for you daily and there's a whole church praying with me." Captured by his wife's determination, Blake felt himself lifted by a wave of encouragement.

Blake bent down to rest his chin on Emily's shoulder as she wrapped her arms around him and held him close. A few hairs tickled his nostrils. Mackenzie was watching from where she had her homework laid out, telegraphing support for his journey in her own unique manner. His senses were overtaken by an intense rush as the kitchen was pervaded by a healing presence. Anchored in the refuge of Emily's arms, a peacefulness came pouring through Blake that offered solace, melting away the angst and refilling its space with positivity and hope. The dream was overwhelming, and he shifted his head against Emily's neck.

Moving a hand to cradle his head, she touched her fingers over what little hair there was. "I'm with you all the way."

"Me too," Mackenzie added.

"Thanks," Blake responded in a gruff voice. He had traveled from opposition to acceptance to what was now a burning sense of urgency. Releasing himself from Emily and inhaling deeply, Blake wiped both eyes with the back of one hand, "I guess we better clean up dinner."

Adopting a playful expression, Emily eyeballed the dishes as she shifted to rest both hands on her hips, "I would love to help, but I have to get some work done for tomorrow." Smiling, she turned in the direction of the door. Exiting the kitchen in a slow saunter, she lifted one hand in a finger wave with her back to him, long tresses cascading down her shoulders as she left.

Shaking his head at Mackenzie in mock disgust, Blake proceeded to clean up, finishing in short order and settling into his chair afterwards with a novel. Mackenzie kept busy plugging away at her homework. An hour later, Blake became aware of her engaging in a flurry of activity as she gathered her books, rising from the table to approach him.

Giving him a peck on the cheek, Mackenzie announced, "Night Dad!" remaining next to the chair as a signal that she desired his further attention. Reaching out to pat his arm she excitedly burst out, "I can't wait for when you use the phone and we can talk!" She was bouncing around as she spoke, choreographing a happy dance.

"Me either! The doctor says the odds are pretty good!" He scrutinized her sunny face.

Mackenzie bent down and whipped out a finger in front of his nose. "I got dibs! Better make sure you call me first or I might not talk to you! Hee hee hee!!" She let out a musical laugh, just like her mother's, before turning to skip out of the room.

Blake watched her go, responding with a belated "Deal!" as she exited the doorway. Mackenzie's excitement was contagious. Forgetting the novel, he was transported to the edge of a precipice where he stood with shaky legs and a tight stomach. Fear and uncertainty remained, but he preferred to try and fail rather than to poison the rest of his days wondering what might have been.

Alone on the edge, thoughts vacillating between anticipation and dread, Blake wrestled with the question of his future. Would it manifest as an uplifting victory or a crushing defeat?

God only knows…but I'm jumping either way.

Chapter 5 – Implantation

Eight days had gone by since his appointment with Dr. Rickerson and it was now Saturday. Blake was at the kitchen table immersed in coffee therapy, trying to decide whether it was more pleasurable to sip the liquid or inhale the aroma. He was dressed for the weekend in black jeans, a University of Cincinnati sweatshirt and flip flops. The morning was cool enough that flip flops and a t-shirt bordered on a case of the shivers, but adding a sweatshirt felt perfect. Outside the window their resident blue jay appeared as a blur of movement, darting back and forth among bare branches. Tracking the streak of blue as it fulfilled some indecipherable mission, Blake was awash with peacefulness.

Yesterday afternoon the doctor's office had called to say that Blake's MRI results were satisfactory and that he could schedule a date for surgery. Emily took the call and informed him when he got home, followed by the two of them dancing around in celebration. The commotion pulled Mackenzie out of her room to see what all the fuss was about.

For the remainder of the evening Blake's mind was consumed with possibilities until he was wound up tighter than a 16-year-old trying to reach third base. Three fingers of whiskey consumed in an effort to encourage drowsiness didn't produce the desired effect. Throughout the night he only dozed off sporadically, laying quietly in between snoozes to keep from disturbing his wife. At 5:30 a.m. he finally gave up when the dawn revealed Emily lost in peaceful slumber. Raven hair spread across the pillow forming a silky backdrop for her exposed neck. He moved closer to inhale her scent and as he did so she stirred and snuggled in. The firm mounding of her breasts contacted his chest and mild tumescence hardened into morning wood. Blake vividly remembered what came next.

One hand explored upward to find his face, "Did you sleep?" She mouthed the words at him with eyes half closed against the morning. He reached out to run his fingers through her lustrous curls and ran his hand lightly down the curve of her backside.

"I'm done sleeping," he whispered as he nuzzled the sexy contours of her neck, sliding a hand underneath her nightgown.

Her answer was to offer encouragement by encircling him with one hand as the other found his neck. She pulled his head down and he gently kissed along the length of her jugular to be rewarded by a shifting to allow him better access. Emily moaned softly under his ministrations, low vibrations strumming from her throat. Blake followed her lead as she took a firm hold to rub him against her opening. As she eased him closer and closer to the edge, his breath started coming in short gasps and his heart pounded in response. He panted into the scent of her curls, prisoner to her grasp. When she was ready, she guided him inside and wrapped herself around him. Released from the need for restraint, Blake matched the undulations of her hips and they moved together in a personal rhythm forged from 25 years together. Rays of sunshine peeked through their bedroom window to caress them both, Emily's body stiffening to arch up in release. She tightened her grip and exhaled hotly against his skin, triggering his own response, their spirits expanding as one before cresting to shatter into a million fragments.

Opening his eyes at 8:00 a.m., Blake turned to his naked wife curled up alongside him and bent down to nuzzle her awake for the second time that morning. Observing him from beneath half open eyelids she straightened her arms above her head and rewarded him with a sultry smile. Her toes pointed out and down as she extended her legs as far as they would go. Emily's muscles tightened, almost to the point of vibrating, then she proceeded to curl up in a ball and pull the sheets back around her. A pair of bright eyes peeked out at him. Blake threw the remaining covers in her direction and rolled out of bed to kick start the coffee maker, but not before sliding a hand underneath the sheets to give her breast a soft squeeze of appreciation.

***

Taking a second pull of coffee, Blake followed the blue jay's movements around the yard, unable to find a discernible pattern. *Maybe I'm too mellow this morning.* Movement registered in his peripheral vision and he looked toward the doorway to see Emily gliding into the kitchen to head straight for the coffeemaker. Silken tresses framed her face with provocative promises and a floor length robe only accentuated her curves. Taking the carafe out and pouring herself a mug she swiveled in his direction to announce, "You're in trouble, mister!"

What a babe! thought Blake. "How so?"

"My right breast is feeling left out." Eyes glittering, she cast him a sensuous reproach that made him wish they were still in the bedroom.

"Sorry, won't happen again." He was powerless to break eye contact, not that he wanted to anyway.

"See that it doesn't." She came over to the table, her eyes claiming him with a possessive gleam and leaning down to clink her mug with his. "By the way, congratulations on your upcoming surgery."

"Yeah. Didn't think I would ever appreciate that sentiment." Understated agreement belied the excitement that had been in the forefront of his thoughts since yesterday.

"What's the plan?" Emily stood in front of him, releasing a yawn that she covered up with the back of one hand. Holding his gaze with a knowing grin, she purposefully smoothed back her hair.

"Tuesday work for you? We can combine Dr. Rickerson and Dr. Archer in one trip." *I'm ok with going back to bed, too.*

"I think so. I can either cancel my afternoon client or call in a favor to get someone to take my place." Emily encircled her mug with both hands and performed a half twirl, causing the robe to puff out below her waist. "This is going to be the most fun appointment!"

Amen to that! Blake took another pull of steaming coffee, captivated by the green and gold flecks excitedly swirling through Emily's hazel irises.

***

Tuesday afternoon Blake and Emily arrived at University Hospital to be deposited in the same exam room as before. Blake was gazing out over the medical campus where a patchwork of yellow, red and orange was evenly split between the ground and the trees. Soon the remaining leaves would be released from their perches and the colors of fall would fade away. His thoughts moved to the holidays and he wondered if this year would be a turning point. *Following the conversation would be an improvement.* He observed Emily perusing the anatomical picture on the wall. She was constantly interpreting for him and it would take significant pressure off her. *And let the fun back in.*

As they waited, Blake remembered Mary Beth mentioning that Dr. Rickerson enjoyed a positive reputation among his patients. According to her, he was known to focus on their humanity, seeing them as people instead of projects. *That may be true,* Blake mused, *but he's pretty rough in the beginning.*

His thoughts were interrupted by a sharp rapping at the door followed by the doctor dashing in with his coat flying behind. *Still at warp speed, I see.* Dr. Rickerson greeted them by getting down to business immediately, "Congratulations! Your MRI is perfect and we can move forward."

"Great!" Blake responded. He could handle the abruptness as long as Dr. Rickerson was proficient at his job. *Maybe I'll change my mind later.*

Emily started off with a question, "How do you handle a situation like Simon's where a patient gets two implants?"

The doctor buried his hands in the pockets of his coat and addressed her query, "For bilateral patients, meaning those with two implants, we generally space the operations five to six months apart. That allows an easier adjustment for the patient, both mentally and physically. I have done both ears at the same time, but only in special cases." He remained standing, "One of my patients was going to lose her insurance so I did both ears together for her. Another was facing multiple surgeries, so it was better to do both ears together. In Simon's case I would prefer to wait six months in between."

"That works for me," Blake commented. "What else?"

"Which ear are you wanting to start with?"

"Whichever one happens to be facing you!" Blake grinned. "At least for the first implant!" He was a little giddy that his operation was a go. *It's on!*

Dr. Rickerson smiled in response, "In that case we can start with the right ear. I'm available on Tuesday, November 3rd if you are free. That should allow you to be activated before Thanksgiving."

"He's free!" Emily burst in. "He's free, I'm free, the whole family is free!" Standing up from her chair, she walked to a spot behind her husband. Resting both hands on his shoulders she blurted, "This is so exciting!"

The doctor addressed them, "Believe it or not, that's it for today. Your case doesn't present any complications, all we need is a date and an ear. Questions?"

"Not from me!" Blake twisted his head around to Emily, "Ready for whiskey?"

"Ha!" she replied. "One of us has to go back to work, buster, so I'll take a raincheck!"

"My nurse will give you information that covers the period before surgery. Please email me with any questions that come up." Dr. Rickerson gave them a few more instructions then turned to pause in front of the door, "Dr. Archer will be in momentarily." He smiled and shook their hands before flying out of the room.

Blake shook his head, "The guy is a brown tornado with a white cape! Mary Beth says he's good though." He could see his wife beaming, "You're pretty happy!"

"Oh, I am! It's the best!" Emily was grinning from ear to ear, eyes dancing above her smile and face glowing with excitement. *I know she's happy for me,* Blake thought, *but I'm happy for her.*

A knock interrupted their exchange and a nurse entered to give them the promised information. Shortly afterwards Dr. Susan Archer peered through the open door. "Congratulations!" As the nurse left she came in the small room to hug them both, a pair of golden hoops glittering from her ears. "How exciting for the two of you! I hope this will be a tremendous improvement!"

"I'm with you!" Blake responded. "What else do we need to figure out?"

"It's pretty important," Susan grinned, her blue eyes twinkling. "We have to pick the color for the processor, cable and magnet!"

"I was thinking either black or grey."

"Probably grey." Lifting an eyebrow ever so slightly, Emily regarded her husband with an expectant gaze.

"Yeah, yeah, grey." Giving his wife a sideways glance, Blake came back to Susan, "Black is second choice."

"Got it!" Susan said, smiling. "We should also set the activation appointment, so how about November 20th, a few days before Thanksgiving?"

"Perfect!" Emily responded, "That would be perfect!" Her smile dazzled with a brilliant glow causing Blake to pause at her appealing combination of beauty and spirit, giving thanks for his luck in finding her. He flashed back to their second meeting when he realized that she was special, displaying a compassion that amplified her allure.

Turning away from his thoughts and back to Susan, he said, "So, three weeks to see if it works?"

"Oh no," Susan answered. "I will be in the operating room with Dr. Rickerson to test the implant. After insertion of the electrode into the cochlea, we stimulate the implant while monitoring the response from your auditory nerve to make sure it functions properly. When you leave the operating room, we already know whether the implant works."

"Good to know," Emily commented. "I will be asking you right away then!"

"We have no reason to anticipate problems," Susan offered. "You don't have any of the risk factors associated with failure so your implantation should be successful."

It's moving along so well! Blake marveled. He reminded himself that after 49 years anyone would deserve a break. The technology appeared incredible. *I hope it's half as effective as Mary Beth says.*

Susan walked to the door, resting her hand on the lever, "I will see you both soon. You're in good hands!" Flashing a smile she left Blake and Emily standing in the room, a sense of anticipation hanging in the air between them.

Blake turned to the wall of glass, gazing beyond the campus to the hills on the horizon. The magnitude of his imminent relief was thrust to the forefront, raising a sword against his long history of futility. In the distance years of struggles piled upon each other to create a living presence that defied description. Emily's hand sought out his, intertwining their fingers, and he found comfort in her touch.

They stood linked together in quiet refuge, staring out across the campus with unseeing eyes.

***

Walking out of University Hospital, Blake kissed Emily goodbye and reviewed his options for the remainder of the afternoon. Emily was going to a dinner meeting and would not be home until late. He considered popping down to Cincinnati's Over the Rhine district to enjoy happy hour with Madison, but a quick text nixed that option. Blake found his vehicle and pointed it in the direction of work, deciding to update George on his surgery schedule. Arriving at the office, he exited his truck to approach the outline of grey brick, set low against the sky. Afternoon shadows were creeping along the blacktop as the sun dropped lower, but George would be in the office for a while yet.

Pushing his way through the door, Blake turned down the hallway towards George's office, remembering how three years ago one of his fishing buddies, Steve, mentioned to Blake that a cochlear implant had improved his mother's life for the better. *That's going to be me soon!* Blake hoped that he could achieve better results than Steve's 87-year-old mother. *Pretty low performance bar there.*

Coming up on George's office, Blake switched to work mode. Blake took pains to ensure that their relationship went smoothly, but George was prone to several behaviors that he gauged irritating, one being a tendency to define situations as black and white. Another was making fun of ideas George didn't understand or didn't care to understand. However, there was no denying that George's tolerance of Blake's deficiencies went a long way towards keeping Blake engaged in useful work, and he was thankful for his forbearance. *George has his faults, but he's also responsible for saving my bacon.*

Reaching his destination, Blake positioned himself at the open door and lightly tapped his knuckles on the doorframe. "Hey, George."

"You're back. How'd it go?" George's head came up from a pile of papers, his tie long gone. A red pencil in one hand appeared more like a toothpick than anything else.

"I'm on the schedule for November 3rd." *Whoohoo!!*

"Congratulations! I can't wait to see how it works for you! The technology sounds mind blowing!" George appeared genuinely happy for Blake.

"I'm still having trouble wrapping my head around it," Blake said, from his spot against the doorframe.

"If it's as good as you say then we'll put a phone in your office!" George laughed out loud, filling the room with boisterous thunder. "Maybe we can even talk instead of texting when you travel."

"Fine by me." *You have no idea!*

"What's that about a phone?" Angela came up from behind Blake to crowd the door opening.

Blake twisted off the doorjamb to see her peering at his face with a curious expression. "I'm having surgery in a few weeks."

"How wonderful! Oh, I hope it makes a big difference for you!" Where George was happy, Angela was ecstatic. Blake was reminded of why he liked working at WEFT. *The people around here can be flat out fantastic. Except for Dan. Even Dan's not mean though, just oblivious to other lifeforms.*

"Thanks! I'm having trouble imagining that I'll achieve normal hearing, but my doctor says the possibility is excellent." Blake took in their smiling faces, "Don't know if I believe him, but I'm not going to miss the chance."

"You better not!" Angela grabbed his elbow and gave it a fierce jiggle. "I've got you on the prayer list at my church!"

"Go for it," George said. "If anyone can make it work, you can."

In the face of such enthusiasm, Blake felt his throat choke off and his eyes tear up. It was all he could do to croak out, "Thanks for the support," while getting out of there as fast as he could.

Gaining the sanctuary of his office he immediately closed the door and sank down into the closest chair, the one positioned for visitors. Taking a deep breath he put both hands over his face and hunched forward.

What's going on with me?

Blake's approach to navigating life was to suppress his reactions until they were properly vetted for release. In the past this strategy had served him well. He vented his stress overload with racquetball and the occasional eruption while portioning out the remainder of his emotions in measured doses.

The prospect of receiving a cochlear implant brightened his life more than anything in recent memory, but it came with an additional complication. Unaccustomed to such positivity, his happiness was beginning to leak out, opening a pathway for buried emotions to explode from containment along with it.

So many years of suppressing his feelings had produced a boiling reservoir that was eagerly hunting for cracks in the dam.

Safely ensconced in his office, an expansion rose from his center, spreading through his extremities and traveling up his neck into his scalp. Blake reacted in dismay as a disturbing surge manifested in his limbs to erupt on his skin in a flush of heat. The outpouring clashed against his wall of restraint and he resisted the leak, afraid to grant recognition to the pressure inside. Newly awakened forces pushed back with fierce energy, causing his heart to beat wildly, forcing him to realize that he was at a turning point.

This can't continue. I have to let this out or it's going to destroy me.

Blake freed his mind to entertain a universe where he could hear and it was a vision that took control of his body. A prickly heat permeated his scalp to emerge in a burn that stood his hair on end. Tears began to flow of their own volition and his throat narrowed to nothing. Blind and mute, sucking in erratic gulps of air, he was subjected to a physical pounding as wave after wave of frustrated emotions slammed his body in a vicious demand for equal recognition. Accepting defeat, Blake surrendered to the power inside as rages from the past merged with promises from the future to pour out of him in a savage river. The purge continued until it was finished running its course, leaving him exhausted, weak and rubbery. He opened his eyes to the darkening office, scared at the strength of what he had allowed to accumulate.

Blake sat numbly in his chair with the door shut, watching the shadows of late afternoon grow longer, wondering where he would find a balance.

***

The weeks passed quickly and Blake's surgery date arrived with a cold snap typical of autumn. Morning temperatures for Tuesday, November 3rd were in the low twenties, the predawn glow exposing frosty highlights on yesterday's green grass. Blake, Emily and Mackenzie left home early in order to avoid traffic, arriving at University Hospital by 5:30 a.m. They exited their vehicle in an upbeat mood, Mackenzie remarking how today marked the beginning of a beginning and the end of an end. *I hope it's a good beginning,* Blake thought.

Navigating a path from the parking garage deep in the bowels of the hospital up to the main floor and from there through a network of corridors, elevators and more corridors, the three of them zigzagged their way to the surgical registration desk. There were plenty of signs to provide assistance, but their minds were so preoccupied that reading was a forgotten skill. After checking in Blake was fitted with a wristband listing his name and birthdate in both written and barcode form. The wristband was made of lightweight plastic and he barely noticed it around his wrist. Following registration they dutifully trailed behind a nurse to be deposited in the holding area, which turned out to be a common room with twelve bays.

Their bay contained a hospital bed on wheels and three chairs situated in an area roughly 12 feet by 12 feet. All the bays were set up to line the perimeter of the common area and each bay could be isolated from the room by blue curtains suspended from a ceiling track. The floor was white linoleum, the perimeter wall was eggshell and the ceiling was white with fixtures that cast a harsh brightness.

Blake was instructed to get in bed after first removing his clothes to don a gown that covered his front and exposed his back. The nurse left, leaving Emily to assist him with the gown. His clothing was to be placed in a plastic bag labeled 'personal belongings' with a label to write in his name and room number. Given the option of removing his underwear or having it cut off in the operating room Blake reluctantly bowed to the demands of the situation. *Modesty is a wasted effort.*

As an added bonus he was required to don a blue hairnet, causing Mackenzie to snigger when he slipped it over the smoothness of his shaved head. His wedding ring was at home and the only personal possessions left were his hearing aids. Those would also be removed before surgery, but for the time being he was permitted to wear them. Once he climbed into the hospital bed a warm blanket provided some protection against the coolness of the room, creating an impression of comfort. *This won't last.*

With his clothes and dignity removed, the three of them settled in to wait for the appearance of Madison and Matthew. Blake occupied a position of honor in the hospital bed which was set up with its head against the perimeter wall while Emily and Mackenzie sat in two of the three chairs positioned parallel to the bed. Blue curtains served as a backdrop. His stomach was rumbling in mild protest at the pre-op restrictions on food and water, but the prospect of his upcoming IV produced a queasiness that made him glad his stomach was empty. *That much less to puke up.* An antiseptic smell hung in the air, contributing an ominous note.

With Emily and Mackenzie sitting close enough to touch, Blake couldn't decide if he was scared or excited. His wife and daughter were perched on the edge of their chairs, neither one able to relax in the overbearing sterility. Emily was fidgeting with her nails while next to her Mackenzie was twirling her phone between two fingers. Blake figured that it was anyone's guess when Madison would arrive. Navigating the hospital could be confusing, but Madison was notorious for getting lost, having been accused by her younger sister of being unable to follow directions for getting out of the bathroom.

A succession of nurses wanting to know his name and birthdate paraded in and out of the bay. It was written down plain as day on his wristband, but his primary job today was to verify his identity to anybody that asked. One nurse oversaw insurance forms, one needed to verify which ear was the target and yet another was tasked with recording his temperature and blood pressure. The constant activity only served to remind him that he would soon be receiving an IV. Whenever the curtain parted, Blake cringed. *Ugh! Get in here, will you! It's sending me over the edge!!*

Then came a lull, all three waiting in expectant silence, wondering who would pop through the curtain next. Mackenzie spoke up, "I wonder how many detours Madison is taking to get here?" An impish expression covered her face, the levity prompting Emily to regard her youngest daughter with amusement.

"Button it twerp!" Madison parted the curtain with Matthew in tow, fixing her sister with a resigned glare, "Thanks for the support!"

"We're all here!" Emily stood up to motion her brood together. "Let's pray before the room gets busy again."

Blake watched from his position in bed as his family gathered about him. Emily positioned herself on one side while Mackenzie jostled her way around to the other. They clasped hands, Blake connected to Emily and Mackenzie with Madison and Matthew completing the circle at the foot of the bed. His wife petitioned for good fortune in a prayer that included the doctors, nurses, family and anyone else within a five-mile radius who could conceivably be involved. A longtime participant in the support ministry at church, her prayers left nothing to chance.

No sooner did she finish than another nurse parted the curtain, pushing a cart jammed full of equipment to announce, "Hi! I'm Jill! Here for your IV." Blake took in a deep breath. *Here it comes!* The warm blanket had cooled off and the reality of what lay ahead began to intrude. Behind her glasses Blake observed a young brunette dressed in dark blue scrubs and the ubiquitous hospital clogs that all the nurses wore. Her clogs were pink, bringing a welcome relief to the sameness of the hospital, but that was only dimly noted by Blake.

At Jill's announcement, Mackenzie paled, retreating to her chair and squirming down into a ball. Madison watched her younger sister's actions with a smirk. Matthew took in the nurse with her cart and quickly decided to bury himself in his phone from the sanctuary of the remaining chair. Madison chose to lean on the armrest of her mother's seat, the two of them prepared to watch the nurse go about her business.

Verifying Blake's name and birthdate, Jill anchored her IV cart close to his left arm, on the opposite side from his family, and proceeded to install the IV drip. She took his arm, strapped on a rubber tourniquet above his elbow and began to massage his forearm to locate her point of entry. Blake turned aside, unwilling to watch. He could feel his heart rate rising and his whole body tensing up as he lay in bed dreading the insertion. Continuing to rub his forearm, Jill said, "Yours will be the easiest IV I've had in months! You have great veins!"

"You're just trying to make me relax, but thanks anyway," Blake said.

"Nope! I mean it. Your veins show up better than a picture in a book." Finding her spot, Jill readied a syringe as she bent over his left arm. "I'm going to numb you before I put in the IV." Taking hold of his forearm, she gave it a hard squeeze while inserting the needle of the syringe near the top of his wrist. Blake was relieved to only feel a light prick. He didn't trust himself to observe, but it didn't take long. Jill was soon hanging up the IV bag and arranging a length of clear tubing between the IV stand and his bed. After she was done, he gathered up his courage to trace a path from the IV bag with its steady drip down the length of tubing to finally arrive at the connection taped on his wrist. Observing the needle sticking out of his skin brought on a wave of dizziness, and he closed his eyes. *Ooooooh.*

"How was that?" Jill stood by the bed. She laid her hand on his shoulder, waiting for his response.

"Way better than I thought," Blake said, opening his eyes to see her inspecting him closely. "It didn't hurt and I can't even feel it. I want you to do all my IVs."

Jill laughed and said, "Thank you! I hope you never have to get another!" She gave his arm a light pat and started to pack up her IV cart. Waving a hand at his family she smiled encouragingly, "It's clear you have all kinds of support! You also have an excellent surgeon!" With a cheery "Goodbye!" she pushed her way past the curtain and rolled the cart out.

Thankful to be done with the IV and its associated trauma, Blake lay back in the hospital bed trying to relax. Even though the IV needle was securely taped to his wrist he made sure to move his arm carefully, afraid to put strain on the tubing. The mental build-up had been far worse than the insertion but having a needle in his wrist was freaking him out. He couldn't feel much other than a light caress from the tubing touching his arm, but he was uncomfortably aware of the alien needle. *Knock me out and get it over with. I want this thing out of me.* Blake sighed, reluctantly ceding that comfort had a different definition while he was in the hospital.

I'm in it to win it, he told himself.

With no clocks around, Blake was unsure how much time had elapsed since his arrival. Surgery was scheduled for 9:30 a.m. and was supposed to take three hours. Afterwards he would be admitted to the hospital and stay overnight to be discharged tomorrow afternoon. He had already lost track of time as the parade of nurses performed their tasks. *I guess it doesn't matter as long as we move in the right direction.*

The cochlear implant was designed to work for the rest of his life, meaning that he was not expected to lose hearing as he got older. Blake was fascinated by the idea that the operation would result in a permanent improvement to his body. *I'll be bionic!* He let go of his concerns with a sense of relief that things were out of his hands. His fate rested in the skill of Dr. Rickerson's team and the prayers that had gone up on his behalf.

Blake's thoughts jumped ahead to life after surgery. *I want to hear in a restaurant. Maybe I'll even understand people after drinking whiskey!*

It was odd how the first whiskey would marginally improve his hearing, but that second pour would quickly cause speech to become a buzz of white noise. Even though his ears crapped out early, the rest of him would still be in good shape, 24 years at Seagram resulting in a high tolerance for alcohol. Blake wasn't the type to become loud and animated when drinking, turning quiet and intense instead. The response made it difficult for others to determine his state of sobriety and Emily frequently referred to him as a high functioning drunk. *Too bad there's no whiskey in the hospital. I could use it to forget about the IV.*

His family was conversing among themselves while Blake's attention was being diverted by the unfamiliarity of being propped up butt naked in a hospital bed connected to an IV. He was watching the steady drip with the eyes of a hawk, trying to determine if the flow was consistent or if the tube was at risk of getting closed off by a kink. Evaluating his wrist, he wondered how the needle stayed open without a blood clot stopping the flow. Blake carefully arranged and rearranged the length of tubing that was laying on the bed to make sure it was not hidden under the blanket or stuck between the mattress and the frame. *I wonder if these things accidentally pull out?*

He reviewed the boundaries of his world, identified by the strict confines of the hospital bed. Foreign circumstances partnered with discomfort wherever he turned. The thin gown with its slit down the back gave scant isolation from the underlying bedsheet which wanted to gather up his butt. Down at the foot of the bed the blanket was getting bunched up around his ankles, and the pillow under his head was too low. There was an air compressor connected to the mattress which automatically puffed up or deflated the bed as a mechanism against bed sores. Blake moved his body here and there checking it out. As soon as he raised his butt, the bed compensated by filling in the space underneath. *How do I fart?*

His circumstances brought a grimace to his face. This morning he entered the hospital under his own control only to surrender his autonomy and become no different than a baby bird, dependent upon the ministrations of those around him. The characterization became obvious as soon as he presented his mouth for the temperature probe. Though he knew it was the price to pay for an implant, his ego was taking a hit. *The sooner the better.*

Isolated from his family scant inches away, Blake withdrew into solitude, deciding that it was better to prepare himself for surgery rather than wasting energy on trying to follow their discussion.

For Blake the act of conversation was a necessary evil rather than a desirable activity. Conversation took a lot of work on his part and with his ability to comprehend operating on a five second delay, he needed lapses in dialogue in order to understand. Nonstop speech was exhausting. It created a massive overload for Blake, making him feel like a nail that someone wouldn't stop hammering. Even when he could understand conversation Blake preferred to take several seconds to evaluate how someone's words matched their body language before formulating his response.

Reading the signs that signaled Blake's separation, Emily intentionally diverted the attention of her daughters. There was no need to distract Matthew, who was banging away at the screen of his phone, a punch monkey imprisoned by an electronic lord. Emily kept one eye on her brood and one eye on her husband as a pre-op limbo settled over the group.

Time crept around the clock, dragging its feet like a toddler unwilling to face bedtime. Relief arrived without warning as Dr. Rickerson made his entrance through the curtains, his energy making the atmosphere come alive. He was dressed in green scrubs with a facemask hanging loosely around his neck and a green cap covering his black hair. Displaying a confident smile, he approached the bed to greet his patient, "Good morning Simon! How are you today?"

Blake abandoned his fixation with the IV tubing to respond, "Ready!" *I was ready four weeks ago!!* He saw that the doctor's normal whirlwind had been replaced by a steadier sense of purpose. Emily and the children came to attention, focusing on Dr. Rickerson.

"It won't be much longer now. I need to mark your ear. We decided on the right ear, correct?"

"Yes sir!" *But I'm sure you want to verify it again! Although I'm perfectly OK with either ear!!!*

The doctor replied, "Good. We don't want any confusion to slow us down." Along with his comment Dr. Rickerson extracted a black marker from a side pocket in his scrubs and inscribed his initials on the skin behind Blake's right ear.

Blake couldn't help thinking that his ear was going to be the focus for a lot of different people today. So someone else's initials seemed appropriate.

Dr. Rickerson took a step back to inspect the IV tubing and remarked, "My anesthesiologist will be here soon to inject a dose of anesthesia into your IV. You'll start to feel that almost immediately. Once you are in the operating room we'll put you under full anesthesia."

"OK." *It's nice to have a little explanation!* Blake was excited. *Whoohoo!!!* The IV took on secondary importance as he realized that surgery was imminent. *Let's go!!!*

Dr. Rickerson laid a hand on Blake's shoulder, "Our surgical team is ready. I'm leaving in a minute or two and Fred will bring you to the operating room."

Blake nodded in acknowledgement. *How about that! This must be the kind and gentle side that I have been hearing about from Mary Beth.*

Turning to Emily, Dr. Rickerson continued, "The operation should take three hours after which Simon will be admitted to the hospital for an overnight stay. Immediately after surgery I'll meet with you and let you know how the procedure went."

Emily nodded in response, not bothering to reply. Her eyes were fixed into a stare and she was clasping her hands together tightly. Blake could tell that the situation had suddenly become real, no doubt causing her to focus on the possibility of complications. All three kids sat quietly, taking a cue from their mother. He was excited, his family appeared to be contemplating Armageddon. *I guess it could go south, life doesn't include a guarantee.*

Before he could chime in, another person parted the curtains to enter. Dr. Rickerson eased himself out with a quick "Goodbye!" and the newcomer moved to take his place.

"Good morning! My name is Fred and I'm your anesthesiologist. Let's verify your name and birthdate before we start!" Fred's booming voice was matched by a beefy physique and red face.

Blake recited the familiar litany and Fred responded with a hearty "Bingo!" as soon as Blake finished. He pulled a syringe from his front pocket, "I have a dose of happy juice for you here. Nobody ever complains about getting this! It goes in your IV and makes your day better." Partway through his explanation Fred took the cap off the syringe and proceeded to inject the contents into a port on the IV tubing.

Turning to Emily, Fred smiled, "Now is the time to collect your husband's hearing aids."

"Of course!" Emily got up to remove both units from Blake's ears. Before taking them off she leaned down to give him a soft kiss on the lips. Gazing deep into his eyes she said, "I love you! I'll be here when you wake up." Her eyes were glistening with flecks of gold and Blake knew she would be praying the whole time.

He lifted himself up to meet her kiss saying, "I love you too!" She slipped off his aids and the world went quiet.

Mackenzie crowded in to give him a kiss of her own, followed by Madison and Matthew. Before bending down to kiss her father, Madison turned to Matthew and motioned him to keep his mouth shut by pantomiming a zipped lip. Blake grinned when he saw her admonition. She might have made a comment too, but he was already encased in silence.

Blake felt the anesthesia take hold and his limbs becoming loose, his family shifting in and out of focus. *Man, that stuff works fast!* The haziness felt pleasant as Emily and the kids stepped back allowing Fred to get the bed ready for their trip. Locking the side rails into position, Fred released the brake and pulled the IV stand closer to the bed. He walked to the curtain to pull it aside then came back to take position behind Blake's head from where he would push. Watching the preparations in a disoriented state, Blake surrendered himself to whatever lay ahead. *Let's doooo it!*

They left the bay, Blake waving to his family as the bed rolled him away feet first. Emily kissed a finger to lightly tap it on his nose. The rest of his family waved back and then he was on his way, wheeling toward a door at the far end of the room.

It was a silent journey, full of adventure. Carefree and ready to roll, Blake looked straight down the bed rails to watch the walls fly by, leaning into the corners. Fred was a phenomenal driver, navigating their way around tight turns and through the flow of medical personnel dressed in scrubs or white coats. A procession of people undulated past his bed no differently than ants, parting at the last minute. He thought it was funny how some people tried to avoid touching the bed and some would sneak a quick glance when he passed by. Then there were those who ignored him like he was a stick of wood on a wheelbarrow. Some people, nurses mostly, smiled at him in encouragement. *I'm on a hospital safari!!*

Blake lost himself in the journey, living in the flow of movement until Fred steered them through a set of double doors into a bright room that was colder than anywhere else. An atmosphere of sterility and purpose penetrated his fogginess. Fred wheeled them up to a table surrounded by a ring of glaring lights suspended from above. It was a strange table - the top was comprised of four thin black cushions about 18" long and 9" wide spaced longitudinally with 4" gaps separating each one. Upon his arrival six unrecognizable people in scrubs and facemasks immediately collected around him. *I think we know what's next!* Blake deduced from their hand motions that he was going to be transferred to the table and that they wanted him to move to the side of the bed. He obliged and six pairs of hands transferred him to the operating room table where his head and body came to rest on the thin cushions.

Before he could get too uncomfortable, Fred's face appeared to shield the glare from above and a mask was slipped over his nose. Fred held up three fingers, tucked one in, and darkness fell.

Chapter 6 – Recovery

Blake drifted back across the border of consciousness with a heaviness on top of his chest and a sluggishness pervading his entire being. His neck was fixed in a vise. Cracking one eye open, he discovered that he was covered with layers of blankets and lying in a bed, one of many spaced throughout a dimly lit room which held a sharp odor of antiseptic. Nurses in scrubs were moving about and he realized that he must be in post op. It was, of course, totally silent without his hearing aids.

I'm alive. Emily will be happy.

His mind registered a warmth from the blankets that shielded him against the coolness of the room. At first he thought that the restraint around his neck was from multiple pillows, but there was something else too. Extracting a hand from under the blankets, he ascertained that his head was encased in a thick cushion of gauze which was held in place by a band. The wrap was 4" wide, ending above his ears to expose the top of his head. Exploring with the delicate touch of a butterfly, he was encouraged that even though his head felt pressurized and swollen, there wasn't much in the way of pain. *Dr. Rickerson did mention a lack of pain receptors up there.* Continuing with his assessment, Blake perceived that he had an unpleasant case of cottonmouth and both legs were being gripped by a strange pressure.

No pain, no nausea...yet.

Probing underneath the blankets, Blake could feel that his legs were encased below the knees in separate pads that were expanding and contracting by themselves. *Weird.* To his left, the IV module stood at attention, his very own guard from Buckingham Palace. Blake closely inspected the hanging bag to ensure that it was faithfully dripping. The effort was exhausting and he decided that the obsession was a waste of energy. *Forget it.* He felt restricted by the multiple blankets and began trying to shift them off his chest.

His feeble efforts attracted the attention of a passing nurse who stopped in front of the bed, "Hello there! I see you are waking up! We have you in recovery." Dressed in dark blue scrubs, the nurse was making exaggerated efforts to pronounce the words. Blake felt he was living in a silent movie. In spite of himself, or maybe because of himself, he started to feel insulted.

Does she treat everybody like a two-year-old or just implant patients?

Blake observed the nurse from under his mountain of blankets while he evaluated the situation and decided that he was overreacting. "K. My family know?" It was hard to get the words out and he couldn't help slurring them.

"Oh yes! Dr. Rickerson has given them the post-op briefing and they are in the waiting area. Are you nauseous?"

"Noooo."

"What about pain?"

"Nuh."

"Do you have any need to go to the bathroom?" The nurse patted a bedpan at the foot of the bed as she queried him.

"Um, no." *And there won't be until I can get up and go myself.* Unfortunately, the reference caused Blake to become aware of a fullness in his bladder. At the same time he realized that the IV had been pumping him full of fluids for a while and his storage capacity was probably getting low. *Lucky I woke up when I did.*

"Can I go myself?" Connected to both the bed and his IV, Blake was positive that an unsupervised trip to the bathroom was out of the question.

"Not without my help. You need an escort when trying to walk for the first time." The nurse smiled at him, "My name is Sandy. I will come back in ten minutes and we can get you to the bathroom." Taking pains to mouth her words slowly, she also pointed to a sign labeled 'Toilet' about thirty feet away.

There's an obvious clue.

"Ok." Blake was determined to outlast the IV and bypass the bedpan. Sandy walked off and he focused on trying to forget about his bladder. Despite his determination to ignore the IV, his eyes were drawn to the tubing to inspect it for kinks. The appraisal provided a temporary diversion until his eyes traveled up to the hanging bag and saw a steady drip destined to enter his veins, pass through his kidneys and fill his bladder even more. Ten minutes suddenly struck him as excessively long. *She better come back soon!*

Sandy returned in less than ten minutes and Blake allowed himself an internal cheer at her reappearance. After clearing the blankets off him, she removed the circulation pads from his calves and began easing his legs over to the side of the bed. His initial attempts to place weight on his feet were wobbly, and Sandy moved a walker in front of him. There was a time lag between when he told his body to move and when it started to respond. He could feel the blood flooding back through his legs as he took tiny shuffles. *I'm going to do this! It's only thirty frigging feet!*

Sandy watched him carefully, and once she was satisfied that he wasn't going to collapse on her, pushed the IV stand in front of him while they traveled the short distance to the bathroom.

They entered the bathroom together where Blake swiveled to a position above the toilet and gathered up his gown in preparation for his next move. Sandy braced the walker to keep it from shifting as he slowly lowered himself until his butt made contact with the seat and melted down into its curvature. She left him alone with instructions to pull on the hand cord when he was finished, and as soon as the door eased shut Blake released his pee in an orgasmic gush. A torrent of pleasure coursed through him, precipitating an involuntary shudder, and he exhaled a sigh of relief for managing to avoid the bedpan. *Thank heavens.*

Once he was done Blake continued to sit for a minute, savoring the tranquility. Eventually boosting himself up off the seat, he noted that the anesthesia was fading away to where he could stand up with a minimum of wobbling and shuffle around with more confidence. Dressed as he was with a gown, socks and no underwear, the logistics of getting ready were limited to dropping the gown and coordinating the IV stand with his movements. *I could use a pair of underwear so I don't have to worry about dripping all over.* After a final inspection of his plumbing he pulled the signal cord.

"Hello!" Sandy poked her head around the door and slowly pulled it open. Once she was certain that she had his attention she offered, "Everything OK?"

"That was a lifesaver."

"Most people tend to agree with you!" Sandy displayed a considerate smile.

"OK, then. Let's get you back to bed and I'll see about moving you upstairs." Together they moved back to the bed, Blake shuffling with the walker and Susan pushing the IV stand in front. *This is different.* Back at the bed Sandy helped him to turn around and instructed him to push his butt as far back as possible before she swung his legs up and onto the bed. As she did so Blake hastily stuffed the gown around his crotch to preserve as much modesty as possible. Recognizing his involuntary reaction, Blake grimaced at the futility of it. *Don't know why I bothered. I'm not selling tickets.* Once in bed, Blake shifted himself around as Sandy slid the IV stand close to his bed, arranged the tubing, and verified that the drip, drip, drip was properly drip, drip, dripping.

With the IV stand in place, Sandy went to the foot of the bed to begin strapping the circulation pads back on his calves. Blake didn't particularly care for how they felt and he queried her, "Do you have to put those on?" The dryness in his mouth made it difficult to get the words out.

"Unfortunately, yes. As long as you are in bed for extended periods they are required to help prevent circulatory issues." She gave him a regretful smile and patted his legs. "The more you get up and walk around once we get you upstairs the less you will need them."

"I'm going to be walking all the time then." *And the first thing I'm going to do is tear that room apart searching for my underwear!* Blake was surprised at how fast he was bouncing back. *This is too easy. I'll probably crash soon.*

Sandy addressed him from the foot of the bed, "If you develop nausea or pain let me know immediately." Her demeanor had shifted from solicitousness to action. "I will let admissions know that you are ready to move to your room and notify your family to meet you up there."

"Thank you! And thanks for making it easy to read your lips." *No sense in being difficult.*

"You're welcome! Sandy smiled again, "Hopefully that will become a thing of the past for you!"

I sure hope so. Blake nodded his head in agreement. He reached up to pat the bandage wrapped around his head, "When does this come off?"

"The doctor will let you know about that." Sandy was regarding him with a pair of practiced eyes. "Are you thirsty?" She tilted one hand at her mouth in a drinking motion.

"I am most definitely thirsty." His saliva production was lacking and the idea of water sounded heavenly. Talking required effort since his mouth was so parched that his tongue could not properly form words. A metallic tang was making its presence known.

"Let me get you some water before you go upstairs. I'll be back"

Blake sank back onto the bed and reflected upon his situation. *Operation is finished and I feel halfway decent. Got the pee thing solved for the moment. I hate to say it, but I'm even getting used to the IV.* He pulled the blankets back over his chest and settled down to wait.

Sandy soon returned carrying a Dixie cup of water. Taking it from her hand, Blake experimented with a tiny sip, followed by another. Cool fluid trickled through his system, tiny rivulets of water in the desert. His tongue came alive, transforming from a shriveled lump back to its normal state. Swallowing half the contents, Blake tracked the flow down toward his stomach where it tumbled out of his esophagus to splash into an empty chamber. The metallic note lingered in his mouth, completely unchanged. He drained the cup and his stomach sent up a small rumble as it began to awaken. *Some food would be helpful.*

"More please?" Handing the empty cup to Sandy, Blake's stomach rumbled with a metallic burp, causing a distasteful sensation. He figured that he was probably experiencing drainage traveling down his Eustachian tubes and landing in the back of his throat. *I did get a hole drilled in my ear.*

Sandy left to get a refill, returning with an orderly in tow. Working on his second cup of water, Blake watched them prepare the bed for transport. He was completely deaf, nodding as they motioned him to move this way and that way while rearranging blankets and the IV for his journey. Soon Blake was on his way with the orderly pushing from behind, but this trip wasn't anywhere near as fun as the last go round. Traveling through the corridors Blake felt self-conscious being on display with his prominent bandage. *I look like hell and I feel worse.* The metallic sensation in his mouth combined with the emptiness in his stomach to bring on a faint twinge of nausea. Blake was excruciatingly aware of how the bed shifted from side to side, traveling in a series of unavoidable starts and stops as they navigated among the obstacles of people, equipment and hallways. When they finally reached the doorway of his room, he sent up a silent prayer of thanks that the journey was ended.

I'm dizzy, hungry and nauseous with a crappy taste in my mouth. My head is swollen and the bandage itches. I'm smelly, dirty and my throat is starting to hurt.

I want my underwear.

Blake's thoughts dwelled on his litany of discomforts as the bed was wheeled into place. At the mercy of whomever happened to be in charge, he loathed the lack of control over his circumstances. Time dragged agonizingly slow as he waited for the bed and IV to be arranged, a second nurse appearing as the orderly finished up.

Walking up to the side of his bed and positioning herself in front of his face, she said, "Good afternoon! My name is Peggy." Reaching out to take hold of his arm, she confirmed his nametag as she introduced herself. "You are Simon Blake, excellent!" Blake watched her lips as she spoke. He couldn't hear her message, but it wasn't too hard to figure it out. Her name was prominently displayed on a badge hanging from a lanyard around her neck. Breasts jutting out under the confines of her dark blue top caused the nametag to be suspended slightly in the air. Peggy was a trim blonde with a ponytail who was around 40 years old. She moved with an air of purpose to the whiteboard on the wall and wrote 'Peggy' in the box labeled 'duty nurse'. After writing on the board she returned to his bedside and queried him, "How are you feeling?"

"I was ok down in recovery, but now I'm worse. My throat is starting to hurt."

"That's a common reaction to the tracheal tube used in anesthesia. I can't do too much about that." She furnished a sympathetic smile along with her explanation. "Describe any pain you are experiencing on a scale from one to ten."

"Two, I guess."

Without his aids Blake was forced to keep his eyes on Peggy. *I think this one's been around long enough to know what's what. She's probably right about the tube.*

"I can definitely tell the anesthesia is gone," Blake said, "Do you know where my hearing aids are?"

"Let's ask your family when they arrive – my guess is that they will have them. In the meantime I'm going to start your medications." Peggy turned to leave and Blake's eyes followed her out of the room.

I wonder how long it's gonna be before I get my damn underpants?

Patting a hand over his bandage Blake thought, *Still there. Still doesn't hurt much.* The IV stand stood by his side dripping faithfully and, although Blake did not particularly care to be hooked up to it, he had accepted its necessity. Lying back down, he waited for whatever came next. *Surgery is done, one night in the hospital and then home.* Blake preferred to stay overnight in the hospital to be on the safe side. He wanted to go home, but he also wanted to make sure he didn't develop any post op complications. *I'm not ready to ride anywhere in a car, that's for sure.*

A surge of motion from the doorway heralded the approach of Emily and the children. Emily was in the lead and as she reached the bed he noticed an uncharacteristic disarray to her appearance. There was a look of relief on her face as she bent down over him, and he closed his eyes when she put both hands on either side of his head to plant a firm kiss on his forehead. The pressure from her lips served as a welcome reconnection to the real world and he opened his eyes to those familiar flecks gathering him into a sphere of intimacy.

Then she stood back and a crowd collected around the bed, everyone smiling and chattering. Addressing the animated group, Blake asked, "Who's got my hearing aids?" As soon as he made the request, Emily dug in her purse to pull them out, only to stand there uncertainly. The implanted ear was now completely deaf and required activation of the implant before it could register sound. That left one ear to receive a hearing aid. Blake saw which one he needed and lifted a finger to point it out, "That one."

Taking the aid from Emily's proffered hand, he slipped it on with a practiced motion and glorified in the white noise flooding back. "Finally! That's a big improvement over nothing." His hearing was pitiful, but there was something to be said for sound replacing silence. *Next step, activation.*

Tapping his arm, Mackenzie said, "Dad. Mom was a basket case the whole time you were in surgery."

"She sure was," Madison added. "We tried to go outside of the hospital for breakfast, but she made us turn around in the parking lot and come back. All we got to eat was some crap from the vending machine."

"And it was crap," Matthew emphasized.

Emily didn't say anything, lifting her eyebrows to deliver a silent rebuttal.

Blake smiled and took hold of Emily's hand. "That's 'cause we roll together or not at all!"

Turning to Blake with an expression that spoke volumes, Emily returned his grip with a firm squeeze, hazel eyes swirling with twin tornados of green and gold.

Peggy chose to show up at that moment, commenting, "You guys got here fast."

"Yeah," Madison answered. "Mom knocked over an oxygen tank on the way up here."

This time Emily cracked a smile and shrugged her shoulders, "Dr. Rickerson said the surgery went well. You took another three hours to get up here after he talked to us though."

"Three hours! I thought recovery went fast!!"

"For you, maybe. The wait was driving me insane!!" Emily rolled her eyes, a reaction Blake didn't often see. Flipping back her hair, she took hold of her disheveled tresses and began smoothing them out. "Thank God that part's over."

Moving up by Blake and Emily, Peggy started in, "Your chart has instructions for an intravenous antibiotic and overnight monitoring. As long as the doctor gives the ok tomorrow morning, discharge will be at noon." Glancing at the clock on the wall she continued, "It's 4:30 p.m., time to start thinking about what you want for dinner." She proceeded to inject a syringe of antibiotics into one of the IV ports, following up by turning to address the family. "Visiting hours are unrestricted for family members, so you may stay as long as you like."

At this Emily gestured toward her children and responded, "Thank you! Now that Simon is awake and settled in, I better feed my kids before they turn on me." At this offer, all three children responded with vigorous agreement.

Turning back to Blake, Emily said, "I'll be back tomorrow to take you home." She bent down to kiss him on the cheek. "Love you!"

"Love you too! See you tomorrow bright and early!"

His family crowded around offering kisses and goodbyes after which they moved toward the doorway, waving as they went. Blake watched them go until the last glimpse. He scanned the hospital room with its beige walls and white ceiling. It was a double room, but luckily, he was the sole occupant. The layout included a bathroom up by the doorway which he could see from his position in bed. On his left, between the bed and the doorway, stood a meal tray on wheels and a recliner upholstered in faux leather, colored olive green. *Now that's butt ugly.* Behind the recliner was a couch next to a series of built-in cubbyholes, one of which held his bag of clothes from earlier this morning. *Ahh Ha! My underpants!*

Having found his quarry, bundling up his privates suddenly seemed to be wasted effort. *If I put them on then I have to take them off when I visit the bathroom. And this IV guarantees that will be sooner rather than later.* He was tired, thirsty and hungry, all of which merited a higher priority than underwear. *I was naked for the operation anyway. What I should probably do is figure out what to order for dinner before Peggy disappears.*

Peggy had busied herself reviewing his chart while the family took their goodbyes and now she came up to his bedside. Standing there to command his attention she queried him, "Are you in any pain, Simon?"

"No." *Just a pissy little throbbing, nothing worth mentioning.*

"Tired or nauseous?"

"A little nauseous, but I'm starting to get hungry. Can you call in dinner for me please?"

"Of course!" Peggy listed the choices for him and he decided on meatloaf with peas, mashed potatoes and ketchup. After handling the logistics of dinner, Peggy went down to the end of the bed and connected the circulation pads to an air compressor that was built into the bed. "If you stay in bed we have to keep these circulation pads on your calves. As long as you get up and walk around regularly they can remain off."

"I can walk around by myself?"

"You sure can! We encourage it! The more you move the faster you will recover."

Another visitor walked through the door. This latest arrival was wearing a white coat but was obviously not Dr. Rickerson, being female for starters. She approached the bed to introduce herself, "Hello, I'm Dr. Wang, surgical resident." Dr. Wang was a petite young woman of oriental heritage with short black hair that framed her face in glossy black. Notwithstanding her slender physique, she held herself with an assured bearing, projecting an air of efficiency.

"Will Dr. Rickerson be coming by?" Blake was curious.

"Not unless we have a problem. I will evaluate your progress and discharge you tomorrow if all goes well." Dr. Wang peered into his face, instructing him, "Give me a smile."

Blake obediently forced a smile while Dr. Wang came in closer to inspect his facial muscles.

"As wide as you can."

He forced his face to the limit and after a few seconds Dr. Wang straightened up. "OK, that's good. We always verify the operation of your facial nerve after the anesthesia wears off."

"Ah," Blake nodded to himself. *I forgot about that side effect.*

The doctor continued, "Do you have any dizziness?"

"Not much." *But ask me again in five minutes.*

"Nausea or a metallic taste?"

"A little of both." *But not enough to puke.* "How long does the bandage stay on?" Blake's scalp was itching in several places underneath the wrap.

"Tomorrow I'll replace it with another that you need to wear for a couple of days. Showering is limited to the area below your neck for three days to keep the surgical area dry, and you should avoid blowing your nose for two weeks." Seeing the confused expression on Blake's face, Dr. Wang offered additional explanation, "The pressure change could cause trauma to the insertion site. It's helpful to let your body develop some stabilizing tissue around the implant." Dr. Wang stepped back. "If you're up to it, try to take short walks spaced two to three hours apart."

"I can probably do that," Blake agreed. *My butt is a bag of bricks from lying in bed.*

"I'll come back in the morning to replace your bandage and approve your release. Your condition is normal at this point." The doctor smiled at him. "We'll get you back home tomorrow!"

"Great," Blake responded. *Tomorrow.*

With a final "Goodbye!" Dr. Wang turned and walked out of the room, leaving Blake by himself. Peggy was long gone, having departed in the middle of Dr. Wang's examination.

Overtaken by a growing sense of fatigue, Blake let loose with a yawn that he quickly cut short when he felt a pulling sensation at the surgical site. *Crap! What if something moved!?!*

There was no shortage of concerns to obsess about. Even though the IV was old news, he kept sneaking glances at the drip. His head bandage made every position on the pillow so intolerable that he was starting to wonder how he would sleep that evening. The lack of underpants reasserted itself each time he tried to shift position because his privates would either get smashed underneath or backflip into some uncomfortable arrangement. Then there was the distasteful plight of being reliant upon the efforts of other people for everything. *I'm an infant. Everyone is helpful, but I can't wait to leave.*

Blake sighed as he settled back to wait for dinner. *I want to go home.*

***

Early Wednesday morning found Blake lying in bed, tired and awake, having discovered that overnight monitoring meant concerns about the bandage affecting his sleep were irrelevant. Hospital policy was to record his pulse and temperature at two-hour intervals, making sleep impossible. Watching the night nurse exit the room, he switched his gaze from the doorway to the right side of the room where the entire wall was a large window fitted with blinds that were pulled back, revealing the first traces of dawn. *They really like their windows here.* Conditioned to wake up in the presence of light, the approach of sunrise guaranteed that his day was about to begin. Greeting the show with a truncated yawn meant to avoid any nasty pulling sensations, he watched with interest as the sky began transitioning out of its starry blackness.

University Hospital was perched on a hilltop above the city of Cincinnati, with his room up on the 14th floor. Rising to the challenge, the architect conceived one side of the room as a single sheet of glass, presenting a spectacular view of Cincinnati nestled into a curve along the Ohio River with the hills of Kentucky rising up on the opposite side. Blake watched the sky begin shifting to a lighter hue in the east while in the west it remained deep black. The smaller buildings of the city below were hidden, their existence revealed by a haphazard sprinkling of brilliant dots. Only the tallest building was recognizable, the Carew Tower, appearing as a massive shaft of lighted squares dominating the surrounding darkness. Moving with imperceptible flow, rays of light edged their way over the horizon, morphing the eastern darkness into a shade of indigo that overlaid a glimmering of coral rising up from below. He lay in quiet contemplation as the lights of the city became less prominent, the outlines of buildings came into view and the meanderings of the Ohio River separating Cincinnati and Kentucky began to materialize.

Directing his gaze past the city and across the river to the Kentucky side, he noted five lines of light flowing over five bridges. The daily commuters were following their normal routines, but his own life was on the cusp. Like the light spreading over the city, hope was unfurling that the implant would grant access to activities that had been out of his reach. He wanted to use the phone to chat with his family the same as anyone else. He wanted to understand what people said without hanging on each word and physical gesture. He wanted to listen to someone behind him without turning around. He wanted to be in control of his own personal interactions without being hostage to the goodwill or agendas of other people. Most of all he wanted to move forward instead of falling further and further behind.

With his procedure complete, Blake's focus was to work as hard as he could on interpreting the signals from his implant. *It may work, it may not, but I'm not going to be the stumbling block.* He made the promise to himself, watching the sky continue its transition, releasing the soft light of morning to illuminate the awakening city. Following the hill descending into Cincinnati, he started to pick out details of buildings and streets. Far below his hilltop perch, tiny residents were wandering to and fro as the population prepared for the business of the coming day. To the east a ball of orange was emerging, turning the blanket of clouds into a cotton candy morning, and he glorified in the colors as they crept across the sky.

To the west he could make out another set of mounds serving as a gateway to Price Hill while in the east he noted the hills of Mt Adams. Known as 'The City of Seven Hills', Cincinnati was planted on one shore of the Ohio River directly across from its confluence with the Licking River, with hills rising up in every direction. The hills created a profusion of impenetrable shadows interspersed with areas that were becoming more visible. As he sought familiar landmarks, a crescent of yellow fire came exploding past the horizon, to be captured by the Carew Tower and reflected to his eyes with a blinding glare.

The burst of light reinforced hopes that his implant would be the trigger for a brightening in his own life. His thoughts were flooded with a multitude of possibilities, formerly considered pure fantasy. The passion of his longings, stoked by a lifetime of denials, released a flow of tears that filtered the sunrise into a blur. Using both hands to wipe his eyes and watching the rays of light illuminate the city, Blake sent up a prayer that his life would be different.

Blake had met those who were happy with their implants and those who were not so happy. By and large the surgery resulted in a significant improvement, but there were also some who failed to get much benefit from the procedure. Dr. Rickerson was at a loss to explain why some people didn't do well. Even with repeated adjustments of the computer program and hard work in rehabilitation an unlucky minority went through the process to come out no better than before. *I'll know soon enough.*

Dropping his gaze, Blake saw that the bottom of the window incorporated a shelf which offered a convenient location for flower baskets and gifts. He didn't plan on staying around long enough to collect flowers. *I'm ready to get out of here.*

Blake took a minute to take inventory of himself. He was a little tired from the constant monitoring last night, but not excessively so. Although it wasn't an ideal situation, he knew that the few catnaps which he had managed to steal would get him through the day. The nausea and dizziness were gone and he was ready to go home for a shower. Making the most of the regular bed checks, he had also gotten up a couple times last night to walk around with the IV stand in tow. As a result the nurses were letting him stay in bed without using the circulation pads and he had already peed on his own. There was no significant pain at the surgical site and he would soon get a replacement bandage to address the itching problem. *Except for the metallic taste in my mouth, I feel halfway decent. I'm going to have some coffee, take a poop and put on my underpants!*

The wall clock was reading 6:15 a.m. Shift change was at 6:00 a.m., so Blake figured that when the day shift showed up he could ask for help ordering breakfast. Last night he had a cup or two of water, but now his stomach was rumbling for some real food. *I could ring for the nurse I guess, but I'll wait a while. It's still early to pester someone.* He waited in bed wondering what to order for breakfast. *This could work, surgery is history and I have an appetite.*

Ten minutes later the dayshift nurse walked in the door and Blake was pleased to find that it was Peggy. "Good morning, Simon! How are you today?" Peggy had a bright smile on her face as she addressed him. She was either in a phenomenal mood or a dedicated nurse. Blake suspected that it was probably the latter.

"I'm OK. Thinking about breakfast, believe it or not."

"Super! Let's get that taken care of and then we can move on with the rest of it! The night shift gave you a clean bill of health so if Dr. Wang is satisfied with her examination then you will be released to go home."

Blake huddled with Peggy to order sausage, pancakes, orange juice and coffee. The rest of the morning passed quickly with Blake getting an antibiotic injection from Peggy and a new bandage from Dr. Wang mixed in with his attempts to eat breakfast. Dr. Wang's examination was OK on all counts and she informed Blake that she was releasing him from the hospital. Emily showed up while he was finishing his coffee and he notified her that they were waiting for the final paperwork to leave.

Around 11:00 a.m. Peggy walked in and said, "OK Simon, you're ready to go home! Let me remove the IV so you can get dressed. Hospital policy requires that we transport you out of here in a wheelchair."

Learning of Peggy's intention to remove the IV prompted Blake to envision blood shooting out of his arm. *How does she stop blood from squirting everywhere when the needle comes out?* Peggy approached his side and he barely managed to avert his gaze once he realized that she was not going to wait. Disconnecting the tubing from the hanging bag, Peggy took hold of his wrist with a firm grip and under cover of squeezing his hand, pulled out the needle to slap a strip of gauze and some tape over the entry point. She was finished in less than three seconds. No longer connected to the IV, Blake was surprised at how relaxed he suddenly felt. *That was by far the worst part of the whole deal.*

Peggy left after instructing him to get dressed and thrilled with his freedom, Blake slipped out of bed. Emily helped him discard the gown, handing him his clothes as he needed them. *Hello underpants!* Wearing his own clothes instead of the hospital gown went a long way towards reestablishing his sense of self. Revived, Blake took a few steps around the room as he and Emily waited for the wheelchair to arrive. Walking to the window he took in the view for one last time, Emily coming up beside him to slip an arm around his waist as they inspected the city, pointing out different places to each other.

Forty minutes later Blake was at the main entrance of the hospital in a wheelchair waiting for Emily to pull up the car. Their journey home passed without incident and Blake was happy when they pulled into the driveway. Emily went ahead to open the door for him and he walked in to the kitchen, going straight to his chair by the fireplace. Riding home, Blake was struck by his lack of hearing, now worse than ever. He didn't like how the world sounded faint and unbalanced, but he figured he could live with it until activation.

Blake sank down into the chair's embrace, reveling in the familiarity of his own house. *I'm going to relax.* He was at peace. For the first time in years he didn't feel the need to conceal his emotions behind a shield, desiring instead to let the positive energy from the last few months filter its way out and be free.

I have a good feeling about this.

All of Blake's life had been a troublesome navigation through a punishing world. Accumulated stress produced a fiery hostility which he either buried or blew off in uncontrolled explosions. He liked to say that stress was a mental condition, but stress impacted his physical body each time he chose to trap an emotion inside. The iron control that he was so proud of applying was responsible for creating an internal tornado of unresolved angst, a black hole of chaos to infect his spirit.

Today he felt a freedom and a calmness that exceeded anything in his ken. He harbored no hateful fantasies begging to be released upon some unfortunate soul. There were no uglies inside requiring suppression, rather, his thoughts were full of tranquility and hope. With the operation behind him and activation ahead of him, Blake sat back in the chair and closed his eyes, setting his thoughts free to savor magnificent prospects.

Chapter 7 – Suspension

T he next day Blake woke up to sunlight spilling through the bedroom window. A tentative yawn triggered a warning jab from his stitches. Grateful to be back in his own bed, he opened and closed his mouth, attempting to define an allowable range of motion. Countdown to activation was in progress, with 15 days to go, at which time November 20th would produce a resolution of some sort. Even though Susan had told him that the implant would require a period of adjustment, Blake's attitude was more upbeat.

Turn it on, shoot for the moon!

He was happy to have survived the procedure without a disfigured smile. An MRI beforehand was supposed to give the surgeon enough guidance to work around the nerves, but there was still a small risk. The operation posed potential problems with balance and losing his sense of taste, but he had dodged those bullets also. *Never hurts to be lucky,* he thought. It was his singular phrase, dating back to one Monday at Seagram when he discovered that good fortune was an effective way to escape difficult circumstances. That day started with Blake employing a backhoe operator to remove tree stumps in the morning and ended with him redirecting the same contractor to excavate a sprinkler system leak that afternoon. *That's the kind of luck I need!*

Turning to his left, he was not surprised to find Emily's spot cold to the touch, having been informed last night that she was fully scheduled for today and planned to be out of the house by 7:00 a.m. Mackenzie would also be gone, since she normally left for Oak Hills High School by 6:00 a.m. *I'll make breakfast and see how it goes.* Traveling to a restaurant was out of the question since he was restricted from driving, but Blake didn't enjoy breakfast in a restaurant anyway. Most of the time he woke up hungry and didn't want to drive somewhere, wait to be seated, wait to order and wait for his food while surrounded by odors that made him even hungrier. He pictured himself at a restaurant and recoiled at the idea.

With this head bandage, no way!

Blake gingerly crept out of bed, wrapping himself in a robe and shuffling his way to the kitchen, all the while thinking, *Get the coffee going, then back to the bedroom.* His movements were tentative to avoid aggravating his stitches, but there were some unpleasant stabs. Standing in front of the coffeemaker, he experimented with twisting his head from side to side. *Yes, no, yes, definitely NO.* He was experiencing a slight dizziness that gave him cause for concern. Finished with the coffeepot, Blake shuffled down the hardwood floor in the hallway back to the bedroom for a shower, discovering that a slip n slide motion worked best and that the dizziness went away if he paused long enough.

I can stand here in the hall all day. No problem.

Continuing his trek back to the bedroom, Blake's goal was to get himself in the shower. A hot shower was enormously satisfying and even though he had taken a shower last night, a second shower this morning struck him as appealing. He liked remaining under the spray until the supply of hot water was in danger of running out, a habit that annoyed Mackenzie to no end. Taking care to keep the water from hitting his bandage, Blake remained in place until the water temperature began dropping. Stepping out of the steamy enclosure, he wrapped himself in a towel, starting to feel rid of the hospital gunk.

After patting himself dry, he exited the bathroom to put on his left hearing aid, clicking his tongue several times to test for audio. *Not much there.* His right side was now deaf, leaving his left ear the only game in town until activation day. Pulling on jeans and a shirt with buttons, he added a zippered hood for warmth against the morning chill before proceeding to slip n slide his way back to the kitchen.

A koala could pass me at this rate.

Fresh and clean after his shower, Blake felt invigorated. Dr. Rickerson said that the implant should work for the rest of his life, ensuring that his hearing would remain the same as he got older. *What a bonus!* All his life Blake's hearing had only deteriorated, and to know stability would be phenomenal. Uplifted by the possibility, he thought back to the hospital and out of nowhere came a vision where patients were required to remove their clothes as soon as they walked in the door. *Ha! That would resolve the modesty issue right away!* He entered the kitchen to take a pan from a cabinet and slide it onto the stovetop where he added some butter and turned on the burner. Figuring that was enough activity for the time being, Blake took up position by the stove, watching the butter melt and letting his mind wander.

With his right ear deaf and his left ear a piece of junk, he was going to need all his coping skills to get by until activation. When Blake was young, his father did him a huge favor, explaining that Blake could try to compensate for his hearing loss by carefully observing people. Taking the advice to heart, Blake focused on analyzing the behaviors of those around him, going down a path where he learned to understand what made people tick.

By quirk of fate, he also came to be aware of his father's manipulative nature. Manipulative people have some common tells. For starters they can be charmers who make a habit of claiming they are looking out for your interests only to swoop in and benefit from your actions. Unsolicited offers that come out of the blue are another warning sign. Manipulators are leery of someone else's suggestions, preferring to pursue a path aligned with their own interests.

His thoughts drifted back to his 18th birthday party, when his father announced that he wanted a divorce, taking advantage of the fact that the entire family was present to push past the point of no return and preclude any attempts by his mother to salvage the relationship or her own fortunes. The rest of the family froze in shock at the unexpected announcement. Blake had become proficient in observing people by that point and recognized the clever trap sprung upon his mother. That day birthed in him a dislike, bordering on hatred, for manipulative behavior. He was highly offended that anyone who was able to communicate would pervert such a gift by taking advantage of people.

Once he came to understand that his father was a gifted manipulator it was impossible for Blake to ignore the behavior. Using his father's actions as a curriculum of sorts, he enhanced his ability to recognize manipulation and became adept at recognizing the different ways that people would telegraph their intentions as they attempted to exert control. *Not exactly a skill to brag about, but probably inevitable.*

Acutely aware of interpersonal dynamics, Blake was more suited than most to stop manipulative behavior in its tracks. Had he so desired, he could have used his understanding to pursue his own efforts at manipulation, however, he chose to play defense, focusing his efforts on thwarting manipulators whenever he could manage it, celebrating each reversal with a viciousness.

My father bested us all that one day though. The remembrance caused Blake to frown as he relived the occasion, his mood darkening.

An aroma of melted butter diverted Blake from his recollections. *Time to crack a couple eggs and get the toast going.* The scent of fresh coffee was filling the kitchen, prompting him to pour a cup and take a few gulps in between monitoring the eggs and toast. If he didn't move too fast the dizziness was manageable, and his stitches felt looser after being subjected to the steaminess of the shower. He observed the kitchen window glinting with frost in the sunshine. It was a cold Thursday, coming up on a colder Friday, but warming rays came through the window to bounce off the floor and project a glow that meshed with the smells of cooking to produce a coziness inside the kitchen. Blake poked at the egg whites bubbling up in the pan, thinking that recovery was going well.

The eggs came out perfect, solid whites with runny yolks, and he settled in to enjoy a hot breakfast. Blake's thoughts went to racquetball as he ate, wondering when he might get back on the court. No sense in pushing his recovery, but it always felt good to hit something. *I'm a happier person when I play regularly,* he mused. *Not to mention that people around me are a lot safer.* Racquetball was a thinking man's game. A player had milliseconds to select a shot, and it was more about fooling your opponent than overpowering them, a concept the younger players had a hard time understanding. His observation skills came in handy on the racquetball court as he tried to determine someone's preferred style of play and then, armed with that information, adopt a strategy that forced his opponent to play differently.

Mopping up the remainder of the yolks with toast, Blake poured himself a second cup of coffee. Settling back in the chair he directed his gaze out the window where a thin layer of frost was dissipating to reveal a gorgeous day, with sunshine bathing the yard in golden highlights and the autumn sky holding a crisp clearness. The brightness almost promised a return to Indian summer, but patches of frost in the shady areas telegraphed that those days were gone. He was happy to be ensconced in a warm house with a full stomach and a cup of hot coffee. Blake's thoughts meandered among Pamela, hearing aids and the cumulative effects of waging a moment by moment battle to claim his place in daily life. Forty-nine years of hearing loss had molded him into an individual with specific traits.

One defining characteristic was an inherent stillness that combined with a flat expression and dark eyes to imply a person better left alone. On multiple occasions he had been on the receiving end of a suggestion to smile more, but his inside voice told him that to force a smile would probably work against him more times than not. As a result, he chose to project an external appearance that offered no clues about himself, preferring to take time to read people before exposing himself to the dynamics of an interaction.

Blake could recognize situations when it was helpful to be charming and sometimes he would attempt to do so. Given his understanding of how easily people could be manipulated it was an easy task to tailor his actions to behaviors that others would look upon favorably. However, most of the time he didn't care to put out the effort. It offended him on the most basic of levels to jump through hoops to relate with others whom, he judged, had chosen to disregard his reality. He believed that at some point people were obligated to recognize that everyone operated under their own unique constraints. The concept was evident to him through simple observation and he would quickly dismiss those in the unenlightened category, pronouncing them guilty of ignoring his personal code of awareness.

If that means I'm an ignorant ass of another sort, then so be it.

Dealing with the constant problems created by hearing loss demanded an uncompromising attitude where failure was seen as a temporary detour. The key was perseverance. Quite often a situation seemed impossible until suddenly it wasn't. Most of the time the stakes were higher for him than the other person, and that was why he was willing to be the meanest one in the room. It also didn't hurt to have a reservoir of rage urging him forward.

One lesson Blake had learned was that he was better off relying on himself to navigate the pitfalls of communication. Some of his friends with hearing aids would regularly ask for help, and in doing so would let themselves become dependent upon the limits of those around them. It pained him to watch their lives become a collection of missed opportunities and regrets. *Nobody is going to show up at their front door in the morning and run interference for them all day. That's their own job.*

Receiving assistance came with its own complications because any help was short-lived, the next problem demanding a different solution. Success was and would always be a moving target. Blake was reluctant to celebrate his victories because he was waiting for the next five minutes to present him with another complication. When the anticipated snag arrived, he was already prepared to figure out his options because he expected to be tested constantly and made a conscious effort to stay on his toes. Planning a minimum of eight hours ahead to preempt problems, he lived in a perpetual state of analysis that kept him multiple steps ahead of most people, leading him to trust his own solutions rather than the suggestions of others. Friends accused him of being hardheaded and unwilling to listen, but often he had already considered their solution and discarded it for one reason or another long before they identified a problem.

I could probably be nicer about it though. Especially with certain individuals.

The eggs and toast were gone. Blake rose from the empty plate to pour a fourth cup of coffee, the bitter aroma matching his train of thought. Cooperation was not much of an option for him because it meant relinquishing control to someone who had only recently identified the existence of a problem, as opposed to himself, who had been preparing for the same problem before it arrived. People meant well enough, but their starting point was too far behind for him to bother bringing them up to speed. Add in the fact that few people understood the unique difficulties presented by a hearing impairment and it led to Blake infrequently putting himself in the hands of others. He preferred to go it alone, and he often paid for that choice by being labeled as arrogant. If anyone called him out he would readily admit the accuracy behind their perception, but he was secure in his decision.

Sometimes people would attribute motivations to him based upon their observations. This particularly annoyed Blake because even though he was constantly analyzing others, he considered his conclusions a guide to help himself navigate through rough waters, not an absolute. It was one thing to attempt an understanding of people, something different to blast that supposed understanding out loud. Verbalizing such thoughts only aggravated people and could easily prove embarrassing. He wouldn't dream of presupposing someone's identity or integrity by informing them of the reason for their actions. *Even if I think I know.* Such comments served to reflect ignorance by the speaker rather than any failings of the target. For people to broadcast an evaluation using what could only be described as limited data and limited effort struck him as the height of arrogance and musing on such thoughts increased his sense of negativity.

He stared down at his coffee with its curl of steam rising off the surface. *Man, I'm stuck in the shit this morning!*

There was a Helen Keller quote that Blake considered insightful: "Character cannot be developed in ease and quiet. Only through experience of trial and suffering can the soul be strengthened, ambition inspired and success achieved." Her comment was misleadingly simple. It applied to internal and external struggles, sometimes both at the same time, and perfectly explained the evolution of Blake's nature.

He drained the coffee and carried his dishes to the sink. The chair by the fireplace was beckoning him to rest, and he made his way towards it, his mind considering the complexities of hearing loss. *I'm obsessing. Why can't I just be simple, stupid and happy?*

***

Emily arrived home to discover Blake asleep in his chair, pausing in the doorway of the kitchen to regard him with a wistful expression. When they met in college Blake was already wearing hearing aids, but his loss now was beyond anything she had imagined possible back then. Those had been the easiest times for talking and laughing, and the intoxicating bond they forged made it easy for his disability to fade into the background. Today it was impossible to communicate unless they were facing each other, and sometimes it was easier to say nothing. Each time she took the easy way out she wound up hating herself a little bit, but that didn't prevent it from happening again. She had yet to say the words out loud, but she was desperate to get their relationship back.

She could tell when events became too much for him and admired his perseverance in picking up to start fresh the next day. *Damn this hearing thing,* she thought. Walking over, Emily gently drew her fingertips along Blake's arm, to be rewarded by his eyes opening.

"Hey." Blake's sleepy response was so low that it was almost a vibration, but he knew Emily could pick it up.

"Hey yourself. You feeling ok?" She tilted her head to one side as she spoke and a waterfall of glistening black fell from her shoulders to hang in the air, mirroring sorrow and offering comfort at the same time. Dragging himself to wakefulness, Blake missed her words, but the sum of her actions served to convey the message a different way.

"A little whiskey tonight and I'll be fine" The words came automatically, without thinking.

Emily's musical laugh lit up the kitchen, "A little or a little and then some?"

"Care to join me?"

"Yes! I'm going to change, make me one." Emily squeezed his arm and turned to leave the kitchen. Blake watched the rise and fall of her hips as she left the room and sighed with appreciation.

Too bad the heels are coming off.

Alone in the kitchen, Blake waited a minute, then cautiously raised himself from the chair, wary of angry stitches or dizziness. He moved toward the liquor cabinet in the next room, adopting a slip n slide to be safe. *Am I really doing this?* Blake hadn't planned on drinking so soon after surgery, but the idea of whiskey sounded appealing. His better instincts remained on the edge of revolt, suggesting that maybe he was pushing too hard for normalcy.

Ahhh, just one then.

Blake opened the cabinet doors to reveal rows of bottles, his mind occupied with Emily. He relied upon her to encourage his softer side and rescue him from the cynicism swirling in his thoughts. In the past he would go on a social media rampage that accomplished nothing more than to reinforce a spiral of negativity. Emily knew how to redirect him before he went past the point of no return. *Hopefully, those days get fewer and fewer from here on out.*

Surveying the contents of the cabinet, Blake selected a bottle of William Larue Weller (WLW) whiskey from the Buffalo Trace Antique Collection, a premium line of five whiskies released once a year. WLW was a strong whiskey that drank smoother than its proof. At 136 proof (68% alcohol), WLW was a pour that went down smoothly, without any burn, ending with a cherry finish that caressed the throat rather than attacking it. The whiskey was a chewy mixture of vanilla and oak intermixed with rich fruit from start to finish. He intended to combine it with Coke, a practice that his purist friends loved to comment upon.

Carrying the bottle of WLW to the kitchen, Blake prepared to take his customary sniff. The bottle had a tall neck and a body so skinny that his fingers could almost encircle it. *Love the way that feels!* Standing at the table, he extracted the cork with a soft pop before lowering his nose to the opening. His olfactory senses reveled in the combination of cherries and vanilla with a subtle touch of oak underneath. Pouring a double shot over ice in his customary glass, he stripped the tab from a can of Coke and poured until foam threatened to overflow the glass. Right before it did, he bent down and drew it off with a timely slurp.

Mmmmm! Cherries all the way!

Blake's whiskey drinking followed an established ritual. He started by popping the cork and sniffing the bottle to verify that it matched his mood. Once the bottle gained approval, he moved on to adding two or three cubes of ice into a short glass with some heft to it. A double shot of whiskey over ice was followed by pouring Coke from a height of six inches until the resulting volcano of foam threatened to overflow the sides, at which point it became a race to stop adding Coke and slurp off the foam before it was too late. Usually Blake accomplished the feat in a continuous flow, bending down to the glass, occasionally lifting it up to his lips if he was being flamboyant. The initial foaming was highly effervescent and tasted distinctly different from the rest of the drink. After a slurp of foam came a robust swallow that powered through the remaining fizziness to include the liquid below, followed by evaluating whether the drink required the addition of more whiskey or more Coke. Swirling the glass in his hand developed a secondary foam that was creamier than the first, and he would take sips while waiting for the ice to melt and bring out underlying notes, swirling up a new layer of foam before each swallow. For most whiskeys vanilla and oak were easily detectable in the beginning, while dilution introduced hints of caramel, blackberries, raisins or a number of other flavors. With each swallow the finish came into play, sometimes lingering and oily, sometimes fleeting and light, depending upon his choice of whiskey.

His attention was captured by the reappearance of Emily who glided back through the doorway having changed to black jeans, a black V neck sweater and black flats. Blake took in her restyling from head to toe. The creaminess of her exposed cleavage contrasted with black clothes and black hair to rivet his attention. *With or without heels, works either way.* A slight upturn at one corner of her mouth left no doubt that she was pleased at his reaction.

Emily approached the table and stopped inches away to rest a hand on the wood. In the same motion she swung her hip out and planted her other hand on its curvature, French nails splaying over black jeans. He could detect the faintness of this morning's perfume in her nearness. Tapping the walnut with a single fingernail, she lifted her eyebrows playfully, "Starting without me?"

Her eyes glinted mischievously as she stood there, waiting.

"Checking out the bottle." He met her eyes straight on, enjoying the game. Smiling, Blake turned to preparing her drink and handed it off as the foam threatened to overflow. He made drinks for his family the same way he did for himself. Except for Madison, who sometimes preferred a neat whiskey, they all drank whiskey with Coke.

Emily accepted her drink with a graceful hand and took a draw. Her lips parted to pull off the foam and she let out a sigh. "Ohhh, that's what I need!" She visibly relaxed, supporting her body on the edge of the table. "It's wonderful to have you home in one piece!"

"Amen," Blake agreed, "You think Dr. Rickerson came off a little abrupt in the hospital?"

"Maybe." Emily pulled a chair out and curled up. "You don't exactly come across as a basket of sweet peaches yourself!" Her eyes flashed green and gold, taking away the sting, "I had to wait a while before I was sure you were the one for me!!"

Blake raised his chin to meet her challenge. "What changed your mind?"

"You can definitely be an ass." Emily tilted her head to the side and collected her long hair behind her, pausing to let him take in the display of exposed neckline. Wiggling further back in the chair, Emily peered up at him with a sensuous expression, "I guess I enjoy watching you bend over." She tilted her drink, eyes conveying future promise from behind the glass.

Blake considered his situation, recovering from his operation with a bandage that had to be downright ugly, and he extended his drink in silent acknowledgement.

Emily met his glass with a light tap, her eyes twinkling in roguish delight, "To the sweetest asshole I know!"

Before Blake could offer his own rejoinder, the moment was interrupted by Emily turning towards the doorway and Blake, mostly deaf, waited to see what would develop. He was rewarded by the sight of Mackenzie bursting through the doorway to the kitchen and landing her backpack on one end of the walnut slab. "Whoa! Is this a party now that Dad is back?"

"It is for me!" Emily answered. She got up from her chair to stand in front of the counter. "Your dad is home and that's enough!" She addressed her youngest daughter, positioning herself so Blake could read her lips, "Your father can't drive yet, are you willing to chauffeur him to and from work if he decides to go in?"

"Sure!" Mackenzie replied. She questioned her father, "Is that happening?"

"It could." Blake came back. "Not tomorrow, but maybe on Monday. The bandage is coming off Sunday."

"Yay!" Mackenzie replied, "Hot damn!" Her smile flashed across the room to smack him square in the chest.

Mackenzie was defined by her positivity; any lack of enthusiasm was a warning sign.

"Thanks toots!" Out of habit Blake swirled his drink while teasing his daughter, "You still need a tool in your hand to cuss though!"

Another musical laugh rang through the kitchen, this time from Mackenzie. When Mackenzie was three years old, she reacted with the shock of the innocent upon hearing him swear during a plumbing job. Thinking fast, he said that it was OK to cuss with a tool in your hand. She took his word as gospel, scrunching down to observe him, and when he swore for a second time not five minutes later, promptly picked up a wrench and handed it to him. The 'rule' entered family tradition.

Blake took a seat at the kitchen table and watched Emily set about preparing dinner as Mackenzie started her homework. He swirled his drink, the clinking of ice too faint to register. There wasn't much sound in his world now. If he didn't read lips he was lost, teetering on the edge of faking it with each interaction. Swirling and sipping, Blake evaluated his condition, noting that the dizziness of this morning was mostly gone, with the stitches not as tight. His thoughts slipped ahead to when he would expose himself to public life, this time with the least amount of hearing ever.

Not looking forward to it.

The days between now and activation stretched before him, a pregnant interlude, shrouding the secret of his future behind a temporary veil. Was he biding his time in a chrysalis that would produce a beautiful tiger swallowtail butterfly or languishing in a cocoon that was holding an ugly tent caterpillar moth?

***

The weekend passed quickly. On Monday morning Blake exited from Mackenzie's Subaru to watch her drive off before pivoting toward the entrance to Worldwide Ethanol Fuel Technology. WEFT was located east of Cincinnati, 20 minutes from his home in Delhi Township. He no longer needed a bandage and was striving for as much normalcy as possible by going without a hat. Regular dress clothes had been set aside for black jeans paired with a black sweater, tacit notice that he was not operating on all cylinders. Sunlight spilled past the roofline of the building, the rays blinding him immediately upon turning around, and bending his head down Blake felt the wind drilling icy needles into his shaved head as he strode across the blacktop. Fall had surrendered its residual warmth to the chill of November. Squinting against the glare, he continued moving towards the protection offered by the low building.

Today was his first day back at work. Angela had called Emily last Friday to make sure that he was recovering properly and inquire if he was returning on Monday. She was happy to learn all was going according to plan and promised to pass the word around. *Good,* Blake grumped. *With any luck they'll know the deal and I won't be badgered.*

Blake was feeling antisocial. Last night he had slept fitfully, anticipating the potential for difficulties this morning, and the lack of sleep combined with anxiety to create a state of agitation. He was even more dependent upon reading lips, as if that situation could possibly get any worse, and figured that he would probably be exhausted by the end of the day. His stitches were healing, the dizziness was gone and he might even be driving in a couple days. The prospect of activation was twelve days away. Unfortunately, his hearing was worse than ever and he dreaded the prospect of struggling through the interim, visualizing complications at every turn. For the next two weeks he intended to hunker down in his office, wanting to avoid as much communication as possible.

Blake entered the foyer to be confronted with the receptionist, Brenda. Her eyes lit up at his appearance and he realized the flaw in his strategy. *Dang!* Stopping in his tracks, he forced a smile followed by a nod of greeting.

"Simon! Welcome back! How you doing?!!"

Brenda's high-pitched voice was hard to understand under the best of circumstances. Blake easily grasped her meaning, but the words ran by without stopping for comprehension.

"Ahhhh, well, I'm completely deaf in the one ear now and waiting for activation." He shrugged and grimaced along with the information, hoping she would take the hint and realize conversation was not on his agenda.

"No problem, I'm happy you're in one piece!" Brenda gave him a wink and shooed him away. "Off with you, I've got a load of stuff to do this morning!"

"Thanks Brenda, appreciate it." Blake headed off to his right, grateful for her perceptiveness, knowing he was being a jackass.

Fuck. Me. Monday. The thought rose unbidden, reinforcing his antisocial mood.

Moving down the hall, Blake sensed a commotion and made the mistake of looking behind to see Dan waving both arms. Blake loathed people yelling at him to get his attention and would purposefully ignore anyone who tried. Trapped by his untimely glance, civility demanded that he wait for Dan. His eyes narrowed to slits as he stopped to let Dan catch up. *Perfect.* Dan was the equivalent of Monday morning all by himself.

"Hey man, welcome back!" Dan blurted out the words in a tumble of unintelligibility while simultaneously slurping his coffee, the delivery making it impossible for Blake to understand him. Standing in front of Blake with a foolish grin, Dan was impervious to his multiple faux pas.

"What?"

"Welcome back! Guess your hearing is still bad, huh?" Dan moved the cup down and Blake caught the gist. True to form, Dan was both irritating and insulting in an attempt to be sociable. Incapable of adjusting to another person's viewpoint, Dan went through life spreading agitation in his wake.

"Yes, it is," Blake responded, simultaneously thinking, *No shit, genius.*

Blake regarded his nemesis from underneath hooded eyes, not bothering to add anything else. Dan recognized Blake's operation as an improvement but didn't have the capacity to fathom its true significance. As he hovered in front of Blake with his mouth hanging open, Blake could feel his heartrate increasing and himself on the verge of becoming irrational. In the space of another breath, irrationality won out, his thoughts exploding in an outpouring of censure.

First he yells at me, then he acts like a dick, then he stands there looking stupid.

How can he do that? Does he not know? Does he know but not care? Does he know and can't stop? How can anyone be so dense? Why doesn't he join mouth-breathers anonymous?!

The thoughts shot through his mind in rapid succession before Blake regained control, stifling his mental tirade. Irritation had been present from the second he woke up this morning, growing exponentially since then to the point where it was now a living and breathing thing.

Back off, he admonished himself. *This is Dan. Not manipulative, not mean, just socially backward with less empathy than a dead slug. As opposed to me, who can be meaner than a raft of fire ants.*

The last thing Blake needed was to have a hallway conversation with one hearing aid in the first five minutes back from surgical leave. Dan couldn't figure that out with a kindergarten primer on thoughtfulness. He decided to switch gears and politely blow Dan off, knowing that the chances of him divining Blake's true thoughts were nonexistent.

Addressing the pile of emotional unintelligence standing before him, Blake said, "Thanks for your concern, Dan. Let me go settle in and take care of what's been piling up on my desk."

Not interested in fielding a reply and hoping to shut down any further interaction, Blake turned toward his office to view Angela coming down the hall at the perfect time to rescue them both. Her appearance reminded him that he needed to start acting sociable if he expected to make it through the day.

"Good morning, Simon! I put some paperwork in your office." Angela gave Dan a pointed stare. "Hey Dan, I'm stealing Simon from you. Excuse us!"

Blake peeked at Angela out of the corner of his eye and mouthed a silent "Thank you!" as she grabbed his arm and steered him down the hall towards his office. He fell in with her, rolling his feet over the soft carpet as they left Dan hanging. To his dismay, even Angela's considerate touch felt intrusive.

Not good.

Angela stopped at his office door and pushed him inside, "Settle yourself in and come find me later, I want to hear all about it!"

"Gotcha." Blake entered the office wishing that he could close his door for the rest of the day. The interaction with Brenda exposed his inadequacies right from the beginning, giving his return a disagreeable start. He stood before his desk feeling miserable. There was nobody he wanted to be around, nothing he wanted to say, and he was rethinking the whole idea of being at work.

All I want to do is turn around and leave.

He plopped down in his chair, dreading a torrent of good cheer. It didn't take long. For the rest of the morning a procession of people stopped by to offer encouragement. They were all polite, all considerate and Blake wanted them all gone. The effort required to integrate words and body language for more than a few minutes at a time was too much for him to handle. After an hour of struggling he was wishing for the peacefulness of the weekend, contrasting it to the intensity of the office, knowing that he should have waited longer before returning. *This was a mistake.*

Robert Nolan stopped in for a hello and made an exit almost immediately. He was happy for Blake and sharp enough to know that communication would be difficult for a while. Offering his help with any calculations, Robert left in under two minutes.

Another engineer, Troy Stevens, stopped in but failed to leave so quickly. He was the same age as Blake, portly where Blake was trim, possessed with a nervous fidget that cycled from hand to hand. Troy had an infuriating habit of picking items up and putting them down in a different spot, causing Blake to mentally catalogue what would be repositioned upon his departure. Watching the relocation drama play out, Blake was tempted to restore each item to its rightful place as soon as Troy released it. *Maybe he would leave sooner!?*

Troy's head was covered in a tangled mane the color of burnt orange, with untrimmed eyebrows resembling a couple of wooly bear caterpillars. The thick eyebrows cast shadows across his face, giving him the appearance of scowling. Having observed Troy to be up one day and down the next, Blake was convinced that Troy was bipolar. He considered Troy tedious to be around because he rarely shut up, blind to the fact that his audience frequently paid more attention to the items which he was constantly shifting around than to what he said. Blake also considered Troy a bit pompous and when he got tired of listening to him would protect his sanity by drifting off into daydreams. Unable to compete for airtime, Blake suffered through the visit by imagining Troy's perfectly pompous posturing to be a mutated version of Mary Poppins, who was practically perfect in every way. Each glacial minute passed slower than the last, Troy's monotonous drone winding him up tighter and tighter until Blake finally called a bathroom break to end the torture.

The parade of callers ended with the approach of lunchtime, Blake taking advantage of the lull to unpack a salami and rye sandwich. His visitors had overwhelmed his capacity for accommodation, and with each well-wisher his mood worsened as he tried to attempt conversation employing a hearing aid that was more decorative than functional. Blake reverted to an old standby, pretending interest and nodding at his tormentors in encouragement while releasing himself to contemplations. It was an effective system that he had perfected long ago. All he needed to do was watch for nonverbal cues that indicated a response was expected, throw in a "Whoa, Uh-huh or Really?" and his colleagues would continue talking, newly reassured that they were the center of his universe.

He stared at his sandwich, the privacy which he had been longing for reinforcing his gloominess rather than providing relief. Alone in his office, the silence which he normally welcomed as a place of refuge was pounding on his shoulders with a rhythmic beat, driving home an understanding that the implant had better work. Blake's ability to focus was shattered by the bald truth of his predicament, his thoughts drifting away to areas best left alone.

As he spiraled down into a familiar list of grudges Blake felt an odd comfort from entertaining thoughts which he knew would only make him feel worse.

One of his sore points was people saying, "Never mind," and moving on without bothering to repeat themselves. While the behavior seemed understandable on the surface, Blake would smolder in frustration at such a cavalier dismissal, vowing to get even at the next available opportunity.

Something else he disliked was practical jokes. Because he was walking a stressful edge most of the time, it was difficult for Blake to understand the desirability of practical jokes, viewing them as another form of manipulation. To see people entertaining themselves at someone else's expense was to him an unforgivable offense, the lack of empathy aggravating him to no end. For the life of him, he could not understand why some victims would respond with enjoyment or appreciation.

Blake's response was to launch a massive counterattack. He returned fire with full force and he did so viciously, not quite crossing the line of physical harm or property damage, but close enough to make people wonder. His reaction was calculated to raise the stakes higher than people were prepared to accept in order to shut them down, and the power coiled up in his reservoir of rage gave him more than enough momentum to follow through.

Embracing the negativity, Blake went back to relive an incident early in his career at Seagram when he had been posted in the engineering department, which at that time consisted of eight engineers located in the basement of the administration building. Their boss was in the basement also, but his office was on the opposite side of the building at the end of a long hallway, leaving half of the basement to the engineers. Being so isolated, not a week went by without some infantile attempt at amusement, usually initiated by one individual who fancied himself a practical joker.

It was early in the afternoon when Blake picked up the phone to make a call and found himself with a glob of KY jelly on his ear. Immediately the office seemed much quieter than usual. He was instantly at a raging boil, his teeth grinding together hard enough to pulverize bricks, but gently put the phone back in the cradle and rose to visit the washroom without saying a word. In the washroom Blake wiped the mess off his ear, seething with a fury that grew with each passing second, so furious at being the butt of someone's joke that his hands trembled as he went through the motions of cleaning up. Evaluating a list of suspects, he decided that the chief prankster was the culprit, and if not, he was involved in some manner. Blake remained where he was for ten minutes, getting himself under control for what was to come.

Upon returning to the work area he went straight to his phone, disconnected the jack and silently approached the desk of his suspect where he slammed the phone, handset and cord down onto the desk with a loud clatter to make it explode, he hoped, into as many separate pieces as possible. Still silent, he picked up the phone of his target, unhooked the connection and went back to his own desk to plug it in. His heart was beating wildly, his insides vibrating in random surges, but his outside expression was unreadable, and he moved with a deliberate slowness. Sitting down, he swiveled toward the object of his wrath and with black eyes boring out of a stony expression quietly said, "Next time it lands on top of your head."

His target, rooted to his desk in a state of disbelief, responded with indignation, "What if it wasn't me? Ever think of that?"

Blake shrugged, "Doesn't matter. You live for that crap so think of it as payback." Turning around, he returned to his work. It took fifteen minutes for his heartrate to return to normal and much longer for his insides to stop twitching. For the remainder of the afternoon he obsessively replayed the episode in his mind. He hoped that he had read the room correctly and identified the actual offender, but as long as the message was delivered, he didn't really care.

Jerk had it coming to him.

As much as he required the cooperation of his coworkers, Blake held a low tolerance for ridicule of any kind. It generated an automatic response that rose from his well of rage to draw a line in the sand with his explicit permission. There were days when nobody had it coming to them, but somebody got it anyway. In the aftermath, regret rarely entered his thoughts. Blake considered his response a necessary protection against the machinations of those who would take advantage of him, and he enjoyed watching his enemies realize that they were in over their heads. His lack of control created more control, and he needed the catharsis.

Criticism was another dislike of his. Blake hated criticism, seeing it as an attack upon his careful planning. His internal response was much the same, but the circumstances were not as conducive to release. He was forced to react in a more socially acceptable manner, the checked emotions serving to intensify his response when he flew off the handle later.

His earlier interaction with Dan entered his mind, the chain of events replaying themselves. He stared outside at the view, seeing nothing. A gorilla could have been washing the window and Blake would have missed it.

Lifting his sandwich to his mouth Blake took a bite, the mixture of salt, rye and salami jolting his senses away from his funk. *I need to switch gears.* Turning to the computer he typed in the web address of the company that made his implant. Now that he was an actual recipient, he had access to all sorts of information from the implant manufacturer's website explaining how to get the most from his device. His unit was made by the Cochlear Company (Cochlear). Med El and Advanced Bionics were alternate manufacturers that Blake had considered, however in the end he went with Cochlear because they claimed to provide superior speech comprehension in background noise.

Until his implant was activated Blake expected his work contributions to be severely limited, but he could research the capabilities of his implant to prepare for activation day.

He began punching at his laptop, which was anchored in a docking station located between two monitors. The layout gave him the ability to use three screens at the same time, making it easy to cut information from one application and paste it somewhere else. Blake hunched down behind the protection of the screens, hoping any visitors would recognize that he was otherwise occupied. Scrolling around the Cochlear website, he came to a section on programming options and settled in to review the information.

Despite his efforts, Blake continued to backslide, staring at the screen while he brooded. His desire at work was simple; he wanted to have a say in decisions rather than being forced to accept a consensus in which he took no part. Personal relationships were the same; he wanted to partake in the daily moments spent with friends and family rather than watching from a separate place. That left everyday communications with the rest of the world where buying a cup of coffee would turn into a catastrophe. He could place an order fine; it was during the response when an interaction became unmanageable. Blake pursed his lips in revulsion. *Pitiful. The minute people talk back to me it all goes to pieces.* It happened so often he could predict it down to the second.

He was wallowing, getting lost in a tidal wave of cynicism that was drowning any productive effort. Blake shoved the salami and rye at his face, packing his mouth so full that he was forced to gulp for air, returning to his research with new resolve.

His implant came with four programs: one for background noise, one for conversation, one for music and one for daily living, whatever that meant. Blake learned that he could adjust the range of the dual microphones, making their sphere of capture larger for distant sounds and smaller for sounds that were closer. There was a provision to raise and lower the volume, which in this case meant that the electrical pulse delivered from the implanted electrode modulated up and down in strength.

The electrode implanted inside of him was a complicated device, communicating volume levels and sounds by stimulating the auditory nerve with electrical pulses in place of the hair cell movements used by normal hearing. Blake had a decent understanding of the theory already, but it sounded more like magic.

Going further, he uncovered an accessory that connected the implant processor to an Ipod or a smartphone using Bluetooth technology, allowing him to adjust a mixing ratio to regulate how much exterior sound was allowed through while he was listening to either device.

There was a separate feature to cancel wind noise that was set to be either on or off. That function sounded intriguing, and Blake was looking forward to experimenting with it.

Processor adjustments were made using a 5" long remote. Cochlear made a smaller remote with fewer capabilities that Blake ruled out because he wanted maximum control.

Cochlear also provided a CD meant for installation on a laptop that contained a training program intended for practice in listening to vowels, consonants and sentences. Successful adoption of the implant required teaching his brain to translate the electrical pulses into sounds, similar to learning a second language. Blake was determined to practice more than Dr. Archer requested.

It's gonna be Go Time.

Consumed by his research, Blake failed to notice the shadows lengthening outside his window. The complexity captured the interest of his engineering mind, providing a welcome escape as he worked on creating his desired configuration, intending to ask Susan if it was doable. When he finally quit it was after 5:30 p.m., prompting him to text Mackenzie for a pickup. By the time she arrived most people were gone and he took advantage of the late hour to slip out unseen. Exiting the building and heading towards Mackenzie's car, Blake hoped that tomorrow would be easier.

Probably won't be, though.

***

As he suspected it would, Blake's first week back turned into a painful state of affairs. His skills at faking it were pushed to the max and by mid-morning on Friday all he could think about was getting away from WEFT. There were a few people, Angela among them, who made a special effort to communicate with him, but for the most part his interactions rated a giant fail. He inspected the weather outside his office window, thankful to be driving again. An overcast sky filled his view, multiple shades of grey threatening flurries for the trip home but navigating his way through a blizzard would be preferable to negotiating the swamp he was mired in at work.

Blake had accomplished his goal of hunkering down, but the misguided attempt to avoid communication served to inject more problems into the mix. In choosing to avoid people, he wound up ostracizing himself, creating a predictable situation. A significant risk of being withdrawn is that people assign their own interpretation to your absences. Blake had left his coworkers to decipher his actions by themselves, and there was no doubt that they were crafting an unfavorable story.

He scolded himself for taking the easy way out. *It was a stupid idea.*

Problem is, next week will be more of the same. The notion ran through his mind with a doleful certainty and projecting ahead, Blake resigned himself to the facts.

I need to be more approachable. The way I'm acting I'll be written off as an albatross or an asshat.

The albatross part could be a problem.

196

Next week he intended to work Monday through Thursday, taking off Friday for activation. It was necessary that he employ his skills to make the best of things, especially since he didn't know if his situation would improve after activation. Blake possessed the ability to get along with anyone in any situation. He spent so much time analyzing the actions of people that it wasn't hard for him to determine how to approach them. Having a single ear did make life more difficult, but he already had the tools he needed.

Just too lazy to use them.

The prospect of activation next Friday occupied his mind constantly. Blake visualized himself with his new implant holding a meeting with three people in his office and temporarily putting his colleagues on standby while he answered a phone call from a client in Germany. He would listen, offer a few recommendations to be implemented in order of priority, and then return to his meeting with a "Sorry about that, where were we?"

What a fantasy. What if it doesn't work? What then?

On the few occasions this past week that Blake had ventured out of his office he avoided participating in conversations, letting others do the talking and nodding in return. His interactions quickly stalled out in an accumulation of dead air, which wasn't normally a problem since Blake welcomed any lulls, using them as a chance to gather and process information. He would take advantage of the fact that silence made some people uncomfortable and they would spit out more commentary to ease their own tension. The problem was that most people were now avoiding him.

His plan was working perfectly if the end goal was total isolation.

Fortunately, George bailed him out by assigning an analysis of six ethanol plants belonging to six different clients. Blake's project was to interpret fermentation data for a group of overseas plants designed and commissioned by WEFT to determine how closely the production rates were matching up between plants. The job involved scrutinizing columns of data listing yeast cell counts, pH values, ethanol levels, organic acid levels and other laboratory results measured at specific intervals in a 72-hour fermentation cycle. Taken as a group, the data told a story of what was happening in the ethanol production process. He was tasked with analyzing the numbers and arriving at the correct interpretation using his experience from producing more than 40,000 fermenters at Seagram. His ability to pinpoint problems and identify the true relationship between cause and effect was a major reason that he was so valuable to George. It was a perfect assignment for him because the yeast cells responsible for producing ethanol didn't talk, at least not out loud.

His assignment released him from the need to attend the daily meetings in the conference room, a situation for which he was grateful. The gatherings began each day after lunch with the arrival of George, who entered the room with a purposeful gait that telegraphed his status as the company alpha. George's presence spanned from wall to wall, matching his intent to dominate the discussion and direct the outcome. Rather than trying to establish a consensus, he viewed the gatherings as an opportunity to fight and win. The participants were male engineers, hired by George, trained by George, and not surprisingly, most of them possessed George's arrogance. Contradictory statements rose up from all corners of the room, making the dialogue resemble a pack of dogs tearing at a piece of meat.

It was an atmosphere that Blake found impossible and tapping a pen on the edge of his desk, he gave a sigh of relief for escaping the gauntlet this past week.

Ready to leave, Blake pushed some papers around on his desk, swiping at his cell phone to kill a few minutes. He kept an eye on the hallway, trying to gauge the lunch exodus. His perception was 99% visual and would remain so until such time as the implant was activated. *And then we'll see.* This week he had been staying later than usual, monitoring the traffic passing by his door so that he could make his exit with as little interaction as possible. Two stragglers went down the hall on their way to lunch. Blake observed them laughing and talking in a loose manner that made him ache. Getting up from his desk, he stood at the window watching happy people gathering in happy groups on the way to their happy lunches.

Pressing his lips together, he scowled in disdain.

Earlier that morning Blake had informed Angela of his intentions to make an early escape under the cover of lunch hour, and she received the information with a conspiratorial wink, promising to pass his plans on to George. Blake felt grateful to have a friend in Angela and an understanding boss in George. He owed it to them both to step it up.

The implant might work and it might not. If I keep this up it'll be that much harder to recover from a failure. If it does work, then I'll be practicing like mad. Recess is over either way.

***

Early Monday, the past week already a distant memory, Blake pulled into WEFT's parking lot determined to get a better start this time around. Thirteen days after the operation he was still in recovery mode. Blake could rotate his head slowly, but if he tried to twist around quickly, he could feel the stitches pull and was subjected to a momentary dizziness. Normally an aggressive driver who would weave through traffic and exceed the speed limit, he was choosing to err on the side of safety by slowing down rather than constantly trying to force an opening. Instead of regarding his fellow drivers as obstacles to maneuver around, Blake was now one of many fish swimming in a school. The change helped him blend with the flow of traffic, allowing him to arrive at work relaxed instead of tied up in knots from pushing the limits of himself or other drivers. Old habits were hard to break though, and Blake couldn't help wondering how long it would take before he returned to his obnoxious practices.

He parked his truck, taking a minute to appreciate the blanket of frost covering the blacktop. Vehicle tracks snaked dark trails across a white canvas, creating a transitory image begging to be captured. Thanksgiving was around the corner and mornings were now chilly with the air holding a bite that promised colder days ahead. As he prepared to get out of his vehicle, Blake observed the tracks of his coworkers leading to the entrance, reminding himself that he needed to employ a new approach this week.

Exiting his vehicle, Blake hunched up his coat for protection against the cold as he made his own tracks across the blacktop. He carried a Starbucks with him, guarding his treasure with care, green plug stoppering it from leakage. This morning was starting out cloudy and grey, matching the bleakness that seemed to accompany most Mondays. Blake enjoyed his job, but Monday could sometimes stir up a desire to be independently wealthy.

Opening the door and walking inside, Blake made sure to greet Brenda with a smile and a wave before she could make a move. She reciprocated from her phone call, giving him a wink in return. *Perfect! One for one.* He was prepared for another onslaught from Dan, but Dan wasn't around to double up on Monday.

Never hurts to be lucky.

Blake made it to his office without any disasters, setting his Starbucks down and proceeding to hang up his coat. This week he was expected to attend the daily dogfights in the conference room, a situation that elicited a resigned shrug. *Worst part of the day.* Moving behind the desk to sit down, he stretched out a hand for his coffee, wrapping his fingers around the warm cardboard and removing the stopper to sniff at the aroma before allowing himself a taste. *Ahhhhhh.* The familiar touch and aroma went a long way towards starting the day off properly. He booted up his computer and got to work, knowing his fermentation project was on borrowed time.

Lunchtime came and went, followed by Blake hustling to the conference room to claim his preferred spot. He needed to arrive early to select a seat that offered him an appropriate vantage point for lip reading.

The conference room was constructed with plaster walls instead of glass, which helped to improve the acoustics. Grey carpet covered a floor that was dominated by a large table finished in wood veneer with rounded corners. Easily 20' long by 6' wide, the table was positioned in line with the entrance. Choosing a seat at the far end allowed Blake to observe the dynamics of the meeting as well as positioning himself in a favorable spot to follow the conversation. Padded chairs with navy blue fabric and swivel seats surrounded the conference table, ensuring everyone's comfort.

Upon entering the room Blake was relieved to see that he was the first arrival, heading towards his desired location opposite the doorway. If all went according to plan, Angela would sit by him and he could read her notes when the discussion became too vigorous to follow. The worst scenario was having to settle for a position in the middle without Angela by his side. Stuck in the middle he would be forced to swivel his head to follow events, invariably choosing to look in one direction while the rest of the room was focused elsewhere. He took pains to avoid the middle, preferring to arrive 15 minutes early rather than paying a significant penalty for arriving five seconds too late. Blake had difficulty keeping up with the flow of conversation regardless of where he sat though, and it was only a matter of time before the dialogue would have to pause while someone updated him in order to get his opinion. Each pause left him feeling uncomfortably exposed by the unwanted attention, the ill-fated guest who spilled red wine on the carpet.

People began to file in, Blake watching with envy as they selected random spots without a thought for the consequences. Angela arrived and made a beeline for his side, aware that he was a fish out of water. She sat down, nudging him with an encouraging elbow and positioning her notepad between the two of them. Dan slouched through the door followed in succession by Troy, Robert and the rest of the engineers. Finally they were all there except for George, who made a point of arriving last. George was the only attendee with a reserved seat, located at the end closest to the doorway.

While they waited for George to make an entrance Blake surveyed the room as was his usual habit, noting who was interacting with whom, who was happy, who appeared stressed. A hum of conversation filled the room, manifesting itself as white noise to his ears. He observed, gauging the mood. Some people brought coffee and some brought file folders, still others brought calculators in case they needed to bolster their arguments. Several cell phones lay face down on the surface of the table, causing Blake to wonder who would forget to turn off their ringer.

George arrived with presence, his bulk filling the doorway, conversations tailing off as he shut the door before sitting down. Watching George use a large hand to swivel his chair into position, Blake scanned the group one last time, noting his colleagues' posture and alertness. All indications pointed towards a normal meeting, an assumption borne out by Angela's notes as the agenda progressed. True to form, the contentiousness inherent to WEFT asserted itself almost immediately, triggering in Blake an internal sigh. Everyone participated with the hubris of a 15-year-old convinced he already knew how to drive. At one point George asked for an update on his fermentation analysis, but Blake begged off until Thursday.

Once the meeting was over, Blake returned to his office. His fermentation project was done, but he preferred to let his conclusions percolate a few days in case additional insights came up. He didn't trust judgements arrived at too quickly because the data could be interpreted a number of different ways.

Blake's analysis followed a specific procedure. He would start by identifying relevant variables, after which he would toss them up in the air and begin to juggle them. As he added variables to his juggling act, the relationships between items would ebb and flow from one possibility to another. His task was to identify the most feasible interpretation that was supported by the most data points and then explain it to a bunch of arrogant engineers who saw it as their mission to question all proposals to exhaustion.

WEFT was unique in that regard. At Seagram the engineering debates had centered on cooperation rather than conflict, with people putting their energy toward supporting ideas rather than tearing them down. Soon after being hired, Blake had learned that the culture here was different, a function of George's confrontational style, and he bemoaned the wasted energy as he watched the participants attempt to beat each other into submission. George thrived on conflict though, appearing recharged after the daily skirmishes.

To satisfy such a skeptical audience, Blake would go further in his analysis and try to identify conditions in the plant that could produce the results he was seeing. Sometimes he would target a specific valve or pump as a possible culprit and other times he would gravitate towards process parameters such as fermenter temperatures. After reaching a conclusion, Blake needed to give his thoughts a few days to ruminate. Driving home, exercising or anything else that offered a change of focus released his mind to wander and make associations that could not be made in the heat of the moment when it took all his concentration to weigh a multitude of variables. Whiskey was good that way. The break freed up his intellect to stumble across a connection that seemed obvious after the fact but was difficult to pinpoint in the presence of so much noise.

*****

Thursday afternoon Blake stood up to give his report, confident that he had his ducks in a row. He had also taken the intervening time to mentally prepare for what he referred to as death by presentation. It was easy for his analysis to appear less valid when he stumbled over understanding questions from the audience. Sometimes Blake tried to address this difficulty by having questions written down, but that wasn't a perfect solution either because people often had follow up inquiries. Some of his audience tended to comment first and think second anyway.

Why can't they shut up for a few seconds instead of immediately opening their mouths to think out loud??

His fermentation analysis compared data from six ethanol plants, drawing conclusions from a large amount of data in an effort to simplify a process that was not simple. The data could appear byzantine to people without his skills, so he expected some queries at the end. Blake took pains to go slowly with his presentation, describing the differences between the various ethanol plants to explain why yeast produced more ethanol in some plants and less ethanol in others. It boiled down to the fact that if the yeast were happy then everybody was happy. After finishing he opened the door for comments, hoping for the best. One danger was that he sometimes answered a different question than the one presented, which was always embarrassing.

When that occurred George stepped in to take control of the situation before it could degenerate too far. George respected Blake's experience and Blake made sure to stay in his good graces. Blake's need to fade into the background meshed with George's desire to take control, so on the outside it appeared that they were working together on the same agenda. Since Blake didn't have the communication skills to survive any other way, he had no choice but to follow George's lead. He didn't always agree, but it was his sole option.

This time around the questions were minimal, making Blake grateful for small favors. In his present condition he couldn't determine the difference between a phone ringing or someone laughing, let alone handle multiple questions of unknown context. After the meeting George hung back, tapping Blake on the shoulder with one finger to signify that he wanted to talk, and they both exited the conference room to head off in the direction of George's office. Today was his last workday before activation tomorrow and Blake followed George down the hall, his thoughts moving ahead to his appointment with Dr. Susan Archer.

They arrived at George's office, a corner unit with two exterior walls comprised of floor to ceiling windows.

Vertical blinds concealed the windows, cancelling out the reverberating effects of the glass. George led the way, maneuvering his bulk around the desk to land in his chair, and as he did so Blake noticed that George's habit of binge eating was catching up with him. He was committed to using the same belt loop, but physics was exacting a price in the form of his stomach overflowing his waistline.

"Go ahead, sit down." George waved Blake into a chair across from his desk, one massive hand swinging through the air and creating a breeze in its wake. White sleeves were rolled halfway up to his elbows, the crumpled shirt already dirty laundry.

Blake sat down, resting his arms upon the chair in silence, his face an inscrutable mask. The confrontational atmosphere of the conference room had caused him to take refuge in observation mode, a place he was still occupying.

"You get activated tomorrow?" George lifted his eyebrows as he got straight to the point. He already knew the answer, of course, and Blake realized this was going to be a courtesy exchange.

"Yeah, 10:00 a.m. Emily's coming with me." Unsure how to describe his activation, Blake was noncommittal. He was unwilling to show excitement, hoping to avoid a public setback in the event that the procedure turned out badly, but on the other hand, he was hoping that tomorrow would be the start of something glorious. Earlier this week Blake had been guilty of quashing Mackenzie's enthusiasm with his refusal to show any eagerness. His compromise was to appear neutral on the outside while hoping for a screaming miracle on the inside, but the contrast between the two was getting harder to resolve.

George leaned forward, his bulk filling the space in front of Blake and making the desk appear small. "I hope the implant works out for you. It sounds phenomenal."

"Hope so. Anything would be an improvement over where I am today." Knowing the futility of trying to conceal such an obvious failing, Blake took pains to be upfront with George about his hearing loss. He felt fortunate that George was willing to look past his disability for the value in Blake's knowledge. Blake gave thanks once more for finding a job with the right mix of people and needs.

The majority of his conversations this week had resembled a standoff between two alley cats. With George he could relax because he trusted his boss and the booming bass of George's voice came through loud and clear. He still had to read lips, but George was among the easier people for him to understand.

"I'll be back Monday and we'll talk." *Or not.* Despite his doubts, Blake winked at George. Tired of waiting, he wanted the suspense to end.

It won't stay a secret much longer.

With nothing else to say, Blake stood up, preparing to take his leave. Standing in front of the desk, he met George's eyes with an air of finality, raising his hands in an unspoken acceptance, George nodding in return. Blake appreciated the tolerance that George showed for his disability, and an expression of thanks was on the tip of his tongue, but the comment failed to make it past his lips. He respected George, recognized that without George he was in deep trouble, but after sitting through the contentious meeting and being commandeered for a private audience his ego rebelled, considering the action overly meek in face of

George's tendency to take control. For a millisecond Blake entertained saying thanks, hiding his mental exercise behind a bland expression.

No.

It was ungracious, he knew, to look down on his benefactor, but he turned and walked away, his thoughts shifting to 10:00 a.m. tomorrow morning.

Blake glided down the hallway to his office, his mind full of questions for Susan. He planned to leave early today, wanting to gather his energies for activation instead of squandering them on work. Despite putting up a calm front for George, his mind alternated between excitement and fear.

What if it works? What if it doesn't? The aftermath seemed overwhelming either way.

Blake tidied up his office and grabbed his jacket to reenter the hallway, conscious of the blood surging through his body in time with his heartbeat. He couldn't help thinking that he was leaving for the last time as Simon Blake and would return on Monday as someone completely different. His veins were pulsing the beginnings of his conversion throughout his body, seeking out each cell to prepare it for a new identity. Tomorrow was his shot at a miracle to correct the chromosomes that failed him at birth.

Forty-nine years. My second chance.

Walking across the blacktop to his truck, Blake was conscious of the afternoon chill cutting through his jacket but heedless to its bite. He was hours ahead of quitting time so traffic going home should be light, and after entering his vehicle he turned on the heater before heading home, operating strictly on auto pilot. Tomorrow's moment of truth consumed his thoughts as he flowed with the traffic. In less than 24 hours he would emerge from University Hospital as Blake 2.0.

Tomorrow…

Blake stared through the windshield at the concrete on his driveway with no recollection of how he got there. Turning off the engine he sat in his truck, his attention going to the Thanksgiving wreath mounted on the front door. Thanksgiving promised family time and fond memories. He wondered whether his kids were conscious of the fact that the memories this year were going to figure prominently on the family timeline.

Madison and Mackenzie, yes. Matthew doesn't think that far ahead.

Tomorrow changes everything.

Which way though?

It could be so great.

I don't even want to think about failure. My hearing is practically nonexistent now. If the implant doesn't work then my life becomes a disaster.

Like it's not already.

I suppose I could try again on the other ear if this one craps out.

It would be so much easier if my hearing got better instead of worse. I don't need perfection. Even a small improvement would help.

Emily will be devastated if I get worse. She didn't sign up for this. Who in their right mind would?

Maybe I should have started with the left ear?

Maybe it'll turn out ok and this is wasted energy.

Maybe it'll all turn to garbage.

Afternoon sunshine was beating down on the truck, making the interior cozy and protected. Ensconced in warmth, lulled into stasis by the comfort of his seat, Blake was reluctant to leave the only refuge he'd found all week.

Fears and dreams competed to hold his attention in a clash that had been going on ever since he left the hospital. Sometimes he imaged himself like Mary Beth, calm and capable, reacting to events in a manner of his own choosing, each new interaction a celebration, made more so by the unexpected blessing of its existence. Then he had visions of himself in the solitude of janitorial work, mopping some hallway as the last shafts of afternoon sunshine streamed through the windows, illuminating golden flecks of dust dancing in the air, too elusive for capture, each radiant mote representing a moment of beauty forever out of reach.

The two possibilities alternated between lifting his spirit to wondrous heights and plunging him to terrifying depths. Alone in his vehicle, sheltered from prying eyes, Blake dropped any pretenses about keeping up appearances. His internal strife manifested itself in a surge of heat that raised the hairs on his neck. At the same time the desperate nature of his desire flooded his eyes, trickling tears of anguish down his cheeks. In the center hope grappled with fear, the turmoil twisting his gut with vicious energy. Tomorrow would see the tide of battle turn one way or another, ending this chapter of internal angst.

Waiting was turning out to be its own challenge, especially now, on the edge of a permanent resolution.

One minute he felt optimistic. The next he did not. His past reasserted itself, driving him back toward the clutches of fear and doubt. There were plenty of reasons to be optimistic, but years of painful setbacks had no problem regaining the upper hand.

Although the warmth offered some small measure of escape, he couldn't stay in his truck forever, and Blake forced himself to get out. It was slow going to the house, a last march of sorts. Entering the front door, Blake went down the hallway to seek sanctuary in the kitchen.

He passed through the doorway, having the place to himself since neither Emily nor Mackenzie were yet home. Thinking that perhaps he could kill some time by reviewing his questions for Susan, Blake sat down and set out his notes. Five minutes spent shuffling paper around disposed him of that notion and he slumped back in resignation. Morning could not come soon enough. A diversion was required, and as he idly drummed the walnut with a couple of fingers wondering if maybe whiskey would fit the bill, his cell phone vibrated, demanding his attention. Blake pulled it out from his pocket to read a text from Tom, one of his fishing buddies.

You home?

Blake typed back, *Yup.*

He stared at the screen, willing it to respond.

Got something for you, swinging by in 30.

Blake perked up, grateful for the interruption. Tom was a friend from Seagram whom Blake had kept in touch with after leaving for WEFT.

The two of them went back a long way, both starting work at the Seagram distillery in 1981. In 1985 Tom suggested that they take a weekend to go fishing and they hit it off, catching lots of fish while discovering that they made a compatible team on the water. Tom, like Blake, was a natural outdoorsman, comfortable around nature, able to improvise and shrug off the vagaries of the weather. Neither got too excited about the logistics of traveling or about who caught the most fish. Their focus was on helping each other succeed, at work or on the lake, and the pair possessed a knack for seeing humor in mundane events.

That first weekend morphed into an annual excursion lasting a full week, the destination being Snowbank Lake in Minnesota. Each year different friends would filter in and out depending upon the logistics of their lives, with Tom and Blake serving as the core.

Their years of fishing together created a bond of trust. The fishing trips were often in remote locations, demanding reliance upon each other to get out of the inevitable jams, some of them dangerous and some of them bordering on the ridiculous. Early in their relationship Blake noted in Tom a fundamental respect for human dignity, and their bond strengthened over time as they grew to be close friends. Tom was one of the few people permitted to tease Blake about his disability without negative repercussions.

Blake slid the cell onto the table in front of him, knowing that Tom wouldn't bother ringing the doorbell. He took another pass through his notes, finding them more engrossing now that he had a diversion in the background.

Here. The phone lit up, Blake rising from the kitchen table after a quick glance at the screen. Approaching the front door, he wondered what the occasion was.

Got to be an improvement over being home alone with lifelong demons for company.

Pulling open the door, he was presented with the sight of Tom standing on the porch with a beat-up cooler.

Tom was a big man at 6'-5" with a barrel chest that matched a beefy physique. The same age as Blake, his head was covered by salt and pepper hair cut close to his scalp. Long arms befitting a gorilla ended in massive hands studded with large fingers that displayed patches of curly hair growing between the knuckles. Blake had seen him on multiple occasions with his shirt off and knew that the hair extended to his arms, his neck and most of his back. Put him in camo gear, give him a gun, and Tom could be Mr. July on the mercenary calendar.

At Blake's appearance, Tom raised his eyebrows, a huge grin popping out of a three-day stubble. The stubble completed the look. Blake had been places with Tom where he watched in amusement as people crossed the street to avoid getting too close.

The truth was the complete opposite. Tom was a friendly dude possessed of an engaging smile and a demeanor conveying tolerance and respect. Blake instinctively recognized an inherent goodness in the relaxed mannerisms of his friend, and it amazed him that anyone would miss it. Once Tom opened his mouth to speak, people would visibly relax. Emily had taken to Tom immediately, declaring him one of her favorites.

Blake swung the door wide open. "What's up?"

"Got a few bass this morning. Figured you would want the babies." Tom winked conspiratorially, the smile starting to resemble a smirk.

"I don't clean fish under four pounds. Thought you knew that." His tone conveying exasperation, Blake spread his hands in mock dismay.

"These should work." Tom flipped up the lid of the cooler to expose three largemouth bass packed in ice, each one easily 22" long. Their green and black coloration showed prominently against white ice as they lay there with fat bellies, trophies destined for the table. Blake caught a whiff of fresh fish, undeniable in its pungency.

Gazing down into the cooler, Blake let out a whistle of appreciation. "Impressive. You finally started listening to me." He nodded in approval.

The two friends stood there eyeing each other and then both burst out laughing. It was the same way every time; big fish triggered pride and bullshit.

"Want a drink?" Blake stepped back to enter the foyer. "Emily won't be home for a few hours. You're welcome to stay until she kicks you out." He grabbed the cooler and dragged it inside upon the rug. "Guess I'm making dinner tonight!!"

"Nah, have to meet the wife. I stopped by to say best of luck tomorrow."

"Appreciate it!" Blake gave his friend a nod, "Never hurts to be lucky." He reached out to clasp hands, taking energy from Tom's firm grip. "I'll let you know how it goes."

"Do that." Tom turned to go, lifting an arm in farewell. Upon reaching his truck, he snapped off a two-finger salute in a gesture of support before climbing in. Blake watched him drive off with a renewed sense of optimism.

Shutting the door Blake inspected the bass packed in ice. A fishy odor wafting up brought back memories and he relaxed, the social call serving to lessen his anxiety. After carrying the cooler into the kitchen, he busied himself cleaning the bass for dinner. Combined with onions, potatoes and butter in aluminum foil, the meal would be a mouth-watering treat for Emily and Mackenzie. He could throw in a side salad for the perfect accompaniment. *And whiskey.* Once done with the dirty work, he submerged the fillets in saltwater and sent Emily a text letting her know that dinner was in progress. She would be thrilled.

Before the smell of fish guts could permeate the kitchen, Blake opened the backdoor and carried them outside for disposal. Afternoon shadows blanketed the yard and as he passed through a section of shade on his way to the garbage, the drop in temperature caused him to shiver. His thoughts turned to Emily and how the two of them were at a place where they complemented each other as naturally as breathing. Their bond had been tested many times, making them stronger together and wiser than in the beginning. Would tomorrow bring another challenge, maybe the hardest one ever? He hoped not. A quietness took over his body as he interrupted his errand to gaze across the backyard, conscious of his surroundings, but focused inward.

If the implant worked then he hoped to rival Mary Beth, talking and laughing and loving like never before. He felt the potential coursing through his body, poised to break loose.

If it didn't work, he would be facing a terrible defeat. Condemned to live in a silence corrupted by stress and rage, he would spend the rest of his days knowing that those who succeeded where he had failed were celebrating their new lives, full of wonder and joy.

The epiphany froze his soul with a stillness born from horror and he felt his heartbeat stutter.
What have I done to myself?

Chapter 8 – Activation

Thursday night Blake slept fitfully, dozing off for a few minutes at a time only to return to a state of wakefulness, eyes closed and heart pounding out a disquieting rhythm. Each time he sought to remain motionless so that Emily could get some rest. More than once he opened his eyes to stare into an impenetrable curtain of darkness, the black void reverberating through his consciousness to create more questions than answers. With a sigh of defeat he would shut his eyes against the uncertainty and concentrate on willing himself back to sleep.

At 4:30 a.m. with the bedroom still dark, he decided to call it quits and make breakfast. Before getting out of bed he bent over his wife and lifted her hair aside to plant a gentle kiss on her cheek. She stirred in response to snuggle in closer, a reaction that normally encouraged him to take things further, but it was a measure of his unsettled condition that all he did was turn to the edge of the bed and ease himself onto the floor.

In the predawn darkness Blake groped for his clothes to pull on a pair of black jeans and a black sweatshirt laid out for the morning. He entered the bathroom and shut the door before flooding the room with light. Evaluating himself in the mirror, Blake made a promise that he would face the day without flinching.

After making his way to the kitchen, two eggs, toast and coffee were followed by seeking refuge in his chair with more coffee. The mood was still, a restful quiet permeating the house while he waited for his wife and daughter to wake up. On Saturdays Blake typically got up early and made his own breakfast, taking advantage of a peaceful interlude before Emily and Mackenzie appeared. It was the same this Friday, and with the kitchen free of distractions he stared out the window, barely able to discern the forms of the backyard trees framing the nights' slow fade from blackness to shadow. Buttressed by the coffee's soothing aroma, Blake allowed himself to hope that activation would mark a turning point for the better.

An hour later, with the sky approaching pale blue, Mackenzie blew through the kitchen on her way to school, favoring him with a kiss and a hug before grabbing her lunch from the fridge. With a final wish for luck she was gone, leaving him another step closer to whatever destiny had in store. He drank in the lingering vitality of her presence, experiencing a stab of relief that Matthew wasn't home to inadvertently contaminate the day. Madison would have said something appropriate, but she was an infrequent visitor these days, caught up in the social whirl of college. Today was the last Friday before Thanksgiving, prompting him to speculate how the family dynamic would change this year.

His meanderings were interrupted by Emily materializing at the kitchen doorway in grey pants and a red top. As she entered the kitchen, Blake was taken by the enticing combination of tight jeans and close-fitting sweater, wondering why he had been in such a hurry to get out of bed. *It's a sad day when I pass up a morning cuddle.* Outside the kitchen window dawn was spilling over the horizon, and he watched Emily approach in the pale light, boots clacking over the wooden floor in a slow rhythm.

"Let me guess, not much sleep." Her eyes met his to read uncertainty, hope, fear and all the combinations thereof. She stopped alongside him, resting a hand upon his shoulder in silence, knowing further commentary would only serve to resurrect a conversation neither of them cared to repeat.

"Nah." Tilting his head Blake peered up at his wife, his expression encompassing a struggle that she had come to know well.

Emily stood above him, surveying her husband of 25 years. She surrendered herself to the depths of his eyes, the fact that they were his most expressive feature pulled her in even more. Plumbing his innermost thoughts, she read the story of their years past and perhaps their years to come. In any marriage there will be times when quitting seems to be an attractive option, but they made a pact to stick to their vows long before they reached the altar, and their relationship was stronger as a result. Neither of them wanted to pick up the pieces of a family torn apart over something that in the long run might easily turn out to be inconsequential. The aggravations of this world have a predictable tendency to melt away with the passage of time and even more so in the presence of death or trauma. Taking his hand in both of hers, she bent down to brush her lips across his skin in silent affirmation before turning to walk to the other side of the kitchen.

She had no idea how the day was going to turn out, but Emily was determined to get it started off in the right direction. Reaching the cupboards she swiveled around, checking to see that he was paying attention. Pointing a slim finger in his direction, Emily fixed him with an encouraging smile and delivered her sermon, "Like you always say, never hurts to be lucky!"

Throwing him a wink, she began making her own breakfast. A beam of sunshine enveloped her in a shaft of golden light, her preparations stirring up particles of dust that danced through the air in swirls of sparkles, joyous fairies playing tag. It was a positive omen to tease the dreams of them both.

Blake watched his wife go about her tasks, finding peace in the refuge of her presence. Suspended as he was in the few hours remaining, he wished for one more day of grace in the event that his life unraveled, and not wanting to contaminate his fortunes, at the same time wished that the day would turn out favorably.

He took a draught of coffee, the fifth cup of the morning, looking past his wife to another place.

For the past few months he had been on a trek through heavy fog to the top of a mountain, and today he was hoping to break through to a spectacular view at the top. Mountain weather being unpredictable, it was also possible that he would arrive at the summit surrounded by so much fog that there was no view to be had, only a disappointing curtain of whiteness signifying that his journey was for naught.

It was impossible to think of one without entertaining thoughts of the other.

***

At 9:30 a.m. Blake and Emily checked into the University Hospital audiology department and claimed their seats in the horseshoe of the reception area. With their arrival the section was full. Lowering himself onto one of the remaining chairs, Blake eyeballed his fellow patients, wondering which of them would go home satisfied and which would be cast adrift. Emily settled herself in close and crossed her legs, sliding a hand over to rest upon his thigh. He glanced down at her French nails, tracing a line from the slim femininity of her fingers up her arm to her shoulder and neck, lingering on the twin curves of her breasts pushing identical mounds out from her sweater, burying his eyes in the raven curls that attracted him in their first meeting.

Nothing stirred and his attempt at diversion ended as fast as it began.

Behind Emily an older couple exited from the hallway where the offices were located and Blake observed them closely, trying to be subtle with his inspection. The woman carried a black case decorated with yellow pin-striping and emblazoned with the 'Cochlear' logo. She was holding the hand of her companion whose short hair clearly revealed a cochlear implant on one side of his head. As the couple walked through the reception area, his eyes tracked them the whole way, analyzing the dynamics of their interaction. It appeared they were having a normal conversation, without the repeats and awkwardness common to his own experience.

He glanced at Emily to find her watching. As if on cue, she met his glance and mouthed a silent, "You and me!" as she waggled a finger between the two of them.

Blake lifted an eyebrow and leaned in to whisper, "Fifteen years, maybe!" He followed up by exhaling gently into her ear, his breath soft enough to be soundless, warm enough to tickle.

Her eyes twinkling, Emily touched one finger to her lips, suppressing a smile. She gave his leg a squeeze, and for an instant they enjoyed a temporary escape from that inherent tension present in all waiting rooms everywhere.

Better than a pity party, Blake told himself. He was attempting to sit quietly with a measured pace of breathing, his physical body under strict orders to reveal nothing. The exterior calm belied his anxiety, heart hammering as if he was playing racquetball. Since the couple now leaving were obviously finished, he figured that Dr. Archer would be coming out to get them any minute.

His pulse pounded with anticipation and he reminded himself that stress was a state of mind.

Except my mind is a mess.

He sat in his chair on the edge of being uncomfortably warm. Rays of sunlight burned past the windows in the sunroom of the reception area to bake the carpet surrounding his seat, and he could sense waves of warmth rising from below as the shafts of light imperceptibly crept his way. The air seemed more stifling by the second, and he was hoping that Dr. Susan Archer would make an appearance to rescue him from the suspense that had become a runaway train.

For the moment he waited in vain.

Bending his head down, Blake closed his eyes and breathed in slowly before letting his breath out even slower, marshalling his powers of self-control to overcome the suffocating atmosphere, the obstinate thumping of his heart and the stress of uncertainty. A mental image of himself standing at a fork in the road filled his mind, enclosing him in its sphere. The fork displayed no signpost and he checked both ways, clueless as to which path was his.

The minutes dragged by, each rotation of the dial a separate burden until Dr. Susan Archer finally emerged from the hallway housing the clinical offices to head in their direction. She was dressed in the universal white coat which hung open to reveal grey slacks and a black top. Her high heels skimmed smoothly across the carpet of the waiting area as she approached them with a wide smile and an outstretched hand.

"Good morning Simon! I have your processor in my office!" Susan's blue eyes exuded confidence as Blake rose to clasp her hand in relief. Forcing a smile that he was only partially sure about, Blake remained silent, nodding through their exchange while his heart maintained its stubborn pounding.

Turning to Emily, Susan extended her greeting to include his wife. "And good morning Emily!" Her eyes lightened as she continued, "I am so pleased the two of you are here together!" Emily managed to do better than her husband, offering a greeting of her own along with a smile that illuminated her eyes, telegraphing more than a little excitement.

Standing before them in a manner designed to take charge, Dr. Archer clasped her hands together, an air of anticipation evident in her expression. "Let's get to it. We have a long list of tasks to accomplish this morning." She turned, white coat swirling in her wake, and headed off in the direction of the hallway. Blake and Emily fell in step behind her, Emily pulling even to clasp Blake's hand in a solid grip.

As they left the reception area, the hallway reverberated with the sound of the two women click clacking over linoleum, a steady rhythm that accompanied their progress deeper down the corridor. The three of them advanced without speaking, each entertaining their own thoughts. *My last chance for a life,* Blake agonized, as they strode down the hallway. *It's this or nothing.* Hoping for the same miracle that Mary Beth described, he felt he was entering an arena to do battle without knowing who or what lay in wait.

At the end of the hall they came to the open doorway of Susan's office, its welcoming light beckoning them to enter a new world. In the twilight of one life and on the threshold of another, Blake was thinking that he would soon learn whether the rest of his days would become a soundless tragedy.

Better not. The anger stirred inside, more than willing to accept release and wreak havoc. Blake assessed the hallway with its unpretentious linoleum and the makeup of his posse. When the Mayans sacrificed someone there was ceremonial dress, feasting, fire, crowds of people. Likewise, any first communion or bar mitzvah was a fancy affair involving formal outfits and parties. For such a momentous occasion it seemed inappropriate that the best he could manage was three people gathered in an office building, two of them in jeans.

We'll do the brass band later, I guess.

Moving through the doorway, Susan headed for her computer station, where she sat down next to the window, the view outside revealing a frigid world with bare branches spreading upward to beg warmth from the sun. Gesturing towards the chairs by her desk, she waved them to their places, "This is the day that we start the real work." She preferred to set the tone by focusing on tasks rather than excitement in an effort to avoid false hopes. For a minority of her patients activation day turned out to be a cruel disappointment. Whether it was due to unrealistic expectations or implant issues, a small number left under a cloud of gloom, sometimes in tears. Those were the days that she hated to go home. Susan was optimistic that today would be one of the good days, but it was still too early to know.

Blake sat down next to Susan's desk, scanning the layout of the room, thinking that he wouldn't mind delivering a hard kick to the audiometric booth located five feet away. Its menacing presence threatened another round of torture and anguish. Peering through the window at the hateful speaker that dished out so much punishment during his initial visit, he queried Susan, "We doing the booth today?"

Susan shook her head once, "Nope, we are done with that for a while. Today is activation. We will test you again later, maybe in three months."

"Humph," Blake offered. *Can't wait.*

He was in no hurry to crash and burn. Offering what comfort she could, Emily inclined toward him to drape an arm over the back of his chair, crossing her legs in his direction as they both keyed on Susan. From his seat close to Susan, Blake saw that her work area was covered with stacks of small boxes and black cables in plastic baggies, a technological puzzle waiting to be assembled. Blake recognized the external magnet and the processor with its earhook that would soon be affixed to his head. A black and yellow suitcase like he had seen earlier rested on the floor.

The room held a sterility that magnified the clinical aura, hinting at unfortunate procedures for the luckless.

Unable to settle on one emotion in the face of so much doubt, Blake fell back on the familiar, adopting his poker face. He figured Susan not only knew the true state of his hearing, but also understood what odds he faced today. She had checked his implant in the operating room while he was under anesthesia and at this point would have a better idea how it was working than he did.

Let's go.

Tired of the suspense, he was ready to get on with it. He was a contestant on The Dr. Archer show, trying to win the life of his dreams. Blake was praying that she would wave her magic wand and bless him with the gift that he so desperately wanted.

Dr. Susan Archer, fairy godmother.

Blake recalled the anticipation that arose on a fishing trip when his vehicle turned off blacktop onto a gravel road. Gravel signified an imminent shift of circumstances, promising that before long he would be flying across the lake, exposed to the mercy of the elements, breathing air filled with the scents of woods and water. There was a similar vibe of impending change inside the office. The difference was that while fishing trips encouraged relaxation, this experience was having the opposite effect.

Sitting close enough to his hardware that he could reach out and pick it up, Blake tried to relax, but his body refused to cooperate. His heart continued its unruly hammering and he massaged clammy hands along his jeans to dry them off. A flow of cool air from the ceiling vent was giving him a chill, but that was nothing compared to the disturbances inside of him.

The range of Blake's peripheral vision was narrowing down to eliminate everything but Susan, who appeared to be sitting at the far end of a tunnel that grew longer and longer while he continued to watch. *All she needs is a psychedelic halo.* His head was floating above his shoulders, his movements mired in slow motion. An involuntary tremble sprung from between his shoulders, passing up his neck to bury itself in his scalp and make his hair stand on end.

I'm in trouble.

Dismayed at such betrayal by his physical self, Blake homed in on Susan, struggling his way past the hallucinations, seeking an anchor before the tension manifested itself any further. Susan's words echoed up through the tunnel. "I want to start by mentioning that if you have questions, either ask them as we go or write them down for later. We are going to cover a tremendous amount of information and it's easy to fall behind." She stopped to affirm they both understood, her far-off voice registering in Blake's brain seconds after she finished talking. Emily nodded in response, as did Blake, but Blake's nod was purely mechanical, gripped as he was in the throes of disorientation.

Taking their nods at face value, Susan continued, gathering her lapels together and leaning forward. Facing Blake, she began, "Simon, you will need to read my lips for a period of time this morning because I have to remove your hearing aid while setting up your processor." Blake nodded again, her eye contact helping to draw him in. He came away with the thought that he needed to read her lips more than he needed to hear her voice, the dose of coherency helping him settle down.

Keeping her focus on Blake, Susan kept going, "In the beginning your processor will be attached to your head but it will not be providing you with any functionality until we finish our configuration. Our first task is to establish the maximum and minimum sound levels that are specific to your situation. This will depend upon the electrode array that was selected, the depth that the array was inserted, the fluid inside your inner ear and a whole host of factors that are unique to you as an individual."

After a short pause to let that sink in, Susan resumed, "During your operation Dr. Richardson inserted a thin wire that we call an electrode array into your inner ear. This wire is a single cable with 22 electrodes coiled together. Each of the 22 electrodes has a gold-plated contact that is designed to make physical contact with the auditory nerve. The auditory nerve extends along the coil of the inner ear and the electrodes have different lengths in order to contact the nerve at different points. On the opposite end of the electrode array each electrode is wired to the chip that was implanted under your skin. That chip is wired to an induction coil/magnet which was also implanted under your skin. Those three components, the electrode array, the chip and the induction coil/magnet are the internal parts of your cochlear implant. Today you will receive the external parts of your cochlear implant after I configure the external processor."

"Right," Blake said.

Sitting in the chair farthest away from Susan, Emily moved closer to Blake, intent on catching every word.

"Before we configure sound levels for the processor, we need to verify which electrodes are functioning and which are not. All of your electrodes may be working or only some of them may be working depending upon how the electrode array is positioned inside of your inner ear." She paused briefly, "Sometimes an electrode will fail due to mechanical reasons but it is unlikely for all 22 of them to malfunction."

Listening with fierce concentration, Blake raised a finger to break in. He was loosening up by degrees as she talked, the need to process information helping him to gain a semblance of control. "Any possibility that I won't be able to hear some frequencies if several electrodes are not making contact with the auditory nerve?"

"I can utilize whichever electrodes are functional to send a complete range of frequencies to your auditory nerve. We may use all 22 electrodes or we may find that only 15 electrodes are functioning and just use those. As we move forward, I will need you to help me determine which electrodes are better for which frequencies."

Blake displayed a puzzled expression, causing Susan to back up, "We'll come back to that later if necessary, for now please be prepared to give me feedback on what you are hearing."

Emily broke in with a frown, "If you only have 15 working electrodes how does that not significantly affect the end result?"

"Our brains have a tremendous ability to adapt," Susan replied. "We are replacing approximately 20,000 hair cells with 22 electrodes. The real miracle is that the brain can use 22 electrodes in place of 20,000 hair cells. If it has to make do with 15 electrodes it will do so."

She paused for emphasis, "The human brain has the biggest capacity for adjustment in this entire process and that is why we encourage our patients to practice with their implant as much as they can. An implant supplies a finite range of inputs. Your brain, by comparison, has unlimited processing power to interpret those inputs."

"Use it or lose it, huh?" Blake spoke up, working his way back to normality. His engineering background was kicking in and the wheels were turning as he started to evaluate his options. *This is it,* he thought. *I am NOT wasting time obsessing about hallucinations or physical anomalies.*

"Exactly," Susan replied. "You don't go fishing with one lure and you shouldn't receive an implant without expecting to practice different listening scenarios."

"He'll practice," Emily piped up. "The computer is waiting as we speak."

"Good!" Susan nodded in approval, "After we establish parameters regarding sound levels and frequencies I will set up the programs for different listening situations. We can install up to four programs on your processor." She began to describe them with Blake listening closely. "Cochlear provides a catchall program for most listening environments, another for music, one for noisy locations and one that dampens the rear microphone in favor of the front microphone. That last program is called 'Focus'."

"To summarize, you will have four programs and they are called 'Everyday', 'Music', 'Noise' and 'Focus'."

"How do I switch between them?" Blake asked.

"That's on the remote control which I will show you later this morning."

Emily and Blake both nodded in unison, two cats perched on the windowsill. Blake had prepared a list of items to query Susan about, but he could tell that this was going to be an intense morning and figured that he better pick his spots carefully. For the time being he was content to sit back and listen.

Susan kept on going, "I will configure the setting for ambient noise, which is called 'scan,' the setting for wind noise, which is called 'wind', and we will adjust those at your next visit after you gain experience with them. Some patients like having them and some don't."

"I want to hear everything!" Blake emphasized.

Susan nodded her head in acknowledgement, "Sometimes people ask for less."

"Not me," Blake responded.

"People have different ideas about what they consider desirable. My job is to customize the implant for you so that you get the most benefit from it."

Blake sat back in his chair, analyzing what he had learned. Physical distractions had faded into the background. His mind was going a mile a minute trying to put the pieces together so that he could walk out of today's appointment with the best setup possible. At some point he would double check his list, but for now he waited to see what Susan would do.

Susan nudged the Cochlear suitcase with a foot, "We are also going to go through the contents of the case that Cochlear provides. You have some user manuals in there that I am going to review rather quickly because I would rather focus our time on adjusting your implant rather than talking about procedures which you can read later."

"I already downloaded the manuals and read them," Blake offered.

"Excellent!" Susan answered, flashing a smile. "I wish all my patients did that much preparation!"

Clasping her hands together, Susan said, "As you can see we have an ambitious agenda. There are other concepts that I will introduce as we go but talking about them at this point may prove to be a case of too much too soon. By the time we are done today your heads will be spinning. Are there questions before we proceed?"

Blake turned to Emily who shook her head in response. He returned to Susan and replied, "Let's do it." His heart began to beat faster, but this time he felt better about it.

Blake wanted to hear today, right now. He could sense a pressure building in his chest and was sure that if the implant worked tears would be making an appearance. It wasn't possible to hold in that much emotion, no matter how practiced he was. The joy would be a thousand times stronger than any rage, and in the face of its power he would no doubt be helpless. Flashing back to the day when he almost lost control in front of George and Angela, Blake resigned himself to the fact that he was going to be at the mercy of his emotions, whether he liked it or not.

It's too much, anymore.

He watched Susan with a mixture of anticipation and apprehension. Sunshine came through the window to create golden highlights in her hair, and those rays that slipped on past illuminated her desk in a shower of light. His processor lay on its side, the grey finish sparkling with promise. Blake licked his lips. The tunnel was gone and in its place were three people lined up at the starting blocks.

Showtime.

Susan picked up his processor and they broke from position.

"This is your processor, grey, as requested." She held it up in the air, acknowledging Emily with a glance. "I am going to show you how the assembly goes together so that you can replace parts if the need arises." Working efficiently, Susan connected one end of a short cable to the processor and the other end of the cable to the coil. Holding the assembly out for their inspection, she said, "Next we connect the rechargeable battery to the processor and add a magnet to the coil. We often refer to the coil and magnet as either the magnet or the coil since they work together as a unit."

Snapping the rechargeable battery onto the processor, Susan then screwed a small magnet into the center of the coil. Holding everything out for them to observe, she let the assembly dangle from her hands while describing it. "Now as you can see we have the processor and its removable battery connected by a short 3" cable to a 1" diameter coil that has a magnet screwed in the center. These are the external parts of your implant." Blake observed that all the pieces were the same grey color. The processor, rechargeable battery, coil and magnet were painted in grey epoxy with a shiny finish, and the cable was covered with a rubberized coating in grey.

Blake came in closer, "Not that big, even with the battery."

"Similar to your hearing aid. A little heavier, but not by much. This earhook on the processor hangs on your ear while this outside coil/magnet gets placed over the internal coil/magnet which is located under your skin." Susan manipulated the equipment in the air as she spoke, showing the two of them how it was going to fit on his head. "At this point, Simon, I need to place this on your head, but before I do that, please remove the hearing aid from your left ear." Her eyes addressed him with reassurance, "You will be reading my lips for the next part."

Blake laughed, confident that he could read Susan's lips from now until the end of time. Surprised that he was starting to relax and enjoy himself, he slipped his aid off in one smooth motion before turning to Emily. "Guess you can throw this out now!" Emily took his hearing aid and depositing it in a case brought for that exact purpose, returned her attention to Susan, anticipation covering her face.

Taking hold of an audio cable, Susan plugged one end into the bottom of his processor. It was a long cable, approximately nine feet. Gathering its length in one hand, she moved to stand in front of him, reaching around his head to his right side, hooking the processor on his ear, followed by hovering the outside magnet over the internal magnet until the two magnets attracted each other and came together. They connected with a soft snap, creating a sensation of pressure where the skin was trapped between them. Blake could barely feel her touch as he sat motionless, receiving his equipment. She draped the wire around his shoulder, making sure that there was plenty of slack to avoid pulling on his ear, her hands moving swiftly and lightly to accomplish their tasks, returning to her desk to plug the other end of the cable into her computer.

After she was done, he patted the outside magnet with his hand. It was an alien appendage affixed to his scalp, a button of technology in grey steel. He traced the rubberized cable back to the processor, running his finger along the smooth finish of its case. Blake turned toward Emily to find her watching in fascination, an odd expression appearing on her face as she evaluated his apparatus.

"Good thing that internal magnet wasn't installed upside down!" he said with a grin.

Before either of them could respond he queried Susan with a question that sprang into his head. "How do I keep the outside magnet from breaking the skin? I don't have much hair up there."

"Excellent question!" Susan commented. "Obviously, an impact to that area has the potential to cause trauma and break the skin. Regular rubbing on the exterior magnet, from a baseball cap for example, can also stress the skin held between the two magnets. You do have to be careful."

She took a second magnet from a box on her desk. "Here, the magnet has a number stamped on it." Susan held out her hand to Blake and Emily so that they could inspect the tiny device gripped between her fingers. The magnet was a cylinder approximately 3/8" long and 1/8" in diameter with the number two stamped upon one end. On the sides of the cylinder were threads covering half of its length, the surfaces coated in grey epoxy with a shiny finish.

"We have the ability to control the strength of the magnet so that it is strong enough to keep the coil from falling off your head, but not so strong as to cause the skin to break down. Cochlear makes five different magnets with strengths from one to five. I start my patients out with a three and then go up or down from there as necessary. If an intermediate strength is required, then we make that adjustment by screwing the magnet further into the coil or further out of the coil."

"This is starting to get complicated!" Emily interrupted.

Susan's lips pinched together, "Yes, and this is the easy part!"

"Now I feel dumb!" Emily commented.

"It's OK," Susan assured her. "Think how confusing it gets for patients who try to navigate through this by themselves. Your support will prove to be invaluable!" She paused to flash an appreciative smile at Emily.

"Now I need to run some diagnostics and verify which electrodes are working. Simon, please sit quietly until I'm finished."

Blake and Emily sat side by side in silence watching Susan tapping away at her keyboard. After a few minutes, Blake shifted his gaze to the window where the sky exhibited a vibrant blue. Bare branches stuck up in the air, sending him back to the days of his childhood when he would be cast aside, left to his own devices and imagination. A recurring fantasy was to imagine that the bare branches of winter were actually roots, and that there was a completely different world underground where the same trees were in full foliage. Then it would reverse each year, becoming winter in one place and summer in the other.

No less a fantasy than being able to hear.

Ten minutes went by, then fifteen, Susan alternately tapping on her keyboard and scrolling her mouse. All her attention was concentrated on her computer screen. Blake watched her working, hopeful that whatever spell she was weaving would grant him entrance to the hearing world, contemplating how the physical body could be so unappreciated yet so miraculous.

When we take our lives and gifts for granted are we really living? Isn't that another form of death? I'm afraid my life will be destroyed if this doesn't work, but is it worse to have such a gift and not be mindful of its blessings?

He was jolted from his meditations by Susan taking her hands from her computer and turning to face him. She was displaying a satisfied expression that stoked his speculations, her next words confirming his hopes. "Simon, you have 22 electrodes operational, which is a great start, and we are ready to calibrate your T and C levels." Blake mentally pumped his fist.

There was no opportunity to celebrate though because Susan kept going.

Sliding a ruler onto the desk where he could reach out and touch it, she began another spiel. "We have five dots on this ruler that are labeled 'intolerable', 'painful', 'uncomfortable', 'comfortable', and 'insignificant'. These dots are for you to indicate how you feel when we set your C levels, which are used to set the upper range of volume for each frequency." Blake took a few seconds to inspect the five dots on the ruler, looking back up when he was finished.

Regaining his attention, Susan continued, "I am also going to set your T levels, which we call threshold levels. T levels are soft sounds, the sounds that you can barely hear. We set T and C levels for each frequency, then use the range between them to create a map of the sound levels available to you. That's where the term 'mapping' comes from.

Mapping also includes adjustments to additional settings such as rate and pulse width."

Blake gave Emily a sideways glance. "My turn to get confused!" he said ruefully.

"I'm sorry," Susan said. "Some of my patients ask me to repeat this every time they come in. Others eventually stop asking, but it's obvious that they still don't understand." She paused to wait for the two of them. "Questions?"

"Gotta be easier than the testing booth," Blake grinned. "Can I have some whiskey while we do this?"

"You're the first to ask," Susan responded, her professional demeanor softening. "But if I can't have wine, then you don't get whiskey!"

"Say, that's right. I remember seeing a picture of you in the paper at some wine tasting down in OTR."

"Just dabbling, but I do enjoy a glass of wine!" Susan pushed her hair back, allowing them a glimpse of another dimension.

Emily relaxed, listening to the interchange. The atmosphere created by Susan was fostering a team effort, with the three of them working side by side on a common task. Victory would mean different things to each of them, and if the activation was successful, its significance would be magnified with the passing of each day.

Susan turned to her computer and analyzed the screen, followed by swiveling back to face Blake. "We are going to do T levels first. What you are going to hear in your processor is a series of beeps, three at a time, each series of beeps identical. I want you to raise a finger for each beep that you detect." She raised her own hand to demonstrate. "Starting with a fist, you extend a finger for each beep, thumb first, index finger second and middle finger third. Then close your hand back to a fist and wait for the next series. Eventually the sounds will get so low that you won't hear anything."

She added more explanation, "You will encounter lower and lower volumes for each frequency until I determine your threshold for each one. I also randomly switch between frequencies to prevent patients from figuring out a pattern and skewing the results."

"Got it," Blake answered. He waited in his chair, conscious of the processor hanging over his ear, the wire strung across his back. Seconds ticked off, at least ten if not 15, and his fragility was such that he started to assume the worst. Susan was fully engaged with her scrolling and tapping, causing him to question whether the testing had already begun without him knowing.

Is it working or what!!?

His eyes drilled into Susan, willing something to happen, and he was rewarded by her meeting his gaze. "OK, Simon, we are ready to start."

Shoot! Blake exploded internally. *You took that long to push a button? I'm dying here!!*

His reaction was cut short by a blast of "Beep! Beep! Beep!" loud as a foghorn and so startling that he missed lifting a finger. Blake caught up by raising two fingers on the second beep, finishing off by raising the third and final finger with the last. He raised his eyebrows in delight, checking with Susan for confirmation and then switching his head toward Emily to give her a wink.

Susan nodded in approval, a single finger tapping a single key while Emily watched, spellbound. The unique aura of technological magic suffused the room, promises blossoming through the air.

Another series of beeps came through the processor, but this time Blake was ready and he flipped his thumb out immediately. The next two fingers followed, spaced the same amount of time apart, about the 'One' in One Mississippi.

Inside he was cheering. *Houston, we have sound!!*

The beeps continued, Blake flipping out his fingers and Susan tapping her keys. He felt a surge of pure joy run through him. Blake was thrilled to detect tonal differences in the sounds. It may have been his imagination, but he thought that Susan tapped at her keyboard before the next series dropped in volume. She was smart to introduce the randomness because the beeps went low, then high, then low until his natural tendency to find patterns was thoroughly defeated.

I got this, I got sound, I got a new life coming round! Lalalalalalalala!!!!!

Blake was happy, practically bursting. A swell of exuberance was building up, one that was spreading to include every cell in his body. *This is good, we're not anywhere near done yet, but this is good, good, good!*

As the testing progressed, the beeps became lower and lower in volume until Blake found it necessary to hone his focus to an intense concentration. He closed his eyes and rested one hand on Susan's desk so that she could easily watch his fingers. It seemed that he was getting repeats now and then. Occasionally he would miss the first beep because it was so low, catching up on the second beep by raising two fingers. The pattern of tones echoed in his head, becoming phantoms of perception. Once or twice he started flipping out his fingers only to become aware that there were no beeps at all, just his imagination going wild.

Finally there was an extended silence and Blake opened his eyes to find Susan busily working her keyboard.

My fairy godmother has a computer.

Blake looked at his wife, wanting to share his success. She nodded excitedly, neither of them putting their thoughts into words, unwilling to tempt misfortune.

Beeps are a start; I'll need more than that though. The euphoria began to fade as Blake considered his progress, the silence reminding him that there was a long way to go.

His attention was captured by Susan tapping on the desk with one finger. "The next task we are going to perform, Simon, is setting your C levels, which define the upper ranges that you can hear. T levels are the low levels, they define the minimum levels of current being sent to your electrode array. As you can probably figure out, the chip sends more current with louder sounds, and our goal is to avoid sending a signal so strong that it overloads the auditory nerve."

Emily broke in, "What happens if the signal is too strong?"

"Two things," replied Susan. "If we overstimulate the auditory nerve, Simon may experience anything from mild twinges to a painful stabbing in the presence of loud noises. If the current from the implanted chip is excessive, the signal may leak out past the auditory nerve and affect the facial nerve, causing his face muscles to twitch."

"Ouch!" Emily was shocked at what she was hearing. Blake raised an eyebrow, his expression begging for more explanation.

"It's something that we watch closely," Susan reassured them. "Facial twitches show up right away in the office, less so for twinges and pain. If you develop a problem, contact me and I will fix it for you the same day. In the meantime, taking off the processor or lowering your volume with the remote control is a temporary solution."

Blake swiveled to face his wife, "If I do get facial twitches then you'll know I can hear you!"

"Funny," Emily responded. "Laughing inside." Her sour expression encouraged him to drop dead, the faintest of flashes detectable behind her irises.

Susan continued, "Ok, Simon, we will run through the beeps again, except this time they will be going up in volume each time. As before, I will cycle through each frequency so that you hear each one at different volumes. Ready?"

"Born that way." Blake answered. One of his biggest fears had been a complete failure of the implant. That hurdle was gone and he was having fun. The testing booth was out of the picture, all 22 electrodes were functional and the implant was pumping sound into his brain. *So far, so good.*

"I want you to place your finger on the dot that describes how you are feeling."

"OK." Blake rested four fingers on the edge of the desk, using all of them but his thumb, ready to reach out and tag the appropriate dot. He tapped a finger on the desk, anxious to begin.

This time there was no waiting or maybe he felt more relaxed. In any event it wasn't long before his senses were assaulted with a sustained "Beeeeeeeep". It lasted a full three seconds, time enough to reach out and place his index finger upon the dot labeled 'comfortable'.

He switched his eyes from the dot to Susan, catching a nod of approval. While he watched, she clicked her mouse and as she did, another sustained beep came his way. *Love it!!* He rejoiced, tapping his finger on the same dot.

Before he could take his finger away another beep followed almost immediately. *Hmmm,* he mused, *not much difference there,* so he lifted his finger up from the 'comfortable' dot only to put it down in the same place.

Susan appeared perplexed at his choice but continued without commenting.

During the next three minutes Blake rated each beep, but instead of moving past 'comfortable' to the dot labeled 'uncomfortable', he would raise his finger up to put it back down in a location fractionally different than before with the result that he never wound up more than halfway between 'comfortable' and 'uncomfortable'. The 'intolerable' and 'painful' dots were out of the question, and 'uncomfortable' was a stretch, making him wonder what Susan was thinking.

His curiosity was answered when Susan took both hands off the keyboard to rest them in her lap and said, "Simon, are you not having any problem with the sound levels?" Her eyes bore directly into his with a mixture of professional concern and maybe, he thought, a bit of wariness.

"They're fine," he answered. "I can distinguish different frequencies, but as far as the volume levels go, no problem. It's a little loud, nothing that bothers me though."

"Hmm," she replied, "I have taken the volume levels up fairly high, even exceeded the levels of some recipients that have had their implant for a full year, and you are my only patient who has not indicated discomfort with higher volumes on activation day."

"Does that mean something is wrong?"

"I don't believe so," Susan said thoughtfully. "It does mean that if we stay at these settings then you will be starting out with more power and probably more sounds than the typical recipient."

"Works for me!" Blake could not stop himself from grinning. One item on his list was to ask Susan for the highest settings possible, and that one could be crossed off. *Yes!*

"I'm not trying to be tricky," he continued. "I don't have a problem with the volume at those levels."

"All right," Susan came back. "We'll continue on this way. It's more difficult to know where your limits should be if you stick to the lower dots, but I can work around it." She added, "The processor has a feature that clamps down on loud noises in order to prevent damaging current being sent down the electrode array to the auditory nerve. Even if I do set your volume levels high there is no physical danger involved. The issue is primarily one of comfort."

"Comfort is where I'm at." Blake blurted out in his excitement.

"Yes, well, your experience may be different outside of the office. Please keep that in mind." Susan returned to her keyboard with a renewed focus while Blake sat there wondering if he had overstepped with his flippant comment. He felt a faint flush on the back of his neck and was relieved that her attention was directed toward her computer.

Smarty Pants.

Before he could chastise himself any further the sounds resumed, Blake welcoming the diversion. The beeps were still short of 'uncomfortable' and Blake bent his head down to apply himself.

Nothing changed on his end for the remainder of the calibration, Blake sticking to the area between 'comfortable' and 'uncomfortable'. The beeps ended, Blake resting in his chair as Susan's fingers flew across her keyboard. Left in silence, Blake relived the soft sounds, the loud sounds, the different frequencies and had a hard time containing his excitement. He inspected his hands, now clasped together in his lap. There was a ballooning of hope inside of him, an elation that he had taken pains to hold at arm's length, but it was rising up, threatening to break loose with or without his consent.

Susan interrupted his reverie with a single finger tapping the desk. She was holding up a slim device that was 5" long by 1 1/2" wide and 1/4" thick. It was finished in black matte with six pushbuttons located below a display screen that was 1" square. "This is your remote control for the processor. I have already loaded the four programs into your processor and am going to explain how to operate them with the remote."

While Blake and Emily inspected the remote control, Susan continued to speak, "Your four programs are named 'Everyday', 'Music', 'Noise' and 'Focus'. Each of them has a dedicated button, you press the button and the screen displays which program you have selected." She pointed at the display screen as she toggled between programs. "When you leave here, I want you to switch between the programs in different listening environments to determine which of them you prefer to use in different situations."

"No problem," Blake responded, the change in topic tempering his excitement. "I was wondering if I would need to haul that thing around or not."

"At least in the beginning," Susan said. "It has a rechargeable battery that lasts about a week." Positioning the remote control in her hand, she kept going. "I am going to cover two more functions of the remote, leaving the rest for you to read about on your own."

"The first is volume, which is easy to understand. Volume is regulated from 0 to 10, the higher number corresponding to a higher sound level. Higher sound levels mean more current is being delivered to the implant, but it's easier to think of volume instead of current." Susan used the pushbuttons to adjust the volume up and down while Blake and Emily watched. With volume set at 6, the display screen on the remote showed a stack of ten horizontal bars, the six bottom bars in blue and the four bars above them in white. Above the stack of horizontal bars the number six was also displayed.

"Neat!" Blake commented. "Why can't I hear?"

"Because your processor is waiting on my computer. In a couple of minutes I will activate your processor so that it can receive sound from its own microphones."

"Then I will be able to hear?" Blake queried Susan.

"Then the processor will take in sound from its two microphones, run the sound through an algorithm that converts the sound to electrical pulses, send those electrical pulses through the external cable to the external coil where the pulses create an induction loop with the internal coil that allows the signals to be received by the internal chip from which they are sent down the electrode array to contact the auditory nerve at the 22 electrode locations. After that your body takes over and the pulses are transmitted to the brain."

"Oh."

Susan pinned him to the chair with a penetrating gaze, "What you need to remember is that your brain is accustomed to translating movements from 20,000 hair cells into sound. It has zero experience translating electrical pulses into sound. The processor configuration which I am setting up today will give your brain access to better hearing. Understanding the input from your processor will take practice in order to train your brain to convert the signals into something that makes sense."

"Ahh," Blake felt himself deflating. His outlook had reversed 180 degrees, ending any sense of celebration.

Susan regarded him with a professional calm. "My intention is not to be discouraging. Your brain is capable of interpreting the signal properly, but I need you to realize that it will take effort on your part."

"Got it," Blake answered. "Anything worthwhile and all that." He straightened up in his chair and nodded ruefully. *Nothing I didn't already know.*

"One last bit on sensitivity and we are ready," Susan said. Pushing another button on the remote control, she showed them the sensitivity adjustment which was scaled from 0 to 24. It was also displayed in bars, same as the volume. Moving the sensitivity adjustment up and down, she said, "Think of sensitivity as a sphere around your head that captures sound. If you are listening to sounds close to you then you want to use a low sensitivity so that you are capturing a small sphere of sound in your immediate vicinity. Sounds outside that smaller sphere are partially ignored by the processor. Listening to something farther away requires a higher sensitivity that pulls in sound from a bigger sphere around you."

Emily had been sitting quietly, but now she spoke up, "So listening in the kitchen requires a small sensitivity for a small sphere of sound because people are close together but listening to a sermon at church requires a higher sensitivity for a larger sphere of sound to capture what the preacher is saying from farther away."

"Correct."

Blake chimed in, "Whoa! Different programs, different volumes, different sensitivities."

"You have quite a bit of flexibility," Susan placed the remote back on her desk and stood up. "I encourage you to take advantage of it. Any questions before I activate your processor?"

"Plenty, but the biggest one is whether it works." Blake sucked in a breath, his mind filled with an image of himself standing in front of a high striker carnival game where the goal was to swing a mallet hard enough to ring a bell at the top of a column. There was nothing left to do but take a swing and hope the pulses turned into words. He prayed they would. Blake had talked to recipients who had been able to understand on their first day and to others who said activation was a disaster. It was difficult to know whether some people made their own luck or whether some people were unlucky. He was prepared to practice till he dropped, but he didn't know if he could handle failure despite his practicing.

"Let's find out." Susan approached him to take the processor off his ear, pulling the magnet gently away from his head until it detached, leaving her holding the processor and magnet in her hand. Taking a battery out of her pocket she held it up with the comment, "Fresh battery" before swapping it out. Then she returned the processor to its position hanging on his ear, hovering the outside magnet over the internal magnet until the two of them snapped together.

As the magnets made contact Blake felt them click into position, the last step on the last mile of a journey that he never thought he would take. He went motionless, his mind blank, his body still. Beside him Emily sat poised on the edge of her chair.

They both tracked Susan's return to her desk, where she sat down to place one finger on the button of her mouse, the scene branding itself in Blake's memory.

Susan's finger moved then, and with the click of her mouse a kaleidoscope exploded inside his head, birthing more kaleidoscopes in the milliseconds that followed.

The background erupted with a multifaceted presence that he wanted to reach out and touch as the dull roar of white noise splintered into an assortment of vibrations, chimes and snaps.

He breathed in through his nose with a robotic trill, making a connection between his intake of breath and its associated sound.

One foot shifted to produce a series of beeps and clicks. At the same time he smoothed down his pants to create whispers of static that ebbed and flowed with the touch of his hands.

This is the hearing world?

His mind was being assaulted from all directions as Blake struggled to grasp the universe of sound exploding into existence around him. It was beyond description, impossible to comprehend. Catapulted through a wormhole, he was flung onto the surface of an unfamiliar planet, landing on his knees before Lucy in the Sky with Diamonds. The thought came to him that his brain had a lot to decipher.

Blake's attention was drawn to a harsh cadence of clicks and whistles coming from the direction of Susan. With a shock he realized that she was talking to him. Her lips were moving and he understood what she was saying only because he was reading her lips. The speech itself came across as an alien garble. She was taking pains to speak slowly, and as she did, he could tell that the garbling matched up with the rhythm of her lips, each word being its own combination of unintelligibility.

Some of the sounds repeated as she spoke, encouraging him to focus on making a connection between specific sounds and specific words. As a check he glanced away and the clicks and whistles degenerated into random noises, any pretense of rhythm gone. Without lip reading he was lost. He watched her, struggling to make sense of the gibberish, knowing that it was supposed to translate to words comprised of different syllables. The language on this planet made no sense whatsoever. Blake eyed her lips with the intensity of a jungle cat stalking its prey, afraid to look away, caught between wonder and a fear that this was all there was going to be.

Then his synapses skyrocketed into the galaxy, taking his breath away.

In the midst of his concentration, Blake felt a doorway fling itself wide open inside his head and discovered that he was suddenly making a connection between the sounds coming from Susan's mouth and the words they were supposed to represent. It happened independently of time, faster than the speed of light, and he was off and running. Her voice snapped into specific units, forming words organized in coherent thoughts and complete sentences. The quality of sound was different from that produced by hearing aids, very clear and precise. He was reading Susan's lips in a foreign dialect, one that made perfect sense, a divine language that restored comprehension of the spoken word to his life in the space of mere seconds.

It's working…

Struck dumb with awe, Blake listened to her tell him that she could adjust the programming if he needed to hear less.

Blinking once, then twice, Blake was overtaken by a tidal wave rising up to topple any resistance, leaving no option save surrender. Digging out his hankie he attempted to wipe his eyes, jamming the cloth into his face, knowing that it was a lost cause if there ever was one. Mocking him with its power, the yearning that he had held back for so many years broke free to sweep him away, leaving him exposed to the joy of answered prayer. His throat constricted so that it was impossible to speak, and he yielded to a massive wave of redemption.

A shell of darkness that had ensconced itself deep inside his psyche shattered to release a fire from his center that expanded until it touched each individual cell with its healing purge. He could feel absolution coursing through his being, burning away years of mental angst like flames devouring dry grass. The bad things were outmatched and they knew it, slinking away in shame and defeat.

Emily and Susan observed his reaction, exchanging glances. Susan offered a small shrug in response to Emily's silent question. She wasn't ready to comment one way or another and the office fell quiet as time drew out to infinity. Ambiguity was hanging in the air, a red velvet curtain preventing the two women from seeing past its folds.

Blake continued mopping up his face, a task that he figured might drag on, while giving silent thanks for Pamela's refusal to sell him more hearing aids. He was suspended inside a bubble of calm, filled with a peace that made time meaningless. A second out of body experience came teasingly close as his perception drifted upward to adopt a bird's eye view of the office with its three occupants. From his perch above Blake saw himself nod his head and croak out a weak attempt at speaking, "I can hear. It's amazing."

The statement was so inadequate that he winced inside as he uttered it. *What else is there to say? It's happening so quickly that I can't explain it to myself. Words take too long to express and some of the words I need don't exist in this dimension. Did I just learn a new language in seconds? Is there even a way to describe that properly?*

Looking at Emily he made a second effort, knowing that he could only give her a fraction of the story. "It's working." The two words signified a sea change, triggering possibilities that danced through his imagination. He continued, struck by how alien his voice sounded, trying to move past the otherworldliness of it all. "I have no idea how, but my brain must have switched to a different level and Susan's voice started making sense."

"Excellent," Susan replied. "Exactly how much are you comprehending?"

"It took about ten seconds," Blake informed her. "After that you sounded like a duck that learned English. It started with clicks and whistles and then I could understand you." The act of describing his transformation helped bring him down from a transcendental high, back to the mundane surroundings of the office.

"Oohhhh!" Emily grabbed him by the arm. "That's so exciting! I can't believe it!!" Her eyes glistened and flashed, multiple emotions competing for expression.

"I have to read lips, but the sounds are translating into words."

"Congratulations, you're one of the lucky ones!" Susan said with a smile. The question had been answered, in the best way possible. She had known that he would hear something, just not what it would be or the speed at which he would adapt. *It's such a wonderful gift,* she rejoiced. *When it happens.* Happy to be out of the danger zone, she said, "Let's talk about practicing."

Blake received her affirmation with joy, interpreting the words as final confirmation that surgery had indeed gone according to plan. His thoughts gleefully abandoned the darkness, leaving it behind to swirl in futility, a devil needing another host. *I can move on.* A sense of peacefulness brought him to an unfamiliar place. He thought to himself that it was going to be a long time before anything bothered him. The way he felt now, if someone rear ended his car on the way home, he could shrug it off, no problem.

Right. Let's not get crazy here.

He addressed Susan with his typical deadpan, "How much should I do?" Calm on the outside, inside he was building up for a primal scream lasting forever.

"As much as you can stand. I tell my patients that an hour a day for the first six months is a good start. In a few minutes we'll discuss some of the ways in which you can do that." Susan's voice held a reverberation, similar to what came out of a megaphone. The words were clear, but they were different from what he was used to hearing. Blake couldn't decide if her voice sounded robotic, tinny or if she was Minnie Mouse on helium. "It's important to wear the implant all of your waking hours. If possible, try to keep your hearing aid off for at least three weeks so that your brain does not attempt to use it as a crutch."

"I'll try." Blake addressed Emily, "Hide that thing from me."

"Easily done," she said, with a glint in her eye. Emily's voice resembled Susan's, but he thought that he could catch a slight difference, some small note on the edge of perception.

Susan stood up to approach him, "Let me disconnect the cable and turn you loose."

"What else is left?" Emily interjected.

"A few items," Susan responded. "The good news is that we are ahead of the game since Simon can understand us, even if he is reading lips." She reached out one hand to remove the processor and coil from Blake's head, plunging him into a familiar quiet. The silence was a jarring reminder of his old existence. A sense of loss fell over him, and he wished that she would hurry it up.

"Here." Susan unplugged her cable and held the device out to him in the palm of her hand. "This is yours now. I have set your volume at 6 and your sensitivity at 12."

Blake gingerly removed the processor from her palm, holding it in one hand while studying its configuration. Then he took hold of the processor with his index finger and his thumb, trapping the coil in his palm with his little finger and hooked the earhook over his ear. The coil was dangling off to the side and he stumbled through a momentary clumsiness until he ran his fingers along the short cable to arrive at the coil. Moving the coil towards his implanted magnet, he was surprised to have it jump out of his hand to seat itself against his skin with a soft impact.

No science fiction movie was ever this cool.

In the blink of an eye the two magnets built an electronic bridge that connected the processor signal to the electrode array, stimulating the auditory nerve to send information down its neural highway. Months later, when Blake was trying to explain the sensation, he likened it to stepping into a rainbow.

Silence yielded its grip to the music of life, expressed in a multitude of ways. The air came alive with clicks, whistles, vibrations and chimes, all of them signifying something different, a playground of sound that shot a ripple of exhilaration through his chest. He reached out to unfold the invitation that awaited.

Simon Blake online.

A huge grin spread across his face as he turned to Emily in delight, "I can get used to this!"

Emily returned his look of triumph, the expression on her face saying it all, offering her fist up for a celebratory bump. The day was a glorious success, far beyond the reach of their imaginations. Excited for her husband, she freed herself to open the doorway to her own dreams.

"What now?" he queried Susan.

In response she reached down to lift the Cochlear suitcase up onto her desk. Unzipping the lid, she flipped it open and said, "We need to review what's in here."

Obviously familiar with the contents, she proceeded to go through the suitcase with an expeditious flow as she put her hand inside to pull out a battery charger and two additional batteries. One battery was identical to the unit already on his processor and the other was a bit smaller. "You have three rechargeable batteries. Carry at least one spare with you and make sure to charge all three at night. Cochlear also gives you the option to use disposable batteries." Susan held up a battery pack that came apart to accept two disposable batteries, showing him how to insert the batteries and put it back together.

"There are some manuals in here, but you said that you downloaded them already so they should not be a surprise to you."

"Yes."

"We have spare microphone covers in case yours get dirty, a couple of earhooks in case you break one, and a case to keep the implant safe at night. Another item is the phone clip which is used to Bluetooth your cell phone directly into your implant. After a week or so you may want to try using the phone." As she made the comment her eyebrows came up in an encouraging lift, making Blake wonder how long it took most patients.

"Got it," Blake said. As far as he was concerned phone calls represented the enemy. *Texting suits me just fine.*

"The last item is a computer program," Susan said, pulling a CD out of the suitcase and holding it up for emphasis. "It contains six types of practice sessions and 20 levels of proficiency for each session. One of the sessions is listening to sentences, one is single syllable words, one is vowels, one is consonants, one is for environmental sounds and the last is music. Each session is structured so that you listen to sounds and then attempt to identify what you heard. This may be the most useful item. In order to get the most from your implant you need to take advantage of the tutoring sessions on the CD."

"I can do that." Burning with urgency, Blake didn't need any prodding, intending to start this afternoon as soon as he got home. He was awash in wonder at the sounds coming through his implant. *I'm walking out of this office able to hear!* A second chance was there for the taking, the biggest do-over of his life. The exhilaration of the last few minutes had strengthened his resolve to push himself to the next level, and the next level after that.

"That's the formal practice, but the more you practice the better it gets. Trying out books on tape, having someone read to you or listening to the radio are all beneficial. Some people try to listen to speech without reading lips, some people use captioned movies. Exposing yourself to different auditory sources improves your capabilities. You can try listening to music, but music normally takes a little longer to understand."

"Music isn't my thing." He remembered back in high school when his friends enjoyed playing the radio while cruising. It was a noisemaker to him, another complication. His friends though, were incapable of leaving the radio off, forcing him to suffer its interference.

"Some people have trouble with environmental sounds masking the sounds of speech. When you come back for your second mapping, we'll determine if that's an issue. That particular problem can be addressed by a change in your mapping or by practicing in a way that encourages your brain to ignore the competition from environmental sounds. Practicing with the CD using high levels of background noise or by yourself in noisy environments will make it easier for your brain to understand speech in the presence of noise."

"OK."

Susan continued, "The first year is the critical window for success. Don't slack off when you get better, work harder by making your practice more difficult. Increase the background noise level on the computer program or raise the volume of the TV while you are trying to listen to someone talking."

"OK."

"If there was a magic button that would help your brain to understand, I would use it. You are fortunate to get off to a fantastic start today, but that doesn't mean you can skip practicing. Those who practice do far better than those who don't."

As Susan talked Blake was amazed to realize that he could follow her without needing information repeated. Words rippled from her mouth to his brain in an effortless stream, giving him time to flip them up into the air and behind his back before sending them on for processing. It was necessary for him to read lips, but this was the easiest listening of his life, requiring a fraction of the effort he was accustomed to using. The day didn't have enough hours for him to ride this magical carousel of sound. He strolled along in time with her voice, pausing to peruse a dancing bear here, a unicorn there, wondering if he should climb up on the snow goose or continue down to the giant butterfly.

I never thought it could happen. Tears welled up as the magnitude of his change in fortune came rushing home.

Finishing with the suitcase, Susan put the contents back inside and zipped it up. Facing Blake, she said, "Remember to experiment with changing programs for different situations and try raising the volume."

"What about sensitivity?"

"You can adjust that also, but the implant will help you more if the signal delivered to the auditory nerve is stronger. Raising the volume delivers more current and a stronger signal to the auditory nerve. The stronger signal will make sounds louder and maybe create some discomfort."

Blake thought about what she was saying, wondering what it would take for him to object because he was hearing too much. *How is that a problem?*

"Once you get to the point where you are regularly using a higher volume, I can increase the strength of your baseline signal which will allow you to increase the volume even more. With increased power you will be hearing things that you can't even imagine today."

"Wow."

"In a year's time, today will seem like nothing," Susan said. "The combination of daily practice and additional mappings should boost your capabilities much higher."

"How many mappings will there be?"

"Three or four. Plan on coming back for your second mapping in one month."

Blake was determined to beat her schedule, thinking that he could max out the volume in a week and come back in two. *Probably better to wait and see.* He kept his mouth shut, resolving to turn the volume up with the remote.

I want to hear it all.

"This is so wonderful!" Emily exclaimed. "How can we ever thank you?"

"Helping someone is the only thanks that I need."

Susan rose from her chair to slide the Cochlear suitcase across to Emily. Standing in front of them she said, "Today was exceptional. Dr. Rickerson will be pleased to learn how well Simon did. Not everyone starts off so successfully."

Taking the hint, Blake and Emily stood up, Emily giving the suitcase an exploratory heft. Reaching out to shake Susan's hand, Blake said, "Thank you sounds so inadequate." He was holding back an urge to run and shout victory from the rooftop while simultaneously wanting to acknowledge a tremendous debt of gratitude to those involved in granting him this gift. From the researchers who invented his device to the technicians that built it, to the medical professionals involved in applying it, he owed them all a favor that was impossible to repay. Blake felt humbled by the fact that so many people had combined efforts to create such a difference in his life. Pamela's refusal to sell him another set of hearing aids, Mary Beth talking about her experience, so many individual actions cascaded in purpose to forge a new destiny for him. Standing in front of Susan, Blake's resolution to make the most of his implant kicked up a couple of notches. This miracle was bigger than himself, bigger than anyone who played a part. It was an example of the best humanity could offer.

"It's a lot to process for one day," Susan said. "Enjoy the weekend and contact me if you have any problems."

"Definitely." Blake was at a loss for words. Trains of thought were leaving the station one after the other, heading out to different destinations. He considered the people that only knew him as he was yesterday, evaluating potential changes in each relationship. *That's just part of it. What about people I haven't met yet?*

On another tack, if this morning was an indication of things to come, Blake could already identify an obligation to give back in return.

Then he started to wonder whether his peacefulness was here to stay or whether he was too ornery for it to stick.

He was confused about the speed of his adaptation, so much so that he was afraid it would vanish when he woke up tomorrow morning. *Has that ever happened? Can it disappear as fast as it materialized?*

Lacking focus, he made for the door, taking the return journey along the linoleum with Emily by his side. Lost in the future, Blake walked in silence, distracted by the clamor that chased him wherever he went. Emily tugged on his arm as they passed through the waiting room, a second version of the couple from this morning.

"How is it?" she asked.

"It's different. Robotic and tinny when someone speaks. Other noises are similar to bells and whistles with a few sounds that I can't begin to describe, snaps or chimes maybe."

"I can't believe it works!" she said. "We're talking. The first day!!"

He turned to meet her eyes, thinking how lucky he was. Emily more than anyone knew the rage that swirled inside of him, the futility of trying one more time only to fail miserably yet again. Staring past her shoulder at the possibilities that were opening up, he could see a light at the end of the tunnel offering an invitation to restore his life and relationships under his own terms, and his gaze returned to find her waiting for him. "I can't believe it either." *I never expected to hear like this.*

He clasped her hand with fierce energy, channeling his hopes and joy with a squeeze that branched off into a thousand tangents.

"Thanks for having my back all these years."

She shook her head slowly, the regret evident. "It kills me that I didn't understand how awful it was for you."

"Not your fault. I could have told you, but that's not my style." *Sad as that is.*

Arriving at the elevator without anyone else around, Emily went to push the button. "I'll get it," she said.

"OK."

She turned to him in wonder with a cry of delight, "Simon!"

Blake's face broke out with a broad smile and they both stood there with their mouths agape, speechless.

Just then the elevator opened behind her, about three quarters full, and they moved in to stand along the side wall. Blake leaned his head back where cold steel chilled his scalp. A woman across from him whispered to her companion while from above he could hear a hissing noise above the trapdoor. The doors slid shut with a metallic click. *Are all elevators this noisy?* With an audible lurch the elevator began its descent to the garage, Emily snaking an arm around his waist and he gathered her in closer.

It works. Thank you, God.

Chapter 9 – Rebirth

Descending to the second level of the parking garage, Blake and Emily exited the elevator to make their way out of a lobby that, with the exception of the elevator shaft, was constructed out of glass. Opening the door to enter a world of concrete, Blake cocked his head at the onslaught echoing off the hard surfaces. An automobile drove past them with its tires squealing in protest as it wheeled around the corner. He was startled at the screeching, wondering how tires could make so much noise and still maintain traction. *Wow!* he thought, watching the vehicle disappear. Gathering his coat against the frigidity of the garage, Blake headed in the direction of the car with Emily, drowning under a deluge of clicks, whistles and squeals.

"What's that zooming noise that comes and goes?" he asked Emily.

"Cars above and below us," she responded, pointing a finger up and down. Her voice was clear enough to register as a separate noise and reading her lips he could pick out the words, despite the competition from all around.

"This is incredible! I'm hearing a drone in the background, almost a vibration." *Wow!*

"That would be the exhaust fan in the garage." Emily's face displayed an amused expression at his excitement.

"Whoa!" Blake scanned the garage, seeking to associate sounds with their origins, spinning his head around and trying to make sense of the bombardment. Somewhere in the garage a horn beeped, causing his face to explode in a grin. "Hey! That must be an elephant passing gas!"

Grinning at her husband's rare display of innocence, Emily laughed in delight, "Yeah, this place has a ton of them!"

"Listen to this." They were at the car and Emily was holding out the key fob. She pressed a button, prompting the horn to honk twice and the parking lights to flash.

"That's obscene," Blake said with a laugh, drunk with exhilaration. He unlatched the door to enter the passenger side, pausing over the roof to meet a pair of hazel eyes that were dancing with happiness.

Blake was walking on air. Slipping into the freezing car, he ignored any discomfort from the hard seat. Dr. Rickerson and Dr. Archer claimed that there was no predicting the speed at which each recipient adapted, but it appeared that he was one of the fortunate ones, stoking his resolution to push himself to the max. *I want to be the fastest to hear the mostest.*

Burning to get home and begin rehabilitation, Blake's mind was consumed with the potential. *I wonder how the TV will sound? What about Mackenzie?* Some recipients commented that the amount of stimulation was excessive and that they needed to remove the processor to take a break. He wanted to hear as of yesterday and was willing to push himself in order to shorten his learning curve. When Emily activated the key fob there was a millisecond where the beeping from the horn lanced into his brain, but it disappeared as fast as it came, and he was determined to ignore it. *A little pain is ok by me if it gets me where I want to go. Susan said it was a matter of comfort and my comfort zone is where I hear the most.*

Emily started the car and he opened his mind to their progress, tracking the car up the ramp and out onto the street, trying to interpret each noise. Cracking the window he was inundated by a roar of confusion, but he reveled in the commotion. Blake closed his eyes, turning his focus inward.

"You ok?" Emily threw him a glance, tapping his knee before returning her attention to the road.

"Yeah, taking it all in." *How do you describe a reality you have never known?* "When we get home I'm going to practice first thing."

He kept his eyes closed for most of the drive home, attempting to track their journey, opening his eyes once or twice to see if he was correct about their location. It was a strategy he employed to avoid conversation, but now he tuned into the muddle, seeking to identify the thrumming and buzzing that accompanied their trip. Recognizing when Emily pulled in the driveway, he opened his eyes to see her smiling. "I'm so happy! It's our greatest gift since Mackenzie!" She sat in the driver's seat beaming at him. Her voice held a tinny quality, but to Blake it was heaven. The words came at him with the clearness of a bell and he wondered how soon it would be before he could listen without lip reading. *That would be sensational.* Outside the car a wintry blast was doing its best to validate the season, blowing leaves across the yard with savage energy.

Leaning closer he said, "Maybe tonight we'll have our easiest conversation since forever." He winked at her. "As long as you say something worth listening to!"

"Ha!" Emily retorted. "Big words for a newbie!"

They sat eye to eye, ensconced in a bubble of well-being until Blake broke it up by saying, "OK, time to practice." His eyes narrowed with purpose and he adopted a determined air. "It's showtime."

Getting out of the car, they moved toward the front door, a fierce wind chasing them up the sidewalk. Over the short distance the wind blew against his implant, drowning him in a hurricane of static. He tried shielding his implant with one hand, but the wind was not so easily defeated, chasing him to the house where he finally found refuge. Once inside he was gratified at the return of his hearing, taking the Cochlear suitcase from Emily to say, "Give me an hour or two."

"Good luck. I'll be in the kitchen."

Walking through the house was an adventure, his footsteps mixing in with a hum that he thought might be coming from the furnace and a distant buzz that could be an airplane outside. The constant racket put his imagination into overdrive. *I can see why people say this is overwhelming, but I love it!* He went down the hall to his own office, which was on the same side of the house as Emily's but in a different room, anxious to get started, his fingers fumbling with the zippers on the suitcase. *This is glorious! It's really working!*

Perusing the contents of the suitcase, Blake found the CD case tucked in its slot and pulled it out, flipping the case open and removing the disc with two fingers. Booting up his computer he sat there impatiently, the disc pinned between his fingers, waiting for the desktop to load. The computer finished its routine, displaying a pop-up notification from his email and he read a message from Mary Beth congratulating him on his activation and wishing him a successful day. She was also inviting him to the next Cochlear meeting for a presentation on accessories. *For sure,* he thought. *You can't keep me away. If it's this easy it would be a crime to disappear into the community without helping to spread the word.*

He began to install the program, the computer accepting the disc with an audible click and whirr. *We're in!* Blake figured he was good for two hours as a starting point and once the program finished its installation he got down to business.

Reviewing the program Blake saw that he was presented with a choice of sentences, words, vowels, consonants, music and environmental sounds. Figuring that he wasn't interested in the radio and didn't care about listening to the sounds from zoo animals or a fire truck, he ruled out the last two choices. That left four categories and he settled on sentences as the place to start. With sentences selected, the program displayed a blank screen labeled 'Step One' that lasted about seven seconds after which a new screen appeared with a list of four sentences. Blake was confused at first and then figured out the problem. *Maybe turn up the volume, dummy!* His normal practice was to keep the speakers on mute. *Guess that strategy isn't going to work anymore.* Tapping the key for speaker volume, Blake cranked it up to 100% and restarted his session. This time the blank screen was accompanied by an electronic voice blaring out nonsensical garbage followed by the appearance of four sentences in boxes with a prompt to select one of the four as the sentence that he heard. *Perfect – another version of the audiometric booth.* He shook his head at his naivete.

What else did you think was going to happen? The memory of his spectacular failure gave him pause as he sat in front of the screen. *I do have an implant this time though. Let's see how it works.*

The rehabilitation program was in step one of level one and the sentences were simple. Blake's choices were "Bill went out to go fishing", "Bill went hunting for a turkey", "Bill tasted his ham sandwich" or "Bill went after the school bus". He selected "Bill tasted his ham sandwich" only to have a simulated explosion blossom on the computer screen signifying that he made an incorrect choice. *I guess Bill's not hungry after all.* Three of the sentences disappeared leaving the answer displayed, which was "Bill went out to go fishing". At the same time the program repeated the sentence giving him the chance to verify word associations. *Bill's going to have a lot more fun than me.*

There was no second chance, his score was listed at the bottom of the screen as zero and the program advanced to step two, displaying another blank screen with 'Step Two' displayed at the top. An electronic voice narrated the second sentence followed by offering four boxes to choose from. *That's a little sneaky,* Blake thought as he inspected the sentences. *They all have close to the same number of syllables and the words sound similar.* The four selections were "Molly wore a red dress", "Molly was a hot mess", "Molly swore a blue streak" and "Molly tore her new dress". He sat there considering his options until the screen exploded as he ran out of time. His score remained at zero with the program notifying him that the correct choice was "Molly was a hot mess". *She's not the only one,* he thought, as the program moved on to step three.

Blake wasn't a fan of listening to the radio or TV, preferring to avoid the radio entirely and employ captions for the TV. Using the phone was a lost skill since electronic voices were far beyond his comprehension. Announcements in the airport, movie theatres, any situation that involved an artificial voice required a work-around of some sort and his enthusiasm sagged as he realized that rehabilitation was going to be tough. Same as in the testing booth, there were no lips to read and he was being dropped into the deep end without knowing how to swim. *I'm a virgin picking a condom here.*

The program kept on going, the screen kept on exploding and Blake watched his score remain at zero. *I guess it's too much to expect that I might get lucky? Is it always going to be this hard??*

Shaking his head in frustration and reminding himself that he was already ahead of the game, Blake switched to a pep talk. *Time to put on the big boy pants. Maybe I can ignore things that sound the same and focus on words that are unique.*

Blake renewed his attention for the next step, number seven, closing his eyes and willing himself to get over the hump, even if it was just for one step. Listening to the sentence, Blake thought that he could pick out the word "duck" and reviewing the choices saw that there was one sentence with "duck" in it. *OK, do that.* Making his selection he was rewarded by a shooting star arcing across the screen and his score bumping up to one. *One for seven. Killing it.* The program repeated the sentence and he listened closely, hoping to kick start the beginnings of comprehension.

Wielding his new strategy, Blake progressed through the program until he finished step 25, achieving a final score of nine for 25, which amounted to 36%. After completing step 25 the screen switched to a display showing a graph of his success rate which was plotted as a blue line showing his score in percent. The graph began by flat lining at 0% for steps one through six, then shooting up to 14% at step seven. His score went down to 12% at step eight, which he missed, and then zig zagged its way to step 25, recalculating after each step, before ending at 36%. Most of the selections that he got correct were a result of picking out individual words, but closer to the end he was able to understand a couple of complete sentences. *Not very good if you ask me.*

Given a choice by the program to stop or continue, Blake chose to continue. *Yeah, as if there's something else I should be doing.* Notifying him that he was in level one, the program asked if he was ready to start. *Yes! And this time I'm going to do better than 36%!!* It wasn't the first time that he faced problems and it wouldn't be the last. He felt encouraged to be attempting a task that was impossible one day earlier, confident that he was resilient enough to tough it out. Regardless of what happened next, 36% was lightyears ahead of the 2% he scored with Susan. *I'll get past this and when I do it will be goodbye lip reading!*

The program restarted at level one with sentences, and this time Blake performed better, utilizing his strategy of identifying unique words. He wasn't happy that his progress depended upon recognizing one or two words, but complete comprehension continued to elude him. As the program ran through its 25 steps he became acclimated to the electronic voice, understanding more each time. Unfortunately his understanding skewed toward words that were repeated rather than words differentiating the sentences. After a number of trials he reached a score of 75%, but the trial after that dropped him back down to 55%, which was discouraging. Each session was unrelated, so that when the program restarted the sentences were different. It was becoming obvious that the program was designed to be confusing because he could mark at least three separate speakers. One of them spoke fast, one spoke softly and the third speaker appeared to have a cold. Three times he reached a score of 85% at the halfway point, only to have the speakers switch and his score plunge by the time he finished. This is hard! And aggravating! How many variations are there anyway? *What do I have to score before this stupid program advances out of level one?*

Glancing at the clock, Blake saw that he was up to 90 minutes. The exhilaration of this morning was gone and he was getting more frustrated with each attempt. *I need a break. Stay here much longer and I'm going to explode.* Mired in level one, Blake recognized the familiar rage lobbying for a foothold, a reaction he was better off nipping in the bud. Evaluating his latest score, he wished a pox upon the designer of the program, rolling his eyes at the unpredictability of his results. *This is designed to be as difficult as possible. If I knew who developed this torture device, I'd be tempted to key their car!*

Thoroughly disgusted, he snapped the laptop screen closed, almost pinching his fingers in the process, and reached down to grab the Cochlear suitcase. *I'll set up the battery charger and see what else is in here.* His eyes landed on the phone clip, triggering a derisive snort, *There's an accessory I won't need for a while!* The battery charger and overnight case took priority so he pulled them out for an inspection. They seemed to be self-explanatory and Blake headed for the bedroom with the intention of setting them up. He was in a contentious mood, ready and willing to pounce on whatever inanimate object offered the slightest resistance.

So much for butterflies, unicorns and dancing bears.

Surveying the bedroom, he decided to put the charger and overnight case on his nightstand within easy reach. His remaining hearing aid, which Susan recommended that he not wear for three weeks, went into a drawer. The overnight case consisted of a drying box that came with its own desiccant and a small fan that blew air over the contents. Plugging it in, Blake took a step back to inspect the assembly and felt a tap on his shoulder.

He turned to find Emily's smiling face a couple feet away. "How did practice go?"

Adopting a blank face, Blake stifled his mood, reminding himself that he was already reading lips and understanding words at the same time, an achievement that most recipients took weeks to accomplish. *This thing is still pretty marvelous,* he thought, *as much as I hate to waste a good mad.* "It was tough," he said. "I have to figure out how to understand an electronic voice without any chance to read lips and I'm stuck on level one."

She moved in, putting her arms around his neck and flipping her hair over her shoulder with a toss of her head. "You can do it. I can already tell that you're hearing better."

Blake slipped his arms around her waist and pulled her close, grateful for the encouragement, thinking that there were worse problems than being consoled by an attractive woman. Emily's gentle coaxing was a soothing tonic to his disposition. The gracefulness of her touch burned hot on his neck and her eyes swallowed him up while her breasts nudged his chest with a provocative firmness to bring on stirrings of recovery. Giving in to her enticements, he submitted to the validity behind her statement. "Yeah, you're right." He buried his face in her tresses and held on tight, the scent of her working its magic so that he was inspired to give her a test bump. "What else can you tell?"

"Somebody's happy," Emily touched her hips to his crotch while lifting her lips to his neck and giving him a deliberate nip. The nip gave way to her lightly dragging bare teeth along his skin, raising goosebumps. Any thoughts save for his wife were blasted to oblivion as her allure took front and center. "Mmmm. Maybe you'll get lucky tonight if you play your cards right."

"I got a full house." *With your name on the front door.*

"I can see that," she said, releasing him to look down at his pants. Her face registered a sultriness that gripped his attention. "You certainly do. But then, nobody was kicking you out of bed this morning. I would have been happy to help you start the day off properly."

"My bad," he said. "There's always tonight though, isn't there?"

"Maybe." Emily shifted her weight to one foot, crossing her arms across her breasts. With a teasing glint sparkling from her eyes she said, "We'll see."

Blake stood in place with his pulse pounding, desire ruling his thoughts. His implant kicked in, registering an unfamiliar sound. "What's that beeping?"

"The timer for the chicken."

"In the kitchen?"

"Yup."

"Wow! From the bedroom?!" Blake brightened up, his mind returning to thoughts of rehabilitation, discouragement melting away. *I'll give it a shot tomorrow.* "Fried chicken!" He could smell the telltale aroma starting to waft through the house.

"With mashed potatoes and a salad," said Emily. This time Blake focused on her eyes and a small thrill of excitement coursed through his veins. Emily met his gaze with a curious expression on her face, "Are you not reading lips?"

"Trying not to. That time I understood most of what you said. Maybe practice helped after all."

"Didn't I tell you!" Emily reached out to tug his hand. "Come in the kitchen and talk to me while I'm cooking!"

She turned to leave the bedroom and Blake followed behind, losing himself in the enticing roll of her hips. Her jeans might as well have been painted on and he gave his thoughts free rein. *Don't fight with your wife on a Friday night!*

Entering the kitchen, he settled into a chair at the table while Emily took her place at the stove. They talked for an hour, Blake trying to understand her speech. He would look away from her lips, pushing his comprehension to the limit, delighted to find that his requests for repeats were getting less frequent. Emily made a game out of it, covering her lips to make it harder, her playfulness sending his thoughts in other directions. Practicing with her was more fun than staring at a computer screen. *The view is better too.*

Considering where he was yesterday, today was a voyage of discovery, with the kitchen a cornucopia ready for sampling. He asked Emily to help him identify what he was hearing and she willingly obliged, identifying sounds from cutting up an apple, the furnace turning on and off, even the clock ticking on the wall. Blake was aware that clocks made a ticking noise, but today was his first time experiencing it. When Emily walked him through the refrigerator dropping ice cubes into the ice bin followed by water coming on to refill the tray he was astonished. Her words became easier to understand the longer they talked and he began to listen without looking, their interaction taking on a dynamic give and take that brought life to the hope tingling inside of them. The fluidity of exchange lent a carefree mood to their conversation, Emily serving as his guide, giving him a teaser of what lay ahead as the comments flowed back and forth with an ease that lightened two hearts, bringing joy to them both. Astounded at the miracle unfolding before their eyes, they chatted spontaneously with a dialogue that flowed easier than water.

How is this happening so fast?!

The frying pan bubbled and popped with pieces of chicken, and Blake commented how he could hear the intensity rise and fall with each piece put in the pan. He spoke to his wife, eye to eye without glancing at her lips, "I can't begin to describe how amazing this implant is."

"I can't believe it either," she said. Emily approached him to put both hands on his face and bent down to give him a deep kiss, clasping him tightly in her grip as the years melted away, the magic of college coming back to fill the kitchen with a glorious aura that signified a second beginning. The power of dreams come to life poured into their spirits and nudged desperation to the side, his implant making a way where there was no way before. She let go and stood before him, her eyes meeting his to race toward the future, fantasies darting around like a thousand dragonflies flashing golden in the summer sun. "But I love it," she added, turning back to the stove.

Blake sat there watching her flip pieces of chicken, a jumble of thoughts going through his head. *What about work?* he wondered. *Will I be able to hold my own against George and the rest of them? How about my friends or people I meet for the first time? Can I order Starbucks without sounding like a clown? Is this just for us or will I understand everyone?*

A bang interrupted his meanderings, and he raised his eyebrows, intending to question Emily. She beat him to the punch with a musical laugh. "That's your daughter home from school!"

They didn't have long to wait before Mackenzie shot into the kitchen to say, "Well? What happened? Mom said you were home, but I don't know what's going on!" She cast back and forth between her parents trying to figure out where to start. Making up her mind she turned to her father, searching his face, "Does it work?!"

Blake surveyed his youngest child, with whom he shared a silent language of gestures and glances. Her words were clear as a bell and he understood right then that the implant was going to be the biggest home run of his life. There was finally a cure, and he sat for a second, savoring the wonder. Family, work, church, it was all going to change for the better in a substantial way. The last few months his hopes had been a freight train speeding toward a junction between two destinations, one leading over a cliff, one leading back home, and in that moment he took the spur heading for home. *This is going to be spectacular.* He watched his daughter standing there impatiently, wanting to wrap her in his arms and hold her tight, recognizing the chance for a relationship exponentially better than the one they shared today, and meeting her eyes he saw that she had already figured out the answer but he said it anyway, "It's a miracle." With those three words he claimed his path, embracing the future for all it had to offer.

"I knew it!" Wild with excitement, Mackenzie jumped up in the air to smack both hands together, charging in to give him a hug. "Can you talk on the phone? I'm going to call you every day!" Mackenzie was happy for him, but the comment went deeper than that. Closely connected to Blake since she was a toddler, Mackenzie was jealous of her friends having phone conversations with their fathers. Her friends told her it wasn't so great, but she had her own ideas on that.

"Working on it. I'm doing OK as long as I can read lips, but the phone is going to take a little longer."

"I'm first though, right?"

"Sure," Blake laughed, turning to Emily. "As long as it's ok with your mom!"

Emily stood at the stove, watching them, "I guess this one time." She directed a mock frown at her daughter, "Don't get used to it though."

"Ha!" Mackenzie performed a twirl in the middle of the kitchen. "Wait 'til I tell my friends! Do Madison and Matthew know?"

"Yes, they do," Emily replied. "I already told them. They're coming over Sunday for dinner." She turned to address Blake, "You can show off then."

"Perfect." *I hope.* Blake sat at the table, elated at how easily he could understand Mackenzie. She was easy to read though. He could figure out the general direction of her thoughts by watching her mannerisms, giving him a context with which to frame her dialogue from the start. *I almost know what she'll say before she says it.* Most people won't be so easy to interpret, he mused, but the implant was working incredibly well. At this point he could understand both Emily and Mackenzie and that was enough for the first day. It was more than he expected, but not enough to satisfy him tomorrow. *Tomorrow I'm getting past level one.*

The mood in the kitchen was upbeat as the three of them prepared dinner. Mackenzie went to her room to drop off her books and came bouncing back into the kitchen, happily planting a kiss on his cheek before assisting her mother with place settings and laying out food. For his part Blake took care of the drinks, sliding them onto the table for his wife and daughter. They took their places and Blake lifted his glass in preparation for a toast, one he felt lucky to make, thinking that the day could have turned out differently, grateful for his success and determined to grab this chance with both hands to wring out every last bit of performance from his implant. His wife and daughter picked up their drinks and waited for him to gather his thoughts, recognizing the need to acknowledge something so remarkable. Out of habit Blake swirled his drink, tightening his grip on the cold glass and reveling in the sound of ice cubes crashing into each other as they swam in the foam, mulling what to say and the ways to say it. He pondered whether he should give recognition to the past or cast it off. Should he mention the people that made this gift possible or focus on those who had stood by him through the years? Emily and Mackenzie sat patiently as he deliberated, entertaining thoughts of their own, dreams expanding to fill the room, and Blake finally concluded that he could hold forth until the Coke in their drinks went flat and the chicken cooled down to room temperature without doing adequate justice to his change in fortune.

Allowing a smile to replace his customary inscrutableness, Blake cleared his throat. His world was new and exciting, full of wonder, and it was fitting to mark the occasion by breaking out of his old mold. He was about to celebrate the unthinkable and to do that it was proper to free his emotions from their shackles.

Extending his drink he said, "Here's to starting over and making relationships better."

It was a vow that extended far into the future and touched on a belief that was teasing its way to the forefront of his thoughts. For the rest of his life Blake would be indebted to those who made this gift possible and as he moved forward he was committed to keeping the magic of his transformation alive. *Human nature being what it is, I'm sure it will be easy to start taking my new hearing for granted. That would be shameful.*

The clinking of their glasses set off a familiar routine, Mackenzie rattling off a recitation of the day's events and Blake hopping on the carousel to take in her narrative with ease. She possessed the clearest voice in the family and he tried turning away from her face, attempting to pull her words out of the air and assemble them into a coherent flow. With three of them in the kitchen and one person talking, Blake easily followed the conversation. Mackenzie inspected him with a growing intensity, questioning him with her eyes as she talked to understand how he was doing and he nodded to let her know that he was keeping up. None of them could escape the magnitude of what was transpiring, the suspense growing until after ten minutes Mackenzie finally spoke up, "Is it that good?" Her face held a mixture of perplexity and intrigue as she posed her question.

"Unbelievable," he said. "Don't forget though, it's quiet in here and only one of us is talking. I'm sure listening won't be so easy with all five of us." He was thrilled that there was no need to ask for something to be repeated and the unbroken flow of conversation was an unexpected pleasure. A typical conversation was filled with awkward silences while he struggled to catch up and interruptions when he fell too far behind. *I can't wait to try this at work!* "It's fantastic to get it the first time," he said, lifting his whiskey.

"Amen!" Emily cheered.

"Yes!" Mackenzie added, and she took off from where she had stopped. Blake watched her with a sense of peace, grateful for finding a doorway to a better life with his family and thinking that compared to a few months ago, his future was shining brightly. *Today is just the beginning,* he thought. *Who knows where this will go? Should have taken the jump a long time ago.*

Dinner turned into an experiment as Blake followed the dialogue instead of being stuck in isolation and receiving periodic updates. *I'm only missing one or two words here and there. I can live with that!* Presented with the option of commenting or listening, Blake felt more comfortable sitting back quietly while evaluating scenarios in his mind. Mackenzie was going over the logistics of her evening prompting Blake to consider the options, something that wasn't possible before since he could never be sure that he was aware of all the details. He was content being onboard with the train of events, feeling no need to jump in with his own opinion because he figured both Mackenzie and Emily had plenty of practice operating without him. *They've been doing it long enough.* The same principle would apply with his other two children. Why upset a family dynamic that was already working? It was better, and more fun, to sit back and enjoy the show without shoehorning his way into a different role. *That won't be the case at work though,* he mused. *Some people are due for a surprise.*

The meal came to an end, with Blake and Emily being informed that Mackenzie's plans for the night involved cheerleading at the football game that evening, followed by an overnight with another group of friends from the dance team from which she would go straight to Saturday morning dance practice, arriving back home sometime Saturday afternoon to do homework. "Maybe we can watch a movie tomorrow night?" she said.

"No date?" Emily responded.

"I do have an offer, but I'm thinking that I could invite him here?"

"Not a problem, we can get a pizza and chill."

Blake listened in, loving that he didn't have to be updated after the fact. Also loving that he could count on having the night alone with his wife. *Yes!*

"Is it OK if I leave then?"

Blake chose to jump in, "Sure, we'll clean up."

"Thanks Dad!" Mackenzie threw him a look of appreciation.

He winked at her, then directed his gaze to his wife, "I'm at your service." *All night long.*

"You'll be busy then," Emily responded with a grin.

"You could at least wait until I'm gone!" Mackenzie protested.

Emily addressed her daughter, "That was your cue to leave."

"Ok, Ok, I'm out of here!" Mackenzie leapt out of her chair and headed for the door. "Please don't embarrass me tomorrow night!"

Blake turned to Emily, "How would we do that?"

"Accidentally on purpose, maybe. Depends on who she brings."

"How come?"

"Also depends."

"Huh?"

"Forget it," Emily said drily. "You may have better hearing, but you're still a guy."

Mackenzie reappeared a few minutes later loaded down with gear, pausing to give them both a kiss before disappearing from the kitchen with a cheery "Bye!"

Blake cocked his head at the banging of the front door, "She's gone." *Time for the main event.* He got up with a load of dishes to deposit in the sink and returning to the table, bent down to give his wife a kiss. "As much as I love your fried chicken it doesn't turn me on as much as your special perfume."

"Let's get this mess cleaned up and I can fix that for you." The huskiness in her voice made his heart thump as he watched her walk to the sink. It was insanely arousing to focus on her bottom and the lustrous mane of black hanging down her backside while having a conversation, precipitating an involuntary hitch in his breathing. Without looking at him Emily said, "What's left?"

"Stuff that goes in the fridge." Blake stood behind her with his pulse speeding up, drinking in the curves of her hips, captivated by the hem of her sweater floating above the waistband of her jeans to reveal the smallest strip of bare skin and letting his imagination dive beneath her clothes. "You did that on purpose, didn't you?" he said.

This time she glanced back over her shoulder, the arch of her neckline pulling his gaze into a forest of raven curls. She was wearing a set of gold hoop earrings and they bumped the curve of her neck, flashing an invitation to come and nuzzle. "Yes, I did," she purred. "What are you going to do about it?"

He ran his eyes down her neck to the swell of her cleavage and over the curve of her breast, partially hidden by her arm, his throat starting to tighten. There was something incredibly sexy about her standing at the sink with the sleeves of her sweater pushed halfway up to her elbows and her hips tilted skyward from wearing boots. His unsettledness from this morning was gone, and Blake could feel his erection growing with nothing in the way except the arrival of morning a long time from now. Moving up behind her, he pressed himself into her curves. "I've never fucked a fried chicken before."

"Not happening." She shoved her butt backwards with a firm push, making him groan at the deliciousness of the contact. "Finish cleaning up and we'll do this the right way."

"How's that?"

"Sober, clean and slow," she said. "In that order." Emily locked eyes with him and their bodies remained in contact as dancing flecks of green bewitched him to her command.

Intoxicated by her allure his thoughts spilled out, "What about fast, hard and sloppy?" Blake whispered. The warm contact coupled with the prospect of having the night alone with her threatened to dissolve his brain, and he pushed her against the sink, his erection leading the way, sliding one hand forward to cup her breast through the softness of her sweater.

"No," she said, bumping back for emphasis. Rolling his eyes in defeat, he let out a low groan and released her to turn around, his pants throbbing with the sweet torture of denial.

They soon finished in the kitchen and Emily took him by the hand to lead him to the bedroom. "Wait here." She went to the corner to kick off her boots then returned to where he was standing. Brushing up against him with intent, Emily's eyes shone out from underneath dark eyelashes with a shimmering mixture of hazel and green, "Get in the shower and save me a spot." Taking a step back, she pushed him in the direction of the bathroom.

Blake did as he was told, stripping off his clothes and removing his implant to place it bedside. His processor was supposed to be waterproof down to five feet, but there was no sense in being stupid about it. A curtain of silence fell with brutal impact. Their lovemaking had been a soundless ballet for years, at least for him, and he didn't expect tonight to be any different. Entering the bathroom, he opened the shower door to reach in and start the water, adjusting the temperature as hot as he could stand it before stepping in under the showerhead, lifting his head up to the spray and closing his eyes while the deluge of warmth ran down his body. He felt a pair of arms encircling him from behind and Emily pressed up against him, hot water splashing over the two of them. The flow created a slippery sheen between their bodies and she took advantage of the lubrication to slide herself up and down his back. Slipping one hand down his front and snaking the other between his legs, she brought him to size with an experienced caress. Her head came up and although he couldn't hear, she meant for him to read her lips.

"I want to play with your full house." She was smiling in a way that made him rigid.

"Uhhh," he said, imprisoned by her touch.

"Uhhh," she mimicked, the look in her eyes claiming ownership of his member. Grabbing a bar of soap Emily lathered him up, moving her hand slowly up and down his length, French nails disappearing beneath the foam only to reemerge, rotating his balls in her other hand until he stammered out, "I don't think you want to play that game much longer." *Or the night will be over before it starts.*

She smiled with satisfaction, squeezing him hard at the base, "That'll do for now." Emily stood in front of him and proceeded to wash his body, starting at his chest, working her way down his stomach to his legs and back up to his neck. Her hands slid across his skin, lubricated by a thick layer of suds. His penis bobbed up and down before her, but she pushed it out of the way, concentrating on the rest of him. When she was happy with his front she stepped behind to do his back, finishing up by leisurely probing between his cheeks, and Blake's heart thumped faster, his erection rising to point straight up into the air. Completing her efforts, Emily moved in to cuddle up against his backside, sliding her arms around to pull herself tight.

Held firm in her grasp, he twisted around to face her, the lubricity between them accommodating his movements, positioning his cock flat against her stomach to see her smiling up sweetly. Slicked back hair ran from her forehead down toward her bottom in a satiny sheet of blackness and water came past his shoulder to bounce off her upturned face in silver droplets. The wet carnality of her curves was mesmerizing, and her eyes radiated a sultriness that made his member throb with need. "My turn," she mouthed.

Blake picked up the soap and lathered her breasts, covering them in a citrus scented foam, positioning his hands underneath to cup their slipperiness and massaging her nipples in gentle circles. She withstood his ministrations with her head tilted back and eyes closed, water splashing over her face. Gliding his hands across her skin up to her neck he worked his way down her body, caressing her stomach and hips in a cascade of foam, his penis bumping her curves, urging him to take her on the spot. *I wish.* Kneeling down to wash her legs he devoted attention to her crotch, washing her pubic mound with a delicate touch, moving up to address the enticing rise and fall of her belly and returning to the voluptuous flaring of her hips before reaching through her legs to return the favor from earlier. Emily widened her stance as he did so, resting her hands upon his shoulders while he performed his services. At the end he stood up and swiveled her around so that he had access to her backside, dousing her hair with shampoo and then piling it up on top of her head, massaging her scalp with the tips of his fingers as he kneaded the shampoo through her hair, the scent of lavender filling the shower. His penis did its best to distract him, insistently bumping up against the valley she presented, and it wasn't long before he gave in, sliding himself up and down the outside edges of her cheeks as he washed her hair.

Emily braced herself on the tile, tilting her head back to let out a sigh of contentment. He rinsed her off and added a dose of conditioner, rinsing that out too and succumbing to desire, took her by the hips to bury his erection between her cheeks. Blake began to thrust slowly, aware that his heart was pounding out a warning as he pushed himself against the slickness of her body. *This might not be a brilliant idea.* She responded by pushing back, rotating up hard against his stomach, bringing him so close to the edge that he was forced to step back with a sudden intake of breath.

She peered behind with a teasing smile, "Too much?" The silent query rolled off her lips to produce an effect that was overwhelmingly erotic.

He nodded his head in rueful surrender, heart punching out of his chest with each pulse.

Emily swiveled around and took hold of his penis, fondling its tip and tracing the length of him down to his stomach where she proceeded to twirl circles in his pubic hair. "It's nice that you've recovered from this morning." She switched to stroking the underside of him with a delicate finger, sticking out her tongue to drink from the water droplets landing on her face.

Glowing with a desirability that made his heart race, Emily stood before him in the shower, water splashing off her body. She moved closer to drape an arm over his shoulder, wrapping the fingers of her free hand around his erection. "I'm dying to celebrate your superpower, so why don't you get in bed and wait for me?" With a provocative twinkle in her eyes, Emily tightened her grip and deliberately pumped him, opening her fingers with a brazen look as his body convulsed in response and he fell away from her grasp.

Recovering, Blake reached behind her head to pull her in for a kiss, pushing his tongue deep inside her mouth while dropping his second hand between her legs to knead the warm slipperiness of her mound. He gained entry, sliding two fingers inside to be rewarded by Emily letting out a gasp, exhaling into his mouth. Holding her in his grip under the hot water, he proceeded to massage her inside and out until she began to kiss back in earnest, then released her to step back, satisfied at the need evident on her face. "Don't be long." Blake stepped out of the shower and closed the door, turning back to catch a glimpse of Emily standing under the water watching him go. *Touché!*

Blake dried himself off and rolled into bed naked, sole inhabitant of a silent universe, covering himself from a chill in the bedroom. His erection tented the sheet and he regarded it with amusement and a sense of pride. *Welcome back!* Reliving the expression on his wife's face as he exited the shower, a quiver of anticipation shot through his loins.

Emily came out of the shower and he watched her through the open door of the bathroom as she bent forward to towel her hair off while letting it hang down in front of her. Still bending over, she proceeded to blast the hair dryer through her tresses, standing naked in front of the mirror with her legs spread out. Blake admired her outline from the bed, his penis twitching in arousal. *Oh. Wow.*

Finishing with the dryer, Emily flipped the mass of curls over her back with a practiced motion as she stood up to turn in his direction, fully expecting an audience. He stared at the stunning display of beauty, drinking in her voluptuous body framed by a backdrop of untamed tresses and crowned by a lovely face. With a smoothness that made his heart skip a beat, she gave her neck a shot of perfume before gliding out of the bathroom to the side of the bed, proceeding to climb up on all fours and straddle him with her face above his, trapping him under the sheet. Her breasts hung down, tempting him with their lusciousness, but before he could react Emily moved in to plant a kiss on his lips, hair falling to either side and enclosing their faces in a dark curtain of silkiness that held a dampness infused with the scent of lavender. Loose strands drifted across his neck and arms, tickling him with strokes of coolness and she pushed his head down into the pillow with her own, seeking out his tongue to coax it into her mouth with a gentle suction. Blake surrendered to her embrace, running his hands over her back, cupping her behind and roaming the softness of her warm skin. The touch of her breasts against his chest and the intoxicating scent of her perfume recalled memories of other nights, his penis hardening in response. She kissed him with intent, taking her time, and he felt himself straining underneath the sheet.

Emily felt it too and ended her kiss to sit back on his legs, a layer of cotton between them. Reaching up, she yanked the sheet down to his thighs in a quick motion so that his erection popped out, bobbing up and down crazily. She grinned, pleased at her accomplishment. When it finally came to rest Emily teased one finger under the tip, making his tool bounce in excitement before coming to a stop pointing up to the ceiling.

"Having fun?"

"I could do this for a while," she said, treating him to a sensuous gaze, her breasts a couple of ripe fruits hanging in front of him, prompting his penis to twitch without any additional encouragement. Blake met her eyes, a willing captive. Her next move took him by surprise as she leaned forward to brace her hands on his chest and set her face in front of his. "Simon." The seductive manner fell away and her face turned serious, "Can you put on your implant so I can talk to you in bed? Would that be OK?" A yearning passed over her face and he read raw vulnerability in her eyes as she sat on his legs, naked and warm, hair askew, and he wondered how long she had been holding back, allowing him to make his own decision without adding to the angst. *Ahhh.* Their pillow talk had faded away years ago, replaced by taps and nudges performed in the darkness, a casualty of the insidious silence that had crept into their lives. Accepting the loss as collateral damage, Blake had never bothered to ask if she felt differently. He laid underneath with her beauty poised above, magnified by the request, her unselfishness authenticating their relationship to pierce him deep in the heart.

"Sure." Rolling her off his legs he turned to the side of the bed and opened the case holding his processor. He connected the magnets, hearing three beeps signifying their handshake and braced himself for the coming explosion. A tidal wave broke over him and Blake automatically clicked his tongue to tune himself in, supporting himself on one elbow to look back in her direction. She sat on the bed with legs crossed, hands in her lap, eyes swirling with twin tornadoes of green and gold.

"Is it on?" Her voice conveyed a tone that he had not heard in a long time.

"Yeah."

"Yes!" Excitement clearly evident, she ripped the sheet down to the end of the bed, throwing most of it on the floor. Emily pulled him towards her and rolled onto his chest to pop herself on top of him, reaching a hand between their bodies to flatten his penis under her stomach. Planting both elbows on top of his chest she said, "Is it ok if I touch it?"

Blake laughed, "I guess so. Didn't know an implant would turn you on or I would have gotten one a lot earlier!"

"Shut up. You're what turns me on, I want to know where it is." Emily reached behind his head to run her fingers around the circumference of the magnet, tracing the cable that ran back to the processor on his head with the delicateness of a ladybug's footsteps and returning to the magnet to rest her fingers upon it.

"It's not going anywhere."

She bent her head down to kiss him softly on the lips. "Thank you." He kissed her back, gathering a handful of her tresses and pressing her lips into his with a firm grip that left no mistaking that he was ready. Emily responded eagerly, opening her mouth to reciprocate.

"Where were we?"

"You have this thing that keeps poking me," Emily said. She rolled to the side and took hold of him, stroking her hand up and down his length while kneeling by his crotch. Pulling her hair to one side, she positioned her head over his penis and grabbed him firmly by the base as she took him in her mouth, watching him out of the corner of her eyes as she began working her tongue.

He rolled his head back, overcome by the sensation, knowing that as good as it felt, she was just getting started. Thirty seconds later he was hard as a rock and grabbing at the mattress to keep himself from exploding.

Before he was too far gone Emily lifted her mouth off him, causing him to exhale in relief. "You're about ready. Ladies first."

"Thank God," Blake gasped. "I can't take much more of that."

They switched positions, Emily moving up to lay down on her back with Blake taking position above her. He started by nuzzling her neck, nipping at her skin until goose bumps rose on her arms. Kissing his way down her body, he came to her nipples, taking one into his mouth. Her head rose up from the bed to watch as he pulled on her nipple with his lips, feeling it extend under his touch, tasting the freshness of the shower. Still holding her nipple inside his mouth, Blake flicked his tongue off its tip and she let out a sigh, extending a hand over the stubble of his hair, finding the side opposite his implant and pressing him onto her breast.

His fingers toyed with her remaining nipple, rolling it gently until she began to breathe harder. Suckling one nipple with his lips, he slowly pulled away until it fell out of his mouth. Then he switched to the other, Emily supporting her breast with one hand to give him better access. Next Blake brushed his lips down her stomach, running past muscles that were already clenched and pushing her legs apart to expose her muskiness. Taking his time, he kissed his way up and down her cleft, moving away to address the sensitive areas inside her thighs, returning with his tongue to be rewarded by her lips spreading apart easily, presenting a warm wetness that extended to the rim of her opening. Encouraged, he pushed his tongue inside, probing the ridges of her tunnel and hearing a groan of pleasure from above.

Cupping a hand behind his head, she gazed down at him. "Move your tongue in a circle," she instructed. He obeyed, moving slowly inside of her, and Emily began to moan softly, matching the rhythm of his circles, her hips rising to meet his mouth and the pressure of her hand getting stronger as his own touch got softer. Blake ran a hand across the tightness of her stomach, moving it up to cup one of her breasts. "Deeper," she said, and he obliged, pushing his tongue in as far as it would go until his lips were pressed in hard, the noises from Emily getting louder and louder with each circuit of his tongue. "Up," she ordered, tugging on his head, and he advanced his lips to cover her clitoris, tongue still circling inside. Arching her body up off the bed she began to pant in time with the revolutions of his tongue, breathing harder and harder. Waiting for that magic moment when she began to go rigid, he continued to rotate his tongue inside of her while teasing her engorged clitoris with his lips, alternating his touches between hard and fast followed by soft and slow as she thrust her hips toward his mouth. Her moans escalated to an insistent whimpering, signifying that she was almost there, and when she stiffened, he clamped down with his lips to begin a sustained humming. Emily let out an exclamation, her legs jerking off his shoulders and hips vibrating under his mouth as her eyes went rolling back. Pushed over the edge and beyond, she spasmed against him, her body lost in the throes of orgasm until he finally had to stop for breath. Released from his urgings, her cries subsided, and she collapsed onto the bed, head rolling to the side, arms laying loose, legs quivering from the intensity.

Spread out beneath him, Emily was his for the taking, and Blake opened her legs to enter his wife, sliding himself in up to the hilt with a long stroke of deliciousness until he felt the tip of his penis bump against her, stopping deep inside. The warmth and tightness felt glorious and he stayed in place, pushing himself hard against her body to claim his prize. "Ahhh," A rapturous sigh escaped her lips and he stared upon her beauty, hair splayed out across the pillow, half lidded eyes encouraging any liberties he wished to take. He remained above her, captivated by her loveliness, holding his throbbing penis in place, the contact hardening his member into a solid piece of steel. Reading his state, Emily smiled knowingly, and her muscles contracted to pull him in tighter, Blake's eyes going wide as he felt her taking him over the cliff. From deep within his loins a billowing of pleasure broke free, destined for release whether he moved or not, and he withdrew once to pump back inside her, losing himself to her expert nudge and arching up to convulse with his own orgasm before slowly collapsing on top of her. She gathered him in with her arms and he buried his face in her neck, closing his eyes to breath in the intoxicating scent of her body, perfume and hair, mingled together in an irresistible blend of anesthesia.

*****

Blake came back to consciousness with Emily pushing on his shoulders. "Roll over so I can breathe."

He complied, falling onto his side while pulling her leg across his hip, wanting to stay inside of her. They lay on the bed face to face, wrapped up together, and he pushed himself against her because he wasn't ready to pull out.

"You're noisy."

"You would know!" Emily snickered. She kissed him lightly, touching her hand to his face, then drifted it down his neck and over his shoulders, tracing the curve of his spine to rest her hand on his bottom. He felt a stirring between his legs and Emily did too, squeezing his rear as a naughty smile blossomed on her face. "I bet you could take it in the ass without a peep." Her smile turned deliciously wicked. "You might like it. Some guys do."

"I don't think so."

"Pity." She kept her hand where it was, tracing one finger along the valley between his cheeks with the lightest of touches. "A girl can dream."

His penis responded and he pulled her against him, pushing her leg higher over his hip. With a mischievous smile Emily took his face in both hands and kissed him, pushing her tongue deep inside his mouth and causing his erection to grow in earnest, expanding inside her tunnel. She moved her hands down, twirling his chest hair and exploring around his nipples, tweaking them playfully with her fingers. He caressed the curves of her shoulders and neck, exploring the hills and valleys of her breasts and hips, delighting in the voluptuous offering before him and marveling at the fact that there was not a flat surface anywhere on her. Curls of hair covered her breasts and shoulders, teasing him so that he pushed them aside to see what lay beneath. Stoked by their petting, his member grew larger to graze her tip and she stilled, snaking a hand behind his neck to seek out his eyes. "You're really deep."

He shifted his hips, "Better?"

She bit her lower lip, pushing her forehead onto his chest, "Umm." He made as if to shift further only to have her grab his hips. "Hold still."

He lay in bed with her folded into his arms, waiting for her to catch up. Blake nuzzled her luxurious mane, burying his fingers in waves of starry blackness, exiting the pile of silkiness to drift his fingertips down the smoothness of her back. Finding a rhythm, he repeated the caress, starting at the top of her head and going as far down as he could. When Emily started to rotate her hips against him, Blake cupped her bottom, matching her movements, and they began to undulate as one. They went slowly, feeling each other out, Emily raising up as he pulled out and pushing down as he moved forward. She moved her hands onto his shoulders and angled her hips into his thrusts, giving him a kiss that lasted multiple strokes. Breaking away she whispered, "Slower," squeezing his shoulders for emphasis, and his heart skipped at the eroticism of her voice, the hushed tone adding a new dimension to the union of their bodies.

Blake moved with a new confidence, thrilling to the freedom of not having to second guess where she was or worry about ruining the flow with an untimely movement, thrusting inside her with a security that made him want to shout in celebration. Emily kissed him again, a lingering clasp, and he could sense a difference, their coupling renewed by a sense of oneness, her words restoring an essence which had faded so slowly over the years that neither of them knew exactly when it was lost. Closing her eyes, Emily pressed her head to the side of his neck, encouraging him with a bite, and Blake sped up his movements, feeling her match his change in tempo. Moving faster, he pulled her hips to his with each thrust, anticipating the increase in her breathing, waiting for that point in time when she stiffened in his arms, the moment signaling her peak, and when she arrived he plunged in deep and hard, pulling out to slam back in, knowing that he was dangerously close himself. He felt her shudder against him, fingers digging in urgently. She was quiet this time, her shuddering accompanied by a soft "Ohhh" breathed hotly against his neck, and it was all he needed to join her in a fall that seemed to last forever. Holding her tightly, he emptied himself into her as she submitted to his grasp. After he was spent, Blake rolled onto his back, pulling his wife on top of him where she molded herself to his body, breasts flattened against him, head burrowing into his chest, their hips and legs joined together in a crazy tangle.

"Mmmmmmmmmmm," Emily's lips vibrated against his skin.

"Mmm?"

"I thought I liked fucking you before, but I really like fucking you now."

He kissed the top of her head, gathering her hair aside to expose the skin of her back. She snuggled in, seeking every point of contact and they lay entwined on top of the sheets. Blake drew a fingertip up and down her spine, feeling her breathing slow and waiting for the twitching that signaled the beginnings of sleep. Her leg jerked against his body once, then twice, and he closed his own eyes, surrendering to the afterglow.

***

Waking to a cacophony intruding upon his rest, Blake vaguely remembered separating to fall asleep. The furnace was emitting a steady hum occasionally broken by a whistling noise which he didn't recognize and lying in bed he stared into a curtain of blackness, fielding a slew of sounds that blended together. From the front of the house a roaring came and went, Blake guessing that it was a car going by. Before the roaring could fade away a screech split the darkness and he wondered if the neighbor's cat was having a showdown with another creature of the night. Above him a cargo plane was taking off on its nightly mission and as it grew fainter in the distance Blake imagined a tick tock coming from the kitchen. *People can sleep in this?* Deciding that he was done, Blake rolled over to pop the magnet off his head, securing his implant inside its case on the nightstand, and a blanket of silence fell on the bedroom granting welcome relief. He looked sideways to admire the dim outline of Emily sleeping beside him, closing his eyes in bliss.

***

Light crept through the window, penetrating the silence to coax him awake and opening his eyes Blake observed Emily laying on her stomach in the same spot as last night. *She hasn't moved a millimeter.* Sitting up in bed, he drank in the tranquility of dust motes suspended in sunlight before remembering that he was now part of the hearing world. *Oh boy!* Turning to his nightstand, Blake picked up his processor to turn it on, placing the earhook over his ear and lifting his hand to place the magnet near his head. The magnet jumped out of his hand to seat against the magnet under his skin, the processor emitted three beeps and a nuclear explosion blew up his brain, stabbing him with a million lances of fire. *Holy Shit!* Blake doubled over from his sitting position in bed, clenching the air in front of him until the noise fell off to a dull roar and the pain disappeared. It didn't take more than a second but while it lasted he was on the edge of losing his mind. *I signed up for electroshock therapy!* Tentatively clucking his tongue, Blake winced against a blast that failed to materialize. *OK.* He tapped his fingers on the nightstand, picking out the impacts as separate dings within the environmental din that surrounded him. *Not bad.* Emboldened, he tapped harder, seeking a threshold in there somewhere, but nothing hurt and he exhaled in relief. *Maybe it's only a problem after being off for a while. Wonder if I should lower the volume before taking it off?*

He sat in bed listening to the ever-present furnace, confident that he could identify when it turned on and off in addition to pinpointing the background hum produced by the fan. *That one's in the database now!* Blake clucked his tongue, wary of the stabs, becoming hopeful that the initial blast was an isolated occurrence.

"Testing, testing," Blake spoke to the bedroom. *Be gentle, please!* The words came out in a squeak, but his brain processed them without complaint. Brushing his hand across the sheets, he sat there admiring the hissing noise he was making until Emily put forth a delicate snore and he turned his face toward her in amusement. Watching her chest move in and out, he was rewarded by another, softer than the first, and Blake laughed to himself. *That's hilarious! I wonder if she knows?* He stayed where he was, enjoying the incongruity. *Drop dead gorgeous, snores in her sleep!*

Blake pulled the sheets off himself, listening to the whistling and hissing as he gathered them to the side. *It's going to be a busy day cataloging all this stuff.* He took a peek at Emily, still asleep on her stomach, taking a second to admire the raven curls covering her back. Unable to resist, he ran the back of his hand over her hair, twining his fingers through her tresses and reveling in their luxuriousness. *That was some twofer,* he thought, and decided that he better get out of bed before his thoughts could filter down to his penis.

Entering the bathroom to sit down on the toilet, he released an urgent flow. The splashing gave him a start, filling the bathroom and bouncing off the walls to reverberate around the room. *Is it that loud all the time??!!* Through the doorway he saw Emily up on one elbow watching him sleepily, causing his sphincter muscle to contract and shut down his flow. A few last drops trickled out weakly, plopping into the water and making him even more self-conscious. *Come on!* "Please tell me that my peeing did not wake you up!"

"Ha-ha!" She laughed from her position on the bed. "I've been listening to you pee for the last 25 years!"

"Oh." He thought about it. "Guess that kind of makes sense."

Emily pulled the covers closer to her breasts and grinned. "Let me get this straight. We have three kids which means I've received an enema from you before each one, pushed for hours until the sweat is pouring off me followed by popping out a baby in front of an audience while I'm screaming uncontrollably but you're embarrassed that I can hear you pee?!" She slipped a hand over her mouth, trying without success to stifle a giggle. "Right!! You know the rest of the world can hear you too?"

"That's the weird part. All those times I had no clue."

"Welcome to real life. You make noises when you poop too." Emily fell back on the bed giggling out loud.

"Thanks for the tip." Blake swung the door shut against his wife's laughter. Suddenly snoring seemed to be a non-issue.

Super. Wonder what else I don't know about?

He performed his morning toilet, analyzing the bathroom noises. Some of them, like water coming from the faucet were familiar, but the effect was slightly different with his implant. Flossing produced a peculiar hiss, something that was brand new, but the electric razor was pretty much the same, a mechanical buzzing. Flushing the toilet temporarily drowned out anything else, then sounds began to filter back one by one as his brain added them in. *Maybe that's the program clamping down on sudden noise?* There were no more stabs of pain, for which he was grateful. Blake opened the door to exit the bathroom, detecting a squeak in the hinge. *Perfect, something to fix.* Scanning the bedroom he saw that Emily was gone, so he proceeded to get dressed before making his way from the bedroom to the kitchen. Normally Emily slept in on Saturday and Blake took advantage of the time alone, but today it was going to be breakfast for two.

Turning the corner to enter the kitchen Blake was presented with the aroma from a fresh pot of coffee, the table already set and Emily at the stove in a floor length robe that suggested desirability underneath. *She would look awesome in a burlap sack covered with mud.* The memory of their coupling filled his mind, making him wish they had stayed in bed. *Except I'm probably out of bullets.* His thoughts went to college where their chemistry was so evident that he was considering how to propose after the third date. *Easiest decision ever.* There was a story that Emily liked to relate about transferring out of history class to sign up for geography with Blake, disappointing a potential suitor in history that had eyes on her. Running across him on campus two months later, she turned down his request for a date because she was already engaged. *I sure wasn't going to wait!* Blake never considered holding back, thinking that she was the total package and remembering his grandmother's comment that the greatest gift of marriage is walking through time with someone by your side. *And a fantastic piece of ass doesn't hurt, either!*

Sunshine was flooding the room, matching his mood, and the kitchen was alive with a symphony of morning music coming from the coffeemaker. A scraping noise caught his attention and he determined that it was Emily sliding a pan onto the stovetop. Blake walked up to her and took her in his arms, wrapping her in a bear hug that she returned with fierce energy. "You still got it," she murmured next to his ear.

"Likewise," he said, nuzzling his face into her hair. "What's for breakfast?"

"Whatever you make!" She kissed him on the cheek. "I'm waiting."

Blake laughed, "Sit down then and get out of the way." Normally he would make an early breakfast on the weekend, getting up ahead of Emily, and Mackenzie too, if she was home. After a few hours they would magically appear and he would make them the same breakfast as his own, eggs over easy with toast and coffee. Starting his routine, he opened the toaster oven and slid in two pieces of bread. The door clanged shut with a bang that made him wince, but the pain disappeared as fast as it came. *Ooooh! That hurt a little bit.* Standing in front of the toaster oven Blake listened to the timer ticking away. *Nice beat. Shuka, shuka, shuka, shuka!* Losing himself in his preparations, he focused on identifying new sounds, listening to the frying pan screech in protest as he centered it over the burner. Pouring olive oil in the pan from above, Blake tried raising the bottle up higher and higher to see if he could isolate the oil falling. *Nope.* He could feel the heat from the pan, but there were no bubbles forming and no popping to offer any hints on temperature. *Butter is fun, olive oil just sits there getting thinner and thinner.* Hovering a hand above the oil, he decided that it was hot enough and cracked an egg against the stovetop, reveling in the sustained crumpling as he pulled it apart, hoping to hear it plop into the oil, but disappointed at the silence. Cracking a second egg, the ripping noise that followed from tearing apart the inside membrane was extremely satisfying. On his way to the garbage can, he crumpled the shells in his hand, celebrating the crunch of their destruction, passing Emily at the table drinking her coffee.

"What's everything sound like this morning?"

"Completely different." Glancing back in her direction he said, "You're old news. I can understand you without even trying."

"How romantic. Hope you got your fill last night then."

Not hardly. Returning to the stove, he stopped to plant a kiss on the top of her head. "Maybe I'll make some progress with Matthew."

Seeing that the eggs were getting ready to flip, he watched them diligently, waiting for the degree of doneness when the albumin was colored brilliant white around the edges and a snotty yellow surrounded the yolk, signaling that time was of the utmost. He flipped them over and stood back to wait his customary 60 seconds, discovering that at 45 seconds a delightful groaning came from the pan as the egg whites fluttered up and down to release bubbles of hot oil. *Ah ha! There's a couple of stingrays swimming around the pan and they're complaining it's too hot!!* Laughing, he carried the pan toward the table to tip the eggs out onto Emily's plate, returning to make his own. *Talk to me!* The groaning manifested for a second time, and he tilted his head in glee before sliding his own eggs on a plate and sitting down to join her.

Ensconced in a glow, they sat and talked, Blake realizing that he could hear himself slurping on his coffee. *Not so great, that.* He could make out the ticking of the clock and a beep from the coffeemaker when the warming element turned off, building up a database of recognition while they conversed. The amount of information previously hidden in the fog of white noise was staggering. Blake looked outside to where the blue jay was performing its morning flybys, surprised that he could perceive its call. *Through the window, no less!*

Sitting across from Emily, Blake stole a glance at the time, basking in his progress, reluctant to leave her for the day. *Guess I better start round two. Time to hit the dungeon.* He knew better than to try skipping practice based on his results this morning. Experience had shown him that trying to avoid pain guaranteed a static situation at best and sometimes resulted in situations getting worse.

I can't psyche out a computer program, but I do have the capacity to learn and adapt. And I will. He reflected how a person's true capabilities are only developed under fire because a smooth pathway has a single outcome, and that is to rob someone of the chance to grow by calling on the same skills repeatedly. Pain fostered growth by forcing a person to come out the other side stronger or accept defeat. There is no middle ground. Defeat signaled change was required, only becoming a problem if it forestalled additional effort. Blake was familiar with how the process worked and not afraid of defeat, having come up against it many times. *Like all damn every day.* On the racquetball court there was nothing more satisfying than losing to an opponent, trying again with a different strategy and ending up the victor. Fishing was a perfect example of the need to change in the face of defeat because those who limited their efforts to being pole holders went home with small stringers more often than not.

He was dismayed to see some of his hearing impaired friends get trapped in a circle of comfort, convincing themselves that they were doing fine while avoiding efforts to get better, choosing to deflect opportunities to stand up and fight their disability. Hearing loss was an insidious disease, creeping in slower than the morning fog, advancing so stealthily that abilities were lost without obvious indications and after a while life was different than before, regardless of what people were willing to admit. Comprehension never got better without some type of intervention, but it did a remarkable job of getting worse, so it was better to work constantly against deterioration rather than trying to rationalize the status quo. In the absence of any concrete improvements, success was defined by a refusal to give up.

Emily helped him clean up the dishes from breakfast and they prepared to go their separate ways. While his wife was holding an open house in Green Township, Blake was determined to advance to the next level on the computer. His motivation was ingrained by his mother, who would spout off a number of clichés daily, seeking to influence the thought process of her brood. The lesson presently looping inside his head was a holdover from his early days, "If at first you don't succeed, try, try again." *Story of my life.*

Blake went down the hall to his office, aware of his slippers shuffling across the hardwood floor. He experimented with a slip and slide, the skimming of his slippers along the wood creating a cross between a hiss and a scrape. Entering his office, he booted up the computer and selected the Cochlear program, designated by a grey icon with a yellow 'C' inside. *And away we go.* Selecting sentences, he found himself back in level one, step one. *Thanks for remembering. Let's see if kitchen progress translates into computer progress.*

On the first step he was rewarded with a shooting star, prompting an internal cheer. His success continued with step two and Blake began to think that he might have a chance this time around. *Yes! That's more like it!* Blake got up to step six without an error, but then the program switched to a different speaker and he missed step seven. The screen exploded and he chastised the software. *I know what you did, changing speakers on me to make it more difficult!* Listening to the new speaker at the sentence repetition, he tackled step eight with renewed purpose, achieving another shooting star. *Ha! Got you!* He finished with a final score of 80%, a record, and sat back after choosing 'continue', pleased at such a good start and waiting for what came next.

The program returned to level one, step one and Blake rolled his eyes. *Of course you would.* He finished the second trial with a score of 80% and immediately started his third. *Right on the edge here.* This time he ran his score up to 98% halfway through, dropped to 90% on the last step, and was elated to see a message appear above the graph congratulating him for his advancement to level two. Shooting both fists into the air Blake yelled out to the room,

"Yes! LEVEL TWO!!!" *Boom!* Pumping his fists up and down, Blake yelled in triumph, screaming in the face of his emotionless tutor.

Level two incorporated more background noise and four speakers instead of three. The four speakers in level two were different from the three speakers in level one, comprising a mix of genders and ages, with the fourth speaker being a child with a foreign accent. Background noise varied for each step, sometimes even changing intensity within the same step. His initial run through resulted in a score of 25% with the program offering him the option to return to level one. *Not a chance!* Blake sighed to himself. *This is going to be hard in the beginning followed by harder in the middle and even harder at the end.* Originally Blake was thinking that he could practice most of the morning, but it was obvious that he needed to set limits to keep from wearing himself out. *I can do about an hour a day of this. Anymore and I'll go nuts.* Mary Beth told him that he would get frustrated and now he understood why. *Small wonder people don't enjoy practicing.* There was significant difference between levels. *It's the same as going from high school to college. And advancing from a level is like hooking a five-pound bass only to watch it shake free at the bank!*

Inspecting the time Blake gave himself another 30 minutes, encouraged that he would at least be stopping at a higher level than yesterday. *Moving up one level each day is fine by me.* Thirty minutes later he had lost count of how many trials that he had been through but was keenly aware of having achieved either 75% or 80% for the last four, being repeatedly stymied by the little stinker with the foreign accent. *So close!!* The next attempt left him at 80% and Blake pounded on the desk in frustration. *10% more!!!* He started again, fighting to get over the hump and was dismayed to end up at 60%. Blake stood up and slammed the lid of his laptop shut, disgusted at the drop in his performance. *That's it!*

With nobody home it was the perfect time to let off some steam, so Blake put on his work clothes and headed out to the backyard where he kept the firewood. On the way he stopped in the outside shed to pick up iron wedges used for splitting wood and a three-pound sledgehammer fitted with a four-foot handle. Going directly to his work area, he rolled a few logs into place and proceeded to beat the frustration out of his body. As he went at his task, the sledgehammer pounded the wedges with a resonating clang, the impacts ringing across the yard. The effort required to swing the three-pound hammer off the ground, above his head and down onto the wedges involved his whole body, the impact traveling down his legs and out his boots to take the tensions out with it. His breathing sped up and he increased the pace, transferring his vexation to the wood. Eighteen logs disappeared into a circle of kindling, by which time Blake was panting with exertion and his legs were shaking with fatigue.

Stopping to lean on the handle of the sledge, he paused to catch his breath, becoming aware of the wind blowing through the bare branches above him and knocking them into each other. It was a magical interlude, and he tilted his head in appreciation. The blue jay spoke to him from the far end of the yard and he peered up to find it. A flurry of blue shot over his head and Blake scuffed his boot through the wood chips surrounding his work area, listening to the scrape and clatter created by his feet. *This is pretty darn remarkable.* He was relaxed, far enough removed from the practice session of this morning to tell that his progress was going in the right direction, and his thoughts drifted back to a few weeks earlier when he feared for his future.

Was it so long ago? Last month I was struggling through each day without much hope, angry all the time, but this is a complete reversal. I can hear so much more today, more than ever before, and it's only the second day. There's no way to repay the people that gave me this gift. I'm living a celebration that'll last until the end of my days.

A surge of gratitude passed through his body and the backyard dissolved into a blur of shapes, Blake letting it roll over him, giving thanks for the years of weight being lifted from his soul so unexpectedly. Inside his heart a kernel of happiness was sprouting, tiny for now, but it appeared to have enough potential to reach higher than a California redwood. Hour by hour his brain was adapting, understanding more the second time than the first and better yet on the third. *What an impossible thing to ask for, yet here I am.* He bowed his head, scuffing the wood chips under his feet, inhaling their freshness, humbled by his change in fortunes and vowing that one goal in the days ahead would be to find a way to validate the efforts of those who helped him. *I need to give back somehow. Walking away into a new life won't cut it.*

A sound traveled over the roof from the front of the house, the slamming of a car door, he surmised, triggering him to speculate whether Mackenzie was back from her slate of activities. He cocked his head, waiting, listening for the front door but failing to pick it up. What he did hear was a beagle from four houses down bellowing in response, a cacophony that shredded his brain with a harshness that couldn't be ignored. The animal was a familiar adversary from his walks around the neighborhood. Blake disliked being subjected to the dumb dog barking its head off, rushing at him from the fenced in yard as he passed by, continuing to yelp frantically from behind its protective barrier, its body jerking so hard with each fit of barking that the animal had trouble staying in one place. If he approached the fence the beagle would immediately begin retreating, all the while yelping like mad. After observing the dog react the same way over and over, Blake was convinced the yapping translated to nothing more than a continual refrain of, "I'm Stupid! Stupid! Stupid!"

He had little patience for aggressive animals or their owners, tagging the latter as even dumber than their untrained pets. *Especially if they have a sizeable dog.* His implant was doing an unbelievable job of picking up the barking from this far away. It was four houses down and halfway around a curve, yet the yelps were easily recognizable. *Now I know what noise pollution means.* Blake surveyed the split wood, wishing for the animal to shut up, caught up in his aversion and unaware in the grip of his disgust that he would only encounter one sound which he could live without and that it would prove to be the idiocy of a barking dog.

He stood among the disarray of his efforts, filtering out the bellowing and trying to concentrate on the wind whistling through the branches to be interrupted by Mackenzie yelling, "Hey Dad! I'm back!"

Her words carried across the yard and he turned to Mackenzie sticking her head out of the back door, 140 feet away, short brown hair falling to the side, understanding her words without the benefit of lip reading. *Wow! That's got to be a record.* "On the way," he said. Before bending down to gather up his tools he casually threw in, "No need to yell."

Mackenzie's smile made her whole face glow, "Showoff!" He made himself a promise that when he tried the phone he would call her. *But I want to be sure that I'm ready first.*

Heading back inside, Blake came into the kitchen where Mackenzie was camped out with her schoolbooks and emptying a plastic bag. She wadded it up and pushed it to the side, giving her attention to a snack bar that came out of it, and Blake marveled at how loud the crumpling of the plastic bag registered in his brain. *It sounds like an aluminum can being crushed!* Mackenzie was engrossed in unwrapping her snack bar and the kitchen was silent, as silent as it could be in this different world. He could easily pick out the furnace running in the background. *Got that figured out.* The clock was ticking, loudly he thought, but there was something else too, and he was flabbergasted to perceive that the plastic bag was unfolding itself from a crumpled state and producing a series of clicks in the process. *I don't believe it!* Blake spoke to his daughter, "Is that plastic bag making a noise?"

"Uh huh," she replied, munching on her snack. Then she studied him with amazement, "You can hear that?"

"First time in my life!!" He poked a finger at the bag, listening to the whisper of it skidding across the walnut surface, his finger making the plastic crackle even more in response, and a grin of amazement appeared on his face.

"Wow," Mackenzie exclaimed. "That's awesome!" Not missing a beat she kept going, "I bet you can use the phone, Dad. You have to try it!"

"I will," Blake promised. "Not today, but soon."

"Dad!" she groaned. "Come on!" Her face pleaded with him, puppy dog eyes coming out full force, but he stayed firm.

"Almost there. I want to get a little farther with the computer. Want a whiskey?"

"Yes!"

"Me too, I feel like celebrating!" He caught a gleam in her eye at the unexpected offer and although he didn't mean to intentionally change the subject, the invitation effectively sidetracked her request. Blake inclined his head toward his daughter, eyebrows raising up. "Don't tell Mom, though." *Better safe than sorry!* It was still early and despite the fact that booze was a common fixture in their family, he wasn't sure what Emily's reaction would be.

"Deal!" She lowered one eyelid in an exaggerated motion, their shared language of silence lending the word an added richness.

Blake left the kitchen to open the whiskey cabinet and pull out a bottle of Blanton's, carrying it to the kitchen and slipping into autopilot. He popped the cork to take his customary sniff and proceeded to get out the ice, his thoughts analyzing the last day and a half.

Friday morning had started out less than perfectly but ended with him leaving the hospital on cloud nine. The first round of practice brought him back to earth with a rude awakening, but in retrospect the implant was working, he was just pushing the envelope. *Understanding electronic voices after only 12 hours may be asking too much.* Once he got away from the computer, he was able to see that the implant was performing spectacularly, and his second day of practice was a definite improvement.

Thinking that he was in excellent shape, Blake focused on the music he was creating, his daughter watching contently. Ice cubes fell into the glass with a ringing that reminded him of bells, sliding over and around each other in a search for their final positions. Bourbon splashed in from above and the cubes shifted, creating a faint tinkling as they adjusted positions. *Yes!* Coke came falling in, accompanied by more tinkling between the ice cubes and a series of sharp snaps as the cubes developed cracks followed by foam rising with a ferocious hiss in its attempt to overflow the glass. *Neat! Well, not really neat, but neat to me!* He slid a drink across the wood toward Mackenzie in time for her to catch the foam and proceeded to pour his own. After sampling the foam, Blake swirled the glass, listening to the clinking between cubes chasing their neighbors in a circle, the motion generating a new layer of foam. *Love it!* Mackenzie was observing him over the edge of her glass, soaking up the ambiance and Blake lifted his drink, watching her beam with pleasure as they tapped glasses.

Mackenzie set down her drink to begin shuffling around her schoolwork while Blake put the bottle back in the cabinet, coming back to take a seat at the table and savor the whiskey, his thoughts moving ahead to the next day, Sunday, when the three of them would be going to church. They sat in companionable silence and lifting a hand, he traced his fingers around the magnet on his head, wondering how he felt about being in public.

Guess I'll find out.

Chapter 10 – Liberation

Sunday morning Blake opened his eyes to sunshine burning frost off the window, a quietness cloaking the bedroom and emphasizing his reconfiguration. Pain from connecting his implant yesterday morning was fresh in his mind, and he lay in bed dreading the next step. *Am I going to fry the inside of my head every morning?* Last night before removing his implant he remembered to lower the volume from 8 to 4, which seemed to be a good idea at the time, but now he was wondering why he didn't take it down to level 1.

Hope I'm lucky enough to be stupid.

All right. I survived it yesterday. Positioning himself on the edge of the mattress he prepared for the shift, hooking the processor over his ear and holding the magnet far enough away that it couldn't jump out of his hand to make contact. He traced the smooth edges of the magnet, savoring a few seconds of grace before reluctantly releasing it to link up with its mate. Three beeps ticked off from the processor during its handshake with the internal components followed by an explosion of sound inside his skull approximating the blast of an M80. His teeth clenched and his body coiled up into a fetal position, but in less than a second the blast subsided, causing his frame to sag in relief. *Better.* Blake exhaled a breath that he didn't know he was holding, standing up to relieve his tension. The inputs entering his head separated and he began trying to identify specific components, immediately recognizing the clock ticking away on Emily's nightstand. A car was traveling down the street and Blake listened to it fade into the distance. *Never hurts to be lucky.* Sunlight spilled through a bare spot on the window to illuminate the room with a beam from heaven, boosting his spirits and bringing an image of angels singing in the background. *Let's do it.*

Padding across the cold floor in his bare feet to enter the bathroom, he reflected on today's trip to church, his first time out in public. Leery of being on display for the masses, he contemplated the bus stop episode from kindergarten, when he attempted to hide his hearing aid in his pocket.

Sure. Then I'll look stupid when I finally put it on. Might as well grow a combover.

Nobody's going to care, and if they do say something, I'll blast them.

Emily will probably beat me to the punch.

Blake began to shave, encouraged by a vision of Emily on the warpath. He smiled to himself as he remembered being on their honeymoon, long before the concept of accessibility hit the mainstream, when a server in a noisy restaurant told Emily that he was too busy to waste time with Blake having trouble understanding the specials and could she please order for him. Emily spent the next five minutes educating the waiter on the realities of hearing loss until he became desperate to escape. *Major mistake, dude!* Lost in recollection, Blake bumped a can of hairspray off the sink, its impact against the floor generating a clang that lanced a bolt of fire through his brain for a microsecond. *Oww!* The pain came and went so fast that by the time he could react, it was already gone.

OK. Susan said that it was a matter of comfort. I'll be comfortable then.

Finishing in the bathroom, Blake got dressed, approaching the bed and shaking Emily's foot to wake her up, receiving an unenthusiastic grunt in response. He headed out of the bedroom to the kitchen, giving Mackenzie's door a sharp rap as he went down the hall. Sunday morning's routine was to eat and go, breakfast being a simple affair and sometimes bypassed altogether in favor of coffee. Pulling out the coffeemaker to get started, he put in a filter and started pouring coffee straight from the bag, the grounds producing an intriguing rush that caused him to stop in mid pour. *Wonder if I can hear just one?* Intrigued, Blake poured the coffee back in the bag and then reached in to pinch out a few grains. Dropping them into his palm, he made his selection and held it above the empty filter. Releasing a single grain to the grip of gravity he watched it bounce off the sides of the cone on its way to the bottom with a "bip, bip, bip, bip", a grin spreading across his face as it ricocheted its way down. *How mind-blowing is that!* Picking up another, he did it again, dumbstruck at the tiny pops following it down to the bottom. *Hot dog!*

Thrilled at his discovery, Blake dropped additional grains down the filter, having a fine time with his game, then poured the rest of the coffee in, listening to the grains cascade over themselves. He turned on the coffeemaker, which acknowledged his command with a beep. It began to gurgle, and he stood in front, reveling in the feedback, before directing his attention to making toast. Right before the door to the toaster oven slammed shut, he cringed, recalling yesterday's bang too late, but his implant failed to register any discomfort. *Maybe my brain is getting smarter!* Blake poured himself a cup of coffee, timing his actions by pulling the pot out while it was still filling and sliding it back in before the filter basket overflowed, taking a seat at the table in order to monitor the gurgling from the coffeemaker and the ticking of the toaster oven. This Sunday was different from last Sunday. Today he could track the progress of his toast by listening for the finishing ding of the toaster oven or monitoring its ticking. When the coffeemaker was finished the gurgling stopped and a vigorous sputtering began as the remaining water turned to steam and shot out the top. The coffeemaker also notified him with a follow up ding, which seemed to be a moot point after its eruption. Accustomed to watching his preparations closely, Blake judged the amended routine infinitely more relaxing. *Coffee tastes better too!*

Blake sat in the kitchen drinking coffee and waiting for his family to appear. A soothing aroma curled up to his nostrils as he reflected how today's expedition to church would be his first contact with those who saw him as hearing impaired. The old Blake required handholding to participate in a conversation, but that Blake was gone. *At least I hope so.* If his progress yesterday was any indication, church would be an adventure, and he was eager to test himself in background noise. Practicing with the computer seemed to be working, but he was curious how his progress would translate to the real world. His church friends were tolerant people and Blake felt sure that they would be accommodating of his issues. Today would be useful prep for Monday when he would be forced to navigate the swamp. Angela would have his back for sure, also George to some degree, but the rest of them were less reliable, despite having good intentions. *Dan is a train wreck of stupidity all by himself.*

He wanted to stand on his own, without having to rely on assistance from Emily or anyone else, just like Mary Beth. *Maybe it's too early for that?* All indications from the last two days were pointing in the right direction, making him hopeful. Pulling out his remote control, Blake bumped up the volume, trying to decide where it sounded best. Moving the sensitivity adjustment up and down was supposed to adjust his sphere of capture, and he was planning on using a large sphere of capture during the sermon when the minister was far away, changing to a small sphere of capture when talking to someone who was close to him. The 'Focus' program was designed to dampen sound from the rear microphone in favor of the front microphone. Hopefully, 'Focus' would make it easier to have a conversation in a crowd, the typical situation once worship was finished and people congregated in the gathering space.

Alone in the kitchen, he experimented with the remote, an ambivalence creeping in about exposing himself to the world with a magnet attached to his head. *Yeah. I thought I would be fine, but it's definitely strange.*

***

Emily, Mackenzie and Blake arrived at Shiloh United Methodist Church, located at the corner of Anderson Ferry and Rapid Run, merging with a flow of people heading toward a set of eight doors on the outside of the building. Entering the church provided welcome escape from a blustery wind in the parking lot and they passed through a gathering area, moving toward the sanctuary with the rest of the crowd. From the gathering area they were able to see all the way to the altar of the sanctuary, through six doors that were propped open and arranged in pairs. Shiloh Church was built in the fifties with stained glass windows lining both sides of the sanctuary. Morning sun entered from the east to flood the interior with multi-hued bands of light. The sanctuary was 200' long by 60' wide with two rows of sandy brown pews on either side of a red carpet leading to an altar positioned seven steps higher than the pews. Soaring high above in the shape of a triangle, the ceiling was supported by thick beams of dark wood that blended into a background that was every bit as dark, with chandeliers hanging down at regular intervals to illuminate the worship space with pendants of white. Their pastor, Jon Seagrave, was standing outside the center pair of doors greeting people as they entered. Joining the line stacked up in front of Jon, the three of them smiled and waved to several families on their way inside, but the need to find places forestalled any meaningful exchanges. As their spot in line inched toward the minister, Blake could feel the protective isolation of the last two days dissolving away in the face of public interaction. *I've been on his prayer list for weeks, so a simple "hello" is going to be impossible.* Positive that the magnet on the side of his head was glowing fluorescent green, Blake took position behind his wife and daughter, watching the pastor greet Mackenzie.

The pastor was a charismatic person, *an advantage in his line of work,* Blake thought, with short black hair who was in his fifties. He had been Shiloh's minister for the last 12 years during which time Blake and Emily became friends with both him and his wife, attending the same share group, bonding over potlucks at church and working together to serve the community meal which was held on Friday evening for those who needed a boost in their circumstances. Their families had grown close and Blake considered Jon exceptional, not because he was pastor, but because he possessed a tremendous empathy. Time after time Blake had seen Jon drill down and get to the concerns on someone's mind by focusing on the meaning behind their words. It seemed like common sense, yet Blake had met only a few people who could listen well enough to come out the other side with an understanding of the message being sent. Blake knew what was coming, and as much as he appreciated Jon, he was more comfortable presenting a wall to the outside world. *I'd love to breeze on by, but that would be rude.* This unexpected gift was shifting him out of his comfort zone because reasons for taking up arms against the world were becoming fewer. *You would think it would be an easy transition, but I'm happy with my barriers.*

Jon was wearing a suit and tie underneath his worship robes. Six feet tall, he towered above Mackenzie, but his smiling eyes and graceful movements conveyed a congeniality which was reinforced by a warm tone of voice. Switching his attention to Emily, Pastor Jon clasped one of her hands between his own to bestow a smile and a greeting before turning to Blake, who was standing at the gallows.

"How's your implant, Simon?"

Jon's voice came out with a metallic reverberation, the words rolling over Blake with clarity, and meeting Jon's eyes Blake saw in them an authenticity, reinforcing what he already knew, that the prayers sent up on his behalf were not an obligation but a heartfelt petition.

Lighten up and tell him the news. Why fight it? Don't answer that, stupid question. It works so well that I'd be a fool to minimize it. I'm supposed to be happy now! Caught between his old world of concealment and his new world of wonderment, Blake stood fixed in place while inside of him two personalities fought to pin each other to the mat. *Say something, dummy!*

Blake forced a smile amid his jumbling, taking Jon's hand in a firm grip. "You and Emily are a couple of rock stars!" A sense of peace came from joining hands with Jon, and his trepidations melted away. The ability to understand Jon in the middle of a room that was buzzing with background noise served as additional validation of his progress. One month ago, he would only dare to smile and nod, but here he was on the verge of having a conversation in the middle of a chain saw carving contest. *Don't know what I ever did to deserve this. Nothing comes to mind.* It was too intense for words and his vocal cords froze up while his thoughts shot off on a tangent.

How did I get here? Did it start with Pamela? Before? After? This isn't the same world anymore.

Emily curled an arm around his waist, "He's going to be hearing better than me before long. Yesterday he was fixing a squeaky hinge!"

Pastor Jon smiled in response, "That's fabulous!" Ignoring the crowd waiting behind them, he continued, "Hopefully Simon won't be sleeping through my sermon today then!"

Blake recovered enough to wink at Jon, "Not in the beginning, anyway," and they headed for the sanctuary, blending with the flow of parishioners seeking their seats. *That was half-baked.* Like she always did, Emily took the lead, taking them up front to the second row of pews so that Blake had a chance to read lips. The three of them filed into the pew, Emily in the lead, Mackenzie second and Blake bringing up the rear. As they took their seats, sunlight coming through the stained-glass windows draped a soothing shawl of warmth around their shoulders and Blake began sifting through the surroundings, curious to see what he could identify.

No furnace fan was detectible, *first time for that,* but he could distinguish multiple rhythms in the air from different conversations. *Hello, Mickey Mouse!* One voice manifested with the shrillness of a toddler and somewhere else in the room a firm declaration announced the possibility of an argument. Directly behind them a pair of elderly women were huddled close and whispering with a discordant hiss. Their speech was too low to understand, but the cadence of their voices was irritating. *Put a plug in it, ladies! You sound like a couple of drunk raccoons!* Last time Blake attended church he sat in a bath of white noise that was easily tuned out. White noise was still present, but it was now reduced to a rustling in the background and he was being bombarded by a multitude of perceptions.

From his position in front Blake realized that those behind him could see his implant but flicked the concern away. *So what.* He imagined people pointing it out between themselves, then decided that he didn't care. *If they can see it, fine, saves me the trouble of breaking the ice.* Blake wanted to stand up and lead a cheer to show how excited he was. *I'm not going to cheapen it with concerns for personal vanity.* Everyone in this room except for his wife and daughter probably thought of him as deaf, but that horse was dead, shot between the eyes and hauled away.

Two acolytes came up the aisle side by side to light the candles, causing the buzz in the sanctuary to fade away except for the raccoons behind them, and Blake locked eyes with Mackenzie in disbelief. She grinned and nodded her head in agreement, rolling her own eyes. Knowing that he could read her lips she mouthed a comment at him, "All the time!" and he broke out into a grin. Church was suddenly fun. A thunderous roar erupted with the beginning hymn and Blake adjusted his remote. Bumping his volume from 6 up to 7, he kept going up to 10. *I can handle this, sounds better at 10, actually. No pain, no gain.* He ran the volume down to 1 then back to 10, playing with the range. Satisfied that more was better he left the volume at 10, watching the choir file up the aisle to take their seats to the right of the altar, Pastor Jon following behind.

The hymn ended, Pastor Jon stepping up in front of the congregation to start in on the announcements, Blake adjusting his remote while listening to Jon. Tweaking both volume and sensitivity, Blake settled upon a volume of 8 and a sensitivity of 18. Raising the sensitivity helped significantly, increasing his sphere of capture to include Jon standing some thirty feet away.

Finishing the announcements, Jon remained in place to receive the weekly offering and then stepped aside for a scripture reading by the lay leader. Afterwards he took his place at the pulpit, pausing to look out over the congregation before launching into a sermon about Jesus feeding the 5,000 with five loaves and two fishes. Listening closely, Blake found it easier to dissect the vagaries of Jon's voice as the sermon progressed, detecting additional coherence in the patterns of his speech. The Mickey Mouse effect was more pronounced in the beginning, but then gradually began to resemble the richness that Blake remembered from his hearing aids. Behind him the raccoons kept on jabbering, and curious, Blake activated the rear microphone, sitting back in the pew to find that their voices were more understandable. From what he could gather, the first lady was having problems with a sick cat and the second was thinking about getting a scarf. *And to think I missed last week's issues.* Redirecting his attention to Jon's sermon, he marveled at how clearly the words flowed together without straining on his part. *I can dig it!* A child wailed in the background, causing Blake to remember when his children were young, squirming throughout the entire sermon. Mackenzie glanced sideways to see how he was doing, and he gave her a wink. She winked back and a veil parted, inviting him into a vision where a set of double doors stood glowing with promise. As he watched, they swung open to reveal an epiphany waiting on the opposite side, arms crossed impatiently.

The sanctuary was engulfed by thick bars of vibrant light coming through the windows, and in a flash of insight Blake cast off his protective shield, ripping it apart and flinging it aside. *I can do this!* With no barriers to hold it in, his angst spilled out, burning away wherever it encountered the sunlight, and with its departure he found freedom. *No more living behind a curtain of sadness.* Inspired by the kaleidoscope of light and sound swirling through the air, he considered the riches available to him in this chapter. Each of the parishioners in this church represented a rebirth. He no longer had to wait for whatever interactions the day would parcel out; he could embrace the magic by striking first. If he could understand Jon, the raccoons and a large portion of the randomness surrounding him, who knew what lay ahead. Stepping through the doors of his vision, he saw a road with his name on it disappearing beyond the horizon of his experience. *Yesterday is gone.* The magnet on his head was a symbol of power, a transformational device, and Blake vowed to step up and seize this chance to be counted as a person who could no longer be ignored.

All day, every day.

It's such a simple thing, being able to hear, but it means that my destiny can flow from my own choices. If I don't agree with someone, I can express my opinion. Why should I accede to someone else's judgement when I can evaluate what's going on around me? No more looking stupid because of missing some comment, no more being held hostage to anyone's choices but mine! Blake inhaled deeply, sliding back against the smooth wood of the pew. *I can take control and it's going to be magnificent.* Jon's sermon filtered through his consciousness, conveying a message of how love and faith can override insurmountable odds, and Blake heard the message speaking directly to him. The impossible was becoming real, with no explanation except the grace of God.

Jon's message joined forces with Blake's awakening to construct a ladder rising out of the darkness, and as he climbed up Blake's thoughts shifted to those who had brought him this far, a list that spanned the world. Manufactured in Australia, Blake's device was installed at University Hospital in Cincinnati, Ohio. In between was a long list of researchers, programmers and manufacturers who dealt with the hardware issues and a multitude of health care professionals involved with the considerations presented by each patient. On a more intimate level, support from family and friends eased the way forward. It was easy to say that his implant represented time and energy offered for the benefit of someone else, but that was far too simple of a description.

I never dreamed this could happen. Asking for my hearing to return – that's asking for a miracle. It's so incomprehensible that I never saw it as an option. This is so much more than I expected. It has the power to defeat my despair.

Jon was wrapping up his sermon with the raccoons finally silent and Blake was filled with a sense of awe. *I can't wait for work tomorrow! Every minute brings a revelation.* The beginning chords of the ending hymn flooded the sanctuary and Blake stood up with the rest of the congregants, reaching for his remote. *Lower the sensitivity and keep the same volume. Works for me!* He felt a tugging on his elbow and turned in the direction of his daughter.

"How was it, Dad?" Mackenzie was talking along with the music and his brain was isolating her voice. Somehow.

What planet is this?

He shook his head in disbelief, "If I had a nickel for every word I understood, you could go to Harvard!" *And Mickey Mouse has left the building.*

"Yes!" Mackenzie squeezed herself into his side. "I'm so happy for you!"

Emily was watching and Blake met her eyes above the head of their daughter. They stood in the pew with the music rolling over them, sunshine wrapping them in a cloak of grace. Friday and Saturday had been terrific days for Blake, full of amazement and discovery, leaving him full of gratitude. Today was different, solidifying an understanding that his implant was more than an accessory to get operating at full capacity. It was his passport to creating a new identity. With Mackenzie tight against his side, Blake stood tall and invincible, a different person than when he sat down, the shell of his sadness lying in pieces around his feet.

I can feel it in my whole body.

It's like my soul is several shades brighter and the dirty parts got cleaned.

Here, put this on and take your life back. Reinvent yourself or go for a rebirth – your choice.

Welcome back to a relationship with your family.

Let your personality shine through instead of being suppressed.

Rip that cage apart and step forth to meet the rest of your life.

His reverie was interrupted by a hand clamping down on his shoulder and Blake turned his head to see his friend, Bill, standing in the aisle. Grey eyebrows peeked over a pair of wire frame eyeglasses with temples that tucked underneath a pair of hearing aids resting behind his ears. The two of them were friends, connected by hearing loss. A 65-year-old widower, Bill was wearing grey corduroy pants, a blue cotton shirt with a button-down collar, and he was one of those skinny guys that would barely tip 130 pounds. Bill packed away a full meal with dessert at the community dinners, but the potbelly common to most seniors was absent from his frame.

Blake stepped out of the pew to greet his friend.

"Hey Simon! How's that cock leer implant?"

Blake smiled. The correct pronunciation was something different, but Bill had the same problem with words that Blake had lived with for years. "It's really a 'coke leer' implant, bud, although I might need the other eventually."

Bill nodded and bent closer to say, "I hear ya!"

"It's amazing. I'm progressing faster than most patients, but I could understand the whole sermon today and I can talk to Emily and Mackenzie without problems. You're easy to hear!" His wife and daughter were squeezing their way past, heading for the gathering space with the rest of the parishioners, so he moved toward the altar steps with Bill, knowing that it would be easier to converse as the sanctuary emptied out. They were accustomed to finding a quiet spot and having their own conversation away from any interferences. Blake was impatient to find how he would do among the background chatter in the gathering area, but he tamped down his excitement to spare a moment with his friend.

"Does it itch?"

"Nah. I can't tell that it's back there to tell you the truth." Pulling the processor off his head, Blake held it out for Bill to inspect, subjecting himself to temporary deafness in the process, taking a minute to point out the various components before sliding the processor back over his ear and hovering the magnet in place until it jumped out of his hand to seat itself with its mate. His brain came alive with an explosion of fireworks and he picked up the last few words that Bill was saying.

"do that someday."

Blake responded, "It might be worthwhile. I can hear sounds now that I've never heard before." He tapped Bill on the shoulder. "You want to know what the ladies are saying!"

"That's a reason not to get it," Bill cackled in glee. "This way they have to get close to me and I can tell who's with the program!" Bill winked, "Picking up the check doesn't hurt either! A man's wallet is the best cologne in the world. I tell the women they can be the pretty half and I'll be the rich half. That's why I'm so popular!" He continued, "Maybe it would help me with the ladies if I tell them it's a cock leer implant!"

Fully aware of what was happening, Blake let his friend run on. Oftentimes hearing impaired people try to monopolize a conversation to avoid listening. The more talking they do, the less they need to worry about understanding others and the more they feel in control. Blake had been guilty of the same behavior in the past. Today Blake was keeping up with whatever Bill was saying, and it was wonderful, pumping his heart so full that he wanted to break out into song. With a smile, Blake came closer to his friend, "This is between you and me, now." Bill moved in, turning serious and Blake said, "It really is a cock leer implant, if you know what I mean!" *And I know you do!*

"Yup," Bill nodded, and he gave Blake a light punch in the shoulder. "The ladies can be tricky. We need all the help we can get."

"Amen!" Blake agreed. "Come on then," he said. "I want to test myself in the crowd." He was fired up and couldn't wait a second longer. There was a spring in his step that had been missing for a long time and he was eager to experiment.

It's Showtime!

The two of them headed out of the sanctuary, Bill peeling away and Blake practically skipping toward the crowd in the gathering area.

Time to reel in the big one!!

Conversing with Bill had been easy, without the stutters and starts that he was used to experiencing, and he couldn't wait to immerse himself in the crowd. *Talk to me, Scotty!* A babel of conversation surrounded him, but he could pull snippets of coherence from the madness as he passed by different groups. Heading toward his wife and daughter who were with a cluster of 'church ladies', as Blake called them, he squeezed himself in next to Emily. Nobody paid him any mind, which was par for the course, so he stood by his wife trying to take in the conversation, making sure his implant was in 'Focus' mode and determining that the topic of discussion was the Christmas Boutique. Fascinated that he could hear, Blake was content to stay in the background, reading people and listening to the conversation. *I can understand them, they just don't know it yet.* He was living in a world where everyone thought of him as deaf, but he was someone else now. *There's a new freight train coming down this track.*

One woman was monopolizing the discussion, a heavyset matron whom Blake referred to as the dominator. She spoke nonstop with a fast delivery, pausing to breathe only reluctantly, and when she did it was to suck in air as fast as she could before anyone else had a chance to jump in. He liked to amuse himself by monitoring her habit of going "uh, uh, uh" between sentences, keeping count each time. Whether the idiosyncrasy was a conscious effort or not he didn't know, but the effect was such that it was difficult for others to participate because without natural pauses between sentences the sole option for her listeners was to interrupt. *Who needs ears when no one else can speak?* The dominator's voice registered so easily that his brain was searching for something else to do, and before he knew it, was adding another layer to the mix. *I'm dying to interrupt this soliloquy. Maybe I should ask her to stop speaking so fast because it's making my implant vibrate? Wonder what she would do?* Blake was tickled to no end that he could follow her narration and his own train of thought at the same time. *Whoa!* As he listened, Jon came through the area, pausing next to Blake.

"So?"

"Thanks for the sermon, Jon," Blake said.

"My pleasure. You seemed to be doing ok."

Exhilarated at reeling in one victory after another, Blake let himself loose, "You know, I never realized it before, but you're pretty good up there!" He felt Emily poke him from behind, but he was on a roll, "Next week I'm going to get here early so I can try listening from the back!" Jon laughed in response, his face mirroring Blake's happiness. Clasping Blake on the shoulder in a show of camaraderie, Jon moved on to touch base with the rest of his flock and Blake caught Mackenzie's eye when the dominator broke for air, "What's for lunch, toots?"

"Skyline!" Mackenzie piped up immediately.

"Works for me!" He tapped Emily's arm to extricate her from the group of church ladies caught in the grip of the dominator. Blake could read body language enough to see that nobody was truly engaged, and Emily willingly turned to join them. *This is too easy,* Blake thought, *butting in like that. Normally I'm standing there like a statue until someone runs out of patience and starts the exodus. I can get used to this kind of power!*

The three of them headed out to the parking lot, Blake ecstatic at the results of his public foray. *Whoohoo! Mickey Mouse is becoming a memory and I'm communicating at will! I even turned a conversation to my advantage! When's the last time that ever happened!!? Look out Starbucks!*

***

The family returned home from lunch at Skyline Chili and Blake went down the hallway to his office for a bit of practice. Today he would be talking with Madison and Matthew at dinner and reaching another level on the practice program would be a boost. He was convinced that he would have no problem understanding Emily and Mackenzie, but family conversation during dinnertime would be different than eavesdropping on the dominator. His last session of practice had ended in level two and Blake booted up the computer, brimming with confidence after his successful morning. Navigating his way to sentences, Blake resumed practicing. *And away we go.*

Thirty minutes extended to 45 as Blake wrestled with the computer program. He was performing erratically, achieving a score of 80% on one go round followed by a score of 60% on the next. Just when he thought that he was on the edge of success with two trials at 85%, he crashed to 55%. It was a discouraging performance after doing so well at church and he sat back in his chair thinking that maybe it was time to call it quits. *Tomorrow is another day,* he reminded himself. With a sigh he reluctantly ended the program and rose from the chair to walk off the tension. *Better let go of it before I feel like killing something.* It wasn't the result that he hoped for, but it was the result that he needed to live with, at least for today. *I'll be back tomorrow. And the next day. And the next. By the time I'm done the program will be giving up.*

It was late afternoon and Blake wandered into the living room to watch football. The Cincinnati Bengals were playing on the West Coast and he cranked up the volume, experimenting with whether he could understand the announcers without reading the captions. *Susan said captioned TV was good practice. The more practice the better. I guess it's all practice from here on out.* His comprehension was hit and miss without reading the captions. *It would help if they didn't say stupid things. I get distracted when they yak to fill up the air.*

Blake killed the rest of the afternoon in front of the TV, adding in a glass of bourbon and trying to follow the dialogue without reverting to the captions. The game ended with the Bengals pulling defeat out of victory and he got up, following his nose to the kitchen where Emily was preparing white chili.

She watched him come in, "Ready for your next performance?"

"Church was incredible. I have a good feeling about dinner." Blake moved up behind his wife to slide his hands around her waist.

"Madison and Matthew are on the way. We'll eat in ten minutes, enough time for you to get the drinks going." Neglecting to turn around, she spoke with him facing the back of her head.

"How quickly we adjust."

She turned around then and gave him a peck on the cheek. The peck turned into a kiss and when their lips parted, she said, "It's magical."

"Yes." He separated from her, leaving the kitchen and going to the living room to stand in front of the liquor cabinet.

"I'm one up on you already," Blake spoke to her from the other room, hoping for a comeback. *Practicing might be tough, but real life is working out fabulously.*

She didn't disappoint, calling out from the kitchen, "In that case I want some Booker's 25."

"Done." He pulled the bottle out from the cabinet and returned to the kitchen. "I love it when you talk whiskey to me."

Emily laughed in response. The mood in the kitchen was light-hearted and Mackenzie walked in to see both of her parents grinning at each other like fools. "Now what?" she said, observing the bottle. "How many of those have you guys had?"

"Not nearly enough!" Blake said in return. "You ready for a drink?"

"Yes!" Mackenzie replied, and she took a seat to watch, eyes alive with anticipation.

Blake pulled out the cork and nosed the opening, offering the bottle to Mackenzie for a sniff. Bookers 25 was a limited-edition anniversary whiskey issued by the Jim Beam Company to commemorate the 25th anniversary of their Bookers brand. It was aged for ten years, three months, and packed a punch at 130.8 proof (65.4% alcohol). Beam did a superb job on the packaging, employing dark brown glass covered with shiny bronze script and topped with a 4" section of wax at the top in the same color as the lettering. Both Blake and Emily preferred not to display their collection of booze, thinking the effect was tacky, but the Bookers 25 bottle blended in anywhere it was put down. The whiskey quickly moved past the burn and smoothed out into a combination of oranges and brown sugar mixed with caramel and topped with a hint of oak. Vanilla was also evident and the mixture of flavors together with a long finish brought to mind a creamsicle that wouldn't melt. After sliding a drink in front of Mackenzie he proceeded to make one for Emily.

Having served Emily, Blake was in the middle of making a drink for himself when he heard the front door open and close. Glancing at Mackenzie he said, "We have company!"

She nodded in agreement and they both turned expectantly to where the hallway joined the kitchen. Blake tracked the clicking of heels coming down the hall followed by Madison entering the kitchen with Matthew close behind. Madison made a beeline for Blake to embrace him in a hug and say, "Wow, Dad! Mom has been telling me how much you can hear and it sounds unbelievable!"

"It is! I even heard you enter the house and come down the hall!"

"Pretty cool, Dad," Matthew said.

"Thanks bud! Never hurts to be lucky! I think I got a couple years' worth of lucky these last few days!" Blake gave his son a hug and slipped him the drink that he finished making. "Here, let me finish making drinks and we'll toast!" He winked at his youngest, "I think Mackenzie is ahead of us already!"

"Neat for me, please," Madison interjected.

"Got it." Blake pulled out a Glencairn for his oldest daughter and filled it up. He set about making the last drink for himself and before it stopped fizzing, he lifted his glass, "Cheers to Cochlear!"

"Amen!" said Emily, the rest of them echoing her words and the family clinked glasses all around.

A buzz of activity followed as the family pitched in to set the table, the kitchen filling with conversation and Blake eavesdropping anywhere he chose. Madison and Mackenzie were talking about clothes with Emily putting in a word at random times. The three women were moving around the kitchen and he was grabbing their voices out of the air. *Wow. This is how people talk without looking at each other!* In between commenting on her daughters' topic Emily was asking Matthew about his weekend, Blake learning that it involved music and clubbing in the district around the University. He took a swallow of his drink, enjoying the melding of flavors and smacking his lips on a finish full of oranges that lingered forever. *Mmmmm!*

Listening to Matthew interact with Emily, Blake saw a person who was drifting aimlessly while surrounded by the richness of the university environment, failing to realize the variety at his fingertips. *What a wasted opportunity.* Blake realized that people needed to mature at their own pace, but it was painful to watch Matthew restrict himself to a limited sphere of activities, mostly associated with an electronic subculture.

His son presented an air of disinterest, blending into the background so well that it took a real effort to notice him. Matthew's t-shirt was usually clean, his mother demanded that much, but his lack of muscle definition meant that the shirt hugged him flat in both the front and the back. He was majoring in electronic media which led to hours spent in front of the computer. His son's current focus on videos and clubbing made it difficult for Blake to find common ground, and he wished for simpler days when it only took ice cream or a trip to the amusement park to connect. Blake observed Emily battling Matthew's indifference and decided that it was time for a change.

It's been tough for me to talk with him, but that ends now.

The family was taking their seats and for once Blake stood back from the rush. Pressure to grab a seat was off. He wanted to experiment, so he remained standing by the counter as his family sat down.

Even at home Blake was accustomed to making a special effort to claim the perfect spot, positioning himself adjacent to the head of the table, a location that put him in the middle of the action with the best view. The remaining spots rotated among his wife and three children depending upon the day, because for some reason they played musical chairs instead of sticking to the same location. Today Emily was at the head with Madison and Mackenzie on one side and Matthew on the other. The girls' heads were bent together and Emily was in conversation with Matthew. Blake watched the ballet evolve as the three women sat down and Matthew, engaged in conversation with his mom, pulled out the chair by Emily. That left Blake in the remaining chair next to Matthew at the end of the huddle, a situation that he tried to avoid at all costs.

It didn't matter to him today though, and he strolled up to his seat, pulling out the last remaining chair. He spied hesitation on Emily's face as her mouth started to open and knew what she was thinking. Mackenzie beat her to the punch and addressed her brother, "Matthew, you're in Dad's spot."

"Oh, sorry," Matthew turned red but before anyone else could speak Blake pushed down on his son's shoulder to keep him where he was.

"Not a problem. I'm trying this end out for a change." He sat down by his son and said, "My hearing is so good now that I can hear what you're going to say before you say it!"

The room erupted with laughter and Blake, taking advantage of the spotlight, went off in another direction, "Did I ever tell you guys that we used to pull pinochle all-nighters when your Mom and I were at UC?"

"We have a group that plays that too!" said Madison.

"Boring," Matthew responded, drawing looks of scorn from both sisters.

Blake saw Emily tighten her lips and dove in, "Hey Matthew, nobody minds if you think it's uninteresting, but you ought to run that stuff through a filter before shooting it out there."

"I've been trying to tell him that for years," Madison said.

"It's going to take another ten," Mackenzie added.

"I'm sure Matthew already knows, it's just a matter of slowing down." Blake picked up his drink. The dynamics were changing, he could feel it in the air and discern it in the eyes of his family as the mood lightened. He tapped his drink against his son's glass and addressed Emily, "As I recall we were a pretty good team back then."

***

Dinner was a success as far as Blake was concerned. He had managed to diffuse Matthew's negativity and was hopeful that today signified a turning point. *Maybe another point of view will make a difference.*

During dinner Blake tried focusing on his plate, loving how the voices registered beside his ear. His implant was on Matthew's side, who was next to Emily, and the girls were directly across from him, but with the correct orientation of his head they all felt right alongside him. The microphones were on his implant, which was on his head, and all he had to do was twist his head to put the microphones in line with whomever was speaking. The furnace fan was attempting to distract him by turning on and off, but he was able to separate it out.

The conversation resembled a stroll through the park instead of rock-climbing and he luxuriated in the ease of it. Listening to Mackenzie refer to Queen Latifah, Blake was surprised to realize that it was pronounced La <u>tee</u> fuh and not La tee <u>faa</u>. *Huh.* They discussed Madison's apartment in OTR, the streetcar, and the music clubs that Matthew visited up at UC. When the family entered a discussion about whether it was appropriate to put pepper on macaroni, all of them except Madison agreed that pepper was the way to go, whereupon Mackenzie commented that her older sister was an acceptable role model as far as bourbon went, but a failure at macaroni. The comment triggered a round of laughter, Blake included, and the camaraderie of being on the same page was the missing link that completed his day. He could sense a thread weaving its way through their lives and drawing the family closer.

Dinner finished with Madison and Matthew taking their leave, Mackenzie disappearing into her room to put the finishing touches on a school project and Emily announcing that she needed some downtime. Blake was left to cleanup by himself, a task that was simplified by dinner being mostly bowls of chili, and he set about his task, welcoming the chance to reflect. Standing at the sink he heard a rushing from the other side of the wall and deduced that Emily was taking a shower, *That's gotta be what that noise is,* finally understanding how she managed to time dinner so perfectly with his washing up. Tomorrow was his first day back at work and he was eager to know how Blake 2.0 would perform. Once more he would be testing himself among those who thought of him differently than he knew himself to be.

I absolutely cannot wait.

He made himself a nightcap and sat down in his chair, his mind cycling through one work scenario after another

until he finished the whiskey and stood up to go to bed.
Putting the glass in the dishwasher he gave the kitchen a
final inspection to make sure that it was ready for the
morning and headed down the hall. Mackenzie's door was
already shut, and the light was out in his own room. Blake
turned off the light in the hallway and quietly stole into his
bedroom, shutting the door as gently as he could, getting to
the bathroom before being stopped by a question from the
darkness.

"Coming to bed?"

Emily's hushed voice sounded like she was leaning over
his shoulder, raising the hairs on his neck. His eyes stared at
a wall of inky blackness, "Thought you would be sleeping
by now."

"Not yet."

"Guess we're both a little slow." He peered in her
direction, the darkness yielding no quarter.

A whisper drifted from the shadows, "The slower, the
better."

***

Blake's first stop on Monday was Starbucks, walking
through the door and taking his place in line to be greeted by
a robust aroma and a bustling crowd. At 5:45 a.m. the place
was full and holiday cups were back, reminding him that this
week would be short, with Thursday and Friday reserved for
Thanksgiving. His preference was to order at the register
instead of using the mobile app because it gave him a chance
to interact with the servers. The register was difficult for
him, but he considered it insulting to blow in and out,

treating the baristas like automatons who existed solely to provide cups of coffee. Once he was done ordering he would occupy himself by observing the parade of customers.

Customers at the register were a random mix, but mobile customers fell into two categories, the wimps, who crept toward the pickup counter cringing, practically apologizing for making human contact, and the warriors, who bullied their way through, demanding service. Both types evidenced a minimal desire for personal connection, not bothering to learn the names of the people serving them and according other customers the barest acknowledgment of their existence. There were multiple variants of wimps and warriors and the show was free entertainment, a boat ramp on Memorial Day weekend. Displaying a sense of manners was the exception to the rule, and he was annoyed when mobile customers would plant themselves in the middle of the traffic flow waiting for their order. The number of them burying themselves in their phones made Blake question the future of humanity.

Blake was convinced that mobile ordering fostered a detachment which led to apathy, and even though Starbucks itself came up with the idea for the mobile app he considered its use an exercise in social destruction. Racing through Starbucks without any need to speak fostered a sterility of experience that separated people from the world around them, resulting in missed chances to touch the lives of others or know the richness of serendipity. Likewise, monkey hammering on a cell phone was a formula for isolation, not connection. The practice was no different in Blake's mind than giving the finger to those in the vicinity and it irritated him so much that he would purposely bump into anyone rude enough to block a doorway or aisle while engrossed in their phone. *Which of these meatheads would stop to help someone who dropped something? Would they even know?*

He moved up in line, now second from the register, his implant defining the environment differently than last week. People were yakking, the barista was hollering out names and steam lances were blasting into the drinks or roaring out unimpeded for cleaning. The lances sounded like a procession of planes taking off, and Blake had observed on earlier visits that they interfered with everyone's hearing. Sometimes Emily was with him and ordered for them both, but she was on the other side of town today. Trying to tune out the din Blake stood in place, attempting to eavesdrop without much luck, figuring that he might have a chance if he could order between the blasting of the lances. His moment of truth arrived, and he stepped up to the counter.

"Hi Priscilla. Triple venti nonfat no-whip mocha, please."

"The usual." Priscilla was an older woman with grey hair whom Blake appreciated because she didn't mash her words together.

"Yes, please."

"You in town for Thanksgiving?" Priscilla changed the subject, and Blake went along with her, swiping his card at the same time.

"We're at our place with the three kids. What about you?" Blake was encouraged to be holding his own. The background noise was hammering at him, but his implant was set on 'Focus', which amplified sounds in front.

"I'm going to my daughter's. She has a group of 18 this year. Better her than me!" Priscilla gave a relieved smile just as a steam lance blew out an explosive screech. His implant clamped down on the overload, cutting off all other sounds, but it was no different from the old days.

Counting down until the lance went quiet, Blake nodded, timing his response perfectly to take his leave, "Have a safe holiday!" He moved down to the pickup counter after Priscilla's goodbye, happy with the outcome. Sometimes the employees would repeat his order back too fast for him to understand or look elsewhere while talking to him, and those were the occasions when his interactions went south in a hurry. This time he understood Priscilla without reading her lips despite the surrounding noise, an excellent sign.

Now all I have to do is catch my name.

Blake employed a system to figure out when his coffee was going to be ready by monitoring the first in, first out sequence of those customers from the register who placed an order before him. Mobile customers were in a separate line, so he didn't need to worry about them. His system worked perfectly unless the staff received a crush of orders, at which point everyone behind the counter pitched in, disrupting the normal workflow and making the output less predictable. Unable to recognize his name in the din, he was left wondering which drink was his. If a drink sat there long enough, he would reluctantly walk up and inspect the name on the cup, hoping nobody else tried to claim it. Sometimes he was right, but most of the time he was wrong. *Bet on it.* The best scenario was when the barista recognized him and waved him over, but that wasn't going to happen today since the barista, Stephanie, was new. *Whatever.* He stood back from the fray, analyzing the flow, surrounded by organized disorder.

"Triple venti nonfat no-whip mocha for Simon!"

Having let his attention get diverted by the circus of mobile customers, Blake was spellbound when the words magically registered inside of his head. *That's me!!!* Moving up to the counter, he grabbed his drink, throwing off a "Thanks, Stephanie" before walking out like a normal person. *Score!* He was probably the only customer in Cincinnati who equated understanding the barista with winning the lottery. Sliding behind the wheel of his truck, Blake took off for work, thinking that the day was starting out flawlessly.

Arriving at WEFT, he sat for a moment in the parking lot, scanning the grey building that held his professional future. Blake was happy to be here instead of Seagram since the move had broadened his design skills and allowed him the opportunity to work in exotic lands. The ownership change at Seagram had turned out to be a blessing in disguise because he had been getting jaded after 24 years in the same location and the distillery was steeped in a tradition that kept change to a minimum. Several of his ideas were shot down because they were a departure from the way things were normally done, generating frustration. *Why not? Because that's the way we've always done it!*

How about trying something else besides the missionary position!?

WEFT's client base was international, offering a mixture of different locations and cultures that made each job unique. George also gave him free rein when he was onsite, a situation facilitated by Blake's inability to talk on the phone. Blake possessed the right skills and an excellent sense of judgement, but sometimes he wondered if George regretted hiring him when remote communication became difficult. Pulling the green plug out of his cup, Blake took a sip of coffee, warming his hands around the cardboard container while he watched several people enter the building.

Deciding he was ready, Blake exited his truck and strode across the blacktop, unbuttoning his overcoat in defiance to the frigid morning. *Let's do it!* He was clothed in tailored pants, dress shirt and Jerry Garcia tie, the professional garb firing his mood. Halfway to the entrance he took another pull of coffee, the hot liquid trickling down his insides.

Nobody in there has a clue what's going to happen today.

Pulling open the door, he walked up to the receptionist, Brenda. "Hey, Brenda! Happy Thanksgiving!"

"It's Monday, Simon."

"Must be the coffee." He winked at her.

"Must be." Brenda rolled her eyes in return. Blake snapped off a mock salute and headed down the hall. *Rock on!*

Last Thursday Blake had left work on the bubble, not sure how activation would turn out, but this morning his unease was gone, and he was excited to start pushing his limits in a place that would be his toughest test to date. Friday, Saturday and Sunday had served as time in the nest and today he was ready to spread his wings. Starbucks was a harbinger of the future. He arrived at his office to hang up his coat, turning around to Angela standing in the doorway. *Hello!*

"So?"

"You know those fairy tales where the guy gets the girl?" Blake stood by his desk holding his Starbucks.

"Uh huh." She regarded him skeptically, waiting for the punchline.

"This is better," Blake broke out in a broad smile. "Everything they told me is true. I'm ahead of the curve and my hearing is back."

"No way!" Angela crossed her arms and stared in disbelief. "That fast?"

"Yeah, I guess it happens," Blake spread his arms. "I didn't expect to hear this well." He shrugged. *I can't even begin to explain it.*

"That's amazing!" Angela put her hands up to her face. "I'm so happy for you!" She came inside the office and grabbed him in a fierce hug. Blake put his coffee down in a hurry to keep it safe, not sure where to put his hands, but Angela released him almost immediately and stepped back to what he considered a safer distance. "What does Emily think?"

"Oh, she's loving it," Blake blurted out, knowing Angela was a master at reading between the lines.

"I'm calling her today! Conference room after lunch?" Angela was moving back to the doorway as she spoke.

"Sure."

She paused at the doorway to shake her head in amazement, "How wonderful!"

Angela left and Blake picked up his coffee, moving behind his desk to sit down. He booted up his computer, regarding with distaste the Ipad abandoned on his bookcase. Each engineer received an Ipad, but Blake didn't care to waste time keeping current with a second operating system to perform the same functions he was already doing on his Windows laptop. Blake considered the device about as useful as a second girlfriend, sucking up time and energy to make his life more complicated. *No thanks.*

He was due to check in with George for their Monday update and Blake sat back thinking about what he would say this morning. *I'm back? It works? Thanks for putting up with me?* Even though his inability to use the phone didn't seem to be an issue for George, Blake's goal was to fix that deficiency and assume more of the load. *If I were in his place, I would be bothered a little bit by me not being able to use the phone.*

Outside his window Blake saw Dan, bundled up against the cold, getting out of his car. The sky was dark, a fitting backdrop for the figure crossing his field of view. *Hey train wreck! Have I got a surprise for you!* Rising from his desk, Blake picked up his coffee and moved toward the doorway, intent on visiting George.

Shoes were scuffing the carpet in a slow trudge of warning and Blake stopped to peer out into the hall. *Traffic alert.* Troy appeared, stopping in front of Blake.

"I hate Mondays."

"Cheer up, Troy. There's always tomorrow!"

Troy's mussed up hair and bleary eyes gave evidence that he was not fully awake, and it was way too early for fidgeting. His words came out in a mish mash of mumbling that served to highlight the sluggishness, "Bengals lost again at the end." The HVAC system was humming in the background and further down the hallway Blake could grab snatches of conversation drifting their way. Filtering through the environmental interference, a boost of optimism filled his heart as the content of Troy's words took form in his head, despite the sloppy delivery.

"The last two minutes are the only part worth watching," Blake said. "Anything earlier creates false hope." *It's mostly quiet around here,* he realized. *Not like Starbucks.*

"Losers," Troy grumbled. "Can't trust them for a second." He trundled down the hallway toward his office, Blake stepping out in his wake. Catching movement from the far end of the corridor, Blake realized that the short time spent chatting with Troy had given Dan enough time to complete his journey from the parking lot. *Perfect.* Blake started walking, the back of his neck tickling with a warning.

It took less than a second before Dan began hailing him from the far end of the hall, demonstrating more effectively than words could ever convey his inability to consider the needs of others. "Hey! Simon!" *What kind of blind stupidity lives in that moron?* At the same time he was castigating Dan, Blake was hit with the sensation of each syllable carving itself into sandstone to create a physical presence inside his head. With carpeted floors, no windows and ceiling tiles made from mineral wool, the hallway environment possessed excellent acoustics, and he flashed back to last night's interchange with Emily in the darkness, thinking that it had been far more of a challenge than his current environment. Blake suddenly felt certain that this conversation was going to be fun. *Like catching bluegill off the nest.* He stopped walking, pivoting in place to address Dan who was 50 feet away.

"Where's your coffee?" Blake called out in return.

"Huh?"

"It's Monday, we all need coffee." *I'll start the meeting, thank you. A little foreplay wouldn't hurt, either.*

"Got a question," Dan blurted out while approaching, ignoring anything outside the confines of his own thinking. His hair was sticking out in all directions and his tie was set too short.

How does he survive? Blake thought, visualizing Dan trying to get out the door in the morning. Feigning interest, he said, "Oh?"

I love hallway questions on Monday. Especially the rude ones.

"George and I were talking about changing the fermentation recipe for the Brazilian plant," Dan said, the words tumbling over themselves in his haste to get them out.

"Why is that?"

"To improve the yield in the fermenters. They're not making enough ethanol."

Blake stood in the hallway examining Dan, knowing that it was dangerous to encourage him because his point of view employed such limited focus. *Micro mind,* Blake thought to himself, remembering the times when he had allowed himself to be misled by Dan's illogical fantasies before he knew any better. Dan could take a single point of data and extrapolate it into a justification for reconfiguring an entire system, ignoring other variables in play. *That's your reasoning? How do you think they've survived up to this point?* There was probably something else going on here, but it was difficult to ask Dan to explain himself just once. Most of the time Blake needed to ask the same question five different ways before Dan would stop pushing his own viewpoint and produce a relevant response. *Stupid engineers need to learn how to listen instead of playing king of the hill. I guess we know who to thank for that.* He regretted the dearth of rational discussions which he had known at Seagram, thinking here at WEFT too many conversations turned into a pissing contest. Having neither the time nor the inclination to baby step through a minefield, Blake said, "Then set it up with George."

"He told me to ask you."

Why am I not surprised? "You did. Not buying it." *Especially since you're not giving me all the facts. I'm standing here listening if you change your mind.* The conversation was a fantasy come to life as the words rolled off his lips, Blake hearing in real time with his brain in overdrive.

I'm two steps ahead instead of five steps behind!

"Can we sit down before lunch?" Dan persisted.

"I have to get some stuff done this morning, so let's get together after the daily meeting." Dan appeared disappointed, but Blake didn't care. Unwilling to accommodate Dan's lack of transparency, Blake nodded in confirmation, eyes seeking a reason for the curious behavior. *What's so important that you feel the need to ambush me first thing on Monday?* With no additional information forthcoming from Dan, Blake turned to go down the corridor, exposing the magnet on his head.

"Hey, what's that?" Dan said.

Blake didn't say anything, just smiled, looking over his shoulder with his hands spread apart. *What could it possibly be? My new hat for the Kentucky Derby?*

"That mean you can hear?"

"Maybe, maybe not." *Maybe I'm a dick.* "Catch me this afternoon and we'll talk."

Free of his nemesis, Blake continued on his way to George's office. He took a drink of coffee, enjoying its bitterness on his tongue as he walked down the hall, evaluating what had transpired. The interaction with Dan was unmarred by the typical hesitation on Blake's part, permitting him to function at a higher level. If the conversation had occurred last week then Blake would have been asking Dan to repeat himself, maybe more than once, and probably would have asked follow up questions to ensure his understanding. That approach invariably led to a student / teacher interaction which put Blake on the subordinate end, minimizing his skills and ceding authority to the other person. Blake burned with frustration at his inability to manage events that demanded his expertise. Just now, free to process the conversation without excessive effort, he was able to get ahead of Dan's agenda and focus on what was missing instead of surrendering control and allowing himself to be led somewhere by the nose. *One for me.*

Arriving at George's office, Blake rapped lightly on the doorframe, walking in to observe George pouring over sheets of fermentation data. Stopping in front of the desk, he noted that the worksheets were in the same format used by their Brazilian client. *Let's see what Dan 'forgot' to mention.*

George's head came up, "Hey, Simon! Angela gave me the news. Is it true?"

"I think so," Blake said. "It's going incredibly well. Hard to believe." He slipped into one of two chairs in front of George's desk, resting his Starbucks on the armrest.

"Have you tried the phone?" A quick study, George's mind was used to jumping ahead. He was the bear that nobody wanted to try outrunning. Blake lost himself in the smooth warmth of the coffee cup in his hand, considering George's adaptability. The atmosphere in the daily meetings was a disaster and most companies would probably suffer from the culture of confrontation that George fostered, but George could reverse his position on the fly when the facts warranted it, a skill that enabled him to make smart decisions time after time. *Not sure what it would take to affect his feelings. Warm and fuzzy doesn't apply.*

Knowing he was in the wrong place to get sidetracked, Blake stopped musing and addressed George's question before his meanderings caused too much dead air, "Probably next week after I get a little farther with rehabilitation."

"Got it," George sat back in his chair, pencil disappearing into his fist, "Your timing is either really good or really bad. The shit hit the fan last Friday."

"Brazil?" Blake queried.

George nodded, "Yeah. They finally shot themselves in the foot."

"Been watching them on the computer."

"There's several ideas floating around the office, but I want to know what you think."

Taking a short pause to sample his coffee, Blake sat quietly for a second. "I think I've probably seen this before," he answered. A trend had started to develop months ago, but sometimes a client needed to prove things to themselves before they were willing to listen. Having set more than 40,000 fermenters with Seagram, interpreting process data was second nature for Blake, and he made decisions faster than most. Once at Seagram the plant manager attempted to put him on the spot regarding a fermentation problem, but Blake had already been prepared, explaining to his boss that the required solution was to keep their dry yeast in cold storage, an action which he recommended a year ago. He sent the data sheets backing up his position that afternoon and his boss authorized his use of cold storage before the day was out. Blake had already collected enough information to identify Brazil's problem, figuring he would wait until they were ready to pay attention.

"After lunch then," George waved him away, "I got other stuff to do, let's get it settled at the meeting." He swept the data sheets together and gave them to Blake. "Here, this'll give you a head start."

Picking up the worksheets Blake took his leave, intent on formulating how to present his analysis. Dan's ambush in the hallway made sense now. There was a fire and Dan loved jumping into chaos. Humming under his breath on the way back to his office, Blake realized that he was being presented with a golden opportunity. *First day, no less.*

***

Blake munched on a sandwich at his desk, finalizing his proposal for the daily meeting. He was ready to be tested, and suspense was starting to build. *If I can finally hear* *what's going on it would make my day!* His initiation to the chaos of the conference room had been a painful experience and just walking by the place was normally enough to twist his stomach in a knot. After the string of successes this past weekend Blake saw no reason why he shouldn't be able to keep up, and dread was taking a backseat to curiosity.

Finishing the last bite of his sandwich, Blake gathered up his files and strolled to the conference room. Excited to showcase his abilities, he walked through the door even earlier than normal. With a confident step he went to his seat opposite the doorway, pivoting around to face the spot where George would preside. He aimed an imaginary gun at the chair with his hand. *Bang! Time to make it rain.* Pulling out the chair, he got comfortable, swiveling back and forth, his notes in front of him.

After tracking the data for months he knew what to say, and this afternoon was the ideal time to present his conclusions. The plant in Brazil was a fresh startup, only recently gaining enough expertise to operate consistently. Once a customer got to the point where they could sustain a baseline of efficiency, it became time to focus on second level improvements. Brazil had achieved their baseline and was now struggling to maintain it, creating the perfect opening for WEFT to ride to the rescue. He couldn't believe how events had coincided to afford him the perfect chance to unveil himself.

Blake thought back to Brazil, remembering the food. In South America the big meal was served at lunchtime in the churrascarias, beginning with a massive spread of vegetables and salad items filling up a long table which was laid out in tiers. In addition to the vegetables, which were fresh, steamed or fried, there was a selection of cheeses, pasta, bread and fish. Bowls of berries, fruits, pigeon eggs and other miscellaneous offerings came at the end. After filling up a plate, one took it to a weigh scale that charged so much per gram, collected the ticket, and then found a seat in the dining area where a waiter would take drink orders. At that point the waiter asked if you wanted meat service, which was a selection of ten or 12 cuts of meat carried around the dining room on skewers which servers braced against your plate in order to carve off pieces. Normal practice was to use tongs to grab slices of meat as they were carved off the various skewers, declining those skewers you didn't want. Meat service used a system of cardboard discs which were red on one side and green on the other, the idea being that if the disc was turned green side up the servers would keep stopping at your table until you flipped the disc over to display the red side. He enjoyed going to lunch with the locals because they would let him know when his favorite cut, filet mignon, came around. His second favorite was the roasted chicken, which was juicy and tasty, rivaling the filet mignon. Dessert followed the main course, consisting of puddings, cakes and ice cream at the buffet plus a special treat of grilled pineapple covered with cinnamon sugar that also came around on skewers. Whenever he took lunch at one of the churrascarias, dinner was a small affair, sometimes skipped altogether.

As he rotated back and forth in the chair, dreaming of Brazilian food, Robert entered the conference room, walking over to Blake and claiming a seat next to him.

"How's the new toy?"

"Crazy good," Blake replied. "I'm thinking of raffling off my hearing aids so that the rest of you guys can listen better!"

Robert laughed, "Amen to that!" Dan passed through the doorway and Robert commented, "I know who should win."

"Win what?" Dan said, coming to their side of the room.

"A Deadhead t-shirt," Blake said, causing Robert to grin.

"Don't care for 'em." Dan slouched down one chair away from Robert, hair no better than it was this morning.

"It would be perfect on you, though," Blake answered, waving to Angela as she entered the room. *In more ways than one.*

Angela took her place on the opposite side of him from Robert, setting down her notepad to say, "Are we going to make history today?"

Blake paused for a second, smoothing out his tie, then veered over to whisper, "We're gonna kill it!"

Angela's eyes sparkled, "I can't wait!"

Blake flashed a thumbs up, nodding in response. *You and me both!*

Everyone was on pause waiting for George to arrive and Blake studied the room, observing who was sitting with whom, eavesdropping on the buzz. He caught snatches of conversation, even determined that a couple of engineers at the far end were dissecting the Bengals' loss from yesterday. The conference room was filled with the hum of the HVAC system and the hiss of papers, coffee cups and calculators being pushed around the table. Six chairs away Troy was clicking his pen in a rhythmic cadence. *It's magic!* His heartrate sped up and he wondered what was taking George so long. *Get your butt in here big boy, I got things to prove!*

Finally George's bulk filled the doorway and he entered the conference room, closing the door in his wake. Attendance was already at 100% because nobody was willing to chance arriving after the door was shut.

The buzz tailed off and Blake sat back in anticipation when George called the meeting to order. From his spot opposite George at the far end, he possessed a clear field of view as George began with some housekeeping items. Comments came from all sides and Blake could hear those at the end of the table as if they were talking next to his ear, like dinner last night. *Yes!* His need for Angela's notepad went by the wayside as Blake tracked the conversation and he experimented with switching his gaze in another direction to see if he could understand. Voices on the same side as his implant registered better than those from the opposite side, and Blake compensated by turning his head to aim the front microphone on his implant in the direction of whomever was speaking. Curious how he was doing, Angela gave him a tap on the forearm, and he nodded at her in affirmation, returning his attention to the discussion.

George finished with the preliminaries, announcing that he wanted to review the situation in Brazil and come up with a recommendation for action. *Not necessarily a consensus,* Blake reflected, *because that's not how we roll. Let the games begin!*

The Brazilians called last Friday with a contamination problem that was reducing the plant's ethanol yield, on the same day that Susan Archer was giving Blake superpowers.

Their production manager had spent the last two months fighting low yields and chose Friday to turn his problem into an emergency. According to the Brazilians, the bacteria counts in the fermenter were too high and some of the sugars that would normally get converted to ethanol by the yeast were being metabolized by bacteria instead, resulting in less ethanol being produced. Less ethanol meant less product to sell to the oil companies for blending with gasoline and therefore less money coming in.

Chaos exploded like it invariably did, the discussion degenerating into engineers talking over each other in attempts to support their viewpoint. The standard interruption was, "I understand that," which really meant, "Shut up, so I can talk." Unfit to compete, Blake never took part in the insanity, compensating for his deficiency by reading Angela's notes. He felt no desire to overextend himself on this day, so rather than trying to inject himself into the fray Blake concentrated on trying to keep up, knowing George would call upon him sooner or later.

Outside the conference room many of the engineers used the same confrontational style, and Blake didn't bother to compete then either. His strategy was to let someone run on until they were begging for validation, at which point he took the opportunity to weigh in. Those conversations were less contentious, and he was sometimes able to drive his point home, but in the conference room he was outclassed.

Blake focused on understanding the brawl, ecstatic at how he was doing. At times two or three people would be scuffling for the floor, but once someone took control, they kept it long enough for him to home in on their point. *I love it!* There was no question that the situation was a mess, a textbook case of how not to run a meeting, but it was George's way, and nothing was going to change. The gatherings were a fight to the death where the winning strategy was to grab hold of any opposing ideas, rip them out of the conversation, throw them on the ground and slaughter them until yours was the last one alive. Watching several engineers stew in frustration after dropping on the battlefield, Blake listened to the clashes, marveling how the company ever managed to function as a team. *Excellent seminar on how to throw your coworkers under the bus!*

There was one exception to the process, another reason why Blake disliked the meetings, and that was when George asked Blake to speak, a situation where the rest of the attendees were expected to back off and listen in deference to his disability. He hated being singled out and could emphasize with the resentment on some of the faces. *Except for train wreck.* Another aspect that rankled him was that even when he offered a viable option his inability to respond on the fly allowed other viewpoints to come out on top. The discussion would ramp up again after he stopped talking and his opinions were subject to becoming collateral damage among the dissension.

Several ideas were still alive, volleying back and forth across the room. Some of the engineers wanted a yeast expert to analyze the performance of the yeast strain. One engineer wanted to raise the cook temperature, another was pushing to revise the antibiotic dosage and there was a group lobbying to test the effectiveness of the enzyme.

Dan wanted to change the fermentation recipe by adding phosphorous, a comment that prompted Blake to wonder if he could cut off the top of Dan's head and throw in a sack of brains. Phosphorous was a trace mineral necessary for yeast to thrive and adding it to the fermentation was a good idea only if the feedstock was shown to have low levels of that particular nutrient. *Since Brazilian corn normally contains enough phosphorous for fermentation and we don't have the feedstock analysis to prove otherwise, how can we justify throwing a bunch of phosphorous at the yeast?*

An ethanol fermentation is a biological process which involves multiple variables and Blake was aware that at one point or another each of the proposals had proven useful to WEFT in various plants. However, to be effective the solution needed to have more relevance besides having worked somewhere else. It needed to have some connection to the data coming out of the plant because the fermentation couldn't be treated like a car where the engineers replaced random parts in an effort to make it run better.

The camp favoring enzyme analysis was currently on top, with Angela scribbling furiously as the comments became increasingly technical. Catching George's eye, Blake signaled his disagreement with a slight shake of his head. Waving a hand to interrupt, George broke up the discussion, "Ok, let's hold that thought for a minute. Simon, do you have anything to add here?"

"Yessir," Blake responded.

"Need any clarification?"

"Don't think so." *Nothing here has a chance of working.* Blake rested in his chair with an air of assurance, the trepidation that normally accompanied his moment in the spotlight completely absent. Most of the free for all had registered clearly and his ability to read body language made him confident that the things he missed weren't critical. He could tell who was winning and who was losing, but none of that was going to matter.

Just another page in the deaf guy story and nobody has a clue. Yet.

A calmness filled him as he took center stage, fresh haircut giving him a glowing dome that projected a vitality. Starting today he possessed the ability to go head-to-head with anyone here and he decided to stand up. Some of the engineers had gotten a look at the implant on his head and some had not, but they were all curious because something about him was different. He normally didn't stand, although it wasn't unheard of, and he appeared to be taking control with an authority they had never seen before.

There was no hesitation on his part as time slowed to a ridiculous crawl. It was intoxicating not needing to verify what had gone before and Blake reveled in the confidence that arose from his center like sunrise in the desert. He was finally on equal footing with everyone else in the meeting, and his body language spoke volumes as he stood up straight, placing his hands on the table, owning the room. *I can do this all day long.* Gathering his thoughts, 49 years of struggles coiled inside of him, a powerful force circling impatiently for release, tingling the hairs on his neck as he took charge, claiming the floor with a face that was carefully blank, not caring if some of the engineers were resentful. *Maybe they'll learn how to share the airtime.* He drank of the intrigue hanging in the air, combining it with the potential waiting to burst free, forging the energy into a weapon that would smash his previous life into dust.

Leaning forward, he began.

"Here's what I think. Brazil has a contamination issue, supposedly two months old, but six months earlier I noticed the starting pH of the fermenters beginning to drop, which is an indication that bacteria have a foothold somewhere in the cooking and fermentation system. This drop could be due to the pH probes being out of calibration and if so, we would expect it to eventually disappear as the instruments receive their normal maintenance. Over time the pH drop has been increasing to the point that we are now far below normal, failing to bounce back after maintenance, so instruments are not the problem. Data points taken during the course of fermentation support a thesis of bacterial contamination and the low pH of the first sample tells us that contamination exists right from the start. The remaining data points in the first sample are within range so pH should be our focal point. Conditions halfway through fermentation act as a red herring because low pH at the beginning is the critical data point. Unfortunately, the Brazilians waited longer than necessary to seek advice, but that's par for the course because most of our clients do the same." Stopping to take a breath, he spread his hands apart. "In addition, this plant is stopping for their annual maintenance shutdown in two weeks and any of the proposed changes to yeast type, fermentation recipe, cook temperature or other variables won't give us enough data to figure out if the change is working in the two weeks they have left to run because we would need a week to get organized and the remaining week would be cut short by the shutdown. More importantly though, none of the options discussed so far address finding and eliminating the source of contamination showing up in the initial pH sample, so while it may be possible to attain a higher ethanol yield by changing the fermentation environment and temporarily overpowering the bacteria population, the increased production will create a false sense of security. Bacteria will remain in the system and acclimate to the new environment, propagating to higher levels than today and reemerging as an even bigger problem later."

Blake paused, "Make sense?" He didn't expect an answer but wanted to take a minute to let his comments sink in, watching the dawn of realization on the faces of his audience.

Too bad yeast can't talk. Would eliminate a lot of confusion.

"The shutdown is scheduled to last three weeks. My suggestion is that we ask the plant to empty all fermenters and cook tanks before the outage begins and drain all the piping in the cooking and fermentation areas so that the bacteria in the equipment and piping dies off as the system dries out, giving them a clean process at startup. Before start-up we should have them implement a program for monitoring acid levels throughout the cooking and fermentation areas. We have five weeks to get a system in place, which is doable. When the contamination reappears after start-up, as it most likely will, we'll be able to see where it originates by identifying the equipment which is the first to show elevated acid levels as the processing train transitions from a clean system with low acid levels to a contaminated system with high acid levels. This approach will give us the best chance of identifying where the contamination is starting and let us target our efforts where they will do the most good instead of making changes that produce temporary results without addressing the real problem."

He stopped talking, making eye contact with George and reading an endorsement in return.

There you go - simple, effective and cheap.

The room was silent, and he raised his Hammer of Victory to smash it down onto the table, pulverizing the last vestiges of Blake 1.0 into nothingness.

Ka-Boom!

"Done," George's hand slammed the armrest of his chair, emphasizing the finality of his decision. "Makes perfect sense." He began to gather his papers, signaling that the meeting was over. "I'll call them today and, Simon, I want you to get started on developing a list of sampling points."

Blake nodded and sat down. On the outside he was calm, but inside there was singing and dancing to celebrate lifting of the curse. He felt a nudge from Angela as she bent her head toward his, "Yay, Simon!" Her smiling face dominated his field of view as she tapped her notes, "I got it all down here in black and white!"

Robert leaned in to say, "Looking good," and Blake dipped his head in thanks.

People began to filter out, but Blake stayed where he was, savoring his victory. *Did that really happen?* He could spot a new appreciation on the faces of his fellow engineers. *I guess it did.*

Thanks, Pamela, for not giving up on me.

Next time I won't wait for an invitation.

Blake stayed in his seat, swiveling peacefully back and forth as the room emptied out. He finally got up, following the stragglers out the door into a universe that was expanding with each step down the hall, shoes hissing across the carpet, colors glowing vibrantly, oxygen powering his lungs and his body poised for action.

Endless possibilities were his for the taking.

***

Three days passed in the blink of an eye, and Wednesday afternoon Blake was sitting in his office, killing time on the internet before Thanksgiving break. The week had been one triumph after another, and he was planning to walk out on a high note. Outside his window the sky was a brilliant blue with sunlight filling the air, matching the sense of wonder and gratitude in his heart for how quickly the implant was transforming his life. In less than a week the fluorescent green magnet on the side of his head had become an indispensable part of his identity, a symbol marking his retreat from the edge of an abyss that was threatening to swallow up every relationship in his life a few short months ago.

New sensations flooded his brain each day, adding to his transformation, and he cocked his head at the traffic noise outside. A semi drove by, notifying Blake of its presence ten seconds before it appeared, blustering down the road with the belch of its diesel engine detectable long after it was gone. *Wonder how far away Emily can hear that?*

In the trash can his Starbucks cup from this morning peeked out from underneath a collection of crumpled paper, signifying one less battle to be fought, and Blake reviewed his work relationships, in the early stages of change.

Conversations were easier, lacking the start, stop and retracing of steps that used to be the accepted norm. He was adding verbal information to his reservoir of behavioral observations, framing a quicker understanding of the world around him and offering incisive comments at the proper time, even daring to interrupt on occasion. Some of the engineers were not sure what to make of him because he wasn't one to interrupt and it threw them for a loop as they attempted to adjust. Earlier this week Blake held a conversation with his boss, stifling an urge to break in before George finished. *It's only a matter of time.*

His ability to offer an opposing opinion rather than going with the flow was creating conflict because many of the engineers didn't react well to being challenged. *Not in this training ground for arrogance.* Unwilling to be a doormat any longer, he refused to back down despite the distress he was creating in his co-workers. Blake could be as stubborn as the rest of them and now that the playing field was level, payback was effortless because his ability to keep emotions out of the equation while limiting his comments to the facts under discussion meant that conversations were skewed in his favor. *Most of these characters need a tour guide to control their feelings.*

Among the cliches that his mother used was "Honey catches more flies than vinegar", and Blake knew that it would be worthwhile to soften the effect of his reshaping on the group instead of rubbing it in their faces.

My asshole coefficient may need some dialing down.

He thought back to his formative years when his mother spouted off a cliche for each occasion. "Waste not, want not", was usually associated with eating dinner, "That's the way the cookie crumbles" was her stock phrase for handling misfortune and "Little bit by little bit" was an admonition to keep on forging ahead. The expression that he claimed for his own though, had proven to be the best one of all. *Never hurts to be lucky.*

Transfixed by rays of sunshine playing over a corner of his office, Blake savored an occasion from yesterday when he acknowledged a conversation taking place behind his back, breaking in to offer an unsolicited comment of his own. The event cemented the fact that he was a force to be reckoned with. No longer would he answer questions that had not been asked or require an invitation to participate.

Angela chose that moment to pop her head inside his office on her way home, her face glowing with cheer. "Happy Thanksgiving, Simon! I hope the weekend turns out lovely for you!"

"Thanks Angela," he said. "Same to you!"

She left and he stayed in his chair, watching her appear outside the window to cross the blacktop and get in her car, sunlight glinting off the doorframe. Blake was eagerly awaiting his family's Thanksgiving traditions, hopeful of participating to a greater degree than before. There would be a turkey that he made on the Weber grill, his opening of a special bottle of whiskey, Black Friday at Kenwood Mall with dinner at Maggiano's, card games, board games and the bedlam of charades, where he might finally have a fighting chance. Normally he played charades with an assist from the audience to make sure that the shouted responses didn't go over his head, but this year he might not need help. *We'll see.* The weekend was brimming with potential.

With more than half the office gone and his own exit fast approaching, Blake listened to his coworkers passing down the hallway on their way to the parking lot, taking pleasure in an unexpected bonus that became evident soon after activation - the lack of feedback from a hearing aid or discomfort from an earmold. His ears felt wonderfully free and unencumbered, the cherry on top of his sundae. Shuffling the papers on his desk into a pile, he got up from his desk to leave, dragging his fingers across the sheets to enjoy the gentle hiss, his eyes misting over in gratitude. There was a lightness to his heart brought on by the lessening of his struggles and the continuous parade of magic.

His reservoirs of angst and anger were draining off to be recharged by an entirely different set of emotions and Blake suspected that he might come back after Thanksgiving shedding peace and happiness with every breath.

Chapter 11 – Breakout

Months later Blake was walking back to his office after talking with George. The time was 3:00 p.m., the first Friday in June, and George's request for an audience this late in the day had been unexpected, giving Blake cause for concern that something was wrong at one of WEFT's ethanol plants. Traveling at short notice was part of the job, but the timing would be terrible since Mackenzie was attending a formal dance hosted by a local charity this evening and Blake was supposed to help chaperone with Emily.

Blake pondered the situation, wanting to discuss it with his wife. He could call her, of course, but it would be better talking face to face. The problem was that this evening was booked solid with the logistics of dressing, pictures at the house and the formal at 7:00 p.m. Even though Mackenzie was the fastest dresser in the family, he was supposed to be home by 4:00 p.m. so that the three of them could have an early dinner. Having been through the formal dance routine multiple times, Blake wasn't optimistic about finding time to talk with Emily. *Maybe after we get there and settle down.*

Entering his office, he moved behind his desk to prop his feet up on a corner. Paperwork lay in piles before him, but the brilliance of the afternoon outside his window was distracting and he let his mind ramble. Ever since the day when he made his mark in the conference room, he had been living an impossible dream, and the months following that triumph bore witness to the best days of his life.

Hands down.

Blown away by the miracle that allowed him to reclaim his life, he savored the restoration of his sovereignty.

Six months ago Blake left the office on Wednesday, the day before Thanksgiving, planning to get an early start on the holiday. He was so wound up from the success of his transformation that he slept fitfully that night, and his eyes popped open at 4:00 a.m. the next morning, reality every bit as wonderful as the dreams he left behind. Lying in bed, his mind cycled through one prospect after another, stoking his excitement. Blake eased out of bed into the bathroom, his implant allowing him to perform his duties with stealth, then wandered a dark hallway, wondering how to occupy his time. A quietness filled the house that magnified his ability to detect each step upon the floor, each scrape of a cup, each intake of breath, and he experimented with his power to move as a ninja. Knowing his solitude would last several hours, he entered his home office with the goal of advancing his rehabilitation, using a Bluetooth connection between the computer and his implant in order not to wake his family. Clicking through the Cochlear program, he completed his first trial to score 95% and was promoted to level three. *Whoop! Whoop! Whoop!* Excited by his advancement he kept going, achieving a score of 85% after 45 minutes. His next attempt ended at 90% and he was bumped up to level four. *Yes! Two levels in one day!!* Pumped full of optimism, he closed the lid of his laptop, deciding to quit while he was ahead. Skating his slippers along the floor to the kitchen, he noted the backyard trees barely discernable outside the window, a sign that dawn was approaching, and he busied himself at the stove with a couple of eggs while waiting for Mackenzie and Emily to appear. The coffeemaker gurgled at him, finishing with an eruption of sputtering that he adored. *Every single time.* After breakfast he settled into his chair by the fireplace, watching sunrise turn the sky pink. Thanksgiving was starting off nicely and he was hopeful that his advancement on the computer meant more dreams would come to fruition this weekend.

"Hey," Emily walked in with an air of purpose, robe flowing around her ankles, bending over the chair to give him a kiss. Her hair tickled against his face and the residual of her perfume emptied his brain of all thoughts save one.

"Mmmm," Blake pulled her in for a second kiss. "I got coffee for you, but there's only two eggs left."

"Leave them for Mackenzie. We'll need to get a few things for tonight's dinner."

"No problem, the liquor store is releasing a bottle, so I was going out anyway." Blake grinned up at her.

"As long as you have enough time to grill the turkey," Emily said. "Madison and Matthew will be here at five."

"On my way." Blake got up from his chair to head out. He was in an excellent mood after gaining level four and the prospect of a new bottle of whiskey left him feeling even better.

Arriving at the grocery store, the parking lot was full of last-minute shoppers and he drove around searching for a place where his truck would fit. His odometer listed 95,000 miles and he was past caring about dings. *Now that it's old though, nobody comes anywhere near it.* Circling around, his phone chirped with a new ringtone. The choice of 'Lollipop' seemed to be working out. Selecting a spot and pulling in, he tapped on a text from Mackenzie.

Get some orange juice, please.

Blake lifted a finger, thinking to send a smiley face in response, but in a flash of inspiration decided to tap the phone icon up at the top, his heartbeat accelerating. *Why not?* Holding the phone up close to the microphone on his implant, he listened to it ringing, manipulating the slim pad of plastic so that the speaker on the phone rested directly above the microphone on his processor. *Here we go.*

It rang once, twice, pumping him full of anticipation, and then Mackenzie was on the line with an excited scream, "Dad!!! Is that you?!"

"Think so, but I can doublecheck if you want."

"You can hear me OK?" Mackenzie was yelling so loud that he was tempted to roll down the window and see if he even needed a phone.

"You bet."

"Oh my God! I'm calling you every day now!!"

A laugh of delight came across the line, a celestial tinkling, and his eyes flooded as he listened to her chatter, saying a prayer of thanks for yet another gift.

My heart is full. The phrase took on new meaning as he sat listening to his daughter.

Blake choked out a laugh of his own, mostly because there was no way that he could form any words with the lump that was blocking his airway. Mackenzie kept on talking, but he was only capable of throwing back platitudes in response. The simplest of tasks which he had observed other people doing and spent years longing to perform himself were gaining a foothold in his own life, and the spirituality of the moment manifested so strongly that he scanned the passenger seat for a guardian angel. He finally recovered his voice enough to interrupt, "Hey, I better get this stuff for your Mom, but let me say something."

"What's that?" The words came across crisp and clear, a ticker scrolling inside of his head.

"Call me."

A musical laugh came over the phone and Mackenzie said, "Oh, I will!"

Remembering the joy of that conversation, Blake smiled. His foot was falling asleep propped up on the desk, so he stood up, walking to the window in his office that faced the parking lot. The parking lot was separated from the street by a grassy section and beyond that traffic was flying past, but Blake was lost in the flow of his memories.

The week after Thanksgiving Blake went to Susan for his second mapping. She originally told him to wait one month, but since he was already using a volume setting of 10 on his remote, Blake asked for an earlier appointment. At the last minute Emily was detained by work, so he walked in by himself. He met Susan at the reception area and followed her on back, gliding over the linoleum thinking happy thoughts. Thanksgiving was all he hoped it would be, with Blake handling the noisy environment of Maggiano's restaurant when the family went out for dinner on Friday. That was where he bumped his volume control up to 10 and after a few moments of discomfort his brain gave up and accepted the increase. From then on, he left his volume at the maximum. They entered her office and Blake took his seat next to her desk, the testing booth looming large. *I can probably whip that thing,* he thought. Susan waited for him to sit down, her blue eyes sparkling at him, "From your email it appears that you are progressing quickly!"

"I'm practicing regularly. My volume is set on 10 and I figured that was a good sign."

She nodded, "That's excellent, some of my patients won't use that level. Are you reading lips?"

"A little. I still catch myself reading lips, but I stop when I realize what I'm doing."

"Any sounds that are painful or unpleasant? Physical pain from the unit itself?" Susan was making notes as they talked. Between her comments Blake picked out the scratching from her pen.

"In the morning I'll get twinges from my shoes clicking on the floor or a door shutting, but that goes away before I leave the house." Blake remembered how he felt when Pamela was about to work her magic and he was getting a similar feeling now. This time around, instead of barely maintaining the status quo he was on his way to new heights. Fear was gone, replaced by a thrill of adventure. *I'm getting better! And better!!*

"How often do you use the remote?"

"Not so much for volume, but I do switch between programs. Most of the time I use 'Focus' because I think it sounds better. 'Music' I don't use."

Susan sat back, "Understanding music is hard for most patients. Tell me how you do on the phone."

"I love talking with my daughter and Emily called me a minute ago to say that she got held up at work."

"Are you wearing the hearing aid?"

"Nope, it's in the drawer. I put it on once and it sounded so dull compared with the clarity of the implant that I don't wear it."

Susan stopped writing to smile at Blake. "The speed of your adjustment is unusual. Most recipients need months to get this far."

"Awesome!" Blake said, hoping that he wasn't jinxing himself.

"Let's get started on your mapping. We need to calibrate your T and C levels so that I can increase the strength of your baseline signal. After that I may adjust scan and pulse width depending upon your preferences." The easy confidence in her voice gave him a tingle.

Blake observed Susan's desk, evaluating the equipment spread over its surface, switching his gaze to the testing booth. The speaker was peeking out from the window, and he could have sworn that it was trying to hide. He spoke up, "When do we do the booth?"

Susan said, "Probably at your third mapping. No need to quantify your progress today since you are doing admirably."

Lucky for you. I'm going to dropkick you to the moon, Blake promised the booth.

Susan held out her hand for the processor, "Let's plug you in and we'll start."

Blake removed the unit from his head, plunging himself into silence, watching Susan connect one end of the audio cable to the bottom of his processor. His gaze went to the wall behind her to inspect a row of three diplomas which escaped his notice on previous visits. She stood up to position the processor over his ear and join the magnets. There was no explosion of sound since his microphones were deactivated and he was waiting for the computer to start sending T level beeps. T levels were the soft sounds, used to set the bottom threshold that he could hear. A question popped into his head and he asked, "I'm confused why you need to test for low levels? Why not use the lowest level for normal hearing and go straight to the high sounds?"

"Good question. The reason is that adjusting your pulse width depends upon the range which you can detect. Identifying your lower range also allows me to prevent the processor from sending signals which you can't hear and avoids wasting battery power." Blake was reading her lips, like riding a bike.

"Ahh."

She continued, "Battery usage is affected by many settings, so we spend some time trying to maximize the life of your battery and allow you to go longer between charges. It's common for patients with two implants to have differences in battery life between processors because the mappings are unique to each ear. One battery may last ten hours while the battery for the other ear may last 19 hours."

"I'm getting around 18 hours now."

"That will drop off as the battery wears out, but it's within normal range." She tapped at her keyboard then turned to face him, "Here we go."

The beeps began and Susan gave him a wordless reminder that she needed some feedback, raising her fist up to pop out thumb, index finger and middle finger.

"Sorry!" Blake laughed as he attempted to catch up. "Guess I'm too excited!" He copied her actions with his own fist, and they continued.

They ran through the T levels followed by Blake sitting in silence afterward while Susan worked at her keyboard. Next Susan slid the ruler with five dots onto the desk, tapping it to signify that she was ready to begin C level testing. Blake examined the five dots on the ruler, labeled 'intolerable', 'painful', 'uncomfortable', 'comfortable', and 'insignificant'. *Now for the win!* C levels defined his upper ranges and he wanted them as high as possible. Susan looked at him questioningly and he gave her a thumbs up. *As long as there's no facial twitches, I'm good.*

Like his first mapping, Blake rated each beep somewhere between 'comfortable' and 'uncomfortable'. The beeps registered inside his head, rose in volume and then his brain upshifted to another scale of comfort. Watching Susan pursing her lips, he grinned to himself. *Nobody said it had to be easy!* Her head came up from her computer with a wry comment, "I remember this part now." C level testing continued with Susan switching between different frequencies, taking time to make adjustments, and he thought that she was repeating frequencies multiple times. *Guess that's my punishment.*

The beeps stopped and Susan addressed him, hands suspended above the keyboard, "I'm going to turn on your processor now so that we can talk."

She returned her hands to the keyboard then held up a finger to signify that she was ready. With a click of her mouse his kaleidoscope unfolded, and Blake grinned in pleasure. Lucy in the Sky was back, and he loved her. In the quietness of the office there was not much difference from before, but he was eager to take a test drive. Susan spoke, "How is that?"

"Similar."

"It's not as abrupt the second time. Your improvement from here on out will be incremental." She continued, "I have expanded your baseline significantly so I would expect that you will be gaining some new sounds. Since you have no complaints, I'm going to leave well enough alone and keep your wind noise, pulse width and rate settings the same as before."

"OK."

"Let me try another test." Susan picked up a coffee cup and rapped the bottom edge against the top of her desk. Bending forward, she rapped again twice, carefully observing his face. Each time he could feel a stab of pain, but it went away immediately, and he figured if he complained she would reduce his settings. *Not happening.* Fortunately, he was well versed in keeping a straight face so that when the stabs shot out from his ear, he did no more than blink. Straightening up, she said, "No twitching. Have Emily keep an eye on that for you since it's possible for your face to twitch without you being aware of anything. If you start twitching, let me know."

"Gotcha." *Dodged that bullet.*

"Questions?" she queried, and seeing him shake his head, said, "I'll disconnect you." She stood up to remove the processor from his head and a silence echoed between his ears. Unplugging his processor and offering it back to him in her hand, she said, "Here you go. I have set your volume at 6 and your sensitivity at 12. When you reach a volume of 10, we will do our third mapping."

Blake took the processor and slipped it on his head. The magnets came together, and the heavens came back. It was an otherworldly switch to go from deafness to hearing in the space of a second. *So excellent.*

Susan's voice brought him back to earth, "It's critical to practice even though you are doing well." Blake sat listening to her instructions, the words relegated to one part of his brain while another part indulged itself in a Walter Mitty fantasy where he was standing on a plain brandishing a spear, his battle cry urging a line of warriors to victory.

A horn blasted from the flow of traffic, bringing him back to the present and drawing his attention to the intersection where three cars were temporarily at odds. Still standing in front of his office window Blake remembered how easy it was to get to a level of 10 after his first mapping. *The second mapping was just as fast,* he marveled. *A little pain in the morning and then, Boom!*

Never hurts to be lucky.

The intersection started to clear, his recollections of those early weeks reclaiming his thoughts.

At the beginning of December Blake returned to University Hospital for his third mapping, this time with Emily. They walked into the office behind Susan, taking their seats by her desk. Sunshine flooded the room from the window behind her and Blake wondered how many lives she had improved, feeling fortunate to be on the list. Susan regarded them with a smile before saying, "That was fast! How did you get to a volume of 10 so quickly?"

"I'm forcing myself to adapt. After an hour it's fine, but the initial blast in the morning is a hit." Blake shrugged in an attempt to downplay the severity of it, because he wouldn't change a thing. He was determined to go as fast as possible.

Susan responded, "It's mostly a matter of comfort and those who push themselves wind up doing better than those who don't. Remember that you can back off if you experience discomfort."

Emily broke in, "That's what I said, but he's too stubborn." She shook her head at her husband, but he gave her a wink in return.

Susan continued, "After we finish your third mapping today, I want to test you in the booth."

"Deal!" Blake said. He was all in, figuring that understanding the speaker shouldn't be any harder than the phone or the practice program, both of which were getting easier by the day.

They went through the third mapping, same as last week, and Susan returned the processor to Blake. After he put it on, she said, "These settings will give you significantly more stimulation and regular practice will help you interpret what you're hearing. I know you're probably tired of me telling you to practice, but it's critical in the early stages of adaptation. Now let's test your performance with the implant."

She rose to open the door of the booth and Blake entered, taking his seat on the stool to face the speaker. He fixed it with a stare, willing the plastic and metal to melt before his eyes. *You're going down, dude.* Blake visualized himself ripping the speaker off the wall and stomping it to pieces. *In victory this time.* Confidence straightened his shoulders as he watched Susan shut the door behind him and move to her desk.

He returned his gaze to the speaker. *You're toast.*

Susan's voice came out of the speaker, "Simon, we are only going to test you with the implant so please remain seated and we'll start. We are going to do words first followed by sentences." Her mechanical voice registered clearly and Blake listened to the instructions. *Let's do it.* He nodded to let her know that he was ready.

With a click of Susan's mouse, the speaker began its recitation of 25 words, spaced ten seconds apart, "Hog."

"Hog," Blake replied instantly, then sat there waiting. *Speed it up, dipstick,* he addressed the speaker. The first word was phenomenally easy and he was slap happy with excitement.

"Shuck," was the next word.

"Shuck," repeated Blake. *I got enough time to blow my nose in between words here.*

The words rolled out of the speaker at a rate that seemed ridiculously slow and Blake peered out the window of the booth, making eye contact with Emily. The speaker was easier to understand than the computer program because Susan was dialing in a minimum of background noise. *I'm starting to understand why she says to make practice as hard as possible.*

"Shelter," came out of the speaker.

"Shelter," said Blake. *Bring it on. That the best you got?*

He nodded at his wife, watching her sitting by Susan with a huge grin on her face. *You ain't seen nothing yet,* he thought. *And this time that's a good thing. A hang on, here we go flying down the biggest hill you've ever seen, thing!*

Individual words issued from the speaker and Blake attacked each one viciously. He was so quick with his responses that he spent most of his time fiddling, counting cars at a train crossing waiting for the caboose. Finally, the speaker was done with its 25 words and Susan spoke up, "That was outstanding, Simon. Now we do sentences."

Damn right! It was fucking fabulous! "Ready when you are," Blake responded. His heart was pounding, and he was full of determination. *You got about as much chance as a seal surrounded by a pod of killer whales,* he threatened the speaker. *I'm gonna yank your wiring out your asshole!*

The speaker began its emotionless recital. Having been shot full of holes in round one, it was a ship waiting to sink in round two, and Blake could smell the desperation.

I'm the one who's going to win this time.

"She went for a long walk in the park."

He rattled off the sentence, pinning the speaker with a death stare to let it know who was king.

Give it up, loser.

"Mary bought me a bouquet of flowers" followed a few seconds later, Blake having plenty of time to prepare.

"It's a windy forecast for Iowa today."

"My heart belongs to a longtime lover."

"Can you pay me today for a hamburger tomorrow?"

The speaker tried every trick in its arsenal and failed to come out on top. Blake got a couple words wrong here and there, correcting himself if he had enough time, but for the most part sentences were no problem. He could tell that he did better on the individual words, but he was still crushing sentences.

"My friends decided to go hiking in Arizona during the holiday break."

Slamming the speaker's final attempt at a Hail Mary to the ground, Blake watched gleefully from his seat on the stool as the small box of black fell silent in defeat. It hung off the wall, an inanimate object, void of its former power. *Never again.* Blake clenched a fist in victory, standing up to exit the booth on his own. This time around there was no rage to bury or negativity to channel. His heart was wild with joy and Emily rose from her chair to embrace him as he came out the door.

"I'm so happy for you," she said, her eyes flooding with tears. Her arms locked around his chest and she squeezed him fiercely, Blake squeezing back.

The miracles keep on coming, he thought.

Emily let go and turned to Susan, "Thank you so much!"

"It's not all me," she said. "Simon is pushing himself harder than I ever would." Laying out two scoresheets on top of her desk she said, "Today's performance is nothing short of amazing. Before surgery you scored 7% on word comprehension and 2% on sentences. With your implant you scored 98% on word comprehension and 92% on sentences. At those levels context and observation provide the missing information. You're functioning at the level of a normal person who doesn't bother to pay attention." She smiled at the two of them sitting together. "That's why I love this job."

Emily squashed Blake's hand and her excitement coursed through his body.

Blake said, "Mary Beth asked me to come to the cochlear group and help out, so I'll probably be giving that a shot." *It's the least I can do.*

"Maybe I'll see you there," Susan said. "Each year either myself or Dr. Rickerson give a presentation to the group." She paged through her calendar, "Let's plan on your fourth mapping in January, so give me a call after the holidays." Standing up, she offered her hand to them. "Enjoy your new hearing!"

Blake and Emily took their leave to head for the elevators, Blake remembering how lost he felt in the beginning. University Hospital had grown to be a place of triumph for him, and he floated down the hall with Emily by his side, finally comfortable in his own life.

Emily intertwined her fingers through his while they walked in silence and when they arrived at the elevators, she turned to face him, speaking softly from the heart, "It's so normal to talk with you now, but it's the best gift in the world."

He met her eyes, their history rising up to enfold them, "That's how it feels to me too."

"Where would we be without this?" she said. Every fiber telegraphed relief at their escape, and he mirrored her emotion because the cruel twist to hearing loss was that its silences destroyed intimacy. The years had stained them both with a list of failures that defied counting. Each trial had been followed by another but giving up was unthinkable since it would have signified an ending that neither of them desired. Their pledge had been for better or worse, and sometimes worse was the winner. Lucky for them a path to victory appeared out of nowhere to restore joyfulness to their lives, a timely gift of grace that rescued them both from a place of heartache.

"I can't even imagine," he replied.

Memory of that day in front of the elevator came back full force, blurring his view of the traffic outside his window because the magnitude of their near miss was still fresh in his mind. *We were lucky.* That last appointment was nothing like the first, when his future held question marks wherever he turned. It was so inadequate to say that the implant had turned his life around. The truth was that he no longer felt a crushing despair or a boiling rage, and there was no need to present an inscrutable exterior to hide whatever vileness was mangling his soul. His shields were slowly falling away as he needed them less and less, the ugliness fading to a memory as his implant led him out of the darkness. Each step was now an adventure and discovery waited around each corner. Before the implant, his day had been an endless queue of struggles but riding this carousel from dawn to dusk was generating a tranquility that was erasing the past.

Mackenzie phoned him almost every day, checking in to rattle off whatever was on her mind, and her calls were buckets of fun, dropping into his life without notice.

He could laugh now, remembering his trick of smiling and nodding when comprehension became too difficult, hoping that he hadn't just confirmed someone's wife was unfaithful or agreed to help them move. His initial thought in the morning was to wonder what victory he would be celebrating by nightfall and there was a thrill in knowing that a new triumph lay over the next rise.

Turning from the window, Blake picked up a pen off his desk, twirling it around his fingers until it slipped out of his grasp. He watched it fall, anticipating the thud when it hit the carpet.

He patted his front pocket where he kept his phone, wanting to call Emily but knowing that the timing would be wrong. *Dang.* Unwilling to address the papers covering his desk, he picked up the pen and resumed its twirling, walking back to the window, reliving the thread of his transformation.

Thanks to the boost Susan gave him at his fourth mapping in January he continued to surpass himself. Blake thought mappings one, two and three were astonishing, but the fourth was sublime, marking a different kind of progress. After number four he emerged from the tree line to find the summit of his mountain lit up in majestic glory. *She was right about my hearing getting better.* With number four he graduated to adjusting his volume control in both directions instead of continually bumping it higher. Sometimes he lowered it to 5 and found that he perceived more at the lower setting, an effect that was surprising.

Friends and coworkers told him that his speech was easier to understand because he was speaking more clearly. He began talking at a lower volume, a change which made his wife happy because she no longer found it necessary to stop him from shouting. His rehabilitation advanced in spurts, with Blake plateauing at different levels for longer than he wanted, but despite erratic progress on the computer, his results in the real world kept improving.

Emily had a front row seat for the changes and was delighted to watch his life becoming easier. Their house was filled with laughter as the two of them explored a new playfulness together and she switched from a supporting role to being a celebratory partner in his success. It was a relief for them both that she no longer needed to monitor his interfaces with the outside world, and his ability to solve his own issues without her intervention was liberating. Car repair was a task that she willingly relinquished, grateful for not having to function as a go between on technical issues that made no sense to her. Phone conversations allowed them to deal with issues immediately instead of having to wait for a convenient time which sometimes never materialized. Blake could order for himself in restaurants, negotiate with hotel clerks, they could even talk across the backyard or from different rooms of the house. She found freedom in being able to leave him alone in social settings and no longer needing to serve as a referee between him and the kids, began to redefine her role in the family.

Still twirling the pen, Blake remembered cranking up the radio one afternoon in the truck when Carly Simon's 'Nobody Does it Better' started to play. It was a lovely tune, but the words had always escaped his comprehension. While he was listening, trying to extract fragments of the lyrics, he suddenly realized that it was the theme song for a James Bond movie. *How many times have I pretended that song was about fishing?*

The world was making more sense as the puzzle pieces of life came together.

A group of teenagers cut through the parking lot outside his window and he watched them transition the blacktop, a school of minnows moving in unison. They were talking animatedly, and he cocked his head trying to hear them through the glass, attempting to collect another sound for his database. The craziest one to date was sitting on the toilet in the basement and hearing a musical tinkling coming from somewhere. It wasn't the toilet because he regularly inspected its workings for leaks. Eventually he deduced that it was water falling down a drainpipe inside the wall behind the toilet. He knew the pipe was hidden back there because he put up the wall himself, but hearing noises come from behind the plaster blew his mind.

Water flowing down a pipe was fun, but the real magic came with turning to the sound of someone calling his name or having a conversation in the dark. He loved tilting his head up to confirm a plane flying overhead or hear surf crashing onto the shore in a movie soundtrack. Turn signals, singing along to the radio with the volume cranked up high, the fizzing sound of carbon dioxide being released from pop cans, it was all a bonus. Come July the katydids and crickets would be harmonizing with the lightning bugs and he was excited for the show. Fishing in Minnesota would bring the sound of aspens quaking in the breeze and the hurrying of a babbling brook.

He turned from the window and walked behind his desk to sit down, rubbing his hands over the leather armrests of the chair, thinking of WEFT and how his situation was changing. The transition was so remarkable that it was like getting rehired.

He could talk to his colleagues without lasering his attention at their faces to read lips and body language, behavior that in the past some engineers misinterpreted to mean he was hanging on their every word without opinions of his own. *Ego. It's all about ego.* The last few months he had reclaimed his mojo at the expense of some surprised coworkers. His relationship with George was changing because he could argue the merits in a timely manner rather than having to acquiesce because he missed what was being said. Blake was restructuring his career on his own terms, one of many aspects about himself that he was reinventing.

Most of the time these days Blake was in a happy place. If a dam is holding something back, it needs to be maintained, but without a dam there's nothing stored up to cause damage and no need for monitoring. His dam was gone, and it left him free to use his energy for other pursuits.

Meeting people was exciting, missing the awkwardness that came from stumbling over the establishment of context. He could start up conversations with complete strangers, which was a marvelous tool to have at the cochlear meetings. For the last two months he had been participating as one of the recipient counselors who helped people navigate their way through the maze of logistics and it felt rewarding to use his experience to help others. Being around the volunteers was fun because they were a unique collection of people who seemed to have their heads on straight. Blake felt privileged to be part of such an effort. Everything was new to the potential recipients and he smiled to himself, remembering an occasion when he removed the magnet from his head and someone's spouse jumped out of her skin because she thought it was screwed into his skull.

The phone buzzed in his pocket and he pulled it out to find Mackenzie on the line.

"Hey Dad, are you coming home at four?"

"No problem, almost ready to leave." The magic of being able to use the phone gladdened his heart. Mackenzie's call triggered memories of a trip to Chicago last March when the hotel reservation got messed up and they had one bed for the three of them. Blake got on the phone himself and solved the problem before Emily and Mackenzie even knew there was an issue. *That was fun.*

Mackenzie was excited about the dance, a rite of passage. There was no shortage of boys hovering about, but he was impressed with her intention to avoid romantic entanglements at this stage of her life. Flirtatious and outgoing, she made it clear that she intended to postpone commitment for later. High school was for having fun, an attitude that both he and Emily supported 100%.

"I made Mom promise that you guys would be cool tonight. The forecast is for rain and I'm worried it will cancel our pictures outside."

"Maybe, maybe not. What's for dinner?" Blake was looking out the window at a beautiful day, wondering if clouds were gathering behind him in the west. He was pondering when to break his news to Emily, wanting the timing of his message to match the content.

"We're making fish that you brought back from Minnesota."

"Perfect." The prospect of fish baked with onions, potatoes and butter made his mouth water. For the last 22 years Blake had been going walleye fishing for a week with a group of three friends from Seagram, and they always returned with their limit. Minnesota regulations specified that the number of fish in their possession was not supposed to exceed the daily limit, but they were in violation for most of the trip because they put aside a few extra for meals. Fortunately, the camp operator only cared if they were legal upon departure, so that meant the last night was a fish fry, where tradition was to relive highlights from the week.

As a boy Blake dreamed of becoming a fisherman, a desire spawned from reading copy after copy of Field and Stream magazine. Learning to fish requires a mentor because trying to figure it out yourself takes more time than anyone has available. A teacher can cut years off the learning curve by giving you the smallest of tips. His friend, Tom, an Indiana native whose father, grandfather and great grandfather were all hunters and fishermen was the perfect instructor for Blake, whose own father was a desk bound economist that only went outside to check the mailbox. One thing Tom taught Blake was that wearing rubber boots in the tall grass around a pond will keep ticks away since they position themselves about 12" high. He learned from Tom that it's more effective to pinch a nightcrawler in half when fishing in the spring because a large bait that time of year didn't match up with the smaller size of the natural forage. By autumn the situation was reversed and a whole nightcrawler produced better results. If you got no bites using a half night crawler, a #6 hook and 6 lb line in any season of the year, then it was better to give up and focus on whiskey.

Tom's dad owned a fishing boat which the two of them borrowed frequently, and on those occasions Blake learned the finer points of boating. He received lessons in how to fish from the front and steer the boat with a foot pedal, how to net a fish for his partner, how to keep an eye on the weather, how to anticipate the wind when casting, launching the boat, docking the boat, reading a depth finder, riding into the waves, anchoring in wind and a host of other skills. Blake and Tom developed a system where each fished differently until the main pattern for the day was established, and then they both switched to whatever strategy was working. His friend was patient enough to repeat himself and the environment offered by fishing made it easy for

Blake to understand. The two of them had some memorable adventures on the water, rehashing the adage that experience is what you get right after you need it.

Those days on the water gave him knowledge that came in handy when it came time to buy his own fishing boat. Thanks to fishing he was an expert captain, and on that first launch in Minnesota, consumed with excitement over the week ahead, he would have the lines off the boat and be on plane before he was 30 yards from the dock.

Sammy and Pete rounded out the rest of the Minnesota group. It was a no-drama expedition where they did what needed doing and enjoyed each other's company. Once fishing was done and dinner was out of the way they would spend the rest of the evening playing cards and drinking whiskey. Upon arriving in Minnesota Blake wondered how he would get through a week of fishing, battling the weather, cleaning fish and staying up late, but before he knew it there was one day left and the long drive home was looming over their heads. Last April's trip was the best yet, with his implant adding a new dimension. Blake had been able to participate in banter flying back and forth at night across 40 yards of open water, giving back as good as he got. He remembered driving home from Minnesota and receiving an email from Dr. Rickerson proposing several dates for an operation to get cochlear implant number two. After receiving it he immediately called Emily to share the news.

"So, do you think it's going to rain?" Mackenzie's question interrupted his thoughts and he got back up, walking to the window for a second inspection of the sky.

"Doesn't matter what I think," Blake said. "I'm hanging up, see you in a few."

"Aaagh!" Mackenzie gave out a wail before he broke the connection, returning to his desk and grabbing his car keys out of a tray. Exiting the building to walk across the parking lot he glanced back to scrutinize the sky behind the building with a practiced eye. Any fisherman worth his salt could predict bad weather and Blake's observations were enough to confirm Mackenzie's concerns. *Sometime this evening, maybe in four or five hours.* He reached his truck and swung himself in, thinking of the fish they were having for dinner. *It'll be an easy cleanup, maybe Emily will have some free time.*

He turned out of the parking lot for the 30-minute drive home, happy to have two cochlear implants for the dance tonight, remembering how easy the second operation had been.

For one thing, I didn't have to worry about the wrong ear being operated on.

But that IV was hell.

Waiting in the hospital for surgery to begin wasn't so unsettling the second time. His family was gathered around his bed and the mood in the bay was optimistic. Fitted with a wristband, gowned up and covered with a warm blanket, Blake was hoping to see Jill again, but the curtains parted to reveal a young man in his twenties sporting a mass of wavy blonde hair. *Surfer dude!* Their interaction started off pleasantly enough, with the nurse introducing himself as Mel, but it went downhill from there. Mel ran into trouble positioning his IV cart next to the bed, fumbling with the unit until realizing that he had inadvertently locked the wheels. After fixing that issue, he strapped the rubber tourniquet around Blake's elbow and started searching for a vein. While Jill had no trouble locating a vein, Mel rotated and poked Blake's arm for an extended period, stoking rise to misgivings. Mel finally pulled a sterile wipe from his cart, bypassing the normal position on Blake's wrist to clean a section of skin 3" higher, which didn't feel right at all. By then Blake's body was fraught with tension and his butt was clenched so tight that any pressure in his intestines would have better luck venting through his belly button. The numbing shot was his saving grace, preventing him from pulling his arm away. Once the IV was in and his breathing had stabilized, Blake reluctantly inspected the result. There was a needle located in the middle of his forearm with a small trickle of blood oozing out to run down his arm. Fortunately for her, Mackenzie was gone for coffee, but the rest of his family appeared aghast. He lifted his head to meet Mel's eyes and they both knew what was coming.

"I think I'm going to have to redo your IV," Mel said, with a fallen look on his face.

Swallowing his dismay Blake said, "No problem, don't think I like it there anyway."

Another numbing shot later the second IV was in the top of his wrist, Mel was gone, and Blake felt like he might be able to breathe again without conscious effort. The curtains swung open with a supervisor coming in to inquire about the IV, confirming Blake's suspicions that Mel was still in training. With a small sigh Blake told her the procedure went OK. He didn't see the need to throw Mel under the bus, but he was glad the experience was history.

When the anesthesiologist appeared to ask if he was ready for surgery, Blake nodded, hoping that Mel's IV would prove to be the low point of the day. Watching the medicine being injected into an IV port, Blake felt the grip of the anesthesia almost immediately, reclining on the bed to prepare himself for the trip through the corridors of the hospital. *I'd walk the halls naked to get the second one,* he thought. Next thing he knew, the ring of lights was above his head and he was being transferred to the operating table. *Here goes nothin'.*

Blake arrived home, pulling into his driveway, thankful at how smoothly the second implant sped through recovery, activation and rehabilitation. The second operation was the third week of April, activation was the end of the fourth week, and he spent the month of May getting his left ear up to snuff. He was now hearing in stereo, a feature that added tremendous pleasure to his listening. His sound localization was far better and he was wondering how he would perform at tonight's event.

He walked inside the house to the smell of fish baking only to walk back out at 6:40 p.m. with Emily. Dinner and pictures had sucked up every available minute plus a few extra and the two of them arrived at the dance exactly on time. As they passed under the archway, decorated in a theme that relied heavily on beaches and seashells, Blake turned to Emily, "What are we supposed to do?"

"Be adults, I think," Emily said with a grin.

"Might be difficult."

"Do your best," Emily said. "I'm going to find the moms so, see you when I see you."

"OK," Blake watched her run off, thinking that his timeline had gotten pushed back. The storm broke soon after and he was enlisted to help relocate the picture booth indoors with the help of the other dads. It rained the rest of the evening and they got home late to fall into bed, tired from dodging the occupants of a crowded room.

*****

Saturday morning, Blake woke up to go into the kitchen and start his weekend ritual. He stood before eggs popping in oil with the toaster oven ticking off its beat in between gurgles from the coffee maker, thinking about how the resurrection of his life was cascading through his family, friends and work, bringing changes everywhere. He was more approachable, happier with himself and less arrogant, although that last part could use some work.

The journey wasn't at an end though, not by a long shot.

Blake was waiting for Emily to wake up so that he could share his big news. The reason that George called Blake into his office yesterday was to offer him the position of project manager for WEFT's new ethanol plant in Uruguay, a job which would task his skills to their utmost. George's first choice had dropped out for health reasons and the assignment was Blake's for the taking. It was an opportunity that would have been unthinkable 12 months ago and he was excited for the chance.

I know I can do it. What's another gauntlet through a jungle full of monkeys?

Walking onto the screened-in porch off the kitchen, he opened the outside door to inspect the backyard, balancing a cup of coffee. A continuous procession of lightning, thunder and wind had filled the nighttime hours, but morning was here to offer clear blue skies dotted by puffs of white with a gentle breeze leaving a fresh scent in its wake. Having survived the winter, seeds were forcing their stalks out of the earth in an eagerness to be born while the buds on the trees and bushes swelled with blossoms. Last night's storm had left the world fresh and clean, washing away the last traces of detritus strewn behind by the bleakness of winter. In this season of renewal, Blake could feel energy radiating from the earth.

Above his head the blue jay was calling to its mate and next door the breeze was tinkling a set of wind chimes. They were the simplest of sounds, magical in their purity, the type of sounds so reliable in their repetition that if you heard them once you knew them forever and it was easy for them to fade into the background to be taken for granted without a second thought for their unique beauty or the memories they could trigger. The notes danced with Blake through the halls of his consciousness as he embraced them with joy, marveling at the depth of complexity inherent in each.

I'm living in a rainbow.

Afterword

I have two cochlear implants, and this is my effort to describe the miracle behind the science. As the novel came together I tried to create a story that people would want to keep reading, because even though cochlear implants are a worthy topic, any narrative with a singular focus is quite boring. You are the final judge, but I gave it my best shot.

This book took me a long time to finish because I kept editing sections to make sure that I was conveying the truth of how implants weave themselves through my life. The writing has taken me back in time and I'm grateful for the opportunities to reflect and understand myself better. Now that it's done, I find myself missing those gifts of introspection.

Earlier I mentioned that Blake does not have any heroes beside himself. For many years I assigned no one that kind of respect because circumstances forced me to solve my own problems and be my own teacher. There were those who offered help, but in the end it always came back to me. That's not a bad thing either, because it's a comfort to know that you can rely upon yourself.

I have heroes now though, for the first time ever, and they are all the wonderful people who have given me this gift. My heroes are using their lives to help others, right down to the janitors laboring in the background. They have allowed me to transform my life in the most beautiful way, and for that I want to say,

"Thank You!"

One Last Thing

I am happy to discuss my experience with cochlear implants. My email is briangallat@gmail.com and additional contact information is available at www.smashwords.com/profile/view/bgallat.

If you enjoyed my book, I would be grateful if you would please take a moment to leave a review at the retailer of your choice!

Live well.

B. GALLAT